CO-AZH-693

st

By the same author:

THE EMERALD TRAP

A FORTUNE IN DEATH

THE
SEADON

FORTUNE

Leonard St. Clair

SIMON AND SCHUSTER
NEW YORK

Copyright © 1977 by Leonard St. Clair
All rights reserved
including the right of reproduction
in whole or in part in any form
Published by Simon and Schuster
A Gulf+Western Company
Rockefeller Center, 630 Fifth Avenue
New York, New York 10020

Designed by Irving Perkins
Manufactured in the United States of America

1 2 3 4 5 6 7 8 9 10

Library of Congress Cataloging in Publication Data

St. Clair, Leonard.
The Seadon fortune.

I. Title.
PZ4.S135Se [PS3569.A43] 813'.5'4 76-27373
ISBN 0-671-22369-0

The author wishes to thank the following for their kind
permission to reprint material in this book:

Bourne Co. for lines from "Yes Sir, That's My Baby" by Gus
Kahn and Walter Donaldson, © copyright 1925 Bourne Co.
Copyright renewed.

Chappell & Co., Inc., for lines from "In the Garden of
Tomorrow" by Jessie Deppen and George Graff, Jr., copyright
© by Chappell & Co., Ltd. Copyright renewed, Chappell & Co.,
Inc., Publisher. All rights reserved. International copyright
secured.

Warner Bros. Music for lines from "Tea for Two" by Vincent
Youmans and Irving Caesar, © 1924 Warner Bros., Inc. Copyright
renewed. All rights reserved.

TO THE MEMORY OF MY GRANDPARENTS
AND THEIR CHILDREN

BOOK
ONE

Chapter 1

THE STEAMER *Hesperia* moved slowly toward the wharves and warehouses of the Embarcadero. The morning's fog was lifting, and the passengers crowding the rail could make out the hills with curious names—Telegraph Hill, Russian Hill, Nob Hill—all thrusting upward from the jumble of squat brick and wooden buildings of appalling ugliness. Cathlin Donahoe gazed at the dismal sight and shivered with disappointment. Was this the fabled city that had lured adventurers the world over? In her mood of disenchantment, Cathlin ignored the fact that San Francisco, in 1864, was far too young to have acquired the appearance of great wealth; it was barely sixteen years since the first cry of "Gold in California!" and San Francisco's entry upon the world stage. If Cathlin had thought about it, which she did not, the city was three years younger than she herself.

She glanced about at the other passengers to see if they shared her disillusionment. No, they were smiling, eager, anxious to be ashore. And they stood carefully apart from her, those men and women whom she had once thought of as friends. Most, like Cathlin and her father, had sailed from Boston aboard another ship, a British vessel which would be safe against the Confederate raiders that maintained a sea blockade of Yankee shipping. Together they had crossed the Isthmus of Panama by railroad and boarded a second British vessel for the voyage north. In the beginning Cathlin and her father had been welcome companions; everyone had laughed at Gerald Donahoe's jokes and admired his daughter's comely face, her sparkling blue eyes and gleaming chestnut hair. In the beginning—until Donahoe, weakened by Isthmus malaria, developed lung fever and died. In Cathlin's grief she had not noted, nor would have cared, that the passengers now avoided her; especially the women, who imagined themselves in her plight, and so kept a frightened distance. Captain Dorrance, master of the *Hesperia*, was the one person who had remained kind throughout. He had conducted the funeral services and her father's burial at sea. He had come to her cabin afterwards and asked, "Do you have friends in San Francisco?" She had been too numb with loss to understand his question and the captain had to repeat it. Then she shook her head.

"No, sir. No friends."

"All your kin are in Boston?"

"My mother died in Ireland, my brother drowned in a New Bedford whaler."

Dorrance had frowned and then added hopefully, "But at least your father left you provided for?"

Again she shook her head. "He intended to. But his partner absconded with almost everything. We were going to California to start over again."

That had unsettled the captain more than her previous answers. "Then there's absolutely no one you can turn to?"

She pondered, then lifted her chin. "Oh, yes, sir. The Holy Virgin."

So she had believed, despite her grief, despite her choking sense of desolation. Through faith and prayer, and with the courage of the Donahoes, all must still come right in time. Her

12

father, too, had clung to that conviction and had rallied from every adversity—first, the great potato famine of 1848 in Ireland; then the death of his wife the following year, when they were about to sail for America and a new future; even after the drowning of his son, ten years later, and the loss of his whale-oil business in the early months of 1865. Each had been the Lord's way of testing Gerald Donahoe, he had told Cathlin, a preparation for some great reward to come. Why, was it not the Lord's guidance that had finally turned his thoughts to California? Every Boston newspaper was filled with glowing reports of a wonder which eclipsed even the gold strikes in the Mother Lode. It was the Comstock. The greatest silver mine in history, just over the Sierra Nevadas, on the shoulder of Sun Mountain. By ox team, by Concord coach, by Sacramento River steamer, hundreds of millions in bullion were pouring into the safe rooms of Wells Fargo Bank in San Francisco's Montgomery Street. The shares of the Comstock mines, according to the journalists, were the darlings of the city's stock exchange. Bankers and bartenders, factory owners and stable boys, chambermaids and seamstresses, all were "in the market," and lavishing their winnings on diamonds and silks and carriages with gold and silver fittings. Then why not so for Gerald Donahoe? San Francisco would welcome a man of spirit; there he would regain his position in the world, and Cathlin, with her looks and education, would marry a millionaire. A Catholic millionaire. It was an article of faith which he never abandoned, even when he tossed in the delirium of lung fever.

The *Hesperia* warped alongside the Vallejo Street Wharf, the first mate bellowed orders through his megaphone, the crew cast lines to the pier, the gangplank was run out, the passengers pushed forward. Yet Cathlin lingered at the railing, delaying her leave from the ship which was her only home, delaying the moment when she must commit herself to a new life. Then she saw Captain Dorrance striding toward her.

"Next week we leave for the Isthmus," he said. "I'll save you a cabin."

"Thank you, Captain, but no."

"Still, you may change your mind."

"I mustn't. The passage home would cost what money I have. Better San Francisco with two hundred and eighty dollars than Boston and penniless."

Captain Dorrance extended his hand. "Then be careful of your hotel. Try the What Cheer House. It's plain but decent." He tipped his cap and added, "God keep you."

"The What Cheer it is," the hack driver agreed dubiously when Cathlin finally descended the gangplank with her straw suitcase and stepped into the carriage. From his expression, he had discarded the hope of a tip from one whose shoes were cracked at the toes, whose hat was last year's fashion.

The hack jounced westward through the mudholes of Vallejo Street, then turned south along the artery whose name was famous even in Cathlin's own Boston. Montgomery Street. But where were the handsome bank buildings, the temples of finance? Here, only ugly piles of brick, more mudholes, dray horses struggling with overloaded wagons, Chinese coolies shouldering long poles from which baskets of laundry dangled and swung. Then, as the hack approached the California Street intersection, the prospect improved. The buildings were taller, the men on the sidewalks wore tile hats and frock coats. Occasionally Cathlin caught the gleam of a gold-headed walking stick. There were men in flat-brimmed hats and riding boots, caballeros from the great Mexican ranchos of the Salinas Valley. Just ahead she saw a throng which spilled out into the street. Now the gold-headed walking sticks were being waved in the air. Men were seizing each other by the lapels and shouting. The hack driver nodded toward a brick building which seemed the center of the turmoil. "The Stock Exchange, Miss. Must be some good news from the Comstock." It was good news for Cathlin, too; here was the first evidence that San Francisco meant money and opportunity.

She devoted her first day to reconnoitering the area within easy walk of the What Cheer House. She traversed Kearny

Street, immediately to the west, where women, haughty and confident in their Paris gowns, drifted from shop to shop. So the newspapers in Boston had not exaggerated after all. There were jewelry stores with windows ablaze with diamonds and rubies and emeralds; there were carriages with gold and silver trappings; there were fine restaurants that boasted they had imported their chefs from Paris. The evidences of wealth merely increased Cathlin's sense of her own lack, her loneliness, her helplessness. But surely somewhere, somehow . . .

She followed Kearny Street until it junctured with Market Street and began to search for cards in the store windows. Yes, there was one: JANITOR WANTED. And another. For a tailor. And another. Counterman. And a dozen which read simply, BOY WANTED. If only she were. Then, finally: SEAMSTRESS WANTED. Cathlin's hand reached for the doorknob, then withdrew. There was a second card, an afterthought. NO IRISH.

It was Boston all over again. Too many Irish with their Popish religion. Resented by the Protestants because they would work for any wage that put food in their bellies; called "flannel-mouthed Micks" and "monkey-faced bog-trotters." Even among Cathlin's own kind, there was the caste system. The "real lace Irish," to which she considered herself to belong, drew aside from the "lace curtain Irish." But in San Francisco Cathlin was not even "lace curtain."

That evening she sat in the lobby of the What Cheer House and read a copy of the *Daily Alta California*. She began with the employment section. Perhaps there might be an opening for a schoolteacher. There was none. Of course, she remembered, the school term was already well along. She turned to the social notes. WIFE KILLS HUSBAND IN PARLOR HOUSE . . . TWO DUEL ON POST STREET. BOTH DEAD . . . AXE MURDER AT BELLA UNION. Then her eyes fell on a less spirited headline: THEY RISKED ALL TO GAIN ALL. It was an admiring article on the city's two leading merchants, Felix Verdier, of the City of Paris Dry Goods Company, and Henri Laprebode, of the Maison Française. In 1850, the account went, Verdier had brought from France an entire shipload of fine silks and satins and cases of champagne and casks of cognac to sell to the luxury-starved settlers. They had swarmed aboard the ship, bought everything in sight and demanded more. Henri Laprebode, in faraway Paris, had read that San Francisco was short of washerwomen; the citizens were sending their laundry by clipper ship to China and waiting a full six months to receive it back. That meant customers needed a half-year's supply of underwear, night clothes, shirts, and trousers. Laprebode filled the shortage when he arrived in San Francisco with twenty tons of clothing.

Cathlin carefully tore out the article and tucked it into her reticule. "They risked all to gain all." It was an appealing idea. But what did she have to risk? And how? Then, as if in answer, she remembered the date. Tomorrow would be the feast day of St. Jude, the patron saint of hopeless cases.

She went to early Mass and lighted a candle to St. Jude and prayed for his guidance. Then, as on the day before, but now with a feeling of confident expectation, she walked about and observed. Everywhere, it seemed to her, there were women in silks and satins, with diamonds at their necks and wrists. This time Cathlin did not regard them with envy, but with analytical detachment. They were dumpy, they strode with the rolling gait of day laborers; women with broad backs and muscled arms, who had spent more years over a washtub than in the world of fashion. That was the trouble, Cathlin decided; she had arrived too late. The washerwoman had gotten there first; simply because they were female they had snared rich husbands.

She strolled past the City of Paris and remembered the article in the *Alta California*. Mr. Verdier and Mr. Laprebode had both recognized a need and had supplied it; one with simple honest clothing, the other with luxury goods, merchandise of style and status. Luxury, style, status, Cathlin repeated to herself, and examined her reflection in the store windows. Her dress might be worn and out of fashion, but her waist was delicate and her neck and wrists were as slender as any she had seen in the illustrations in *Godey's Lady's Book*. Why, she had been a fool to even consider teaching school, or sewing until her eyes blurred. Boldness was what was needed. Imagination. Mr. Verdier would appreciate that. On the other hand, perhaps not. The newspaper said he was married. What about Henri Laprebode? Yes. He was a bachelor.

Thank you, St. Jude.

Again she went to early Mass. Then she hurried toward the Maison Française. She lingered outside the dry goods store long enough to whisper an Our Father and then a Hail Mary. She added an "Up Donahoe!"—and entered.

The sales clerks were enchanted with the young lady of such refined taste. She selected the finest qualities, the most chic fabrics and designs from the ateliers of Paris. A rust silk walking dress, to set off the chestnut of her hair; an afternoon ensemble of melon pink, to dramatize the blue of her eyes; a mauve velvet from Worth's for formal evenings. And shoes, gloves, handkerchiefs, parasols, reticules, all to match or in contrast. After each selection, she jotted down a description and the price and asked that the article be reserved in her name. Finally she was done. "And now," she said to the awed clerk, "if you will please direct me to Mr. Henri Laprebode's office."

The owner of the Maison Française was an individualist. In a day of beards and mustaches, he was clean shaven. In a city with strong French overtones, he took pains to speak without accent. He was a small man with bones as delicate as his prices were high. He examined some of those prices on the sheet of paper which Cathlin had submitted to him. He looked up and smiled across his desk. "Most certainly, Miss Donahoe. We shall have pleasure to deliver these to your hotel."

"There is one other matter. The terms."

The smile dimmed. "Credit is extended to old and valued customers. Otherwise, cash."

"I understand." Cathlin waited until the smile returned to full brilliance. "I am considering marriage to a gentleman of substance. We shall require all new furniture for the residence, new draperies, silver, crystalware, uniforms for the servants, and so on. In time, there will be children to clothe. We shall rely on your guidance."

The smile blazed now with the intensity of the noonday sun. "Maison Française will be honored. May I add that the gentleman is to be congratulated on his choice of the lady."

"Thank you. As to the terms for my purchases today, I wish to pay the exact amount which they have cost you."

Laprebode's dark eyes widened with surprise, then narrowed suspiciously. "At my cost? Wholesale?"

"In return for my husband's custom, which, as I say, will be quite considerable. I shall be glad to put such an agreement in writing."

The merchant tapped a forefinger against his lips thoughtfully and regarded Cathlin with the shrewd expression of a man used to dealing with bargain hunters and their stratagems. "It is your desire, I take it, to dress well during your period of engagement." He waited for Cathlin's nod, then again tapped the forefinger to his lips. "And the gentleman's name?"

"I don't know."

Laprebode's eyebrows rose. "I beg your pardon?"

"I haven't met him."

Cathlin watched tensely as Laprebode frowned, sniffed, sat back in his chair, then moved forward again. "I see," he said coldly. "Yes, very clearly." Then he handed her shopping list across the desk. "I suggest that you present your requirements to Mr. Felix Verdier of the City of Paris. Perhaps he may have more sense of humor."

Cathlin rose from her chair. "I shall."

Laprebode smiled at her bravado. "Miss Donahoe, a word of advice. San Francisco has seen many fortune hunters. Our men have a great selection at their disposal."

"Of a certain kind, I'm sure."

"Of all kinds. Without wishing to be rude, may I ask how would you compete? How would you be unique?"

Cathlin tilted her chin proudly. "I would be honest. I would be simply Cathlin Mary Frances Donahoe of Boston, whose father lost his business and hoped to begin again in California, but died at sea and was buried somewhere off Acapulco."

"You have my sympathy." Laprebode sighed. "And that, I fear, is all you will receive from others. No, it is not enough to set you apart."

"Truth will set me apart."

"It is not that kind of world. The male sex desires many things of a woman; honesty is not one of them. I strongly recommend that you take whatever money you have and return to Boston."

Cathlin shrugged. "*Où la chèvre est attaché il faut qu'elle broute.*"

The unexpectedness of her retort brought a chuckle, then a laugh. "*Oui! D'accord!* I must use that. 'Where the goat is tethered, there it must browse.'" Laprebode examined Cathlin with new interest. "So your mother was Norman French."

"Irish, as was my father."

"But your accent?"

"From the sister who taught me at Convent."

Cathlin saw that he was impressed. "So, a convent education. That is in your favor." He cocked his head to one side and studied her. "And your appearance is pleasing. Yes, more than pleasing, very much more. I was, of course, aware of that fact from the beginning."

Cathlin permitted a smile. "You're very gallant, sir."

"No. I merely believe my eyes. Also you have a certain wit. And ambition." Having convinced himself, Laprebode added, "Tell me, Miss Donahoe, how do you plan to meet your particular gentleman? How would he find you?"

She had hoped he would ask, and her answer was ready. "I understand that you are a bachelor."

"True."

"A very eligible bachelor, according to the *Alta California*."

"They flatter me."

"And you dine at the Lick House."

19

"It is our best hotel."

"Then you would invite me to dine with you."

Laprebode's eyes brightened with understanding. "And when some acquaintance of mine is also at table, some eligible friend— Ah, Miss Donahoe, you are *merveilleuse!*" Cathlin held her breath. A door had opened for her. Then it closed with the shake of a head. "I could not deceive my friends. It would be on my conscience. Nevertheless, Miss Donahoe, I wish you *bonne chance.*"

"Thank you." Cathlin opened her reticule, tucked her shopping list inside, and said good day.

She hurried by the counters, her eyes averted from the expectant clerks. She stole one quick backward glance at the rust silk walking dress on the display dummy, then passed out into Kearny Street. She stared about, her mind numb with failure, and tried to remember the direction of the City of Paris. Then she heard running footsteps behind her and a man calling her name.

Laprebode, panting from hurry, beamed at her slyly. "Miss Donahoe . . . did the *Alta California* also say that I am a gambler?"

Her throat tightened, then she managed a nod. "I remember that particularly. But your conscience . . . ?"

Laprebode raised a cautionary finger. "Please! Let us not speak ill of the dead."

That afternoon Cathlin signed the guest register at the Lick House. It was, Henri Laprebode insisted, the proper setting for what he called "the campaign" to come. The lobby floor was of marble, there were potted ferns, and Turkey carpets on the grand staircase, and a string orchestra in the dining room that played Viennese waltzes. Best of all, Cathlin's room was no more expensive than at the What Cheer House. True, it was a room in back, over the kitchen and facing into an alley; but when she stood on a chair, she could look beyond the chimneys and water tanks to the gleaming red and black roof tiles of Chinatown.

"It is an evening of great *ton*," Henri Laprebode pronounced with satisfaction as he surveyed the audience from his box at Union Hall. Cathlin, beside him, could not decide which was more exciting—the concert, the San Francisco society which filled the hall, or the fact that she was wearing the mauve velvet gown from Worth's of Paris.

"That is William Chapman Ralston," Henri whispered, directing her gaze to the opposite box, which was occupied by the man who was to be known as the "King of San Francisco," the foremost banker and controller of Comstock mining. In the same box was Darius Ogden Mills, of Wells Fargo, and later to be the United States Ambassador to Great Britain. Leland Stanford and Charles Crocker, two of the "Big Four" of the Central Pacific Railroad, dominated the adjoining box. On the ground floor proper were men in shipping, cattle, sugar, real estate. Most were married and with their families; but here and there in the audience Henri pointed out a "possibility."

"You notice he is watching you. He is curious. During the intermission we shall enjoy the champagne punch and pastries in the foyer. He will come up to us."

"How can you be sure?"

"I know men. And I know my business. The first rule of merchandising is the proper display of the goods; the second rule is to convince the customer that someone else is about to buy it."

His prediction proved correct. Man after man was introduced to Cathlin, and at some time during the small talk Henri Laprebode would say, "Miss Donahoe tells me that our Lick House is the equal to anything in Boston. So it seems we're not such barbarians, eh?" After a few repetitions, it dawned on Cathlin with a flush of humiliation that Henri was advertising her local address. "Of course, my dear"—he nodded—"but our friend does not know that."

Cathlin frowned a warning. Another man was making his way toward them. Henri glanced around. "No. Not that one. He is impossible."

"You mean married?"

"No money. Also, he lives in Dutch Flat."

He was an outdoor man, Cathlin surmised, for his face was tanned and his mass of sandy hair was sun-streaked. He was one of the tallest men she had ever seen. When he threw an arm around Laprebode's thin shoulders, the Frenchman seemed to dwindle to doll-like proportions.

"How's the underwear selling?"

Laprebode winced. "He never lets me forget my beginnings. Miss Donahoe, may I present Mr. Val Seadon."

Val grinned down at Cathlin and then at her empty glass. "May I?" Without waiting an answer, he took the glass, poured a dipper from the punchbowl, and returned it to her hand. "Where you from, Miss Donahoe?"

"Boston." She waited for Henri to add her impression of the Lick House. Instead he asked Val, "You're in town on a buying trip?"

"Partly. I'm looking for a man."

"Would I know him?"

Val wagged his head. "I don't, either. But I will soon." There was a curious coldness as he spoke the words. Cathlin saw Henri's eyes drift downward along the right side of Val's black cutaway coat and come to rest at the fullness on the hip.

Henri smiled uneasily. "Not at the concert, I hope."

"Oh no."

"So it's not a buying trip."

"It was, at first. My number one boy came along with me. He was going to pick up a bride they'd shipped from Canton. A three-hundred-dollar girl. You know what happened, a Chinese carrying all that gold."

"He's dead?"

"No. But in pretty bad shape. He made it to my hotel and I got him to his tong and they're taking care of him. Hop Gee says it was a white man. Lucky it wasn't one of the Sydney Ducks. By now he'd be shanghaied and out to sea on some whaler." Val saw the frown on Cathlin's face, which he promptly mistook. "A Sydney Duck, Miss Donahoe, is a bad man from Australia. They used to burn down the warehouses here so they could loot homes while everybody was fighting the fires. Robbing and killing is their pleasure, when they aren't shanghaiing."

Cathlin's frown remained. "Mr. Seadon, are you saying that it is possible in this age, in a Union state, after Mr. Lincoln's Emancipation Proclamation, for a Chinaman to *buy* a slave?"

"No. I said a wife. The Chinese buy them the same as men do all over the world. Men with money, and women who want it. Only we call it 'romance.' "

Cathlin flushed and examined her glass of punch with sudden interest.

"You got to understand the fix the Chinese are in," Val went on. "The Central Pacific is building their railroad over the Sierras, and they want labor cheap as they can get it. They put up posters in Canton and say, Come to Fah-lan-sze-ko—that's as near as the Chinese can get to pronouncing San Francisco. Come here, they say, and we'll pay you big money. Big money being one dollar a day against the five dollars they pay a white man. So the Chinese come, figuring they can save enough to go home to their families with respect and honor and a comfortable old age. They don't know about the cost of living here. The years go by, and there's not enough money. Just loneliness. So the girls are shipped over. Boat girls, they call the ugly ones, who go cheap. But they're women. Somebody to love."

Cathlin watched him over the rim of her punch glass, both intrigued by his torrent of words and irritated by his lecturing tone. Then he bowed to her. "Nice to have met you, Miss Donahoe"—and was gone.

That night in her room above the alley she lay abed and listened to the muffled clang of the fog bells in the bay. Was there ever a more lonely sound? And why couldn't she get to sleep? She was overstimulated, she told herself. She was not used to champagne, even diluted as punch. Yes, that was why her mind skipped from subject to subject, like a child at hopscotch. The concert . . . the mauve gown from Worth's . . .

the men she had met . . . Henri's belief in her. Tonight she stood on the very doorsill of the world her father had promised her. And yet her mind kept returning to a phrase, two words that insisted themselves on her like a tune one cannot put out of mind. A phrase Val Seadon had used. It was "boat girls."

In the morning the bouquets and cards for Miss Cathlin Donahoe began to arrive at the Lick House. When she reported the number to Henri Laprebode, the small Frenchman bounded about his office, rubbing his hands and chuckling with satisfaction. "Splendid! You see, it is as I told you. We have created a seller's market!"

"But so many invitations, Henri—which should I accept?"

"All!" His dark eyes danced with anticipation. "We must keep up the spirit of competition. Each night a different gentleman; but one night you must reserve for me."

"Of course," Cathlin laughed. "So you can play the jealous suitor."

Laprebode answered with that familiar sideways tilt of his head, and with sudden solemnity, "Perhaps it shall not be in play."

That night, before going to bed, Cathlin wrote an entry in her diary. "Josephus Wainwright. About 40. He imports sugar from the Sandwich Islands. The Duck Maryland was lovely."

The following noon Cathlin lunched in the hotel dining room. As the headwaiter pulled out her chair, she recognized the man at the next table.

Val Seadon smiled. "So we have the same hotel." Cathlin nodded politely, and then, when she saw that his left arm was in a cloth sling, he added, "Ever try to cut up meat with one hand?" She looked at his plate; the meat seemed to be adequately subdivided. "The waiter did his best, but I guess I don't have a big enough mouth. For eating, I mean. Would you mind?"

She didn't, really—especially after his veiled apology for the other evening. Cathlin applied herself with knife and fork and nodded toward his arm. "What happened?"

24

"I got back Hop Gee's three hundred dollars."

"And the other man?"

Val cleared his throat, which was the extent of his answer.

"Mr. Seadon, would you mind telling me just why you would take such a risk for a Chinaman?"

"Probably because Hop would do as much for me. A man's race doesn't figure with me. I'd do the same for an Irishman. They're both underdogs. Or hadn't you noticed?"

Cathlin nodded. "I thought I'd get away from all that when I left Boston."

By the time she had finished cutting the meat, she agreed that she might as well dine at Val's table. "And afterwards"—he smiled—"maybe you'd let me show you the elephant."

"The what?"

"That's San Francisco lingo. 'Seeing the elephant' means seeing the sights. Maybe the old Mexican Presidio and the Mission Dolores." Val noted Cathlin's hesitation. "That is, if you're free."

"I am," she decided. "Until dinner."

The Presidio, Cathlin discovered, was once a Mexican garrison and fortress guarding the entrance to San Francisco Bay. Now its cypress-shaded slopes were studded with Union cannon at the ready for the Confederate raiders that had never come.

Val leaned against one of the cannon and lighted a cigar. "What were we talking about?"

"The Mexicans." Certainly not about her, Cathlin thought with a tinge of irritation. In the ride out in the hansom cab, Val had not once inquired her opinion, nor why she was in San Francisco, nor her plans. Nothing. She was simply an audience.

"Yes, the Mexicans. They were some of the first prospectors in the Mother Lode, you know. Made some rich strikes. Not that it did them any good. The Yankees came along and drove them off. Those that wouldn't go got lynched. The day I arrived in the diggings, they were fixing a necktie party for a boy from Monterrey. Just because he'd found a nugget. Jealous, you see. In spite of all the stories, not many of them found anything except rheumatism from hunkering down in those damned cold streams."

"Then you did hunt for gold yourself?"

"Yep. Walked all the way from Pennsylvania. A crazy farm boy of fifteen. Blame near starved to death. Lived off rabbits and squirrels. You know how I got my first grubstake?" Val frowned and shook his head. "No, it's kind of raw for a young lady from Boston."

"Suppose you let me be the judge, Mr. Seadon."

"How about 'Val'?"

"If you wish."

"Well, I saw that if I kept scratching for gold, I'd be like the rest. Stealing whiskey and getting drunk and maybe shooting somebody. Or shooting myself out of loneliness. There was a lot of that. Well, I decided I'd hit for San Francisco. Along the way there was a pretty good-sized mining camp. Something must have gone wrong with the water, because almost everybody had diarrhea—I told you this was going to be raw. Anyway, all the men were lined up in front of outhouses. There wasn't anything ailing me, but I stood in line, too. When I'd get up to the door of the convenience, I'd look around and sell my place to the most frantic man behind me. Made fourteen dollars." Val paused, expectant of a laugh, and saw in its place Cathlin's lips set in disapproval. "Well, that was my grubstake. Lost most of it playing poker here at the Bella Union. But I sure learned poker. Mostly from a friend of yours."

"Henri Laprebode?"

"That's how we met. He taught me good. In a week of nights I won back my fourteen dollars and enough over to buy a wagonload of flour and shovels and pickaxes and frying pans. Then back to the diggings and my first general store."

"With your ingenuity, I'd think you would have done better in San Francisco."

Val gazed at a fishing boat tacking its way toward the Golden Gate. "Everything good comes out of the earth. Everything real. Gold, silver, timber, coal, food, cotton. City life is differ-

26

ent. People feed on each other's souls." Val's eyes turned back to Cathlin. "Have you ever smelled a pine forest at night? Or watched an eagle soaring in the clouds, or heard the love talk of raccoons during the full moon?

"That's Dutch Flat?"

"Right in the Sierras. And business is good. We're the main stopover for the wagon teams to the Comstock, and the Central Pacific is laying iron almost at my back door."

Cathlin felt a tightening in her chest. This was not surface conversation. He was not talking about Dutch Flat alone. Veiled as it was, she sensed the invitation for her to share Dutch Flat with Val Seadon.

"But San Francisco is the future," she replied. "It's where children can grow up with all the advantages."

"If you mean schools," Val said, "we got a good one. I know, because I've had one of the teachers tutor me after hours. Fanny Holcomb's taken me through Literature, History, Physics, everything."

"She must be a very dedicated teacher," Cathlin said stiffly. And probably pretty. And unmarried.

As if Val sensed her thoughts, he extracted an enormous silver watch from his waistcoat and flicked open the lid. "Say, we better get a move on if we're going to make it to the Mission."

The Mission San Francisco de Asís, known as Dolores, reminded Cathlin of illustrations she had seen of churches in southern Spain. Its design seemed less Christian than pagan Moor. The scent of incense mingled with the stronger odor of its redwood roof, which was lashed together with rawhide thongs. Cathlin knelt at the altar and lighted a candle to the peace of her father's soul. It did not bring her comfort. Perhaps it was the strangeness of the church, she thought; the feeling of foreignness, of wildness, like San Francisco itself. Or perhaps it was Val Seadon, who waited outside and would not enter the church.

"You're not Catholic," she said, rejoining him.

27

"No."

She was halfway glad. It simplified matters. "What is your religion?"

"None."

"But everybody believes in *something*."

He looked at her moodily. "I believe in hell, because I've seen it."

He shifted his arm in the sling, and Cathlin thought she understood. He was remembering the man he had killed.

In the following week, while Val was out of the city buying supplies, Cathlin dined with six different men whom she had met at the concert. They took her to the same French restaurants and ordered the same terrapin and lobster thermidor and saddles of venison and vintages of Krug Private Cuvée. They escorted her to private houses where she saw the same faces and heard herself repeating the same witticisms that had earned smiles on previous evenings. At one party she met Henri Laprebode.

"My dear, you are not enjoying yourself?"

"Oh, but I am!"

"Still, you look discontented."

"I'm dyspeptic."

"Ah? Tomorrow you must stop by the store. You should not be seen always in the same evening gown."

"It's generous of you, Henri. I'm really tired of thinking of clothes."

The little Frenchman cocked his head to one side like a sympathetic lap dog. "I understand. Even in love there are the dirty dishes to wash."

Then late one foggy afternoon, on Kearny Street, she saw Val. He was buying roasted chestnuts from a sidewalk vendor.

"Have some," he said, offering the paper sack. Nothing about it being good to see her. Instead, he was critical. "You look pale."

She felt pale. And dizzy, as if the blood had rushed from

her brain. She bit into a hot chestnut and tried to slow her breathing.

"Hop Gee is well enough to travel now," he said. "So we'll be heading back for the mountains tomorrow."

"Oh? . . . With a bride?"

He nodded. "Mei-Toy is even smaller than you. A real beauty." Val held up his left arm, which was out of the sling. "Now that I got two wings again, you won't have to cut up my dinner for me."

"Tonight?"

"Have to be. Unless you're checking the merchandise again." He glanced around; they were sufficiently distant from the chestnut vendor. "I figured it out. Every night a different one. But you always came back to the hotel early—the desk clerk kept a log for me—which means you haven't found the right man yet."

Cathlin's face grew even more pale. "You've been talking to Henri Laprebode."

"About what?"

She ground a chestnut between her teeth and debated. Dare she confess the truth? Well, why not? Val had done nothing but talk about himself, his life, his opinions. But she, too, had a story to tell; yes, she would make him admire her imagination, her daring.

Finally, when she had finished describing her arrangement with Henri Laprebode, Val slapped his thigh with delight. "I'll be damned! So Henri grubstaked you!"

"Yes! And I'm not ashamed of it."

"Why should you be?" Val put his arm around Cathlin's waist; it was his first gesture of intimacy. "We're all gold diggers, in one way or another. That's why we came to California. Now, how about dinner?"

"If it's not a French restaurant."

It was German. Afterwards Val decided that they should go someplace else for ice cream. He hailed a hansom and whispered an address to the surprised driver. They went north

29

past Portsmouth Square and the raucous gambling halls beyond and turned onto Broadway. Cathlin did not have to be told that they were entering the Barbary Coast; she had seen Val's right hand slip inside his coat and loosen the Colt .36 pistol he carried on his belt. "Saloons have the best ice cream," he said, as if to distract her attention. "They bring the ice down from Alaska for their drinks, and make the ice cream as a sideline." Implausible, Cathlin thought, but interesting.

The hansom halted under a sign which read STEAM BEER, and the driver went through a swinging door and returned with a bucket and two wooden spoons. They propped the bucket between them on the lap robe; then as Cathlin dipped her spoon, someone whistled. Ahead of them, on a balcony overhanging the street, a woman was leaning over the railing and displaying her bare breasts to a man in the street. The man stared up at her with wavering eyes, then fell backward onto the cobblestones. The hansom rattled past the body and Val looked down.

"Must have put laudanum in his drink."

"Who? Why?"

"One of the girls inside. While she was promising him love, she was relieving his pockets. Then a roust into the street." Val licked his wooden spoon thoughtfully. "You know, I think we should have ordered chocolate. Of course," he went on casually, "the parlor houses over on Jackson Street don't do anything like that. Less infection, too. Here it's just crib houses. Girls kept in cages. Naked and drunk and on the poppy pipe. Just walk along and take your pick."

Cathlin stiffened with insult and suspicion. "You seem to speak from experience."

"It's the best teacher, they say."

They returned to the Lick House in silence. In the lobby, beside the grand staircase, Val said goodbye and kissed Cathlin on the forehead. She accepted it quietly, sadly; then, lest he see the disappointment in her eyes, she turned without a word and started up the staircase.

"Cathlin!"

She looked down at him. He was smiling, yet solemn.

"I hope you don't go all through the garden of love and come out with a cucumber."

Christmas was a week away. Cathlin had received invitations to several holiday parties, none of which were any more appealing than the men who had invited her. Whenever she dined with them, she found herself comparing them with the tall man with sandy hair who had offered her chestnuts on a street corner. She preferred not to think of him as the man who had taken her to the Barbary Coast and talked so knowingly of the flesh. He was a complex man, even a little frightening. He believed in hell, but not in God. And he believed in himself, yet could not put into words his feelings toward Cathlin.

Then one night she awakened from a dream. She had dreamed that she was the woman on the balcony with the naked breasts. And Val was with her. She closed her eyes; perhaps the dream would return.

She went to confession. "Father, I have committed the sin of pride, the sin of ambition."

"Venial sins, my child. Three Hail Marys."

"There is a man. He is not Catholic. He does not believe in any God. I think he may have killed a man. I don't care, so long as he loves me."

"Have you slept with him?"

"No!"

"But you lust after him."

"Yes."

"Four Our Fathers."

"But I *wish* to lust after him."

"And four Hail Marys."

"Father, if we married outside the Church . . ."

"You would be living in sin."

"I know. But if it is just for a while. If he comes to believe

31

in our God, if he takes instruction, if he joins the Holy Church . . ."

"Then you would be living according to the blessed sacraments."

"And his soul would be saved?"

"My child, you want me to encourage you. But hope is not reality. You cannot bargain with our Lord."

Later that same day Cathlin received an envelope postmarked Dutch Flat. Inside was a bill of sale from the Maison Française; it was marked "Paid" and signed by Henri Laprebode. Val had written on the bottom of the bill, "How about a grubstake for life?"

That night Cathlin boarded the Sacramento River steamer *Chrysopolis*. The next afternoon she stepped off the stage in front of the Dutch Flat Hotel. On New Year's Day 1865 she was married to Val Seadon. By a judge.

Chapter 2

I T W A S their first week of marriage and the first week of January 1865. They stood in the doorway of their rented house and watched the last of their guests go down the icy path. Val closed the door and Cathlin flung herself into his arms with a wail. "They don't like me! They resent me! They're jealous because none of them got to marry you!"

Val kissed her hair. "Well now, I don't think Hank Bowers ever set his cap for me. I'd say what the women are jealous about—if they are—is you stramming around in Paris gowns."

"All right! Tomorrow I'm going to the store and get the plainest thing on your shelves. A linsey-woolsey!"

It was almost two weeks before Cathlin could make good her promise, for that night was the beginning of the winter's great snowfall. When Dutch Flat next saw the sun, eight feet of snow had packed against the ground-floor windows and doors of the Seadon house. A "normal" winter, Val told Cathlin; she would get used to it. But she did not. The brutal cold seeping through walls and windows; the chilblains and chapped hands; the ice in the morning washbasin, the stillness of the night, broken only by the cries of wild creatures, the monotony of days that seemed never to end and nights that came too soon—all were a world away from the comforts and cheer of San Francisco. There was not even a Catholic church. Cathlin's communion and confession depended upon the monthly visits of the circuit-riding priest. There were times when she began to doubt her marriage, especially when Val was away overnight, sledding supplies to distant mining camps. Then he would be back and gathering her up in a rush and taking her with tenderness, with laughter, or even violence, and Cathlin knew that there could be no other life for her. There was a Divine Purpose to everything; her desperate days as a fortune-hunter had led her to Henri Laprebode, and through him to Val. And some day soon he would discover God. Her God.

"I won't be a hypocrite," Val had insisted, when she had first come to him. "I won't say I believe in God when I don't. I believe in you, I believe in myself, and that's enough for any marriage." Those had been Val's terms and Cathlin, confident that time would bring all things, had accepted them. . . .

With the coming of spring, she finally saw Dutch Flat as Val had described it. Long lines of freight wagons, drawn by ten-mule teams, lumbered through town with supplies for the Comstock; bullwhips cracked, teamsters cursed, people leaped to the safety of the boardwalks as Concord coaches plunged past, outward bound from the Comstock with their green Wells Fargo chests heavy with bullion.

And there was the railroad. From the back stoop of their house Cathlin watched the work trains of the Central Pacific labor up the grade toward the railhead just above the town. She could hear the explosion of blasting powder, the clang of sledgehammers driving spikes into ties. The work force was enormous; it far exceeded the population of Dutch Flat itself. There were, according to Val, 2500 Irish, 7500 Chinese, and 600 teams of horses.

34

One day—it was shortly after the assassination of President Lincoln—Val and Cathlin put a picnic basket in the buckboard and drove up to the railhead. Hundreds of coolies were building an earth fill across a ravine. On the opposite side, along the face of a granite cliff, more coolies dangled in baskets and hammered holes into the rock.

"That used to be Hop Gee's job," Val said. "He was a powder man. He'd pound a hole into the stone, set a charge, and then get the hell up the cliff. One day the charge went off too soon and Hop's basket landed in the river. Busted his leg. After that the railroad didn't want him, but I did."

No wonder he was grateful to Val, Cathlin thought. No, more than *grateful*, almost worshipful.

"You're seeing history," Val went on, nodding toward the railhead. "When it's done, when those two bands of metal connect up with the Union Pacific, the United States will be truly united. For all time. Long after you and I . . ."

"Val, dear."

"Hmmm?"

"Please don't start into another speech. This is a picnic, remember?"

"Oh. Speaking of, I know just the place."

The buckboard followed a steep trail through pines and red-berried madrona. Scrub jays screamed at the intruders, and squirrels leaped from tree to tree overhead in chattering alarm. Finally they came out onto a rocky promontory overlooking a wide canyon. Below, in the distance, they could see hydraulic gold miners at work. Huge hoses as thick as a man's neck, mounted on iron swivels like cannon, hurled jets of water against the canyon sides. Nothing withstood the pounding. Earth, boulders, shrubs, trees, collapsed and washed down into collecting basins where men waded through the slush in search of nuggets.

Val swung his eyes around to the wooded area behind them. "You know, I ought to buy this point, before they wash it down, or some bastard cuts the timber for railroad ties."

"Val, you can't protect the whole world."

"Just my part of it. The way things are going, there won't be forage left for a single deer or raccoon or squirrel. It's a sin against Nature."

Cathlin seized the moment. "If you believe in sin, then you must believe in God."

"Oh, come on, Cath, let's not start on that again."

"God exists, and we are His children. Without His love, and our love for Him, we are nothing."

"So you think He loves us?"

"I know it."

"Well, it's a strange kind of love that heaps rewards on the thieves of this world—the bankers and politicians and war profiteers—and lets the people you call 'good' barely scratch out a living, or suffer disease and starvation and persecution and insanity."

"That's the devil's argument. Jesus said, 'Judge not lest ye be judged.' "

Val threw up his hands. "We *got* to judge. You're judging me right now, just as I'm judging you. And we're not exactly flattering each other."

"Val, I'm not smart enough to argue it. Logic can go just so far, the rest must be faith. If you'd let the priest talk to you, the next time he comes . . ."

"A waste of time."

She could feel the heat flooding into her cheeks, the angry trembling of her fingers. "Aren't you ever going to think of me? I'm living in sin. I'm risking my immortal soul for you!"

He wiped the back of his hand across his greasy lips, then caught her in his arms and drew her face to his.

"*No!* You always think you can answer me with that! You can't! I won't have it!"

It was their first battle. And, as Cathlin learned later, the first month of her pregnancy.

She sketched in her mind the scene when she would tell Val. He would be delighted. He was. They would make such plans for the boy. They did. And it would be a boy. What else? Val would agree that the child should be baptized. He

36

didn't care. They would buy the house they were renting and enlarge the bedroom for a nursery. Of course. And after her own personal version of the Annunciation, they would make love with a special tenderness. They did.

"I'll be damned!" Val grinned down at her. "Wait till I tell Hop Gee!"

"Don't you dare!"

"I got to! He just told me! Mei-Toy's doing it, too!"

"Val, can't you ever forget that man?"

"Why should I? Hop went to San Francisco to get him a bride, and I wound up with one myself. Hop's going to be a father, and so am I! We've both staked out our immortality."

The following week Val appeared at the front door with another Chinese. A frail-looking young man with a bandaged head and a decided limp. "This is Ah Sing," Val said. "He got cut up in a knife fight up at the railhead. He's going to cook for us."

"Val, I'm perfectly capable of doing the kitchen work."

"You're expecting, aren't you?"

"Yes, but—"

"And Ah Sing isn't. So it's settled."

The summer passed into fall, and soon winter would be upon them. A winter Cathlin did not dread, for with it she would welcome her child. She was heavy and uncomfortable and lonely; for Val, sparked by the idea of a family, worked longer and longer hours. He opened another branch store, in Grass Valley, and hired another Chinese to run it. Sammy Lee. He bought grazing land in a distant valley where he could raise cattle for the butcher shops. He spent long evenings playing poker at the Dutch Flat Hotel, in order to "get the drift of what's going on other places." And he made his annual buying trip to San Francisco. Alone. One night he came home and found Cathlin weeping over her newly made bassinet.

"I'm sorry, honey. I guess I was a bachelor too long. I'm always thinking about you, but it isn't the same as being here."

"No, it isn't. I need somebody to talk to. A woman."

The next morning Mei-Toy knocked at the back door. Neither woman spoke the other's tongue, yet they took to each other immediately. They were in the same month of pregnancy, both new to the mountains, both quick of mind and needle. They made baby clothes together, and patchwork quilts, and repaired their husbands' shirts and socks. Gradually they evolved a common language, part pidgin English, part charade. The secrets of Chinese medicines and diet were Mei-Toy's favorite subject. Cathlin must, she said, provide ground tiger bones for Val's strength, snake gall to ward off rheumatism, the skins of crickets to make him eloquent. Most important, there must be prayers to the Kuan Yin, so like Cathlin's Blessed Virgin, for the health of the coming male child.

Snow came early that winter, and so did Cathlin's labor. It was long and difficult, and when it was over, the doctor administered laudanum and Cathlin slept the day away. When she opened her eyes, finally, Val was bending over her, his face somber and haggard. He kissed her check and she whispered, "Is it a boy?"

He swallowed and looked away. Then she was conscious of Mei-Toy sobbing in the background.

"Val!"

"Yes. It was a boy." He reached down his hand and smoothed her hair. "There's still just us, honey. Just us."

She turned her face into the pillow. For the first time in her life, Cathlin knew true terror. Death still pursued the Donahoes; she had brought its blight to the man she loved.

She did not see the burial plot until the March thaw. The cemetery was a clearing among the brooding pines. Val, with his arm around her waist, led her from gravestone to gravestone. JOSEPHINE TAYLOR. AGE SIX MONTHS. . . . RALPH KINDLEBURG. AGE TWO. . . . HARMONY MACFEE. AGE SIX WEEKS.

"It happens to everybody," Val said. "It's not living in sin; it's not God's punishment. It's diphtheria, diarrhea, pneumonia. And bad doctors or no doctors."

38

Cathlin shuddered. "You never told me it would be like this!"

"Why should I? Good God, woman, what do you think life is? A deck of cards rigged so you win every time?"

She did not answer.

In 1869 the golden spike was driven at Promontory Point, Utah. The transcontinental railroad was a reality. Cathlin never tired of watching the trains chuff and clank along the grade on the south side of town. At the first sound she would hurry to the window or the back stoop for a sight of the locomotives and the varnished elegance of the Silver Palace cars. Seeing them, Cathlin felt she was no longer a captive of the mountains; someday she and Val would go aboard one of those Silver Palace cars and return to her world.

Chapter 3

"SIX YEARS! It is not possible!" Henri Laprebode declared "For Cathlin, it is but the blink of an eye. She grows in beauty while we, alas, grow only in weight." It was an evening in September, 1871, and they were at dinner in the Russ House: Henri, Val and Cathlin. Henri's hair was tinged now with silver and his frock coat was cut more amply to minimize a paunch. "But there are changes also in our city, no?"

"I hardly recognize it," Cathlin said. "Val sees the city every year on his buying trip, but for me it's almost unbelievable."

Henri nodded. "It is but the beginning. Soon there will be cable cars up California Street to the top of Nob Hill. There is where the great mansions will be built." He smiled at the prospect. "It will be amusing to see the great rivals in business and politics, who hate each other with such passion, spitting and snarling on that one small bit of real estate!"

As with so many San Franciscans, Henri Laprebode took a perverse pride in the machinations of the city's leading citizens, and now he launched into a recital of the latest scandals and rumors. There were the stockmarket manipulations of Fair and Flood and Mackay; there was the social climbing of the "Big Four"—Collis P. Huntington, onetime whiskey peddler; Leland Stanford, former grocer; Charles Crocker, ex-blacksmith; Mark Hopkins, promoter—who had bribed congressmen and senators and siphoned off millions in federal money supposedly spent in the building of the Central Pacific Railroad. And finally, there was William Ralston, Cashier of the Bank of California, who, with his ally William Sharon, had intrigued to bankrupt the individual mine owners in the Comstock and so gain control of their mines.

"Please! No more!" Cathlin interrupted, at last. "I don't want to hear about evil men."

Henri smiled. "I did not call them evil, my dear. The Big Four took from the government, but they gave us the railroad. And Ralston, with his money and imagination, has done more than any single man to build San Francisco." Henri paused, his eyes narrow with thought. "Val, perhaps you and Cathlin are free tomorrow evening?" Val nodded. "Then let us not speak of the devil; let us sup with him. Ralston gives a great soiree at his Château Belmont, down the peninsula. It is in honor of a visiting British lord and lady. I am invited. And you shall be, too."

The Seadons exchanged looks, and Cathlin said, "It sounds lovely, but I don't have anything to wear."

Henri waved a hand. "Maison Française is at your disposal. Whatever you require." Then he winked. "On the usual terms. My cost."

Château Belmont was marble and marquetry, Turkey carpets and crystal chandeliers, statues and exotic tropical plants, liveried servants and pedigreed dogs. The hundred guests sipped their champagne cocktails in the library and came forward, one by one, to receive a handshake from their host. Cathlin noted that Ralston carried himself with a military

41

erectness, as if to compensate for his lack of height. He wore a close-cropped beard which he stroked while his eyes darted about with the eager brightness of a terrier.

The babble of conversation grew louder with each round of cocktails, then abruptly it hushed. Every face turned toward Ralston. "It is time," Henri whispered. "He has pressed the button. Watch!" The Seadons followed Henri's gaze toward the far wall of the library. There was a rumbling, and the wall, with its panels, its tapestries, its oil paintings, rose like a theater curtain and vanished into the ceiling. Beyond stretched a great banquet hall. A score of Chinese waiters stood at attention beside tables laden with food and flowers and flickering candelabra. The hundred guests stared in awe; then applause and bravos. Somewhere off scene an orchestra struck up a drinking song.

After the dinner and speeches by Ralston and the visiting lord, the guests streamed into the ballroom to waltz and renew themselves with more champagne. Val whirled Cathlin, in her gown of pale rose, around the floor with the sureness of a dancing master. Inwardly, he was less sure. He looked down at the eyes so bright with excitement, the flushed cheeks, the lips following the words of "The Beautiful Blue Danube."

"This is the life you've always wanted, isn't it?"

She glanced up into his eyes. " 'The Danube so blue, so blue, so blue!' "

Val frowned. "But how many Ralstons are there in the world?"

She gave him a coquette's smile. "More important, how many Val Seadons?"

He laughed, swung her up off the floor, and kissed her.

Later he found Henri Laprebode at a roulette wheel in the gaming room.

"History repeats," Henri said. "Our first meeting was at a table of luck."

"Yes. Someplace we can talk?"

"Of course." Henri picked up his chips and led the way out

onto a great stone balcony facing into a formal garden. They lighted their cigars.

"And what do you think of our host?" Henri asked.

"Napoleon before Moscow. Napoleon waiting for Waterloo."

"But Napoleon did not have the Comstock."

"That's what I want to talk about." Val nodded. "The Comstock is making Ralston and killing the Mother Lode. First we lost the miners, now the railroad has connected up with the branch line to the Comstock, and there are no more freight wagons through Dutch Flat. Business is dying, people are moving away. I'm thinking of it myself."

"Solely for business reasons?"

"Not entirely. Cath hates the winters in the mountains. She needs a change."

"And perhaps something more?" Henri watched Val, noting his silence. "Permit me an observation. Last evening and again tonight I was aware of something between you and Cathlin— or perhaps *not* between you."

Val stared down at the cigar between his fingers. "I have not joined the Catholic Church, as Cath wanted. And she lost a son. A stillbirth. Since then two miscarriages."

Henri's hand went impulsively to Val's shoulder. "My poor friends. But surely, next time . . ."

Val looked off into the dark. "Do you suppose there really is a God?"

They saw the glow in the night sky from the train window. As the train slowed for the Dutch Flat station, they could see the flames.

"Jesus Christ!" Val cried. "It's Chinatown!"

Cathlin went home alone while Val raced off to join the volunteer fire company. It was midnight when Val returned to the house. His clothes were torn, his face streaked with black. But it was the look in his eyes which frightened Cathlin.

"Goddamned son of a bitch! They let him get away!"

"Who?"

"Some crazy drunk. Set fire to the houses and shot 'em as they ran out." He buckled on his revolver and a cartridge belt.

"Val! You can't! That's for the sheriff—"

"Hell, what does he care about a few murdered Chinese? This is something for me and Hop Gee."

Cathlin felt faint; she steadied herself against a table. "Mei-Toy?"

"Dead."

"And her boy?"

"Dead."

She did not see Val again for three days. Where he went, what happened, were never discussed. By Val or Hop Gee.

It seemed to Cathlin that the tragedy drew the two men more closely together than ever. Each had lost a son, each had lost his posterity. They made a curious-looking pair as they went about town. Val, so tall and long-legged, striding the boardwalks; Hop Gee, short and squat, pigtail trailing out from under his hat, trotting a respectful two paces behind.

"Do you think Hop will take another wife?" she asked Val.

"Who knows?" Secretly she feared the possibility. Suppose the new wife bore a child, while Cathlin could not bring forth? With each passing month of her barrenness, she felt the growing distance between herself and Val. Each time she recited a Hail Mary, she winced at the words "blessed be the fruit of thy womb."

Val closed his store in Red Dog and, two years later, sold his branch in Grass Valley. Sammy Lee, who had managed the Grass Valley store, was transferred to Dutch Flat and put in charge of deliveries to the outlying settlements.

"They'll all be gone in another year or two," Val said. "People are just walking away from their homes. Those who stay on are tearing down the vacant houses for firewood. Dutch Flat will be next."

44

"There's always San Francisco," Cathlin reminded.

"All right, damn it! Any place that will change our luck!"

Still, it was not until August 1875 that Val could liquidate his properties and was free to start anew in San Francisco. He and Cathlin made the journey by Sacramento River steamer and docked at the same Vallejo Street wharf where Cathlin had first set foot in California. The hack carried them by the same route to Montgomery Street. There was another crowd outside the Stock Exchange; but this time there was a sinister difference. Men and women massed the street from sidewalk to sidewalk, shouting, screaming curses, hurling bricks at the entrance to the Exchange. Mounted police were clubbing heads. "Jesus! Must be a real crash," Val muttered. The hack made a detour and encountered a second riot outside William Ralston's Bank of California. "Holy God!" Val shouted. "It's closed its doors!"

He left Cathlin at the Lick House and went to see Henri Laprebode. It was evening when he returned and spread the newspaper in front of Cathlin.

BANK OF CALIFORNIA FAILS

COMSTOCK REPORTED FINISHED

RIOTS AS MARKET COLLAPSES

WALL STREET CRASHES IN SYMPATHY

WILLIAM RALSTON FOUND IN BAY. POSSIBLE SUICIDE

Val sighed. "Poor Ralston. Poor San Francisco. I'm afraid it's done for." He saw the tears welling in Cathlin's eyes. "But not us, Cath. We're going to be all right. I was walking down Market Street, and I went into one of those land offices. I bought us some farm land." He paused, wanting her reaction. There was none. "It's down the San Joaquin Valley. Place called Weston. It's the county seat. Haber County. Not much of a place, but it's on the new railroad they're building down to Los Angeles. I can start another general store, or maybe a hardware. Hop Gee can help me. And Ah Sing and Sammy

Lee . . ." He hesitated awkwardly, watching the tears course down her cheeks. "Cath, I never was meant to be a city boy. I need elbow room." He stopped again. "Cath, you said you never wanted to see another snow. Now you won't. This can be the beginning of a whole new life."

She sank down onto the bed and buried her face in the pillow. "Honey! What's wrong? What in God's name . . . ?"

He barely made out the muffled words: "I'm pregnant."

He watched her silently. Then: "You're sure?"

She turned her face toward him. "While you were gone this afternoon, I went to a doctor."

He dropped down on his knees beside her and ran his fingers through her hair. "Well! And I thought you were crying because of the news, because you were frightened."

"I am. If it happens again . . . if it's another gravestone . . ."

He held her in his arms and let her cry herself out. Then, finally: "Cath, we're going to stay on in the city for a few days. Long enough for me to at least get started."

She looked up into his face and heard the words that she had waited ten long years for. "I want to see a priest. I want to take instruction."

BOOK
TWO

Chapter 4

I N T H E twenty-four years since Val and Cathlin had moved
to Weston, they had never experienced such a sandstorm. Sand
choked the horse troughs along Central Avenue, sifted into
the lobby of the Pioneer Hotel, mixed with the sawdust on
the floor of the Orleans Saloon. It drifted between the tracks
in the railroad yard and silted around the little wooden markers
in the Chinese graveyard, around the tattered paper flags and
the forked sticks which held offerings of pork meat for those
in the spirit world. It was cold, as well, for this was December.
A sandstorm in winter was unusual, almost as unusual as Val
Seadon going to Sunday services. Yet there he was, reining the
buggy down Central Avenue in the direction of St. Augustine's. Cathlin sat beside him, wrapped in a bearskin robe,
her face veiled against the swirling dust. Val, by contrast, was
without hat or overcoat, and his gray hair and black suit were
filmed over by yellow soot. It was typical of Val, this defiance of nature. The weather and the opinion of his fellow

man were equally unimportant. Who else but Val Seadon would have dared the luxury—the brazen ostentation, according to some in town—of a buggy *and* a surrey *and* a buckboard for one family?

The surrey was following Val and Cathlin. In it were their children, the two grown sons and a daughter. Ross and Owen and Leah. Presently, as the two vehicles approached the center of town, there were more buggies and farm rigs, all proceeding toward St. Augustine's or to the Baptist and Congregational churches. On foot, other townspeople hurried through the chill yellow gloom. As Val swung the buggy toward the hitching post outside St. Augustine's, he marveled at the turnout. Of course, piety was not the only motivation, he reflected; this particular day of worship was really a celebration. This, the last Sunday of the year 1899, was also the last day of the nineteenth century and the New Year's Eve of the twentieth.

The congregation at St. Augustine's was clearly in a holiday mood, eager to forget the bad year now coming to a close. Not one bad year, but three. Three winters with little rain, three summers of such intense heat that the wheat crops had failed and sheep and cattle had died. Store credit was exhausted for many families, and even Val Seadon's hardware store was six months overdue to its suppliers; and Val, in spite of his outward show of prosperity, had to do the unthinkable—pay the wages of his three Chinese house servants with IOU's.

After the Mass, Father Barrie addressed the congregation in the mood of the day. It was, he declared in a voice still flannel-thick from County Galway, a time to forget personal troubles, to look outward, to view with pride the achievements of this great America which had so recently humbled imperial Spain and taken helpless millions under the wings of the eagle. Cuba, the Philippines, Puerto Rico. But the world stood in awe of more than American might; it envied the spirit of adventure, the will to succeed, which had made America and the Far West —and yes, even Haber County and this town of Weston.

Finally the service was over and, as if in agreement with Father Barrie's optimism, so was the sandstorm. The congregation streamed out into Central Avenue and stared gladly at the clearing sky. The wind had died, the dust was no longer settling. Men slapped each other's backs and women called out laughingly to each other, "See you next century!" Val helped Cathlin into the surrey, with Owen and Leah, and motioned his eldest son Ross to join him in the buggy.

"We'll hold dinner for you," Cathlin called, meaning the midday meal common to all farming towns.

Val shook his head. "Don't. The train might not come in on time."

"But, Val—"

"We'll eat later. Ross will want to show his friend around town."

Val flicked the reins and headed Lady, the bay mare, toward the rail depot, some three blocks to the east. It was then that Ross spoke for the first time since they had left the house that morning.

"Why don't we just drive Dave straight to the house? There's no need to show him around."

"Why not?"

"There's nothing to see."

Val glanced curiously at his son, this almost uncanny physical duplication of himself at age twenty-three. Ross had been strangely quiet, almost brooding, ever since that telephone call the day before. It didn't make sense. Ross and David Marcus had been roommates at Stanford; Ross had filled his letters with the virtues of young Marcus. The best track man, the best swimmer, the leader in every class prank, the student with two beautiful sisters and a banker father who had entertained Ross on weekends in San Francisco. Yet when David telephoned from Los Angeles that he had been mustered out of the Army Volunteers and would be passing through Weston on his way home, Ross had not thought to invite him to stop off. That invitation had come from Cathlin.

Val put his suspicion into words. "Dave knows I run the hardware, doesn't he?"

"We never talked about it."

51

"I see. Just what did you tell him about us?"

Ross squirmed on the buggy seat. "We're ranchers."

"Uh-huh. Except ranchers don't live in town. They live on their ranches."

"The big ones don't."

Val tightened the reins and the buggy creaked to a stop alongside the wooden platform of the train station. "In other words, you had to leave Stanford after just one term because I needed you back home. Had nothing to do with a money pinch." Val waited for his son's answer; then his face hardened. "God damn it, I don't have to apologize for my life. To you *or* your friends!"

Ross was out of the buggy now, looking up at his father. "Maybe that's the trouble. You don't care what anybody thinks. But I do. I want people to respect me. I want—" He bit off the words with a sigh. "I'm sorry. Let's forget it."

Val's face softened as he clambered from the buggy. "Don't you worry, boy. I think we're going to make the right impression on your friend Dave."

The youth who swung down the steps of the *San Joaquin Flyer* was dressed in Army khaki. His peaked infantry hat was cocked at a rakish angle; a canvas duffel bag was slung over one shoulder. From the sag of his uniform, it was clear that he had lost considerable weight; the sallow complexion and the hollows under his dark Jewish eyes told of malaria. If he appeared convalescent, David Marcus was thoroughly robust in his greeting of Ross Seadon. They laughed and pounded each other and said it was like old times and they both looked great, just great.

Val thrust out his hand. "We're flattered, Dave, that you chose to spend New Year's with us instead of your folks."

"They're in London, sir. They didn't know I was being invalided home."

"What about your sisters?"

"In New York. Sure no point of my rattling around San Francisco by myself when I can be with the Seadons."

Val chuckled. "With a remark like that, I'd say the Army's loss is going to be a gain for the diplomatic corps."

The buggy with its three occupants made its way back to Central Avenue, passed the courthouse, and turned onto the river road and went north. Gradually the clapboard stores gave place to a straggle of private houses and then to open range land where the only evidence of life was an occasional jackrabbit which spurted out of the dead mesquite and brought a nervous snort from the mare.

David glumly surveyed the arid landscape. "How far is your ranch?"

He asked the question of Ross, but it was Val who answered. "It's not a ranch, exactly. I had in mind to show you something more important. One of my new projects."

When Val did not elaborate, David said, "You sound mysterious. What kind of project?"

"You'll see."

After a while the buggy reached a fringe of dead cottonwood trees and turned eastward. Just beyond the cottonwoods the ground sloped sharply downward to a jumble of granite boulders. Here among the boulders there was a gleam of water.

"The mighty, majestic Haber River," Val said. "Lowest it's been in twenty years." He flung his arm out in a sweeping gesture. "I bought this land sight unseen when Cath and I were living in San Francisco. Fellow swore it was prime farm land. Only thing I've ever raised is dust."

David clucked his tongue in sympathy. "The earth doesn't look too bad. Couldn't you bring some water up from the river?"

"Not worth the effort."

"How about a water well?"

"Like that contraption up ahead?" Val nodded toward a pyramid of wooden uprights and crossbeams just discernible through the cottonwoods.

David puzzled a moment. "It *is* a water well, isn't it?"

"Not exactly. Last year we had an earthquake. Pretty fair

shake. A week or so later Ross and I happened to be making a delivery across the river. I mean, we *happened* to be out here," Val corrected guiltily.

"It *was* a delivery." Ross turned to David, half in explanation, half in challenge. "We got a hardware store, and we were making a delivery to a customer."

Val gazed gratefully at his son. "So we were. That's right. Anyway, we drove the wagon down to the ford, and I saw something coming out between the rocks. The quake must have opened a fissure, and there it was, oozing right out of the riverbank." Val paused dramatically. "What do you think it was?"

David cast a mystified glance at Ross, as if he alone knew the answer.

"Tar," said Ross.

"Oil," said Val.

"We don't know it for sure, Dad."

It was the old argument again. "Oil," Val repeated. "It looked exactly like what I've seen down in Los Angeles. They got a place out west of the city called the La Brea Pits. 'Brea' is Spanish for tar, or asphaltum. They used to caulk their roofs with it. Nowadays they're using it to pave their streets. The point is, if you take some kinds of asphaltum and heat it, you can boil out genuine petroleum."

"Good Lord!" David's eyes swiveled from Val to Ross and back to Val. "Good Lord! Oil! And *you!*"

"Maybe," Ross cautioned. "Nobody's ever found any in Haber County."

He might have added that few men would have tried. To most people, petroleum, or "rock oil," was simply a handy substance to lubricate machinery or to top off dusty roads. True, it could be distilled into kerosene, which was its chief value. But to the people of Weston and Haber County, kerosene was the business of the Standard Oil combine, back East, and perhaps a few mavericks down Los Angeles way. As for the fact that petroleum could also be refined into gasoline, what was the point? That newfangled machine, the automobile, would surely be powered by steam or electric batteries.

"Oil's here somewhere," Val went on insistently. "At first I figured we could dig into the river bluff, tunnel in, until we found the source. But the bluff is soft shale. Could come down on us. We'd have to shore up as we went, and that's killing work. It's a lot easier to drill down from the top. And one of these days, whether it's this third hole of mine or the tenth . . ." Val grinned in contemplation, then said, "Well, we better be getting on home, before Cath thinks we've been introducing you to the pleasures of the Orleans Saloon." He laid a cautionary finger on Dave's sleeve. "And by the way, don't tell my wife we brought you out here."

"Reasons?"

"You might say."

The Seadon house was as individual as the man who owned it. It was the largest residence in Weston, and certainly the most ornate. As one turned in at the picket gate and proceeded up Cathlin's rose-lined walk, the impression was of a house which had been constructed with a giant pastry gun. There were cupolas and turrets and gabled windows and wide eaves, all dribbling with wooden fretwork. The broad covered veranda which fronted the house seemed designed less for lounging than as an excuse for more fretwork and filigree.

David Marcus' first view of the Seadon house was with Hop Gee and Sammy Lee frantically sweeping sand from the great veranda. Cathlin met him at the front door and reminded him comfortably of those hospitable Irish women who were now among the first ladies of San Francisco.

"You must forgive the way the house looks, David," Cathlin said, ushering him into the central hall. "We spent all week cleaning and polishing for New Year's, and then that terrible sandstorm came along and undid everything. Promise you won't look at the windows or my lace curtains." Cathlin glanced nervously at the worn Brussels carpet on the hall stairs and decided there was no reasonable excuse she could invent for its condition, nor for the scuffed and cracked leather chairs David would soon see in the parlor. "Owen! Come meet your brother's friend."

A tall, lanky figure materialized from the direction of the dining room. Although he was barely two years his brother's junior, Owen Seadon's features had not yet jelled into manhood. His blue eyes gave the impression that he was thinking of something else.

"Where's Dad?"

"With Ross. They're putting up the buggy." Cathlin gave a provoked frown. "Owen! Say how do you do!"

Owen blinked owlishly. "How do you do."

They shook hands, and David swung the duffel down from his shoulder.

"Owen, dear, why don't you take David's things up to the guest room?" And at Owen's uncertain look, Cathlin whispered, "You know. *Your* room."

Owen slung the duffel under one arm and started up the stairs. Cathlin hastened into another apology. "You wouldn't know it, but that boy has the most beautiful manners. He's just so absent-minded. Always with his nose in a book, history books mainly." She took David's arm. "Let's go in the parlor, and I'll have Ah Sing fetch us some tea. I expect you'd like some sandwiches, too, missing our noon meal and—"

At that moment a voice—half girl's, half woman's—echoed down the stairwell. "What on earth is *that?*"

And Owen's reply. "A body. A headless body."

"Liar!"

"All right. A woman for my harem."

"I wouldn't be surprised. That's all you and Ross think about."

Cathlin flushed at the exchange and called up the stairwell. "Teatime, dears! Teatime!"

Footsteps pounded down the stairs. White pumps and stockings and a blue and white dimity skirt descended into view, then a white blouse, and, finally, a face. A startled face with wide hazel eyes which locked on the uniform in the hallway. "*Oh!*" Hands shot upward and patted the chestnut hair, shot downward and smoothed the skirt. The footsteps resumed, slowly now, with stately dignity. A slender arm and hand ·extended.

"How do you do, David Marcus." The voice was a full octave lower. "I'm Leah."

The comfortable security of the Seadon parlor that afternoon was cozily reassuring to the audience, which gasped or shook their collective heads at David's tales of the Philippine insurrection. Owen cross-legged on the floor, Ross sprawled on the leather sofa, Leah perched on the bench in the bay window. Cathlin, passing back and forth in the hallway on some mission of instruction to the Chinese, caught snatches about jungle ambushes and poisonous snakes and head-hunters and peoples with curious names. Igorot, Moro, Tagalog.

"Tell us about San Francisco," Leah begged finally.

"It's home. What's there to tell?"

"Everything! The concerts and the opera and Market Street and Golden Gate Park and dining at the Palace Hotel and sailing on the bay and"—Leah cast a glance at the doorway; Cathlin was not in sight—"and the Cliff House and the Poodle Dog Cafe. Why, San Francisco is the Paris of America!"

David grinned. "You sound like an editorial in the *Chronicle*."

"Really, David," she persisted. "you must have *some* social life."

"Not much. I leave that to my sisters."

"How old are they?"

"Twenty and twenty-one."

Leah accepted that information with a smile of pity. She turned her head in profile to David, allowing the afternoon sunlight which streamed in the bay window to emphasize her strong chin, the straight nose, and high forehead. "And still not married?"

"But looking. That's why they're in New York. Everybody calls them a couple of smashers, but they don't know how to handle the fellows. They're always talking about dull things. Read too much, I guess. My father says they're constipated with too many ideas."

It was a mistake. Leah's head swung around and her hazel eyes skewered him. "In other words, you and your father think a woman shouldn't have a brain. Shouldn't have ideas. Shouldn't have a career. And I don't mean just being a typewriter girl." David threw up a hand as if to ward off her words, but she pressed the attack. "There are women right in San Francisco, in case you don't know it, who have law degrees and medical degrees. Fascinating women. Women who want to be more than playthings for men. Women who . . . who . . ." She choked on her words. She sprang up from the window bench and marched stiff-legged out of the room. In the hall she turned and flung the words at David's head: "The kind of woman I'm going to be!"

New Year's Eve in Weston at the turn of the century was not a night for partying. Families spent the evening quietly together; the more devout went in for Bible reading and making long lists of "resolutions" for the new year. Socializing was reserved for the next day, New Year's Day, when people called on friends and neighbors. It was typical of Val Seadon to challenge this custom and, as he put it, "get a jump on everybody." New Year's Eve at the Seadons' was open house. Ah Sing had scrambled up the big elm in the poultry yard in pigtailed pursuit of the tom turkey which now reposed in golden glory in the center of the buffet table. The cooling cellar had yielded up a smoked ham and preserved peaches and pears and apples ready to be candied to crimson perfection. Ah Sing's big oven had disgorged enough pies and cakes and cookies to satiate a church social. Val himself had concocted the great bowl of eggnog, lacing it alternately with amber bourbon and dark Jamaica rum.

The guests who clustered in awe around the buffet table or gossiped in the parlor were a blend of those whom Cathlin considered "quality" and those whom Val had invited on his own. There were the editor of the weekly newspaper, Sloppy Weather Smith, so named for his habitually turned-up trouser legs; Butch Kleindorf, the foreman of the railroad roundhouse; and Dr. Pixley, the town's physician and horseshoe champion. The younger people, Seadon classmates at Weston High and members of Leah's bicycle club, concentrated themselves in what Cathlin termed the "music room," where Leah and David Marcus alternated at the square piano with snatches from *Floradora* and even made a four-handed attempt at "There'll Be a Hot Time in the Old Town Tonight."

"Got to hand it to you, Val. You sure done this up brown." The speaker who had drifted up to his host was Harry Buhlenbeck, the town banker. Then, with a shrewd look, he added, "I got a hunch about tonight. It's just a little too special. Even for New Year's or the end of the century."

Val smiled. "You never take anything on its face, do you, Harry?"

"Don't pay. But you got a special reason. Am I right?"

"You are. You'll hear at the right time."

Buhlenbeck tilted his eyebrows. "Say! Don't tell me those young folks in the other room, at the piano . . ."

Val snorted. "Leah and David? Oh, good Lord, Harry. Leah's only seventeen."

"Well, that's a relief. I know I'd sure put the kibosh on anything like that. Young Marcus may be all right—*may* be, I say—but there's no point in blinking a certain fact." Buhlenbeck paused, then rolled the word off his tongue with a kind of disdainful relish. "Hebrew."

"*No!*"

"Yep. Use your eyes, man."

Val wagged his head from side to side. "That's a heavy load to bear. Bad enough being Jewish, without being the son of a banker."

Buhlenbeck's cheeks went pink, and then to red as Val turned away.

"I still say it's funny," Leah insisted. "Rich boys don't go off to war. Only poor boys, like around here."

They were in the quiet of the entry hall, David seated on the next-to-the-bottom step of the stairs, Leah standing, clasping the newel post between her hands.

"Maybe I had to prove something," David answered.

"About yourself?"

"And to my father."

Leah tightened her grip on the newel post and swung gently from side to side. "So you're just like Ross."

"What does Ross have to prove?"

"That he's different from Daddy. Only he isn't."

"And you aren't, either. You're Val Seadon, Junior, got up like a Gibson Girl."

She hung motionless on the newel post and regarded him thoughtfully. "I believe I'm going to take that as a compliment."

"You should."

They hesitated, as if embarrassed by this growing intimacy. They listened to the buzz of conversation from the other rooms. Then David said abruptly, "Leah, what do you want out of the new year? Out of the new century?"

She released the newel post and rested her elbows on the railing. "Everything. I want to go everywhere, do everything."

"That's kind of vague."

"If you call getting out of Weston 'vague.' I want to go where things happen. I want to do more than read about San Francisco. I want to know for myself."

David rummaged in his coat pocket, brought out a pack of cigarettes, and lighted one. "To do all the things you want could take a lot of money."

Leah tossed her head. "I'm not worried. I have a voice. I've sung in the choir, and next week I'm soloist. The *Agnus Dei*. And when I graduate from the conservatory . . ."

"Where?"

"I don't know. San Francisco. New York."

"And your parents will give you permission?"

Leah smiled confidently, took the cigarette from David's lips, and placed it between hers. She inhaled awkwardly and coughed. Then a hand reached from behind her and seized the cigarette.

Leah glared around at Ross. "Who do you think you are?"

"Number one brother. And the keeper of your morals."

It was midnight. Leah, at the piano, began the opening bars of "Auld Lang Syne." Tenors and baritones, sopranos and contraltos joined in, oblivious at first of Hop Gee and Sammy Lee, who came grinning into the room bearing trays of wine glasses. "Hey! It's champagne!" someone shouted.

"Genuine French champagne!" Val called back. "Paid for by my boy Ross and my boy Owen!" A murmur of astonishment. Val held up his hands. "Friends, this is more than the beginning of the year nineteen hundred. It's the thirty-fifth wedding anniversary for Cath and me. That's right. Back in eighteen sixty-five we decided to start the New Year right. And legal!" Applause and laughter.

Ross stepped forward. "Ladies and gentlemen, the toast is going to be proposed by my brother." Everyone turned expectantly toward Owen, who blushed, chewed his lower lip, and spilled the champagne from his glass. Ross clapped his shoulder. "Go on, kid. You've only been practicing that speech all week."

Owen swallowed and cleared his throat, then said with growing confidence, "Ladies and gentlemen, there is a saying, a saying that goes 'One speaks to one's dog in German, to one's servant in English, to one's sweetheart in French . . . but to the gods in Spanish.' " He smiled, pleased with himself, and raised his glass to Val and Cathlin. "May I, on this special occasion, and meaning no sacrilege, propose this toast: *Querida madre, querido padre, una vida muy larga, saludos, siempre mucha felicidad . . . con todo nuestro amor!*"

Glasses raised, glasses drained. Val drew his arm around

Cathlin and kissed the tears on her cheeks. "Happy anniversary, honey! Happy New Year! Happy New Century!"

Cathlin shivered. "Don't say that! Don't remind me!"

"Of what?"

"The new century. All I want is *now*. Everything just as it is tonight."

Chapter 5

T H E   F R U I T   trees in the back yard were swelling with buds, and the house finches were investigating likely places under the eaves where they might build their nests. Any day now Cathlin would give the dread command for spring housecleaning. It behooved, Val decided, it definitely behooved to enlist Hop Gee's muscle power before Cathlin could lay claim. The well out on the river bluff was waiting. How long had it been? Over four months. First the winter rains had reduced the wagon road to impassable gumbo. Then the March freeze, when a man dared not work up a sweat in the icy winds and chance pneumonia. Val had, in fact, just recovered from an attack of pneumonia's poor relation, influenza. Even now when he exerted himself he still felt a bit lightheaded. What did it matter? he told himself. Enough of dreaming about that hole in the ground. Today would be action.

He was relieved to see that the derrick had survived the winter's storms; no vagrant had chopped down the wooden structure for firewood; nothing had changed except the level of the Haber River. Where it had been a timid trickle in December, now it coursed over the granite boulders with the serene confidence of a Mississippi. Val unlocked the toolshed and handed out the equipment to Hop Gee. Wrenches, rope, a bucket of nuts and bolts, the iron drill head, and ten-foot lengths of rod which had been fashioned for Val by the town blacksmith. The spring-pole method of drilling was as primitive as it was exhausting. A heavy pole—in this case the trunk of a willow tree from the bank of the river—was balanced over a sturdy crosspiece. One end of the pole supported the iron drill stem; the other end dangled a loop of rope. The loop formed a stirrup into which a man could fit his boot. As he kicked downward, the far end of the pole would raise the drill stem into the air. When the man released his boot from the loop, the far end would plunge the drill downward into the earth.

Val and Hop Gee screwed the drill onto the first length of rod, wrenched it tight, and swung the drill over the hole and lowered it. As each ten feet of drill stem was lowered, they stopped to attach an additional length. At the forty-foot level Val paused and frowned. "Something's wrong, Hop. Listen."

Val put his boot in the rope loop, kicked it down, and released it. "You hear that?"

Hop Gee nodded. "Water, boss."

"But we had the hole capped, so it can't be rain water. It's got to be seepage from the river."

They hauled the drill stem back up the hole and dismantled it section by section. Val returned to the toolshed and found a rusty coffee canister. He punched two holes in the top rim, inserted a length of wire, and lowered the canister down the hole. He glanced at Hop Gee and saw his expression of futility. "I know. If it's seeping in faster than we can bail it, we'll have to rig a windmill and pump her dry. And even then . . ." He shrugged. One problem at a time.

Val hauled the canister back up the hole. He heaved the water onto the clay just beyond the drill platform and turned back to lower the canister again. Hop Gee caught his arm. "Boss!" The Chinese pointed at the wet earth. The water still made a puddle on the clay. On the surface of the puddle there was a bluish film. Val dropped to his knees and raked his fingers through the mud. He carried the mud to his nose and sniffed. Perhaps. Possibly.

He dropped the bailer down the hole again. This time he brought it up with such speed that it spilled its contents before reaching the top. He lowered a third time and brought it up slowly, carefully, hand over hand. He could feel the sweat of excitement pouring from his armpits; his heart thudded against his rib cage like an imprisoned wild animal. Then the canister was in his hands. There was no spill. The same bluish film floated on the water. Val skimmed it onto his fingers and smelled again. And tasted it.

"Yes! By God! Yes!"

He flung his arms around Hop Gee and swung him off his feet in a bear hug. "We've done it, Hop! Oil! *Oil!* The real thing! The honest to God . . ."

The words ended in a gurgle. A jagged pain ripped through his temples. He groaned and staggered. The sky, the derrick, Hop Gee spun before his eyes. Then blackness.

Dr. Pixley came out of the bedroom, closed the door, and nodded to the strained faces in the hall. Ross, Owen, Leah.

"Yes, it's a stroke. Your mother is going to stay with him until the sedative works."

Ross asked the question. "How bad is it?"

"Well, he's lost the use of his left arm, and there seems to be some impairment of memory. But he's able to talk quite clearly."

At that moment Father Barrie panted up the stairs. Under one arm was his satchel containing the articles for the viaticum. He disappeared into the bedroom.

Dr. Pixley resumed. "I would say the prognosis is good. Val is tremendously strong for a man of sixty-five. The main thing is to get his blood pressure down. He must have complete rest and"—he emphasized the words with a warning finger—"and no aggravations from his family."

There was a muffled bellow. *"Out! Damn it to hell! Out!"*

Before the doctor could reach the door, it flew open and Father Barrie, crossing himself, scuttled out.

Val's voice followed him: "No damned witch doctor is going to shovel dirt in my face!"

It was unthinkable that Val Seadon should be struck down. Neither Cathlin nor Ross nor Owen nor Leah—and certainly none of the Chinese servants—could conceive of him bound to his bed. It was some aberration in their own minds. And Val's recovery seemed to confirm it. By the second day, his left arm in a sling, he propped up in bed for his meals and a succession of brown and yellow and black liquids which Hop Gee and Ah Sing had fatched from a Chinese herbalist. They tasted vile and smelled worse and were, according to Val, "hundred-proof snail piss" that would jolt a corpse into life. By the third day he was restless and rebellious. Cathlin, he demanded, was to clear the bedroom of her vials of holy water and chromos of the saints and rosaries blessed by an assortment of priests and bishops.

"He never believed," Cathlin wept to Leah. "All these years he's pretended. He's lived a lie."

And Leah answered, "He did it for your sake, Mother. To make you happy. I can't think of a greater compliment." Nor, secretly, could Cathlin. On the other hand, why did he choose now, of all times, to renounce her blessed religion? His mind must be affected. All because of that hateful well.

By the following Sunday afternoon the family was almost back to its normal routine. Val napped upstairs, Cathlin crocheted in the parlor, Owen read another history, and Leah dawdled at the piano. Ross, who had left the house immediately after the noon meal, returned with a slam of the front door and a shout: "Look, everybody!" Wide-eyed, breathless, swinging a rusty pail, slopping its contents. "This is what Dad found!"

Cathlin dropped her crochet hook. "Ross! The carpet!"

"Who gives a damn? It's oil!"

Owen blinked down at the pail and its mixture of water and petroleum. "You've been out at the well?"

"Yes! When Hop Gee brought Dad home, I asked him what happened out there. Hop just said, 'Maybe boss man tell you.' But Dad couldn't or wouldn't. So I went to find out."

Leah turned to Cathlin. "You didn't know? He didn't tell *you?*"

The tears started again. "He couldn't, dear. He can't remember things."

But he did. Very clearly. As they crowded around the bed, Val grinned impishly. "I was saving it for the right moment. When I could enjoy it. And I guess this is it." He caught Ross's hand. "I'm proud of you, son. You figured it out and did something about it." He gestured to Cathlin to arrange the pillows behind his back, then: "I've been doing a lot of thinking. We've found oil—but how much? And are we over the main body? First we get the water out of our hole and go deeper. If it's just a piddling thing, we try another well, off to the west, and maybe another to the east. And I don't mean kicking down with a spring pole. We got to get a professional..."

As Val paused for breath, Owen completed his thought. "You want to talk to one of the water-well drillers?"

"No, none of the local boys. They haven't got the savvy. We want a man who can run pipe down that hole and shut off the water and then drill inside the pipe. A regular rig with a steam boiler, like they use down in Los Angeles. That's where we got to look for our man. I wish I could go with you, boys, but since I can't..."

His sons exchanged looks, and Ross asked, "What will we use for money?"

Val grimaced. "That's what's stumping me. We got a little in the till at the hardware, but we need a couple of thousand. Ordinarily, I might get a loan at the bank, but Harry Buhlenbeck must have heard about my stroke. He'd be afraid he'd have to collect out of my probate..." His voice trailed off.

That evening the solution came from an unexpected source.

Hop Gee, Ah Sing and Sammy Lee filed into Val's bedroom. One by one they came forward to the bed, inclined a head respectfully, and held out a savings passbook issued by the Chinese benevolent association.

Val smiled misty-eyed at his three elderly retainers. "I'm sorry, boys. I appreciate your trust, but it's too much of a gamble."

Hop Gee's wrinkled face broke into a grin. "Long time play fan-tan. Long time lose. This time maybe win."

In the late 1880s oil had been discovered within walking distance of downtown Los Angeles. It was a "town-lot" field, where derricks sprang up in hundreds of back yards. By 1900 most of the wells had pumped dry and many of the drillers had drifted away. One of those who remained listened carefully to the young Seadon brothers. At the mention of one hundred dollars and a round-trip train ticket, Tim Beakley concluded Weston was worth a visit. He inspected the well and called on Val, who had descended shakily to the parlor and his favorite Morris chair.

"It's hard to say what's down there," Beakley began. "I ran the bailer and got a show, just as your boys said. But it could be just a pocket and nothing more."

Val liked his honesty. He was not trying to drum up business for the sake of a paycheck. Val liked his looks, too: a square face with steady blue eyes, and callused hands that meant he did not shove the heavy work onto others.

"Are you interested?"

"Well, nobody's ever found oil in Haber County. Up at Coalinga, yes . . . and at Ventura and Santa Paula and Los Angeles."

"They haven't found it here because they haven't looked for it. But I asked you a question. Are you interested?"

"If you'll let me go down at least five hundred feet."

"How much?"

"Three dollars a foot. And freight for my equipment from Los Angeles."

"When can you start?"

"Soon as I finish out down south. In two weeks."

"We've got a deal."

Beakley smiled. "One other thing. Suppose we let people think it's a water well." He glanced at Ross and Owen, who hovered behind Val's chair. "You haven't told anything different around town?" They shook their heads. "Good. Because if I find something, I'd like to pick up some land myself. While it's still cheap."

The week before Beakley's steam boiler and drilling equipment were unloaded from the railroad flatcar, Ross Seadon brought a legal document into Val's bedroom. It was a grant deed which transferred eighty acres into the name of the Weston Hardware Company.

Val scowled at the legal description of the property and then at his son. "Isn't this the Giolatta land?"

"Yes. Just west of ours."

"You took the money from the till?"

Ross nodded casually. "We paid only fifty cents an acre, and the back taxes. Less than sixty dollars, all told. The Giolattas thought I was crazy. They said they hadn't been able to graze the land the last five years."

"So you didn't tell them about the well?"

"Good Lord, no! I remember what Mr. Beakley said."

"Mr. Beakley isn't Haber County. He's an outsider. But we're local; the Giolattas are local. We've all toughed it out together. We owe them a fair shake."

"Dad, this is business!"

"That's no excuse. From now on there's not going to be any more buying of land. We'll lease it and the owners get a royalty."

Ross's face darkened. "But we're taking the risks; why should we cut somebody else in on a good thing? We're not our brothers' keepers."

"Aren't we? Is that the way you feel about Owen?"

"Oh, hell, I wasn't talking about him."

Perhaps not then, Val thought, and remembered an incident

when the two brothers were small. Ross had begged a bunch of grapes from Ah Sing, saying they were "for my boy." But by the time Ross gave them to Owen there was only one grape left. Val and Cathlin still laughed about it, but suppose the bunch of grapes were an oil well?

Perhaps that was unfair, Val decided. Ross had always been protective of Owen and Leah, although they sometimes called it "domineering." He was headstrong, like his father, and frequently awash with Irish sentimentality, like his mother. Not a bad combination, really. The question, the really big question, was how would his character stand the test of sudden wealth? On that hung the happiness of the entire family.

That same afternoon Val labored downstairs and telephoned Wilmot Caruth and invited him to the house. Of the two practicing attorneys in Weston, Wilmot Caruth was Val's choice for a somewhat bizarre reason—the same reason which caused Cathlin to snub him on the street and to change the subject whenever his name came up in conversation. Mr. Caruth, aged thirty-two, enjoyed the mixed blessing of a beautiful wife who was bored with her existence. Several years earlier Helen Caruth had become secretly involved with a young bachelor named Jerry Blackburn. Her husband discovered the affair and the locale of its frequent celebration, a room, second floor front, in the Pioneer Hotel. One afternoon while the lovers were in the room, Wilmot Caruth strolled into the hotel with the town locksmith. They went upstairs to the lovers' quarters, Caruth knocked on the door, and Jerry Blackburn opened it. He saw the husband, he saw the revolver, and he saw the light—and he bolted for the bathroom. Helen, naked and kneeling, pleaded for her life while the locksmith changed the lock on the door. He gave the new key to the husband, who bowed to his wife and said, "And now, my dear, go screw his brains out." Then he locked the door, paid the locksmith, and returned to court. Once a day for an entire week Mr. Caruth returned to the hotel room, unlocked the door, deposited a tray of food, relocked the door, and departed. As an attorney, Caruth freely admitted that he had committed an illegal act; as a cuckold, he invoked the unwritten law. The hotel manager, squeamish about publicity, professed total ignorance of what was going on—in spite of the town idlers who stationed themselves across the street and stared up at the window with the pulled blinds. On the seventh day the husband unlocked the door and escorted his wife to the home from which she had never since set foot. Her lover left town that night.

The scandal split the town into two camps. A minority sympathized with the adulteress who had suffered such humiliation. Val was one of them. The majority was loudly on the side of the wronged husband. Val, typically, was in this camp, too, although not for reasons of morality. Val admired Wilmot Caruth's ingenuity, and an ingenious mind was what he desired in an attorney.

Caruth sprawled his rangy form in Val's rocker in the bedroom. "I fail to see the point, Val. Why don't you want to make a will?" His voice projected as if he were in a courtroom. It was a voice of theatrical timbre, appropriate to that era when attorneys considered oratory more basic than a knowledge of Blackstone.

"Wills just cause trouble," Val replied. "If I leave everything to Cath, I just saddle her with the same problem I got now. How do we split up things for the kids? If they inherit undivided interests in the hardware, the house, and my land out on the river, then nobody really owns anything. Everybody will be squabbling."

"Perhaps not. You're a close-knit family."

"Because Cath and I made it that way. I don't tell it around, but we spent ten long years trying for a family. When Ross finally came, and Owen and Leah, they meant so much to us and we were so afraid something might happen to them, that maybe we fenced them in too close. I know they got to go free, and yet I'm afraid of it."

"Why? They're good solid kids."

"I hope so. But you're looking at us from the outside, Wil.

71

You don't really know us. You didn't know me when I was Ross's age. This stroke of mine *has* made me face up to things. My boys don't like the hardware business. When I'm gone, they'll want to sell it. They may even leave town. Anyway, they'll be getting married and want homes of their own. Then what happens to Cath and Leah? Two women in this big house." He shook his head at the prospect. "No. Much as I love my wife, she's Irish and she's Catholic. That means the daughter gets the dirty end of the stick. Dollars to doughnuts, Leah would jump into marriage—*any* marriage—just to get away. Or worse, hit the high road."

Caruth tilted back in the rocker and considered Val's words. "What you're after, as I see it, is how to protect your family and still hold them together."

"Exactly! So what do we do, Mr. Attorney?"

Caruth squinted thoughtfully. "I think you just told me. A holding company. A family holding company."

"Like a corporation?"

"Yep. The Seadon Estate Company. You transfer everything to it—the hardware, this house, your land. You'd be president, maybe Ross vice president, your wife treasurer, Owen the secretary. Each one an officer according to his or her abilities and character. Your daughter is under age, so she can't be an officer yet, but she would be a stockholder like all the others. Everyone would be issued the same number of shares, have the same voting power, receive the same dividends."

Val moved to the window and looked out over the trees and the rooftops of Weston. When he turned back into the room, he was smiling. "And nobody can change the lock?"

Caruth chuckled. "Not even me."

Val's family accepted the idea of the Seadon Estate Company with enthusiasm and relief. It was proof that Val was truly recovering and planning for the future. And the future to Val was that well on the river bluff. If only he could watch its progress and not be a prisoner in the house because of that damned blood pressure. The original hole, both Ross and Tim Beakley reported to him, had been dewatered and widened to accept the lengths of pipe which were to seal off any new flow of water. Then began the drilling into virgin ground. It was a slow business, and disappointing. There were no fresh "shows" of oil sands. The evidences of oil that Val had found, as Beakley had suggested, came from a small pocket of no commercial value. At 110 feet the steam boiler broke down and had to be repaired. At 195 feet the drill stem shattered; days were lost until the drill was fished out and a new one lowered. At 270 feet the hole began to sand up before the pipe could be set in place. With each new delay Val's headaches grew in severity. He would pace and curse to himself and stamp out onto the bedroom balcony and stare off to the northeast, although he could see no farther than the belltower of St. Augustine's. "It's got to happen. It's just *got* to," he would repeat to Cathlin. "There's nothing else for me. I'm down to my last dream."

By early May of 1900 the well had reached a depth of four hundred feet. "Nothing new," Ross reported. "Just sand and rock." Paradoxically, Val began to improve. He came downstairs each day and dutifully went through the exercises which Dr. Pixley hoped would free Val's left arm.

Finally the well touched five hundred feet, and Tim Beakley came to the house for instructions. Should he drill deeper? Yes. "The deeper he goes, the better our odds," Val insisted. But tension began to surface in the rest of the household. Ross and Owen quarreled over trifles; Leah pounded away at the piano as if it were her sole point of concentration; the three Chinese, who had gambled their savings, bickered in the kitchen.

Then one Saturday morning, while the family was at the breakfast table, the telephone rang.

Tim Beakley asked for Val. "We're getting gas, Mr. Seadon. I think we're right over it. Can you come out?"

Val hung up and beamed at his family. "Everybody in your Sunday best. This is it."

No one stirred. Ross, Owen, and Leah turned questioning

73

eyes toward Cathlin. She looked sternly around the table. "You heard your father."

"But Dad can't—"

"He *can*. This is his glory, and I won't let anyone cheat him out of it."

The buggy, the surrey, and the buckboard, bearing the five Seadons and the three Chinese, rattled down Central Avenue. As they passed the print shop of the *Weston Weekly*, editor Sloppy Weather Smith leaned out the window and gaped at Val in his favorite cream-colored suit and Cathlin in her blue silk and her wide-brimmed hat abloom with poppies. "Hey, Val!" he shouted. "What's going on?"

"Come on and see!"

Sloppy Weather's buggy joined the procession. Then another, and another. It was a cavalcade. Men on horseback, in hay wagons, livery buggies, even a boy on a bicycle. No one knew the purpose, no one cared. On a dull Saturday morning in Weston even a dogfight rated as a social event.

It was already furiously hot. As they neared the river bluff, the silhouette of the drilling rig was a shimmering distortion through the heat haze. It was a small derrick. Val judged its height at sixty feet. He could see that the drill stem and the cutting bit had been hauled up into the rigging. The vertical bull wheel was motionless. Val made out Tim Beakley and his crew of three waiting on the drilling platform. Arms folded, faces streaked with grime, shirts damp with sweat.

Beakley and Ross helped Val from the buggy and escorted him up onto the wooden platform. Hop Gee followed with a folding chair for Val, which he waved aside. He shook hands with each member of the drilling crew, introduced them to his family and the Chinese, then began to wander stiffly around the platform. He examined the iron pipe with its gaping mouth, which jutted up through the flooring; he peered into the tool-house that was attached to one side of the derrick; he patted the great wooden bull wheel; he considered the steam boiler, now cold and silent; he stared up into the maze of uprights and crossbeams. High above the crown block he saw a turkey buzzard circling curiously.

He turned to Beakley with a grin. "Ordinarily, I'd make a speech. This time I won't. My wife's doing it for me." He smiled at Cathlin, whose lips were moving in a silent prayer.

She crossed herself, and Val sat down on the folding chair. His family and the Chinese assembled behind him, as if they were composing themselves for a group photograph. The crowd, which had dismounted from their assorted vehicles, stood in a ring just outside the drilling platform. A voice from the crowd called out, "Hey, Val! What's going on?" It was Harry Buhlenbeck. "Are you bringing in a water well or launching a ship?"

"Better than that!" Val laughed. "It's Weston's first oil well!"

The crowd pushed forward. "Oil?" "What does it look like?"

"Money!" Buhlenbeck crowed, an instant convert.

Beakley bawled at them. "Keep clear of the platform! And no smoking!"

The reason was clear to Val. He could smell the sulphurous vapors escaping from the wellhead.

Beakley turned to one of his crew. "All right, Luke." Luke came forward with a metal canister; he placed a load of stones in the bottom of it and covered the stones with a layer of cotton. Then he went into the toolhouse and returned with a glass vial, which he held at arm's length. "No jumping around, folks. This is nitroglycerine." Slowly, delicately, Luke lowered the vial into the canister and packed more cotton around its sides. Now it was Beakley's turn. He rolled a coil of wire over to the wellhead and fastened the loose end of the wire to the metal loop atop the canister. He raised the canister to the mouth of the pipe and lowered it inside. Hand over hand, he paid out the wire. Fifty feet . . . one hundred . . . two hundred . . . three . . . four . . . five. At 670 feet the wire went slack. The canister of explosive rested on the bottom of the hole.

Beakley nodded to Luke. "The go-devil."

The object which Luke brought from the toolhouse resembled an artillery shell. Its iron casing came to a brass-tipped point. Beakley took it and carried it over to Val.

"Would you like to do the honors, sir?"

Val got up from his chair. The go-devil was heavy and awkward, and with Val's left arm paralyzed, Ross had to help him carry it to the wellhead. They stood there, holding the go-devil aloft over the mouth of the pipe. They watched Beakley raise his arm for the signal.

"Let 'er go!"

Instead, Val clutched the go-devil even more tightly. As if wanting to prolong the moment. What was he doing there? he wondered. Why was Ross frowning at him? Why was his face blurring and wavering?

Ross nudged him. "Now, Dad! *Now!*"

They released the go-devil. They heard it rattling and banging as it dropped down through 670 feet of iron pipe. Then a muffled roar. The top of the pipe heaved up, then settled back. A wisp of smoke curled from the wellhead.

Beakley placed his ear over the mouth of the pipe. He shook his head. Then sniffed. "At least the gas has stopped." He listened again. "Ought to hear something . . . if it's down there."

The Seadons, the Chinese, the drilling crew, looked at each other glumly.

Beakley's face was still over the pipe. "Wait a minute! I can feel air blowing. Something's coming up." The pipe began to vibrate and hum. Beakley waved his arms. "Everybody back!"

They stood in a wide circle at the edges of the platform. Staring at the pipe, listening to the gurgling sounds. At first timidly, then with growing force, there was a gush of dirty water. It grew. A spout, a fountain, a geyser. Five feet into the air . . . ten feet . . . twenty. Of pure, glistening water.

No one spoke. No one moved. Then Val leaped forward. He kicked the geysering pipe. "*Damn you! God damn you!*"

Cathlin reached him first. "*Val! No! No!*"

They wrestled and splashed in the growing pool of water. Val pulled free and kicked again. "*Damn, damn, damn you!*"

Ross caught him by the waist and was dragged along by Val's fury. *"Damn you to hell!"* Fist shaking at the leaping fountain, at the derrick, at the sky itself. *"Damn! Damn! Damn! Damn!"*

"God save him!" Cathlin screamed. "Oh, blessed Virgin! *Please!"*

Val turned, as if heeding her. He lurched, stumbled, then pitched forward into the pool of water. Cathlin's hat with the poppies floated past his face.

Ross and Owen carried the body to the surrey. Cathlin and Leah followed, clutching each other, weeping. "For nothing! All for nothing!" Then Cathlin saw the three Chinese. Hats in hands, heads bowed. Cathlin threw her arms around Hop Gee.

"Hop! Oh, Hop! He never had the last rites!"

Behind them there was a shout. Then another. Cheers, yells, laughter. Ross and Owen looked back.

The leaping geyser no longer flashed in the sunlight. Now it was a column of color. First a light blue . . . then darker . . . then purple . . . then black. Black oil.

Chapter 6

THERE WERE two funeral services. The first was Monday morning, when Hop Gee and Sammy Lee and Ah Sing bowed before the gilt idols in their temple and burned the ritual silver and gold joss papers. In the afternoon Requiem Mass was said at St. Augustine's. Catholics, Protestants, even a few atheists filled the pews. After the Mass, while the sound of bells reverberated overhead, Val's coffin was carried down the steps of St. Augustine's to the windowed hearse. The coffin was slid within, the door was closed, and the pallbearers stepped back. One of them, Ross, felt someone tug at his elbow.

It was Harry Buhlenbeck. "My boy, in this time of sorrow, I want you to know you can always turn to me."

"Thank you."

"If the family needs money, I'm ready to help."

"Thank you."

"That's what friends are for, isn't it? I'll be glad to buy your river land, and the piece you got from the Giolattas. Say a hundred dollars an acre. How does that strike . . ." Buhlenbeck's voice trailed off. Ross had walked away.

It was but the beginning. On the drive back from the cemetery the Seadon surrey went past the courthouse. Knots of men were talking on the steps. Some had been at St. Augustine's earlier; others Ross and Owen did not recognize. They were out-of-towners with rolls of paper tucked under their arms.

"What's going on?" Owen whispered.

"Just what it looks like," Ross whispered back. "The county tax collector, the assessor, the recorder. Their offices are all in the courthouse. It's started."

That evening the Seadon brothers were on the veranda when Tim Beakley came up the front walk. The oilman hurried through the clichés of sympathy and on to the subject of his visit. "Everything's fine out at the well. I shut it in, and my boys dug a sump to hold the loose oil. But now we got to decide what's next."

Ross shook his head. "Mr. Beakley, we buried our father just this afternoon."

"I know, I know. It's the wrong time, and yet it's got to be said. You see, I just leased a piece south of your land. Unless I get a contract to drill some more wells, I'm moving my rig onto my own land."

"Go ahead." Owen glowered.

Beakley shifted uneasily. "Well, now, let's not be hasty. . . . How about just one well, along your southern boundary?"

Ross understood immediately. "And if we find oil there, that will prove you got it, too, at no cost to yourself."

Beakley grinned uneasily. "You catch on."

"I think so. Right now you need cash. You spent everything in buying that lease."

"Just about. I've got a payroll to meet, you know, and buying firewood for my boiler is like dealing in jewels."

"How much will you charge per foot drilled?"

"Five dollars."

"It was three dollars for Dad."

"Well . . . yeah. Make it four."

"We'll think about it, Mr. Beakley. We'll let you know."

"Tomorrow?"

"As you say, let's not be hasty."

It wasn't until Ross was in bed that night that he realized that he had not only talked business on the night of his father's burial, he had actually enjoyed it. The night of Val's death he had tried to ease his grief with alcohol, with tears shared with his mother and brother and sister. He had spent an hour, only the night before, with a girl at Madame Devereaux's, and it, too, had failed. Business was the one effective solace.

The Los Angeles oilmen had been the first to hear of Val Seadon's discovery well, and they were the first to arrive in Weston. A week later the Pennsylvania men began to register at the Pioneer Hotel. They were not, strictly speaking, oilmen. They were neither drillers nor company men; they were "boomers"—promoters and lease hounds who cared little about "bringing in" wells. They were paper men, intent on leasing land and selling the paper to someone else. Preferably within twenty-four hours. And, often as not, buying back the same paper after another twenty-four hours, at double the price, and reselling it for triple the money. It was the boomers who brought Ross Seadon to a decision. After dinner one night, when the family was gathered in the parlor, he sketched the conversation with Tim Beakley for the benefit of his mother and sister. And he made a proposal.

"*Sell the hardware?*" Cathlin cried. "Your father's business?"

"There is no business," Ross replied. "Our customers are too busy swapping leases with every Tom, Dick, and Harry who hits town. But I've talked to Harry Buhlenbeck, and he's willing to go ten thousand dollars. That will give us the capital to go ahead. So what do you say, Ma?"

"I won't talk about money while I'm making a novena for your father's soul."

Her children exchanged looks, then Leah said quietly to

Ross, "It isn't going to take all that ten thousand to drill another well, is it?"

"No. The rest we use to buy more leases."

"You keep saying 'we'—but it means *you*." Leah turned to Owen. "I thought you wanted to go to college and teach history."

Owen smiled. "And let Ross have all the excitement? Everything's changed now. I want to hire out to Tim Beakley and learn from the ground up." He chuckled. "Or from the ground down."

Leah's face darkened. "Well, that's just fine for you two. What about me? What about the conservatory?"

"You'll go," Ross said. "Just as soon as the money starts coming in. . . . All right, let's consider this a meeting of the Seadon Estate Company and put it to a vote. All in favor of selling the hardware and going full tilt into the oil business, raise your hands."

Three hands raised.

"I'm afraid you're outvoted, Ma."

By the end of the first month after Val's discovery well— and two weeks after the second Seadon well began drilling —the population of Weston had doubled. Boomers stepped off the Southern Pacific trains a hundred a day. Men slept in three shifts in the rooms of the Pioneer Hotel and at Mrs. Ferguson's boardinghouse. They slept in barbers' chairs, on pool tables, in idle hacks at Slim Perry's livery stable. They slept in tents pitched at the north end of Central Avenue, on the porches of farmhouses, and in the parlor of Madame Devereaux's sporting house.

Harry Buhlenbeck, who had offered one hundred dollars an acre for the Seadon land, now boasted that he had paid four hundred dollars an acre for land a mile away—and had sold it for eight hundred an acre within seventy-two hours. By the time Tim Beakley had brought in the second Seadon producing well (with Owen working as a common "tool pusher"), land for three miles along the Haber River was going for a minimum of two thousand dollars an acre. By early fall Beakley brought in the first well on his own lease, followed in rapid succession by a half dozen wells drilled by other operators on nearby properties. Now land went for five thousand dollars an acre. Not a single day passed without the organization of a new oil company; its sole asset in most cases was a sheet of paper giving the right to drill on land which the stockholders had never seen. "It's Dad's Gold Rush all over again," Ross Seadon exulted, "only bigger and wilder!"

The effects of the oil boom on the simple townspeople of Weston were as various as human nature itself. Hop Gee, Sammy Lee, and Ah Sing refused all offers to buy their interest in Val Seadon's discovery well, even the offer made by Ross. "Look, Hop, you'll have enough to pay your way back to China and a comfortable old age." Hop Gee merely smiled. "You mean, even with oil royalties coming in every month, you still want to go on working for us?" A nod. "Then what's the good of having money?"

Hop Gee smiled again. "Bigger fan-tan."

"And that's all?"

"No. We buy a fine new Kuan Yin for joss house."

Butch Kleindorf, the foreman of the railroad roundhouse, still went to work every morning; but in the evening, when he returned to Mrs. Kleindorf's supper of pork and beans, he ate on silverplate served by an English butler. Val Seadon's physician, Dr. Pixley, who also had done well in oil leases, now went about in his buggy with a human skeleton on the seat beside him. As he explained it, "A lot of GP's got a stack of bones in the office, but how many can say they got one that makes house calls? Ralph here is a hell of an ad for new business, and pretty good company besides."

Weston's prosperity attracted the attention of another breed of boomers. Gamblers wearing flowered silk waistcoats, fresh from the Klondike, stepped off the Southern Pacific trains; San Francisco sent her pickpockets; the Arizona Territory and even the distant Dakotas delivered their quotas of men wearing derbies tilted forward over their small cold eyes. They needed no labels; everyone recognized them for what they were—professional killers. They bullied the merchants, shot out store windows, and killed Chinese and Mexicans for the sheer pleasure of it. The sheriff's men and the police, unsure of their own shooting talents, chose to look the other way.

By November 1900 the banks of the Haber River were prickled with drilling rigs. One of them was Seadon Number Three, with Owen acting for the first time as drilling superintendent. It came in flowing five hundred barrels a day. "My first well!" Owen whooped, bursting into the house that evening. "There's no feeling in the world like it! To pick your own spot of earth, to bore down into a piece of ugly jackrabbit land, and then bang! up comes black gold! It's like Christmas and New Year's Eve and my birthday all in one!" When he finally stopped for breath, he noted the family's odd lack of enthusiasm. "What the hell's wrong with everybody?"

There was no answer. Owen stared at Ross, then at Leah, then at Cathlin. "Have I committed some sort of a crime?" Still no answer. Owen swung back to Leah. "Another argument about you and that damned singing conservatory?"

Leah flushed. "For once, no!"

"Ma?"

"It's clear you haven't heard," Cathlin said.

"Heard what?"

"You drilled on the land Ross bought from the Giolattas for fifty cents an acre."

"Tell me something I don't know."

"Don't be rude, dear. It seems Mr. Giolatta heard about your well."

Owen turned to Ross. "Christ, don't tell me there's a flaw in the title, and now he wants it back."

Ross sighed. "It's a little late for that. He just blew his brains out."

Owen sank down onto a chair and dropped his head into

his hands. "Oh, God," he groaned. "Can't there ever be just one single moment of pure joy?"

Whenever Ross thought of Beniamino Giolatta, which was more often than he liked, he reminded himself that Giolatta had been happy to sell his land. After all, no one *knew* there was oil under it. Not for a fact. Damn it all, life was a poker game; you played the cards you were dealt, and that was that.

Cards were a growing fascination with Ross. His father had taught him the rudiments of poker; now he applied himself with the zeal of a religious convert. Poker not only sharpened his judgment of situations and men, it was the means to pick up the latest rumors, and to analyze their truth or falsity and the possible motivations behind them. The "oil game" went on at the wellhead and over a hand of five-card stud. And, to be honest about it, sitting in the back room of the Orleans Saloon, with the susurrus of cards being shuffled and dealt, was far more pleasant than staying at home, where Cathlin mourned her husband and Leah insisted at every opportunity that her voice was "right at its peak." It was at the Orleans that Ross first heard of G. G. Haggerty.

"They say a San Francisco bunch is looking over Section Eleven." The speaker was Sloppy Weather Smith.

"That so? Raise you twenty."

"You s'pose they came down in that private railroad car?" the man at Ross's left asked.

"What railroad car?"

"Hell! The one sitting on the siding over at the depot. Nobody seems to know who it belongs to or who's in it. The window curtains are always pulled."

"His name is G. G. Haggerty." Wilmot Caruth yawned.

"Who's G. G. Haggerty?"

"The owner of the railroad car. He's been getting a lot of telegrams. Seems they're all in code."

"How do you know so much?"

"The telegrapher at the depot told me. He *is* my brother-in-law, you know."

When the game broke up, neither Wilmot Caruth nor Ross felt in the mood to go home. They made their apologetic telephone calls, claiming a "business dinner," and made their separate ways to the Pioneer Hotel. The evening was freakishly warm for November, and most of the habitués of the lobby had repaired to the bar for iced drinks. Caruth was not in the bar, and Ross returned to the lobby, where he spied the attorney talking with a young woman in a wide-brimmed straw hat. Caruth waved to Ross, and the woman, seeing Ross return the gesture, swung around and favored him with the following: "Sir, do you have a wife?"

"I'm afraid not."

"Then a young lady?"

"Sorry again."

"Perhaps some sisters?"

"One."

"Would she be about my age?"

"Well, she's going on nineteen."

"Close enough. Would she be about five feet six, narrow waist, and well developed?" A hand indicated the area of development.

Ross cast a glance of inquiry at Caruth, whose face was a battleground between solemnity and mirth.

Then there was another question: "Do you think your sister would like this dress I'm wearing?"

He surveyed the dress. Blue lace over a pink foundation, high lace ruching at the neck, and puffed sleeves. Ross's eyes drifted to her face. It was attractive. Perhaps too strong a jaw line, perhaps a bit too wide a mouth, but the cheeks were sprinkled with freckles, and Ross liked girls with freckles. And red hair. In the present case the hair which swirled beneath the brim of her hat was more than red; it glowed like a stormy sunset.

"Mind telling me what this is all about?"

"She wants to sell her dress," Caruth explained. "I told her it's kind of fancy for my wife, who's pretty much of a stay-at-home."

"It's almost brand-new," the girl pursued. "It was custom made by one of New York City's finest French designers. If you could find it in a shop, which you couldn't, it would sell for thirty dollars. But I'll take ten."

"Broke?"

She nodded. "I have to pay my hotel bill here and buy a railroad ticket." She saw Ross beginning to smile, which she interpreted in her favor. "I can go take it off right now and wrap it up for you. I'm sure it will cost only a few pennies to mail home."

"This *is* home. I live here."

She gave him the full benefit of her blue eyes. "Ten dollars?"

Ross shook his head. "I think my sister would prefer to buy her own dresses."

The light faded from her eyes. "I guess it would have been almost inexcusable good luck. Thanks anyway."

She turned away, and Ross and Caruth went into the dining room. The place was already crowded. Oilmen and would-be oilmen laughed and talked across the tables, making up in boisterousness for the cheerlessness of the room.

"You think she was really selling that dress?" Caruth asked. "Or something else?"

Ross scowled at his menu, pushed back from the table, and returned to the lobby. She was still there, sitting on a bench, watching the lobby entrance for a new prospect.

"Miss!" She looked up. "Suppose I bought your dress. When you pay the hotel and get your railroad ticket, what's left for dinner?"

"Oh, that doesn't matter."

Just as he thought. "It certainly does. You're eating with my friend and me."

She bounced to her feet, beaming. "I'll be back in a minute."

Ross and Caruth were tasting their first bourbons when she entered the dining room with a neatly wrapped package under her arm. She had changed into a cream velvet suit far too warm for the sultry evening. She pirouetted in front of the table.

"This one would cost at least forty dollars. The beading is genuine steel-cut jet and the collar is real sealskin. I'm sure your sister would love it."

"Sit down!" Ross commanded.

Liz Barnard, it developed, was a non-stop talker, with an appetite that suggested a recent diet of soda crackers and water. She was, she said, a member of a theatrical troupe which had become stranded in Weston. They had played Los Angeles and were on their way to an engagement in San Francisco. On the train north, the three men in the company had become mesmerized by the conductor's tales of instant wealth to be reaped in Weston's oil boom.

"Joe—he played the heavies in our skits—he said if I'd lend him my money, he'd make me five hundred dollars in one day. He knew just the right oil stock to buy. It must have been the exact *wrong* one, because the last I saw of Joe, he was in shirt sleeves in a labor wagon heading out for the oil field." She cut off a piece of steak, chewed it appreciatively, and launched in again. "Marian was the smart one. She played older women. She kept her money and stayed on the train to Frisco. By now she must be heading back to New York. That's where our tour started. And where I'm headed, too."

"Why?" Ross asked.

"It's home. My parents live there, and my married sister."

"What do they think of you being an actress?"

She sniffed. "The usual. I'm straight on the road to hell." She laughed. "If I am, at least the scenery is interesting."

Caruth steepled his fingers and in his booming courtroom voice rendered his judgment. "You won't be seeing much scenery on Ross's ten dollars."

She looked quickly at Ross. "Twenty, if you'll buy this suit."

Ross laughed. "You're on."

"Thank you. Mind if I finish my steak before changing?"

"I insist. But when you change, don't come back with another dress."

"All right. I'll just walk through the lobby in my shift."

Just the right touch of the risqué, Ross thought. She was not a flirt, not a coquette; she was simply a girl with an earthy sense of humor. Redheads had that quality, he decided.

Then she broke in on his thoughts. "Tell me something. Could Joe really have made me five hundred dollars?"

Ross nodded. "Or five thousand, if he bought the right stock or a piece of a good lease."

She studied him with the same wary expression he had seen in coyotes on the range. "Five thousand in a hole like this?"

"What's the matter with it?"

"Everything! It's ugly, it's mean. I couldn't sleep last night for the drunks stumbling around in the hall, and the swearing and fighting and shooting going on below my window." She grimaced. "We had a line in one of our skits that fits Weston. Joe comes on stage and he says, 'Boys, I know heaven exists, because this has to be The Other Place.'"

Her companions guffawed, then Ross said seriously, "This is the frontier, Liz. Maybe the last frontier. That's why it's got so much opportunity. The drunks and fighting and shooting are just part of our growing pains. Weston's going to be one of the most important towns in California, and one of the richest."

"Really? Because of oil?"

"Because of oil. Lord knows how much stuff there may be right under the ground we're walking on. The Gold Rush was penny ante compared to what we're on the verge of."

"Hmmm!" If she was impressed, she gave no evidence of the fact. Instead, her eyes wandered around the dining room. "Why is everyone watching you, Mr. Seadon?"

Ross was genuinely surprised. He glanced around, then said, "I'd say they're admiring you."

"Gallant, but not true. A woman knows when she is *it*."

Caruth bobbed his head. "When our friend is in a room, all faces turn toward him like daisies following the sun." He bowed playfully toward Ross. "It's his due, you see. Ross is not only our leading oilman, he's the son of the man who discovered the Haber River field." Caruth paused, then added with quiet seriousness, "Weston owes everything to Val Seadon. For what he did, and for what he was."

The dinner was drawing to a close when Ross turned to Caruth. "You know, Wil, I think Miss Barnard should give Weston a whirl. Twenty dollars won't get her to New York; but if she stayed on here and put together a show of her own, why, I say she'd make a mint."

Caruth knew the answer Ross wanted. "Might at that. We could do with some fresh entertainment."

Liz smiled. "No, my plan is to get a booking in San Francisco. That will pay my way East."

"You could change your mind."

"I could." She considered Ross thoughtfully. "Do you suppose your sister would like a wedding dress?"

Ross chuckled. "You certainly came prepared!"

"For marriage? That's the last thing I want. No, this is just another of my theatrical costumes, like all the rest. We did a turn where I played a girl left waiting at the church. It's a beautiful dress, really. Your sister could cut off the train and make a lovely party gown."

"How much?"

"Same as the others. Ten dollars."

"On one condition. That you think about staying on here awhile."

She hesitated, then said, "I promise."

After dinner the two men waited in the hotel lobby for Liz Barnard to return with Ross's purchases. Ross grinned at Caruth.

"Well, Wil, what do you think?"

"I think the coyote is in the hen yard again."

But when Liz reappeared, she had changed into a modest traveling dress and carried a straw suitcase. "I thought it over," she said. "Thanks, anyway."

Ross sighed and dug into his pocket for three gold eagles. "Can I drive you to the depot?"

89

She extended her hand. "No, just wish me luck."

"I do."

They watched her pay her hotel bill and walk out of the lobby into the night. Caruth clapped Ross on the shoulder. "How does it feel to be an accessory to a crime?"

"What crime?"

"Receiving stolen goods. She said those dresses were theatrical costumes, which means they belong to her producer or whoever put the show together."

"You're a little late with your legal advice."

"I thought about it, but you were having too good a time. Hell, I'll bet her name isn't even Liz Barnard."

Ross glowered and walked over to the desk clerk. "Could you tell me the name of the young lady who just checked out?"

"You mean Miss Elizabeth Barnard?"

"Thank you."

"Do you wish her forwarding address?"

"She left one?"

"Yes, sir." The clerk checked his file. "Mrs. Ferguson's boardinghouse."

Ross blinked. "*Our* Mrs. Ferguson?"

"Yes, sir. On Oak Street."

Chapter 7

THE FOLLOWING day Owen Seadon brought in his second well. If Owen's first success had been clouded by the suicide of Beniamino Giolatta, surely the new well would be a happier occasion. So Owen thought, and so Ross agreed, as they watched the crew prepare to shut in the flow of oil. That evening, moreover, Ross intended to celebrate the event by a second dinner with Liz Barnard. In his confidence, Ross had not bothered to stop by Mrs. Ferguson's boardinghouse to issue the invitation. Then the unforeseen happened. Whether caused by a spark from the hobnailed boot of one of the crew, or by static electricity that ignited the gas escaping from the wellhead, there was a hiss of flame, and seconds later Seadon Number Four was ablaze. Burning oil spouted from the wellhead, flowed across the drill platform and out across the field toward the other Seadon wells. Owen, Ross, and the drilling crew frantically shoveled dirt onto the spreading oil; but as fast as they blotted out the flames, there was a fresh tide of burning oil.

By nightfall Owen accepted the inevitable. "Explosives!" he shouted to Ross. "We've got to snuff it out like a candle." The heat radiating from the wellhead was too dangerous to employ nitroglycerine, so Owen decided on fulminate of mercury. He filled a tobacco pouch with the granules of mercury, ordered everyone to flatten himself on the ground, and lobbed the pouch toward the jet of flames. There was an ear-numbing explosion, fragments of drilling equipment and boiler soared into the night—then welcome darkness. The men got to their feet and stared in awe. Nothing remained of Seadon Number Four except a smoking crater. Owen turned to Ross with a rueful sigh. "Experience is kind of expensive, isn't it? Next time I'll throw something mild, like a bolt of lightning."

A day later than he had expected, Ross presented himself at Mrs. Ferguson's boardinghouse and asked for Elizabeth Barnard. "Oh, *that* one. She left this morning." Mrs. Ferguson smirked, as if the girl's departure had somehow elevated the tone of her establishment. "No, sir, left no forwarding address."

Ross's disappointment was tinged with relief. Now at least there would be no further cause for Leah's barbs about "your actress friend." Her reception of Liz Barnard's dresses had been more than a little cool. "It's really typical. You can spend thirty dollars to help a complete stranger, but not one penny to send me to a singing conservatory."

And he had replied, "You'll go, damn it. But not now. You can't leave Ma alone here."

"And when will that ever change?"

"Leah, for God's sake—"

"I won't wear those dresses!"

"Fine, okay, good. Burn 'em up!"

On January 10, 1901, the world oil industry was electrified by an event in Texas which ever afterwards was to be summed up in one word: "Spindletop." A well drilled by a certain Anthony Lucas exploded into the sky at the rate of 100,000 barrels of oil a day. Spindletop was the greatest gusher in history. All Weston, including the Seadon brothers, received the news with envy and despair. Texas oil would surely destroy the market for California oil. The fear seemed warranted, for every day the Southern Pacific depot was crowded with men and women bound for the new bonanza. Then, to everyone's bewilderment, people were no longer leaving Weston; instead, the incoming trains brought an even greater flood of boomers. Again the cause was Spindletop. The Texas marvel was proof that the United States finally had petroleum in abundance, and American industry reacted with enthusiasm. The railroads announced that they would convert their coal-burning locomotives to oil; the steamship companies followed suit. In short, the nation went oil crazy, and Weston was the California capital of the dementia. Within two months after Spindletop, there were thirty-odd wells drilling on the banks of the Haber River. The lobby of the Pioneer Hotel was cluttered with desks, each of which represented the "executive office" of a new oil company. Central Avenue was clogged with traffic bound north to the oil field—mule-drawn wagons carrying pipe and timber and high explosives.

It was on Central Avenue one afternoon that Ross Seadon heard a woman's voice hail him. A voice with a musical quality that stirred a memory. "Hello, Mr. Seadon!"

He turned and squinted unbelievingly at Liz Barnard in jeans and a man's work shirt and the red pigtail which spilled out from under a farmer's straw hat.

"When did you get back to town?"

"Never left. How did your sister like my dresses?"

"Just fine. Loves them," he lied. He surveyed Liz with growing disapproval. "I wish you were wearing one right now." She laughed, and he added, "I stopped by Mrs. Ferguson's and she said you'd left without a forwarding address."

"Probably because she wasn't happy that I was going into competition with her. I've got my own boardinghouse. The old Dutton place, out off the river road."

Ross squinted again. "The Dutton place? That was abandoned years ago. Last I saw of it, the windows were smashed and the front door kicked in."

"That's the way I found it. But it had an old coal stove somebody left in the kitchen, and there was a water well out back. I took what was left of the thirty dollars you paid me and bought canvas to cover the windows and make hammocks. I bought some pots and pans and some food, then I went looking for boarders out in the oil field. I made them pay me a week in advance, then I rented the house."

"After you had already moved in?"

She bobbed her head, grinning. "I was a squatter, I guess you'd say. Took me time to find out who owned the place and where they lived. San Francisco. I mailed them a check for a hundred dollars, and they cashed it. Probably think they're taking advantage of a raving lunatic—but I'm collecting seven hundred a month and clearing four." She paused in her recital and smiled curiously. "You don't seem very impressed."

But Ross was. And irritated, as well. "Did you have this idea all worked out that night at dinner?"

"Of course not. But you kept telling me Weston was the golden end of the rainbow, so I decided to find out. Staying with Mrs. Ferguson gave me the idea of a boardinghouse— someplace out near the oil field that would be handy for the workers." Liz paused again. "You *are* upset, aren't you?"

"Yes! Running a boardinghouse is for middle-aged women who can't do anything else. But for God's sake, Liz, not you. You're an actress."

"Who happens to be between engagements. I learned a lot on the road. It's easy to get a job when you don't need it, so now I'm building up a kitty." She laughed. "And getting an advanced course in human nature, as well."

Ross scowled. "That's exactly what I mean. Oil-field rough-necks are a hard lot. Have you got a gun?"

"Something better. The biggest, meanest, blackest dog in the county. Besides," she added with an impish smile, "a thirty-eight bust outguns a thirty-eight Colt any day." She held out her hand. "Well, I got to go buy a wagonload of supplies. Stop by and say hello sometime."

Ross watched her stride across the street. She was different, he thought unhappily. Not the same girl at all. Femininity and grace had metamorphosed into a kind of male bravado. She had become another boomer. With red knuckles and broken fingernails.

Liz Barnard had changed. So had everyone who lived in Weston or came to Weston in those first heady days. The town itself was stepping into the twentieth century. By the summer of 1901, tracks for a street railway were laid down Central Avenue and across town to the depot, and electric trolley cars began to clatter along an eighteen-block route. The Pioneer Hotel boasted a brick annex. The Weston Dry Goods Store enlarged; a three-story building devoted entirely to office space went up, with Wilmot Caruth and his new law partner the first tenants. Progress came also to the Seadon Estate Company. In place of its operation of the oil property, which entailed consultations with Cathlin and Leah in every smallest decision, Ross and Owen formed a wholly owned subsidiary of the Seadon Estate Company, with themselves as the officers, and christened it "Seadon Oil Company." They rented a one-room office next door to Wilmot Caruth and hired Hattie MacFarland, a gentle Southern spinster, to perform the secretarial duties.

"You know what we need now," Owen remarked, feet on the new desk in the new office, "is another oil lease."

"I'm working on it." Ross nodded. "I think Tim Beakley will throw in his property with ours. Makes sense, the two being side by side."

Owen made a face. "I mean a new lease in a new oil field."

"Where?"

"Well, I've been talking to some of the Texas hands. Learned a lot from them. Things like salt domes and clines and anticlines, upthrusts and downcasts, sand blows and diagonal extensions." Owen swung his heels off the desk and crossed to a map of Haber County tacked onto the wall. His finger jabbed at the area of the Haber River field, then traced southwest. "This could be the diagonal extension." His finger came to a stop. "And here's where I'd like to look. Mirage Springs."

"Where we used to go shooting with Dad?"

"And never winged even a buzzard."

"When do you want to start?"

"Tomorrow."

And so, while Owen rode the range west of town, Ross attended the office routine and played afternoon poker in the back room of the Orleans Saloon.

"How many cards?"

"Two."

"Remember that fellow who was here a few months ago with the private railroad car—what's his name?"

"Haggerty. G. G. Haggerty."

"Well, he's back again. Same railroad car, with the window blinds pulled down. I hear he never leaves it until after dark."

"Then where's he go? What's he after?"

"Oil leases, probably. Sure as shooting, Haggerty is Standard Oil. . . . What are you cackling about, Ross?"

"King, queen, jack, ten."

"Shit!"

Following one such game, Ross returned to the office, and Hattie MacFarland handed him a note which had just been delivered.

> Dear Mr. Seadon:
>   The pleasure of your company at dinner is requested tomorrow evening, September 7, at 8 o'clock, aboard the "Phaethon." Informal dress. R.S.V.P.
>   Anson Billings
>   Secretary to Mr. G. G. Haggerty

"*Phaethon* must be the name of his private car," Owen surmised when Ross showed him the invitation. "I wonder who else will be there."

"And who is G. G. Haggerty?" Ross frowned.

Owen studied the invitation again. "He's a cool customer. He's had that private car sitting there on that siding for three days, like an enemy gunboat waiting outside a port. When the natives are finally just about jumping out of their skins, he invites them to a parley."

Ross sniffed. "It doesn't mean we have to surrender. We can always come ashore and order the fort to open fire."

"What will you use for ammunition?"

Ross shrugged. In spite of himself, he was anxious, queasily so. He had never met a man who traveled by private railroad car.

At precisely eight o'clock the following evening Ross arrived at the Weston depot, waved a greeting to the telegrapher in his office, and crossed the tracks toward the gleaming railroad car with the brass-appointed observation platform. The windows were curtained, but here and there along the side of the car multicolored glass ports glowed invitingly. As Ross approached, he saw a prim-mouthed man descend the vestibule steps and smile toward him.

"Good evening, Mr. Seadon. I'm Anson Billings."

They shook hands and went up the iron steps. At the top a butler in tails and white gloves inclined his head and swung open a door into the main saloon. It was as though one were stepping into the drawing room of some millionaire's mansion. Ross had a confused impression of crystal chandeliers, Oriental carpets, potted ferns and flowers, and the sheen of rare woods. Then his attention focused on a young woman in evening dress who arose from a divan. She came forward, extending a hand glittery with diamonds. Ross noted that the left hand wore no wedding ring.

"We're so glad you could join us, Mr. Seadon. I'm Zoe." The voice was light and immature. "Mr. Haggerty will be with us in a moment. Mr. Billings?"

Billings nodded and raised an eyebrow toward the butler, who bowed and moved toward a bar where a magnum of champagne rested in a silver bucket. Beside the bucket Ross counted four champagne glasses.

So he was to be the only guest. There were to be no witnesses. If a woman is a clue to a man's character, Ross thought, as he studied Zoe, then G. G. Haggerty was a sensualist. One barely noticed the poster-pretty face beneath the pile of blond hair, nor the pouting lips and sheeplike eyes; rather, attention was compelled to the luxurious breasts which threatened to escape from the brim of the evening gown. A cameo suspended from a rope of pearls peeped and flirted from Zoe's cleavage, and to further rivet the beholder, a beauty spot (heart-shaped) was pasted to the slope of her left breast.

The champagne cork popped in the background, and, as if it were the required cue, a door at the end of the saloon opened.

G. G. Haggerty was a curious mixture of the ordinary and the impressive. His face was blandly smooth, but the eyes were dark and penetrating. Although a head shorter than Zoe, he walked as if he were a one-man parade. He was young, perhaps no more than five years older than Ross, yet already he had developed a paunch, which was emphasized by a heavy gold chain looping across his waistcoat.

"A pleasure, a great pleasure, Mr. Seadon," Haggerty said in a voice so muted that Ross felt he was sharing a confidence. He waved a hand toward a velvet divan, leaving Zoe and Billings to find chairs for themselves. The butler offered the tray of champagne, and Haggerty raised his glass to Ross. "To friendship."

They drank, then Haggerty rolled his champagne glass between his hands. "I do a lot of traveling, Mr. Seadon. When you travel, you meet people. And I like to meet people. The right people. When I hit it off with somebody, it's like powder meeting flint. Things happen."

Ross tensed, thinking that Haggerty was coming directly to the purpose of the meeting. But no, Haggerty's talk drifted from subject to subject, as elusive as smoke. Horse racing at Saratoga Springs, yachting on the sound, "Mr. Morgan's sloop," a party at Delmonico's. It was a monologue delivered in a semi-whisper, so that Ross was forced to lean forward to catch the words. It was exasperating and done purposely, Ross sensed, to place him in the role of an inferior. Then, at last, the butler announced dinner.

They went forward to another section of the car, which again might have been transported from a millionaire's mansion. The oval dining table was covered with Irish linen inset with Venetian lace. Silver salvers and chafing dishes, heavily gadrooned, gleamed on a sideboard. The dinner itself was proof that G. G. Haggerty traveled with a superior French chef. They ate in silence—Haggerty doing reverence to each dish, Billings with dyspeptic resignation, Zoe with smoldering side glances at Ross.

Finally, during the roast pheasant, Haggerty murmured across the table, "Mr. Seadon, are you a Bible reader?"

"At my mother's insistence, yes."

"In the New Testament, you may remember, Satan took Jesus up onto the mountain and showed him the cities of the world, their riches and glories, and said in effect, All these I give unto you, if you will fall down and worship me. Do you place the passage?

"I do."

"Jesus refused, of course. But suppose he had not. Suppose he had fallen down and worshiped Satan. What then?"

"He would not have been the Son of God."

"But he would have been the richest man in history. The greatest power. The mightiest emperor. He would not have died on the cross."

"And there would be no Christian religion."

"Is there anyway, Mr. Seadon?"

"That's a strange question for an Irishman."

"North of Ireland, sir. An Orangeman."

It was a curious exchange. As a poker player, Ross recognized it as the opening bid. Haggerty might hold a strong hand, but he wished his opponent to think it was a royal flush. Ross dabbed his napkin at his mouth. "I assume, Mr. Haggerty, that you do not hold yourself out as His Satanic Majesty."

"Right! Nor do you strike me as the Son of God."

They returned to their food. A freight train rumbled and hooted by on the main track, causing the wine glasses to dance. The butler served a flaming dessert, baba au rhum, followed by coffee and cognac and rich Havana cigars. Zoe, glad for an activity, clipped the tips for each man and lighted them.

Haggerty inhaled languidly and eyed Ross. "Tell me about yourself."

Ross ignored the patronizing tone. "You already know. That's why I'm here."

Haggerty chuckled. "True. I had Billings nose around. I liked the answers he got. So tell me what you want to be."

"Exactly what I am. An oilman."

"Your brother feels the same way?"

"I think you know that, too."

"Yes. The Seadons are an interesting family. They've had some hard knocks, things weren't always easy for you. Stanford, for instance." He paused, watching for Ross's embarrassment, which Ross did not permit to show. "And now, some very good luck. But what are you going to do with it? You must have some ideas, some dreams."

"Certainly. To grow, to develop, to make a place in the world."

"You grow by merger, by freezing out your competitors, by enlarging your markets, perhaps buying tanker ships, maybe even advertising. First you use diplomacy on the stupid, then you wage war on the stubborn. It all takes a great deal of money."

"Which you are here to supply."

Haggerty sent Ross a smile which Ross returned unopened. "Mr. Haggerty, the Seadon Oil Company is not for sale."

"I don't want it. I want you." While Ross stared his surprise, Haggerty dug into his trouser pocket and tossed a gold eagle onto the Irish linen. "This can buy food and liquor, clothing and lodging. It can buy a thousand baubles. A chance on faro, an evening's entertainment. It can buy a woman. Yet once this coin leaves your pocket, it's not lonesome for you. It does not send wish-you-were-here cards. The only thing you can spend and still keep is . . . brains. That's where you come in."

"Do you speak for yourself, or others?"

"Both. In San Francisco you'll meet one of my group. In New York you'll meet the rest. We're simply men who appreciate what I call the beatitudes of business."

Ross understood completely. "In other words, you are looking for a man who is trusted by the people of Weston. And who better than the son of Weston's oil pioneer? You supply the money and I buy up the Weston oil companies and transfer them to you or to some dummy corporation."

Haggerty laughed. "I knew I'd picked the right man."

"You haven't."

There was a stillness around the table. Billings stared at Ross with slack-jawed awe; Zoe nervously fingered the rope of pearls that dangled in her cleavage. No one, apparently, challenged G. G. Haggerty.

Then Haggerty recovered. "Naturally, I expect you to bargain. And I expect to pay."

Ross shook his head. "It won't work. The moment I try to buy up stock, everybody would guess the truth. They know I don't have a lot of cash; the money must come from you. Don't forget, this little dinner is far from secret. The telegrapher at the station saw me come here, and by now the word is all over town."

"I hope so." Haggerty paused to draw on his cigar, smiling at Ross's confusion. "I want everybody to know. Then we'll leak it out that we had a quarrel, that you refused any part of me. That way people will trust you even more, and you'll buy the stock cheaper. As for the money, you'll say you got a line of credit from some friendly banker."

Ross pushed back from the table. "Thank you for the dinner, and for the pleasant company."

"Now hold on . . ."

Ross smiled quietly. "At least you've shown that you need Weston more than we need you. No. Weston oil stays with Weston people. We're not going to be swallowed up by an Eastern combine. Nobody back East is going to tell us what we can or can't do. We're independents, we're Californians, and that's the way we'll remain. Come hell or high water."

Haggerty glanced sourly at Billings and Zoe. "You know, I believe he *does* think he's the Son of God."

The next morning at the office Ross gave Owen an account of the dinner. "That's exactly what it was, a parley aboard the gunboat," he concluded. "It may go away for a while, but when it comes back it will have an armada behind it."

"Haggerty's that determined?"

"He is. And somewhere in this town he'll find the man he wants."

Owen scowled at the county map on the wall. "Maybe his armada's already here. I spent yesterday going over the county recorder's books. Seems I wasn't the only one to think about an extension of the river field. Somebody's pouring a lot of money into leases around Mirage Springs."

"Who?"

"Well, I recognized some of the names. Tim Beakley, for instance. But others are new; could be dummies for out-of-towners."

"Then we better move. You spotted some good acreage?"

"Most of it's gone. But there's one piece I'd like to have. According to the records, it's already leased." Owen moved his tongue around inside his cheek, thinking. "But I got a hunch you can deal us in on it. You're the one golden voice she might listen to."

"A woman? Oh, Christ, they're impossible." Ross caught the knowing look in Owen's eyes. "All right, what's her name?"

"Elizabeth Barnard."

Chapter 8

THE DUTTON place was a mile to the west of the river road leading to the oil field. From a distance, it looked as Ross had remembered it: a two-story farmhouse of unpainted board, a shingle roof with most of the shingles gone to visit relatives. In what had once been a front yard a small whirlwind twirled and skipped in the afternoon heat, sucking up a column of dust and dead tumbleweed. Ross's buggy drew nearer, and he saw freshly planted geraniums bordering the front porch. Directly in front of the geraniums was a hand-lettered sign: BATH 50¢. SECONDS 25¢.

A large black object hurtled around the corner of the house and bore down on the buggy with a broadside of furious barks. Ross's horse shied and reared; then someone on the porch whistled, and the dog broke off his attack. Liz Barnard, again in jeans and a man's shirt, watched Ross approach on foot, while the dog circled him with warning growls. "It's all right, Blacky. He's a friend," she called out. "At least I hope you are." She smiled, holding out her hand.

"A friend, and a customer." Ross tossed a fifty-cent piece into the air.

Liz puzzled at the coin, then: "Oh, the bath! Just go around the side of the house. You'll see a tin tub."

"If it's that public, I think I'll charge *you* the fifty cents."

They laughed together, and Liz ushered Ross into what passed for a sitting room. A scattering of battered wicker chairs composed the total furnishings of the room.

"Liz, I came to take you to dinner."

"What a lovely idea! But I can't. I'm running a boarding-house, remember. I've got twelve empty stomachs, and you're welcome to be number thirteen. In fact, I insist. It's stewed chicken." She guided Ross toward the kitchen, where a big-eyed girl in her early teens, ladle in hand, gaped at Ross. "Carrie, this is Mr. Seadon. Carrie helps out. Her folks sell me chickens and eggs. Mind helping set the breakfast table?"

She smiled at Ross's look of confusion. "Yes, breakfast. That's for the night shift that will be pouring downstairs any minute. After them the day shift will be back, and then you get your stewed chicken." She loaded a stack of dishes into Ross's hands and pointed toward an open door.

The dining room was fitted out with a trestle table flanked by benches. While Ross distributed the plates, Liz set out the knives and forks and spoons.

"Just when do you sleep?" he asked.

"With the day shift." She laughed and corrected herself. "I mean, at night, and by myself."

"I'll bet you even do their washing."

She saw him looking at her caustic-reddened hands. She made a weak movement to put them behind her, then gave it up with a defiant "It's extra money."

She looked tired, Ross thought. There were hints of circles under her eyes, and she seemed thinner than the last time he had seen her in jeans and shirt. She was aware of Ross's gaze again; she brushed a red curl away from her damp forehead.

"Yes, it's hot, sticky work. When you first told me about

the wonders of Weston, you forgot to mention that the summers are a hundred and ten degrees. And I don't remember anything about the winters. Last January I was a walking icicle."

Ross frowned. "This whole thing is ridiculous. You don't belong here. You belong in town, in dresses, and in the chips. And I'm here to see that it happens."

"By selling you my oil lease?" She wrinkled her nose at him. "Oh yes, I knew you'd come. You aren't the first, you know."

"I suppose not. Liz, how in hell did you wind up with an oil lease?"

She cocked her ear at the sound of pounding feet on the staircase. "The breakfast gang. Come on." She tugged Ross back to the kitchen. "Can you toss flapjacks?"

He blinked. "Well, I used to watch Ah Sing at home."

"Good. Carrie's got the batter made. Don't worry if some land on the floor. You stay in here, and Carrie will take care of the ham and coffee and the serving. I've got something important to do."

With that, Liz was gone and Ross meekly poured the first batter into the skillet. After the first few failures the brown cakes began to pile up on the plates almost as professionally as if Ah Sing were in command. As Carrie rushed back and forth to the dining room, he heard bursts of male laughter and talk and was thankful that no one thought to stick his head into the kitchen. Any explanation Ross might give would sound ridiculous, especially the truth. Flipping flapjacks to get an oil lease!

After a while he heard the thud of hooves outside and the clatter of wheels. It was the labor wagon, Carrie said, bringing the day shift and picking up the night shift. She had barely finished her explanation when there was the noisy scrape-back of benches in the dining room and the echo of boots clumping out onto the porch. It was time for Ross's escape to the sitting room.

The new arrivals ranged in ages from seventeen to thirty-five. They were sunburned, heavy-muscled, and rough-talking.

They had washed up out at the oil field, but there were still traces of grease on their faces and hands, and their work clothes were armor-stiff with dirt. Ross felt awkward in his trim and clean trousers and shirt, and more awkward still in his explanation that he was a hardware salesman (true enough at one time). At least it brought guffaws. Trying to sell Miss Barnard? Hell, nobody could sell her nothing. At that moment Liz appeared in the doorway and there was a startled silence. She was wearing a dress. Not a house dress, but a city dress in butter-yellow linen, floor length, with long sleeves and a fitted vest. Another of Liz's theatrical costumes, Ross concluded, and certainly sweltering. It was clear also that the boarders had never seen Liz except in jeans and a shirt. They were both awed at her sudden femininity and, from their glances at Ross, resentful of the reason for Liz's change. "It's my birthday," she explained to the room, and the white lie had its intended effect. There was a chorus of clumsy birthday wishes, and Ross was forgotten.

The dinner went quickly, with the toolies loudly swapping information about the day's drilling and making cumbersome jokes about Liz's advanced age. Afterwards, while the men smoked on the front porch, Liz and Carrie cleared the table and then Liz returned to Ross and suggested that they take a walk. Better than that, Ross countered, a buggy ride.

Liz hesitated. "I'm not sure it's wise."

"Your boarders?"

"Yes. They've kind of put me on a pedestal. I've never had any trouble with them, because each one thinks he's protecting me from the others."

Ross nodded understanding. "And nice girls just don't go out with a man after dark. Especially when there's a full moon."

"Especially." She gave a light laugh. "But nice girls are allowed a little lie now and then. I'll say we're driving Carrie home."

Which is what they did. Afterwards, Ross guided the buggy

back across the open range, well out of sight of the Dutton place. When they reached the river road, he headed the buggy north toward the oil field. "And now let's hear about that lease," he commanded. "How and when and why."

"Well, to begin with, one of the reasons I started the boardinghouse—besides making eating money—was to figure out an oil stock to buy, or maybe an interest in some lease. I thought if I boarded the toolies, and listened to their talk, I might hear something that would be a good tip."

"And what did you hear?"

"Nothing! But I did notice that when I washed some of the work pants, one pair was always a lot cleaner than the rest. It belonged to a man named Harley Stewart. It always had thorns and prickles and bits of sagebrush sticking to the legs. And smelled of horses. That got me to thinking. Oil toolies don't ride horses; they're picked up and delivered back here in work wagons. That meant Stewart was getting a horse somewhere out at the field. But why? Unless he was looking for something. Maybe he was an oil scout."

Ross chuckled. "You learn fast. But I can't see an oil scout telling you where he was looking."

"That was another thing. He was so close-mouthed. So I started watching him. And that's how I found out."

"How?"

"Chicken shit."

"Huh?" Ross was not used to women using such frank words.

"I saw it on the heels of his boots. There's only one chicken farm for miles around here. The Wilsons'. Carrie's family. I went over and talked to them, and when I described Stewart, sure enough, they said he'd been there. He told them he needed water for his horse, and when they showed him the horse trough he said he wanted it from their well. They thought that was peculiar."

"Not at all. He wanted to check the well water for an oily taste."

"It has. Just a trace. The funny thing is, the Wilsons had drunk the water for so many years that they no longer noticed it. Mr. Wilson told me they used to think it had 'medical properties,' and let it go at that. Anyway, Stewart came back a couple of days later and said he was thinking about retiring to a chicken farm, and would they sell? The Wilsons weren't interested. Then I explained to them what Stewart was really after and asked if they'd lease me the drilling rights, and they did."

Ross swung around on the buggy seat and stared incredulously. "Just like that?"

"Well, not quite. I remembered that night we ate at the hotel, and that your friend Mr. Caruth was an attorney. So I went to him, got a blank lease form, and took it back to the Wilsons with five hundred dollars. It's a one-year lease with an option to renew each year for another five hundred."

"Jesus! For an actress, you're one hell of a mudlark."

"What's a mudlark?"

"A woman who deals in oil leases. We got a couple in town." Ross peered thoughtfully at the moonlit landscape and the silhouettes of the drilling rigs which were thrusting into view. "You told the Wilsons there might be oil on their land, yet they leased to you—not to an oil company."

"We're friends. Good friends. And"—she let the word dangle in the air for a moment—"and I told them I knew an oilman, a very experienced oilman, who just might go partners with me."

Ross made a strangling noise and let the reins go slack in his hand. "Partners! You and I?"

"Why not? Fifty-fifty."

Ross began to laugh; and the more he thought about it, the harder he laughed. "You know," he gasped, "I bought those damned dresses of yours because I was sorry for you. Imagine! Sorry! They should have locked me up as the town fool!" Finally he was aware of Liz's hurt silence. "Look, it costs a hell of a lot of money to drill a wildcat well. My company takes all the risk, and maybe we'll find nothing."

"Then fifty per cent of nothing is still nothing."

"Sorry. Twenty per cent is my limit."

Liz sniffed and made no answer. By now the buggy was bumping along the work road through the oil field. On both sides derricks reared against the moonlit sky like great prehistoric monsters. Most of the rigs were drilling on a twenty-four-hour basis. The sultry air was heavy with smoke and the tarry smell of the oil sumps.

Liz gazed around. "Which are your wells?"

"Coming to them." The buggy turned off onto another work road and drew up alongside the cottonwood trees that were the landmark of Seadon Number One. Ross helped Liz out of the buggy and led her by the hand alongside the sump, which glistened darkly in the moonlight. He took her up onto the wooden drilling platform, and she watched the slow rise and fall of the walking beam. With each pumping stroke, it emitted a long mournful sigh that was almost human. "This is where it all began," Ross said quietly. "The first well in Haber County. And where Dad died."

She pressed his hand. "I'm sorry. I didn't mean to . . ."

"It's all right. I feel closer to him when I'm out here." Then he changed the subject. "How about thirty per cent and seventy per cent?"

She laughed. "Fifty-fifty."

"Out of the question."

They left the well, and Ross led her by the hand through the cottonwoods that bordered the riverbank. On a narrow shelf of rock he pointed down to the spot among the boulders where the asphalt still seeped out into the glittering water. They stood silently, listening to the night sounds—the chorus of bullfrogs and crickets in shrill counterpoint, the burble of water, and the sudden screech of a nighthawk. Then Ross's arm went around Liz's waist. She gave a start, then turned toward him and looked up into his face.

"I'm glad you didn't go back East," he said huskily.

She nodded. "It would have been the mistake of my life."

At first they kissed shyly, delicately, then with growing intensity. His arms around her waist, hers around his neck. The scent of her hair and skin were sweet with the perfume of youth. There was none of the heavy musk of Madame Deveraux's girls, with their hard lips and trained responses.

Finally they released each other. Liz smiled gently. "I'm not really surprised, are you?"

"Not really."

She touched his cheek with a fingertip. "Twenty-five per cent and seventy-five per cent."

He laughed. "That's less than I just offered."

She nodded. "It's the woman's place to yield. I want it behind us."

His arms closed around her again. They kissed for a very long time. Oblivious of the mosquitoes that buzzed about their ears, aware only of their mouths and bodies and their trembling desire. Then Ross's hands found the buttons on the back of her fitted vest. She allowed him only to loosen the collar; then his lips went to her neck, her throat. When at last they separated, their eyes scanned the area with a common purpose. The dense cottonwoods, the clumps of mesquite, the narrow rocky shelf on which they stood, the jumble of boulders along the bank. There was no place to spread a blanket, and no blanket to spread. Then Ross seized her elbow and pointed out into the stream. A few feet from the bank there was a large flattish granite boulder; in the moonlight it vaguely resembled a stone bench.

Liz contemplated it carefully. "You know," she whispered, "we're both stark raving mad."

"Completely. But the water can't be more than two feet deep." He kissed her once more, for encouragement.

She stared again at the rock, as if trying to work it out in her mind. Then she bobbed her head in understanding. "Turn your back."

He did. He could hear her movements, the soft sliding sounds of fabric. She would be slipping off her underdrawers and stockings, just as he was rolling up his trouser legs and removing his shoes and socks.

They slid down the embankment and gasped as their bare feet went into the cold water. Liz lifted her skirt above her knees and waded after Ross. They reached the boulder and scrambled up. Ross found a hollow in the side of the boulder for his feet and sat down. He looked up at Liz, who was still standing. She might be, he thought, a young lady in her Sunday best out for a moonlit stroll. Except, of course, for her bare feet.

She glanced back at the cottonwoods. "Suppose somebody . . . ?"

"They wouldn't believe it."

She tittered. "I don't myself." Then, with a flurry of skirt, she placed one foot on either side of his thighs, paused while he made ready for her, then slowly sank down onto his lap. Her legs, beneath the billow of skirt, locked around his hips. She moaned, just once, and Ross realized, to his profound amazement, that Liz Barnard was a virgin.

They had agreed to meet the next afternoon in Wilmot Caruth's law office to draw up the assignment of lease. At two o'clock Ross and Owen—the latter jubilant over his brother's success—drew up chairs in Caruth's office and explained the purpose of their call.

"I guess this is what you mean." Caruth smiled and pushed a document across the desk to Ross.

"You mean she's already been here?"

"This morning. She told me what she wanted done and I said no; I couldn't be attorney for both sides. But she insisted that I'd really be acting for you. So I drew up the assignment and notarized her signature. A seventy-five-per-cent drilling interest for 'one dollar and other good and valuable considerations.'" Caruth paused and shook his head ruefully. "This sure teaches me a lesson. The next time a young lady stops me in a hotel lobby and tries to sell me a dress, I'm going to buy her whole damned wardrobe right down to her shoe buttons."

Ross felt deflated. He had looked forward to seeing Liz with an urgency that was quite apart from the matter of the oil lease. And she, for some reason of her own, had chosen to avoid him.

The black dog challenged Ross again. Then, recognizing him, it wagged its tail and trotted along beside him up onto the front porch. As Ross raised his hand to knock on the screen door, he saw Liz inside, staring out at him almost as if he were a stranger. He held up the envelope in his hand.

"I brought you a copy of your assignment."

The screen door opened and her hand reached out.

"Liz! What's wrong?"

She made no answer. Ross opened the screen door and she backed away, shaking her head. "No," she whispered. "Please go."

"Liz! For God's sake, stop acting like a child afraid of a whipping!"

The shock of his words had its effect. She hesitated, timidly searched his face, looked at his outstretched arms, then bounded toward him with a whimper of gladness. "I'm sorry! I'm sorry!"

He held her tightly, brushing his lips against her cheek. "What in hell got into you?"

"Sssh! Carrie's in the kitchen, and they're sleeping upstairs."

Ross lowered his voice. "You're guilty about last night, that's it, isn't it?"

She made a weak nodding motion. "I don't know what happened to me. I lost control. I lost . . . well, everything."

"Your virginity, yes. But you found something, too."

She clapped her hand over his mouth and listened. There was a reassuring clang of pots and pans in the kitchen. She took her hand away and looked up at him. "I'm not in love with you."

"So you're guilty about that, too." He laughed softly. "All right, I'm not in love with you, either. Does that make it easier?"

She gave him a frightened look for answer. Then his arms tightened around her and their mouths welcomed each other with hungry abandon. Finally Ross murmured into her ear, "Can we get to your room without waking anybody?"

"It's too dangerous."

His eyes circled the sitting room with its collection of wicker chairs. She understood. "No, not with Carrie," she whispered. "We've got to wait. Get us a room at the hotel."

"The Pioneer? Where everybody knows me? Why not a store window and be done with it?"

There was only one solution. Liz would discharge her boarders who slept through the daylight hours; she would tell them that she was exhausted and needed more rest; they would have forty-eight hours in which to find new lodgings. As soon as they left, Liz would give Carrie the day off. And so it was that on September 14, 1901, the day that President McKinley died of an assassin's bullets, and Theodore Roosevelt became the twenty-sixth President of the United States, Ross Seadon first saw Liz Barnard's bedroom. There were a brand-new brass bed with a feather mattress, a bouquet of geraniums on the dresser, and, within arm's reach on the night table, a gramophone which, at the crank of the handle, would bray and thump its way through Sousa's "Stars and Stripes Forever."

With the Barnard lease secured, Owen Seadon began to drill the first well. After a month's work it proved to be a dry hole. "Barnard Number Two" was a similar failure. "Maybe I was wrong about Mirage Springs," Owen said to Ross one day in the office. "I'm for knocking off and letting some other wildcatter prove the area."

Ross disagreed. "We're after more than just oil; we're building a reputation. I say, drill Barnard Number Three."

"And maybe lose still more money—"

"Oh, damn the money! Just drill that well!"

Owen glanced at Hattie MacFarland, who was shifting papers at her rolltop desk and pretending that she was unaware of the argument. "Hattie, isn't it about your lunchtime?"

She looked at the watch pinned to her bodice and agreed

with alacrity. The door closed behind her, and Owen turned back to Ross.

"Is this well for the Seadons or Liz Barnard? I'll tell you right now, I'm not bound by any promises you've made her. You can pay for your cozy afternoons some other way." He watched the dark look come into Ross's eyes. "You don't think I know what happens every Monday and Friday? You're not in the office, you're not at the Orleans, you're not out at the river. You're not fooling me; you're an ostrich with your head in the sands and your tail sky-high!" Owen's outburst was a release of resentment that he had not consciously realized; it was as sudden as a thunder squall and, like a squall, climaxed with a deadly bolt: "Get your brains out of your crotch and go back to the whorehouse. At least it's cheaper!"

An instant later Ross's fist smashed into Owen's face and sent him reeling against the wall. He shook his head groggily, then hurled himself at Ross, who stood with his hands at his sides, waiting contritely to accept the blow.

Owen hesitated, then dropped his fist and managed a weak smile. "Christ, why didn't you tell me, man? You're in love!"

Ross frowned uneasily. It had never occurred to him.

The stalemate between the brothers was broken, surprisingly, by Tim Beakley. Their onetime drilling superintendent began the foundation for a derrick to the west of the Barnard lease, and Owen, spurred by the competition, followed suit with Barnard Number Three. The Seadon well was three miles from the Dutton place, but the range was flat and Ross could stand at Liz's bedroom window and see the column of gray smoke rising from Owen's boiler into the windless sky.

"This time I'm sure of it," Ross said one afternoon. "Three is my lucky number." He smiled at Liz, who was propped against the bed pillows with her red hair spilling down over her bare shoulders. "Well, Girl of the Golden West, what are you going to do with all your money?"

She stretched her arms luxuriously. "Get rid of my boarders, for one thing. And buy some decent furniture. And some dresses, the frilly kind you like."

That was a comfort; she planned to stay on in Weston. Then he asked, "What about the stage?"

She made a face. "I'm past that. After what I've seen around Weston, and been through, playacting is pretty hollow stuff."

"What happened to the 'magic' of the theater?"

"Ha! That ends when the curtain comes down and you go back to some dingy little theatrical hotel, because the decent places won't take actors and that's all you can afford anyway." She shook her head at the memory. "It's bad enough for the men but worse for women. A girl can have her pictures in the papers and be wined and dined every night—but she always knows that when people look at her they're saying to themselves, Chippy . . . hussy . . . harlot." Liz paused, glanced down at her naked breasts, and laughed. "My, I'm the one to talk!"

He came back to the bed and stretched out beside her. "Feeling guilty again?"

"A little, I guess. Every girl has a silly romantic idea about how it's going to be, that first time. But who ever thought of a rock in the middle of the river?" She kissed his shoulder. "Thank you just the same. And thank all those who taught you. Every last scarlet lady."

"You don't mind about them?"

"Did your schoolteacher mind which books gave you the right answers?"

Ross was tempted to tell Liz that he loved her, but he dismissed the idea. Both avoided the word *love*, as if naming the emotion might be too explosive, might destroy the fabric of their relationship. Yet Ross sensed that Liz returned his feeling. The change in her was proof; where once she had seemed bossy, now she was docile, almost submissive.

Sometimes they talked about Ross's family. He had never introduced her to them, nor had she voiced a wish that he do so. Still, she was curious. Especially about Leah. It was natural,

Ross thought. They were near the same age, and it was Leah who truly lived with Ross.

"She's a very pretty girl," Liz remarked. "I only saw her from a distance, but I recognized her from her resemblance to you."

"Where was this?"

"The dry goods store. She was talking to my old boarder Harley Stewart."

"The oil scout?" Ross shook his head. "Then it wasn't Leah; must have been somebody else. She couldn't possibly know him."

Liz let it go. "With her looks, and if she's got the voice you say she has, it's too bad she's not doing something about her singing. The Seadon money could smooth over the ugliness that I had to put up with."

"She can't leave Ma. I told her that. She can't be left alone."

"You mean, she's got to be watched?"

Ross looked away uneasily. "It's not that bad. Or maybe it is, and we won't face it. Sometimes in the middle of the night we hear her talking to Dad. I think she's with him more than she is with us."

The rivalry between the Seadon and Beakley drilling crews intensified as the weeks went by. When both wells passed the 2000-foot depth without any "shows," the feeling of competition began to change to one of anxiety. At 2300 feet Owen declared flatly that he had been wrong about the area; there was no oil. Then, at 2410 feet, Beakley's well came in. Two days later Barnard Number Three struck oil sands. The Seadons had lost the race, but Mirage Springs was proven oil country. Within a month Ross was able to stand at Liz's window and count a score of drilling rigs to the west. Moreover, he could now visit Liz by day or night, for with her first check from the Seadon Oil Company she discharged the last of her boarders and outfitted her sitting room with the best furniture Weston had to offer. Ross celebrated more dramatically; he bought the first motorcar to be seen in Weston. It was a canary-yellow Oldsmobile with red leather seats, kerosene headlamps, and tiller steering gear. Ross and Owen, and sometimes Leah, in dust coats and goggles, would chuff and snort down Central Avenue, ignoring the black looks of buggy drivers struggling to control their frightened horses. Sometimes when they felt particularly adventurous, they would make the bone-jarring drive out to the river field and even to Mirage Springs. On one such ride, when Ross was setting out by himself, he overtook one of Slim Perry's hacks bearing a passenger from the depot.

Ross glanced casually at the passenger, and then in a flash of recognition he squeezed his bulb horn and shouted, "Dave! Dave Marcus!" He whipped off his goggles so David could identify him.

"Ross! For God's sake!" David stopped the hack, paid the driver, transferred his suitcase to the motorcar, and climbed in beside Ross. "Man, what three years have done for you!" He laughed, beaming his approval at Ross's car.

"What pries you away from San Francisco?"

"Business. Same as every other banker. My father said it was time to come down and see what our competition is doing. And you're just the one who can tell me."

"Sure can! You're staying with us, you know."

David wagged his head. "The Pioneer Hotel. I got to be in and out at all hours. But if you want to invite me for dinner. . ."

"Done!"

When David Marcus arrived at the Seadon home that evening, Cathlin met him at the door, just as she had on that New Year's Eve three years before. "The last time you were here," she began, "the last time Val was . . ." The rest was lost in sobs.

David glanced sympathetically at Ross. The Cathlin Seadon that he remembered had aged three times three years; she appeared as fragile as a leaf pressed between the pages of a memory book. Then, as if an intentional repeat of David's first sight of Leah Seadon, footsteps echoed on the hall staircase and she was coming toward him, her hand extended.

"It's so nice to see you again, David."

She swept by Ross, who was staring oddly at her blue lace dress with a pink foundation and lace ruching at the neck. Liz Barnard's dress.

"My God, you're a stunner!" David blurted.

Leah smiled modestly. "Thank you, but I'm sure it's the dress." Her eyes slid toward Ross. "Any woman can be attractive if she has the right clothes."

Dinner went awkwardly. With Cathlin silent and misty-eyed at the end of the table, the others strained to avoid a reference to Val Seadon.

David confined himself to safe subjects—San Francisco social life, the probability that "Teddy" Roosevelt would bring about the long-delayed Panama Canal, the President's fire-and-brimstone attacks on the steel and oil trusts. Once he broke off in the middle of a conversation with Owen and smiled brightly at Leah. "I suppose by now you must be engaged."

"You suppose wrong. What about your sisters?"

"Married. Finally."

"And you?" Leah tried for a casual tone.

"Still a bachelor."

"Congratulations."

Ross noted the interchange unhappily. Why did Leah have to wear that damned dress? Each time his gaze had fallen on his sister, Liz Barnard became the invisible guest. And worse, he remembered guiltily, he had promised to take Liz to dinner that night and had forgotten to make his excuses.

After dinner David stood in front of the parlor fireplace and talked, not as he had done three years before of his military life in the Philippines, but now as a rising young San Francisco banker. While Cathlin nodded in Val's favorite chair, her children listened to David Marcus sketch his doubts about Weston.

"I'll admit right off the bat that my father and I resent the business our competing banks are doing here in town. But we're nervous, too. We don't like to see so much San Francisco money being invested in one industry in one area. We'd like to see the risk spread. The citrus production in Southern California, for instance. Even tropical crops in Hawaii."

Owen interrupted. "We can't take such a broad view, Dave. Weston is all we know, and Weston oil needs every cent it can raise."

"All right, then get more of your money from Los Angeles. They've got bankers, too, you know. And raise more money from the public. Merge your companies until they're big enough and strong enough to sell stock on the exchanges."

Ross nodded. "That's been my tune all along. We can't keep selling stock locally for nickels and dimes. Trouble is, most of our producers take the easy road; they've got marketing contracts with Pacoil, and Pacoil tells them the right doors in San Francisco to knock on for money."

"But don't you see where that's going to lead? A monopoly on Weston oil. Pacoil will have you at its mercy. It's up to you boys—you, Ross, and you, Owen—to talk to your people. Tell them not to renew their contracts with Pacoil, make them spread their sales."

"That's a ticklish thing, Dave," Ross said. "Seadon Oil needs money itself to develop our Mirage Springs land. Before we talk against Pacoil, we've got to have some facts. All we know is that Pacoil is a San Francisco marketer. But if we could prove that it's a dummy, say, for Standard Oil—"

"It isn't. It's controlled by Petroholdings, one of our Montgomery Street outfits."

"That's what I've heard. But who's behind Petroholdings? Do some digging, Dave. Get us some names. Meanwhile, maybe I can try to line up some credit in Los Angeles."

"How about asking me?" Ross and Owen exchanged looks of surprise, and David hastened to say, "I know. I just said we don't want to commit ourselves to Weston. But for the Seadons . . . yes."

Ross licked his lips in thought. "A hundred thousand?"

"You got it."

"Just like that?"

"We're old friends. Who better to do business with?" David looked at Leah and winked. "Well now, enough of trifles. How's the emancipated woman, and why haven't I seen her at the conservatory in the city?"

The following noon Ross drove out to the Dutton place. He had rehearsed in his mind the apology for breaking their dinner engagement of the night before. The exact truth, he had decided, was the best—with the surprise of David Marcus' arrival, he had simply forgotten. And even if he had remembered, how could he have explained to Liz when she had no telephone? She would surely see the logic of that. Liz Barnard was a sensible woman. But Ross's assumptions went unproven, for Liz was not at home. There was only Blacky to greet him with a happy clamor.

Ross left a note under the front door, promising to return in the late afternoon, and drove back to Weston to lunch at the Pioneer Hotel. It was there that he saw Liz. She was already at table, talking animatedly to a dark heavy-set man whom Ross recognized as Harley Stewart. Ross seated himself nearby, and when Liz chanced to glance in his direction he smiled and waved. She nodded coolly and turned her attention back to Stewart. Attention? That was hardly the word for it, Ross thought; she was downright flirting with the man. For his benefit, of course, Ross told himself. Black thoughts darted through his mind like startled bats in a cave. Why was she seeing Harley Stewart? Was it in sulky retaliation for the broken dinner engagement, or was this one of many meetings?

Finally the meal was over and Liz excused herself from Stewart and came over to Ross. She listened with studied patience to Ross's apology and his hope for that evening.

"I'm afraid not," she answered. "Harley's taking me for a ride out to the Weir in his new motorcar, and I'm sure he plans dinner."

"Liz, I don't blame you for being angry—"

"But I'm not. As you just explained, you have your life and

I have mine. Oh, for a while I enjoyed furnishing the house and painting the walls and planting my garden and waiting for whatever hour you could spare me. But I find none of that amuses me any more." She gave his arm a sisterly pat. "Take care of yourself." Then she rejoined Stewart.

Chapter 9

D U R I N G T H E following week Ross made no attempt to see Liz Barnard. He would show her, he told himself, that he, too, could be independent. He would let her fret over the possibility that he was seeing other women. The thought that she might not care, that she might be involved with Harley Stewart, he dismissed as merely morbid imagining. But was it? He grew ill-tempered around home, and even snapped at Hop Gee. Cathlin especially was aware of Ross's mood. One evening when she kissed him good night she said, "Whatever is wrong will be made right, dear. I'm praying to St. Jude for you." St. Jude, the patron of the lost, the hopeless.

At least there was the routine of the Seadon Oil Company. Ross and Owen executed the collateral mortgage that they had promised to David Marcus and sent it to San Francisco. In return David mailed a bank draft in the amount of $100,000, and attached a note:

Re. Pacoil: All voting stock owned by Petroholdings. Latter controlled 80 per cent by Phaethon Securities, New York. No information on Phaethon.

"I've seen that name *Phaethon* somewhere before," Owen mused after reading the note.

Ross nodded darkly. "I've been aboard it. It's G. G. Haggerty's private car."

Owen whistled softly. "So he's won after all. Haggerty's got Weston's oil sewed up."

"Except for us." Ross chewed his lower lip and brooded over the scene that night in the railroad car. "Haggerty doesn't give a damn about marketing the oil; he wants the companies, lock, stock, and barrel. He wants to nail our guts to his back fence. The only question is How does the son of a bitch do it?"

Owen blinked at his brother's vehemence. "Then thank God we got that hundred thousand. It'll buy us time . . . and maybe some friends."

Seadon Oil Company, the brothers decided, should immediately triple its drilling operations on the Barnard lease. Ross would go to Los Angeles and place orders for the necessary equipment and arrange for the sale of the expected production to the southern marketers. Before he left, Ross made another decision. He would see Liz Barnard.

She was, if anything, even more remote than she had been the week before. She met Ross on the front porch and did not invite him indoors. At any other time, Ross would have protested; but today, he resolved, there would be no argument, no scene, not even a reference to the breach between them.

He extracted a railroad ticket and Pullman reservation from his pocket and handed them to her. "I'm going to be out of town for a week or so, and I thought you might like to amuse yourself in Los Angeles."

She examined the tickets skeptically. "This reservation is for tonight. Is there some reason you want me out of town?"

"Perhaps." He permitted himself a smile. "I'm going north.

To Fresno. I'll lay over there until this evening, and then pick up the southbound train."

"I see." A glint of amusement came into her eyes. "It wouldn't do for us to be seen getting on the same train."

"Weston's a small town."

"And the word might get back to your family."

He shook his head. "It might get back to Harley Stewart and your other friends. What they don't know can't hurt you."

She smiled. "I hope you enjoy your trip."

"I'm counting on it," he said, watching her tuck the railroad tickets into the pocket of her house dress.

In 1903 Los Angeles was the poor country cousin of San Francisco. It lacked one half the population and most of the sophistication of "the City." It was a Midwestern town in love with Victorian architecture. Business and public buildings and the homes of the well-to-do on Bunker Hill and West Adams were brownstone accumulations of turrets and spires and cupolas. Motorcars sputtered along the streets in surprising numbers, thanks to the nearness of oil fields and refineries. Wells pumped on city lots within walking distance of Main Street, while others dotted the countryside west toward Santa Monica and south toward San Pedro. Visiting oilmen filled the hotels, and chose as their favorite the Rosslyn, on Main Street. It was there that the guest register bore the names of the latest arrivals: "Mr. and Mrs. Ross Seadon."

After the bellboy had deposited their bags in the room, accepted Ross's tip, and closed the door behind him, they looked at each other with awkward shyness.

"I think they guessed," Liz said.

"Who?"

"The bellboy, the desk clerk. We don't look at all married."

"We would, if you'd stop acting like you'd just robbed a bank." Ross did not mention his own guilty reaction when the desk clerk had called Liz "Mrs. Seadon." There was only one, his mother. Nor did he tell Liz that he had deceived Cathlin and Leah as to where he would be staying. "I'll be moving about all over the place, so don't try to phone me. I'll keep in touch through Owen."

By the second day in Los Angeles, their feelings of strangeness gave way to a heady sense of freedom. There were no hours to keep, no excuses or evasions to be made, no friends to avoid. They spent lazy mornings in the hotel room, enjoying the luxury of breakfast in bed and hours of carefree lovemaking. Then when Ross had completed his business, had placed his last order for oil-field equipment, they went on a buying spree. At a milliner's he bought her a huge construction of feathers and flowers, and she reciprocated with a silver-headed walking stick which Ross twirled down Spring Street while he sang "Jim Dumps is a man of woe! Constipation is his foe!" People turned and stared, and more than once Ross heard the comment "Newlyweds." They jumped onto trolleys, not caring where they went; they leapfrogged from restaurants to cafes to ice cream parlors; they went canoeing in Echo Park. One day they boarded an open-air trolley and wound westward through the hills to a farming village called Hollywood.

As the trolley traversed the dirt main street (grandly termed Hollywood Boulevard), Liz gazed happily at the barley fields and vineyards and inhaled the orange-scented air. "I could live here forever," she said. "Let's never go back to Weston. No more heat and dust and mosquitoes. No more drunks and fights and shootings. Honestly, Ross, how do you ever stand it?" The real question, he suspected, was How long would *she* stand it?

That evening they dined at the hotel, and Ross watched their reflections in a great baroque wall mirror. Yes, they could be newlyweds, he thought. They looked so right together, contented and comfortable with each other. He reached across the table and took Liz's hand and, almost not believing his own words, he said, "Marry me, Liz."

Her eyes widened, then she recovered. "And spoil all this? It's much more exciting to be wicked."

"Liz, I'm serious."

She studied him for a moment. "The Seadons are too strong for me. They don't need outsiders; they don't want them."

"How do you know? You haven't met them."

"That's *how* I know. You've always kept me in the background, as if you were afraid of your family, or maybe respect them too much. Oh, I can understand that. You come from a good family, a family that's going to be very powerful, and I come from nothing— No, let me finish. I wouldn't want Leah for a sister-in-law. I've watched her following me around town, seeing what I was like, proving to herself that I was trash."

Was it possible? Ross wondered. Or was Liz inventing an excuse? More likely it was she who was jealous of his sister. "Leah will have to accept you," he said, "once we're married."

"And your mother?"

"Good Lord, all she wants is for me to be happy. And Owen, too."

Liz toyed thoughtfully with the food. "Could we have some more wine?" Ross ordered it. And when the waiter had come and gone, she quickly drained her glass, as if to give herself courage.

"I didn't intend to tell you this, but that night when you didn't come for dinner, I was frightened. And the week we didn't see each other. I was frightened because you had too much of a hold on me. I was at your mercy."

She had described Ross's own feelings. "And yet you're here," he said. "How do you explain it? A way of tapering off, a cure, the hair of the dog?"

"Probably. When I was a girl, I used to get sick on candy, but it never stopped me from wanting more." She sniffed thoughtfully and changed the subject. "Drill me some more oil wells, Ross. Make me rich."

"And that will free you from me?"

She looked away. How could he reach her? What appeal could he make? Then it came to him. "Liz, don't you want children of your own?"

She nodded. "Just one. A boy."

"Then don't you want him to be our son?"

She glanced around cautiously; the nearest diners were three tables away, out of earshot. "No," she murmured.

"Liz!"

"I'll adopt one."

"But it's not the same thing!"

"It can't be helped. I won't marry you. You're a Catholic. Probably a better Catholic than you realize. I've heard you talk enough to know that you would never violate the—whatever you call it—the sacraments." She watched him with a touch of sadness. "You still don't understand, do you? I won't be like my mother. She married the man she loved and then fell out of love, and now she's miserable. She made her kids miserable. That could happen to me . . . or to you, Ross."

"It won't," he said.

"It could. That's what frightens me about life. Nothing lasts. Women want it to, desperately want it, because they know it won't. Look how we've changed since we met. How do we know what we'll be a year from now? If we were married, it would have to be in your church, and then if you or I found somebody else, you'd never think of a divorce." She shuddered. "It would be ugly. We would hate each other, and I couldn't stand that."

It was the first time Ross had been willing to commit himself to a woman, and he had been rejected. It was a humbling experience. And paradoxically it acted as an aphrodisiac. He had never desired Liz more. She saw the hunger in his eyes and nodded smilingly. Yes.

They were still in each other's arms when the telephone rang and Ross cursed and said he would not answer it. Whenever he remembered that moment in after years, every detail returned, clear and luminous. The warm night, the breeze that blew the glass curtains into the room, the glow of light on the ceiling reflected from the streetlamps below, the profile of Liz's face beside him. Everywhere there were sounds. A clock chiming the hour, revelers laughing outside the hotel, the clatter of refuse cans in an alley. And the telephone, harsh, insistent, unrelenting. Ross sighed and groped for the instrument. At first he did not recognize Owen's voice; he sounded choked, almost strangling. "Ma fell downstairs. . . . She's dead."

A missed footing on a staircase had, in a matter of seconds, altered family relationships. Leah was now the woman of the family, and her brothers looked toward her, albeit unconsciously, as the symbol of home and security. They were never more closely knit. They moved about in the big house seldom out of each other's sight, as if in combination they might deny their loss. The dining room, which had once echoed with Val's booming voice, Cathlin's laughter, and the babble of three children, now was a silent place which brothers and sister quit at the earliest possible moment, often carrying their coffee cups into the sitting room to avoid the sight of Cathlin's empty chair.

Ross wrote a note about Cathlin to David Marcus, who replied with sympathy. A day later there was another letter in unfamiliar handwriting.

> My young friend Marcus told me of your loss, which is also mine most grievously. If you come to our city, please spare me an hour.
>
> Henri Laprebode

"Wasn't he the man who brought Ma and Dad together?'" Leah asked.

Ross nodded, then with careful casualness said, "One of us ought to take him up on that. How about you, Sis?"

"You mean the conservatory?"

"Sure. Between Laprebode and Dave Marcus you wouldn't be lonely. There's certainly nothing to keep you here now. You're free."

Leah exchanged glances with Owen. They were testing her. "This isn't a time for singing. Maybe there never was. . . .

128

Besides," she added, "somebody's got to run the house for you boys."

And there the matter rested.

The second producing well on the Barnard lease came in, and Liz was at the wellhead with Ross and Owen for the first test run of crude. Ross had not seen her since that night in Los Angeles—partly out of his feeling of guilt, and because Liz, sharing that guilt, had urged it. The new well, Owen told her, was measuring two hundred barrels a day, which would increase her income to seven hundred dollars a month. The next three wells—for which the derricks were already in place and the boilers being cemented into position—would double that figure, Owen predicted. "What are you going to do with all your money?" he asked. She glanced at Ross, who had asked that same question in Los Angeles. "Something very nice. You'll know about it when it happens."

As the Seadons escorted Liz back to her buggy, they saw a column of dust moving toward them along the work road. It was a buckboard with Tim Beakley. Even before he jounced to a halt, he shouted the news. "Pacoil is dumping their crude! Twenty cents a barrel!"

"You're crazy!" Ross yelled back.

"The hell I am! Twenty cents in Weston, Fresno, Frisco, Sacramento! You know what that means!"

The Seadons did. The oil producers' contracts with Pacoil called for the marketer to buy Weston crude for forty cents per barrel, "or at one half the average current retail selling price, at the buyer's option." The producers had gleefully signed the contracts, thinking that the "average current retail price" must surely rise. Now, with Pacoil selling at twenty cents, the producers would receive one half of that price, or ten cents. Since cost of production of the oil was twenty-two cents, the producers were guaranteed a loss of twelve cents on each barrel pumped. G. G. Haggerty had finally played his trump card.

"This won't affect us, will it?" Liz asked the Seadons.

"No, thank God," Owen said. "We aren't signed with Pacoil. Los Angeles is our market."

Ross tugged on one ear and frowned. "I don't like to take anything on faith. Let's make some phone calls."

The telephone calls confirmed the worst. Los Angeles did not want Pacoil for an enemy. All buying of Weston oil was to be halted "until the dust settles."

By midafternoon the word had spread from the oilmen to the Weston merchants, to the city officials, to the gambling dens and sporting houses. That evening a mass meeting was held in the hall of the new Elks Lodge. Wilmot Caruth was elected chairman of the meeting and turned the floor over to Ross Seadon. The audience listened restlessly to his account of the dinner aboard G. G. Haggerty's private railroad car and of Haggerty's secret control of Pacoil. Before Ross had finished, men were on their feet, cursing and shouting. "We won't pump! We'll leave the damned crude in the ground!"

Wilmot Caruth pounded for order, and said when at last he could be heard, "Boys, you got to pump. I've seen those contracts. They're legal and binding. If you don't pump, Pacoil will sue for non-performance. You'll go broke on legal fees."

They booed Caruth. No one would sell at a loss of twelve cents per barrel. How could they pay off their bank loans?

Caruth's gavel hammered the table. "Boys, the only way we can fight Haggerty is by uniting ourselves. I say, let's form a drillers' association."

Applause and cheers. But who should head the association? Caruth was ready. He proposed the one man who knew G. G. Haggerty and who had defied him. A vote was called for, there was a show of hands, and Ross Seadon was elected.

Ross waved for quiet. "The first thing we got to realize is that Haggerty and Pacoil can't hold out forever. They're buying our oil below cost; but Pacoil has got costs, too. They're selling at a loss themselves. Both sides are playing a game of freeze-out."

Someone shouted, "I got a bank loan in San Francisco to pay next week. After that, I'm an icicle!"

Nervous laughter. Ross scanned the hall. "How many others got payments due in, say, the next two months?" Six hands went up. "How many can pay?" Three hands.

"Then there's only one way out," Ross said. "The companies that got cash in the till will have to make a contribution into a general fund—a war chest—and lend it out to the weak sisters." Scattered applause from those who needed the money; silence from those who had it and would not share. Wilmot Caruth moved that Ross's proposal be put to a vote. It lost.

Caruth turned to Ross. "Now what do we do?"

Ross shrugged. "Adjourn the meeting."

The following week one of the oil companies failed to pay its loan to a San Francisco bank and was foreclosed. Pacoil paid off the amount due to the bank and took title to the property. Two weeks later a second company "went under," and Pacoil became the new owner. Ross telephoned David Marcus and asked if his bank would extend credit to the Weston companies. David's answer was "Why throw good money after bad? I'm afraid Pacoil's got your friends where the hair is shortest."

The Weston oil companies began to pass their dividends, and the market for their stocks plunged—in some cases below their original issuing prices.

"Maybe I ought to start taking in boarders again," Liz said half jokingly to Ross one afternoon, shortly after they had resumed their affair.

"If there's anybody to board." Ross gloomed. "We got to shut down your lease on Saturday. The storage tanks are full."

"Los Angeles still won't buy?"

"Not a drop."

"On orders from Pacoil?"

"Could be. Right now I'll believe anything."

The following week a third oil company was foreclosed and sold to Pacoil; the stock prices of the others continued to fall. Stockholders who had pledged their shares for personal loans at the Bank of Weston found their collateral sold out and deficiency judgments levied against their businesses and homes. Finally, one evening when the three Seadons were at dinner, Ross made a proposal: "Let's get out of Weston."

Owen sat back in his chair and stared. "Quit the oil business?"

"Hell, no! But we've sunk half of our loan from Marcus in Mirage Springs; let's take what's left and go for oil where Pacoil isn't operating. You heard about the new discoveries around Ventura and Ojai. I hear they're selling their oil to the Northwest."

Owen brightened. "That's right. Oregon and Washington. Sure! Even to the Hawaiian Islands."

"Think you could find us a decent lease?"

"God, I don't know, Ross. Haber County I understand, but Ventura . . ."

"Why not?" Leah spoke up. "You were certainly right about Mirage Springs, and you can do it again. Harley Stewart says Ventura is reeking with oil."

Ross stared at his sister. "Harley Stewart?" He saw her flustered look. "Since when have you been talking to him?"

Leah hesitated, then she passed it off lightly. "Oh, I've run into him a few times when I was downtown shopping."

Ross's face hardened. "That's all?" He waited for her answer, which was an unconvincing "Of course"; then he leaned across the table and pointed a fork at her. "Listen, if I ever catch that bastard lallygagging around you, I'll kick his face in!"

Leah glared back. "My! Aren't you the protective big brother! Or is it the jealous lover of Liz Barnard?" With that, she pushed back from the table and stamped out of the room.

The brothers frowned at each other and Owen said, "You know what I think? I think it's time we *all* got out of Weston."

Chapter 10

MOST URGENT YOU BE ON HAND   STOP   WILL MEET YOU
VENTURA DEPOT TOMORROW NOON   STOP   OWEN

IT WAS the last day of August, 1903, and the telegram
was the first word Ross had received from his brother in over
a week. If it was "most urgent," Ross reasoned, Owen must
have located some promising acreage and needed advice.

Ross sensed Owen's excitement from the moment they met
at the railroad station; his eyes were bright and he spoke with
an almost conspiratorial hush. "Don't ask me about it now. It's
too complicated," he said, guiding Ross toward the horse-drawn
stage that waited beside the platform. "How complicated?"
Ross pursued, then abandoned the subject when he saw that
there were to be three other passengers.

Leaving Ventura, the stage turned northeast and followed a
dried riverbed through a cut in the coastal mountains. It was
a region of rock and occasional scrub oak. Then the rocky

heights on either side began to recede and widen out into what Owen said was the Ojai Valley. The scrub oak gave place to its majestic relative, the great spreading live oak, under which cattle grazed in fields of clover.

The town of Ojai was small and somnolent. The stage discharged its fares outside the general store, and Owen led Ross toward an old-fashioned closed coach. An elderly Mexican dozed on the high driver's seat. Owen whistled the coachman awake, and he leaped down to open the door of the passenger compartment. Ross noted a design outlined in silver on the door panel. "Looks almost like a coat of arms," he said.

"It is." Owen nodded. "The Delgado family. We're their houseguests."

The Mexican swung Ross's case up onto the driver's seat, and the coach lurched into motion. Ross leaned back against the leather and smiled at his brother. "I take it you've found some acreage."

"Yes."

"Have you leased it?"

Owen avoided a direct answer; he launched instead into the results of his survey of the wildcat drilling between Ojai and Santa Paula. The best production, he said, appeared to be at the mouth of the Alto Valle—the High Valley—toward which the coach was moving. The main oil pool was a higher elevation, Owen suspected, in the Alto Valle itself. It was there he had focused his attention; it was there, also, that he had met open hostility from the landowners. They were Mexican rancheros who ran cattle over the area and who wished no part of oilmen.

"Except the Delgados?" Ross asked.

Owen bobbed his head. "For the damnedest reason you can think of. Remember Ma telling us something about Dad saving a Mexican from lynching up in the Mother Lode?"

"Vaguely."

"He was a Delgado. Some kid cousin. Don Jaime told me the whole story. Seems the kid made a strike, and when the Yankee

134

miners heard about it they decided to jump his claim. Dad heard they were getting up a necktie party, and because he knew Delgado and liked him he smuggled him out of the Mother Lode in his supply wagon. The family never forgot the name Seadon, and when they heard I was in the Alto Valle, they were practically waiting at the gate for me. It was *'Bienvenido'* and *'Mi casa es su casa'* all over the place. They're really beautiful people, Ross."

"What about their land?"

"Fifteen thousand acres. I found an oil seep in one of their creeks."

Ross chuckled and slapped Owen's knee. "Good work!" Then he sensed his brother's lack of enthusiasm. "How much are they asking for a lease?"

"I haven't even mentioned it."

Ross was puzzled. "You mean you hauled me over here to do your talking for you?"

"No. For another reason." Owen hesitated. "They're Mexican. Spanish, actually. They follow the Old Country customs. They won't accept anyone unless they know the whole family." Owen paused again, and Ross saw the excitement return to his eyes. "Ross, I've found the girl I want to marry."

The coach passed between two stone gateposts and under an arch of wrought-iron grillwork which bore the name RANCHO EL ENCANTO. Half an hour later, among the oak-covered knolls, Ross caught his first glimpse of human habitation. First a cluster of cottages—the servants' quarters, Owen said—then barns and corrals where men were tending horses, and finally, atop another knoll, the Delgado house itself. It was a rambling affair of whitewashed adobe brick with pink bougainvillea vining up to the red tiled roof. The coach swung under an entrance arch, clattered into a courtyard, and came to a halt.

As the Seadons alighted, a bell rang mellowly and an Indian houseboy appeared from somewhere and took charge of Ross's suitcase. A man and a woman emerged from the house and waved greetings. Ross's first impression of Don Jaime Delgado was of a man with a black patch over his left eye and a right eye that, as if to compensate, observed everything with a ferocious, darting intensity. He was below average in height, gray of hair, yet giving an impression of both youth and formidable strength. He was dressed in black; his jacket was cut short in the Spanish style; a braid of black leather descended his frilled shirtfront and ended in a tip of silver. Doña Felipa was the feminine counterpart of her husband. Short, plump, gray hair, black dress, dark smiling eyes.

Owen made the introductions, and Don Jaime pumped Ross's hand and said it was a great pleasure, an honor to their house. He spoke without accent, yet with a rhythm and pace that were unmistakably Spanish.

"Where is your sister?" Doña Felipa asked Ross.

"At home. This is a business trip for me."

"Ah? We had hoped—" Doña Felipa interrupted herself: "Owen tells us that you are but three children." There was a hint of pity, almost of condescension. "We are four sons and four daughters. Four wives and three husbands."

Ross met them when they assembled in the cavernous living room for a glass of sherry before dinner. As they stood in a semicircle with the one unmarried daughter in the center, they reminded Ross of a picket fence, a living barrier of Spaniards, to fend off the Anglo intruders. The object of their protection, Maria Elena Cayetana Isabel Ortiz y Delgado—called Tana— was clearly the youngest of her brothers and sisters by at least ten years, the child of her parents' middle age, the last, the unexpected joy, to be pampered and treated with special devotion.

Unlike her sisters and brothers, she was small and delicately built. Her face was round, like her mother's, and her dark eyes shone with her father's intensity. Her jet hair was drawn back tightly into a chignon, which she tossed with every movement of her head. A beauty, Ross thought. But out of Owen's reach.

The introduction of the brothers and sisters and husbands and wives, with their interminable Spanish names, was hopelessly confusing for Ross, and he was grateful when dinner was announced. They sat, all nineteen, at one enormously long table lighted by three silver candelabra. Ross at Don Jaime's right, Tana directly opposite him, and Owen at the far end with Doña Felipa.

From the conversation of Tana's brothers and sisters—when it was in English—Ross gathered that only two of the sons, and their wives and children, lived at El Encanto; the rest lived at nearby ranchos and had come together that evening for the express purpose of meeting Owen's brother. Their curiosity was obvious, and their approval—if such it was—restrained. But not on the part of Don Jaime and Tana. While the father's one good eye fixed on Ross with a gleam of benevolence, the daughter composed questions which she delivered with the solemnity of a Grand Inquisitor. One question in particular intrigued Ross. "It is so, do you not think, that the elder brother is to the younger brother as a second father?" Possibly, Ross admitted; and to himself he said, Our beauty has a brain.

Following dinner, Don Jaime escorted Ross on a tour of the great sprawling house. It was a bewildering maze of rooms for every purpose, and some with none. Don Jaime pointed out a century-old chest which had once carried silver bullion aboard a Manila galleon, a candlestick from his grandfather's home in Spain, the skin of a bear which Don Jaime had lassoed in his youth and which, in its death struggle, had blinded him in his left eye. Everywhere there was needlework of the Delgado women—throw rugs and quilts and samplers and lace by Raquel's and Carmen's and Gabriela's and Isabel's hands. While Ross was dutifully admiring a framed petit-point, he heard Tana's voice behind him.

"What you see, Mr. Seadon, is not needlework, but long engagements. When a Delgado is betrothed, it is a long wait, and she must fill her days and nights with something."

"For how long?" Ross asked.

"Two years, perhaps three. It is stupid, yes?"

"Tana!" Her father's eye shot a thunderbolt and she went silent. "And now, Mr. Seadon, I must show you our chapel," Don Jaime said, taking his arm. They went out into a corridor of archways and thence to an inner patio where a fountain splashed. Don Jaime glanced back to the corridor where Tana stood watching them. "She is still a child, Mr. Seadon. She has seen her brothers and sisters marry according to a custom for which she has no patience. Children are like that. Everything must be *now*. They turn against the old ways. That is Tana."

Ross turned the conversation to the subject uppermost in his mind. "I take it, Don Jaime, that El Encanto is the largest rancho in the Alto Valle."

"Yes. In my grandfather's day it was forty-eight thousand acres. But he had many daughters, which meant dowries; and the daughters had more daughters and still more dowries. Land was sold. Two thousand acres here, three thousand there. Now I have only fifteen thousand acres. In a few years there will be more dowries again, and my children will have to sell more land. In time, there will be nothing."

He's handing it to me on a platter. Ross smiled to himself. "But you won't have to sell off anything, sir, if there's oil on your land."

"There is no oil."

"How can you be sure?"

Don Jaime tossed his head knowingly. "God has put the riches of His earth where there is desolation. But where there are no riches, He gives us beauty. He gives us the Alto Valle."

"The Mother Lode in the Sierra is beautiful country, too, yet God added gold."

Don Jaime's eye blinked. "There is no oil," he said.

Finally the evening was over. As the Seadon brothers walked the long tiled hallway to their rooms, Owen asked, "So what do you think?"

"Of Tana? I admire your taste, but I don't see any future with her."

"Why?"

"Because you're not Spanish. The family is just humoring the girl. No arguments, no opposition; everybody will be friends. That's the way to throw a bucket of water on the blaze."

"We'll see," Owen said. "I'm going to marry Tana."

Ross clapped him on the shoulder. "Tomorrow let's see that oil seep."

The next morning they went riding with Tana. Neither brother felt at home in the bulky Mexican saddles with their high pommels and cantles, and they watched enviously as Tana —riding side-saddle, dressed in a long leather skirt, short jacket, and flat-crowned hat—galloped and wheeled and swept over the oak-covered hills. Always, somewhere to one side, or ahead on a knoll, was another horseman. A watchful brother or an Indian groom. "They never leave her out of their sight for one damned second," Owen complained. "We're never alone. Daddy's there, or Mama, or some brother or sister, hanging around in the patio or behind some bush. Christ, you'd think I was going to carry her off bodily."

Later during the ride, when Tana had ridden out of sight again, they found the oil seep. It was no more than a few feet of black ooze along the bank of the creek, but it was enough to excite Ross. "I found another seep a couple of miles upstream," Owen said. "It's on a rancho belonging to somebody named Alvarez."

"Have you talked to him?"

Owen wagged his head.

"Then let's do it. And to Don Jaime."

"They won't listen, I told you. They're cattlemen."

Ross sniffed. "Nobody turns away from money, not when it's big enough."

Owen started to reply, then he stared past Ross's shoulder. "Quick. Let's get out of here."

It was too late. Tana was galloping toward them. She pulled alongside and looked toward the oil seep, then back at the

Seadons. Silently, somberly. Then, with a flick of the reins, she wheeled away.

That evening Don Jaime and Doña Felipa threw open their house for a *baile* in honor of the Seadons. In addition to the Delgados, there were guests from all the neighboring ranchos. A buffet of food and drink was set up in the inner patio, where a quartet of rancho hands scraped on fiddles and blew cornets for those who wished to dance. Ross gamely attempted a *paso doble* with Doña Felipa, and then, with more assurance, a waltz with Tana. It was during the waltz that Ross sensed trouble. Tana went through the steps with a cool reserve, neither speaking nor smiling; and when Owen approached for the next dance, she turned away and chose one of her brothers.

"What's the matter with you two?" Ross asked.

Owen shrugged. "I've been trying to figure it out all day. Everything was fine until she saw us at that oil seep. Maybe she thinks I just played up to her so we could get an oil lease."

"Hell, that's up to Don Jaime, and he couldn't be friendlier."

"Well, for Christ's sake, don't mention a lease." Owen chewed his lip in dejection. "Ross, I don't know what I'm going to do. Tana is . . . she's . . ." His voice faltered; he was past words.

Ross had never seen Owen so upset, except by the deaths of his parents. The boy who had been so shy with girls was now a man committed with all the passion of a romantic idealist. For a moment Ross debated telling him the events of the afternoon; that everything would be right again. No. Better to wait. It would all come out soon enough.

With the passage of time and the consumption of wine, the decorum of the party waned. The arrival of each latecomer was greeted with shouts and arm waving; women kissed and men embraced in an uproar of Spanish. Among the latecomers were Señor José Alvarez and his wife. Ross did not see them at first, and when he did, he realized what had happened. The house, so filled with laughter only moments before, had gone quiet. Men and women were staring at him with cold eyes; Don Jaime and

Doña Felipa stood with their arms around Tana, who appeared to be crying. Owen was trying to talk to her, and not succeeding, then he turned and made for Ross.

"So that's what you did this afternoon," he said. "You signed up Alvarez." Before Ross could answer, he went on in icy fury. "Mrs. Alvarez says they're going to be millionaires. Is that what you told them?"

"No!" Ross managed. "I made no such promise. And I didn't get a lease. I bought an option—an option to sign a lease if our investigation warrants it."

"Not *my* investigation!" Owen snapped in a voice that carried to the farthest guest. "If you want a lease, if you want to drill, get somebody else! I'm through!"

Ross caught his arm and muttered, "Use your head, man. The Alvarezes are the weak link. They're hard up. If we crack them, the others will follow. Let everybody blow, they'll thank us in the end. Even Tana."

It was not good enough. Owen turned on his heel, pushed through the ring of guests, and disappeared. Ross stared after him and at the hostile faces. It was too theatrical, like a bad stage play. But very real. And wrong. All wrong. It hadn't worked. He started to follow Owen, then hesitated. If Latins loved a dramatic gesture, by God, he'd give it to them.

He walked quickly across the room to the Delgados. "Don Jaime . . . Doña Felipa . . . Tana . . . I apologize. I'm afraid my thoughtlessness has cost me a brother."

Don Jaime flung out his hands. "That must not be! It is not you I blame. It is José Alvarez. The Alto Valle has been as one family—but Alvarez!" His lip curled. "What can one expect? His wife is an Anglo!"

It was true; she had been the eager one. Ross shrugged as if it were beside the point, dug into his breast pocket, and brought out the option. He tore it in half, then into quarters, and handed the fragments to Don Jaime. "Sir, there can be no price on friendship."

Don Jaime's one good eye misted with emotion. He threw his arms around Ross, pounded his shoulder blades, and beamed around the room. "Did I not tell you?" he shouted. "Did I not tell you?"

It had been a near thing, both with the Delgados and with his brother. That night before turning in, Ross pointed out to Owen, edgy but reconciled, that his courtship was not a matter to be hurried. It was not the Spanish way. There would have to be other visits to Rancho El Encanto. Meanwhile, there was the oil business. Owen accepted the logic, albeit reluctantly, and the following morning the Seadons said goodbye to the Delgados and returned to the Ojai Valley.

After several days of scouting they bought a 51-per-cent interest in a producing lease in Sespe Canyon. The property had been badly managed and would need a good deal of re-drilling, which was ideal from Owen's standpoint. He could divide his time between Weston and Sespe, and be within four hours' drive of Rancho El Encanto.

The brothers returned to Weston—and Ross to a letter.

Dearest Ross—

I'm glad you're out of town, because I hate goodbyes. You must understand—although I'm afraid you won't—that my leaving is not easy. But neither is living in Weston. And I have word from Los Angeles that there is a baby I can adopt.

I shall remember you always, as I hope you will me. With love.

Liz

P.S. As soon as I get settled, I'll let you know where to mail my royalty checks. I'll really need them now. So start pumping again and make Pacoil eat dirt. I know you will win.

L.

Ross drove out to the Dutton place. Only then could he believe it. There was no Blacky to bark a welcome. The geraniums bordering the front porch were already withering. The front door was unlocked. His footsteps echoed through the bare rooms. The sitting room where they had talked, the dining room where they had eaten, the bedroom where they had made love. A few loose hangers in the closet and the faint scent of perfume were all that remained.

"How could she do that to you?" Leah demanded that evening, forgetting her own opposition to Liz.

"It's a long story." Ross sighed. "She's afraid of being tied to anyone. She was always talking about being free."

"Ha! How much freedom is there for an unmarried woman with a baby?"

"Maybe you could change her mind, Ross," Owen suggested.

"If I thought that," Ross said, "I'd be on the next train to Los Angeles. I'd find her somehow. But it's useless." He slumped down into an armchair and shook his head. "It's a hell of a note. At the very time Owen finds Tana, I lose Liz."

Defeat seemed to face Ross on all fronts. The situation in Weston was approaching panic. While the Seadons had been in Ventura County, a fourth oil company had been foreclosed and the property transferred to Pacoil. Tim Beakley reported that his operation would be the next to go. The drillers' association, Tim added, was disenchanted with Ross; there was talk of a new head of the association who would "do something" about Pacoil.

But what could be done? Pacoil was G. G. Haggerty, and G. G. Haggerty held all the aces. Ross reviewed in his mind everything said at dinner that night aboard his private railroad car. If he could recognize some chink in Haggerty's armor, some quirk in his personality that could be exploited . . . But Ross could discover nothing. Haggerty was invulnerable. Then one night as he lay awake mulling over the problem, he remembered the curious way Haggerty had explained himself: "When I hit it off with somebody, it's like powder meeting flint. Things happen." But he and Ross had not hit it off; the very opposite. And yet . . . maybe there was an idea in that florid metaphor. Perhaps a way out. Yes. Why not? He rolled out of bed and went to Owen's room and shook him awake.

"You're out of your mind," Owen muttered when Ross had sketched his idea. "When the boat's already sinking, you don't kick another hole in the bottom."

"Maybe it's the only way."

The next morning Ross telephoned David Marcus and asked if G. G. Haggerty was in San Francisco. As a matter of fact, he was, David replied; he had seen Haggerty at the Palace Hotel the night before. Ross hung up and turned to Owen. "I'm going to call an emergency meeting of the drillers, a closed meeting, and we'll put it to them."

"They'll say no."

"We'll see."

Owen hunched his shoulders in resignation. "What if Haggerty calls our bluff?"

"Then powder meets flint."

The meeting was held in the Elks hall, with the doors locked to all except the drillers. Ross outlined his plan and listened to the howls of disbelief and outrage. To every protest his answer was a simple "What else is there? At least we'll have our self-respect." Finally, after an hour of ragged argument, Tim Beakley asked the key question: "Do you think Haggerty will believe us? You know the guy, Ross. When the chips are down, what does he believe in?"

"Power," Ross said. "That's what I'm asking you for." He waited for his answer to sink in. "All right, let's have a show of hands."

The plan carried with one vote to spare. When Ross left the meeting, he sent a telegram to G. G. Haggerty at the Palace Hotel. The message was cryptically worded in case of a talkative telegrapher.

TOMORROW MIDNIGHT YOUR DARLINGS WILL BE CREMATED STOP ASHES WILL BE SCATTERED AT MIRAGE SPRINGS AND BANKS OF HABER RIVER STOP R. SEADON, UNDERTAKER IN CHARGE

Chapter 11

THE SEADON brothers spent the morning in the office. They restlessly shifted papers and stared out the window at Central Avenue, all but deserted in the baking heat. Ross attempted small jokes at Hattie MacFarland's expense, and Owen yawned and thought of Tana. Noon came and they crossed Central Avenue to eat at the Pioneer Hotel. Afterwards they repaired to the Orleans Saloon and joined a poker game in the back room. Now and then a driller would drift up to the table and ask out of the side of his mouth, "Any word?" and Ross, with a slight movement of the head, would indicate no.

"He's going to ignore us," Tim Beakley predicted, seating himself next to Owen. It was unnecessary to specify that "he" was G. G. Haggerty. In midafternoon Sheriff Biernie strolled into the room, passed among the tables, and carefully scrutinized the players. He circled the room several times and went out.

"Looks like the sheriff has heard something," Owen said.

Beakley agreed. "Somebody always talks. Suppose he tries to stop us?"

Ross sniffed. "Has he ever stopped anything?"

A little later Sloppy Weather Smith wandered in from the newspaper office and dropped down into a chair opposite the Seadons. "What's going on?"

"Five card stud," Ross said.

"I mean, what's G. G. Haggerty doing here?"

It was as if the words had the magic power to turn the players into stone. A paralyzed hand held a card motionless in midair; poker chips dribbled from palsied fingers; a match flared futilely inches in front of a cigar.

"Where?" Ross asked finally.

"Depot. The telegrapher just phoned me. A special train in from San Francisco. Two freight cars and Haggerty's private observation car. They're on a siding."

"Any sign of Haggerty?"

"Not so far." Sloppy Weather rose from the chair. "Maybe I ought to go interview him."

"Do that."

Ross riffled his cards and watched Sloppy Weather disappear through the doorway. "I wonder what's in those freight cars."

A few minutes later the editor was back with the answer. The telegrapher at the depot had seen men, "hard customers, maybe ninety or a hundred," leave the cars and get into labor wagons. The wagons had gone north along one of the back streets. "Must be a hell of a story coming up," Sloppy Weather concluded. "I'm going back and bust some space on page one."

As soon as the editor was out of earshot, Tim Beakley muttered, "Ross, let's call it off."

"No."

"But suppose those guys got guns?"

"Suppose they have? It's going to be a dark night." Ross picked up several chips and pushed them across the table. "See you and raise you."

Cards ruffled, chips clinked, the games changed restlessly

from stud to draw to hold-'em. Then there was a hush in the room and men were staring at the elderly Chinese in a black robe who stood beside the Seadon brothers. "Hop! What are you doing here?" Ross demanded.

"I no let Missy come alone," Hop Gee said, nodding toward the doorway where Leah waited. A moment later Ross and Owen were at her side and escorting her out to the street.

Owen said, "Damn it, Sis, don't you know women don't go into saloons?"

"Well, Hattie MacFarland thought you might be here."

"What's wrong?" Ross asked, more to the point.

"That's what I want to know." Leah's face and voice were anxious. "I just got a phone call from Harley Stewart. He said, 'Tell your brothers not to go out to the oil fields tonight.' "

The brothers frowned at each other. "Did he say why?"

"No. He wouldn't explain. Just that he was calling as a friend." Leah searched her brothers' faces. "*Are* you going to the fields?"

"Oh, Harley's just snooping, like every oil scout," Ross evaded. "We're having a meeting of the drillers." He gestured to Hop Gee, who was stationed beside the buggy. "Take missy home, Hop. And tell Ah Sing we're eating downtown tonight." Then to Leah: "Don't wait up for us."

When both brothers kissed her, Leah took fresh fright. "There *is* something! Oh, don't! Please!"

Ross smiled quietly, helped her into the buggy and slapped Lady's rump. As they watched the buggy start down Central Avenue, Ross grumbled, "That bastard Harley. Now he's making friendly phone calls." He glanced at Owen. "I wonder if he stopped by the house while we were in Ventura. What do you think?"

Owen lifted his shoulders. "I think we *aren't* thinking. About Leah. Or Tana."

The rallying point was Slim Perry's livery, at eleven o'clock. But instead of the hundred and twenty members of the drillers' association that the Seadons had hoped for, fewer than fifty had assembled. Ross surveyed them grimly. "Amazing how many gutless wonders there are in the world." But at least they had come prepared. Some carried canisters of kerosene, and all were armed with long stakes around which they had tied bundles of rags. They climbed into a straggle of buggies and buckboards and wagons and, with the Seadon Oldsmobile leading, started north along Central Avenue. At the town limits they were met by three horsemen. Chief of Police Touchstone and two of his men. The Chief rode slowly back the length of the procession, then returned to the Oldsmobile. He leaned on the pommel of his saddle and smiled down at the Seadons.

"Sheriff Biernie asked me to give you a message. To sort of be on record."

"Yes?"

"He hopes this is a peaceable assembly."

"What's it look like?" Ross grinned back.

Touchstone avoided an opinion on the men with stakes and rags. "The sheriff would have been here, but he got a call that there's a train wreck about ten miles south of town. Naturally he had to go render assistance."

"Naturally."

"Of course, this is county territory and out of my jurisdiction."

"We noticed," Owen observed. "By about twenty feet."

"Well, good evening to you." Touchstone started to turn his horse, then pulled up and peered down at the iron pail stuffed with cotton which Owen cradled between his legs. "What's in that?"

"Refreshments," Owen said.

The night was hot and still and dark, as dark as the thoughts that began to plague Ross. How many men were waiting out there in the blackness? Would Haggerty divide his force, sending some to guard the Mirage Springs field? How much could the Seadons depend on those in the procession behind them?

And most important, what would be Haggerty's breaking point? Questions without answers, questions that brought sweat to Ross's palms and queasy twinges to his stomach.

The oppressive smell of the oil sumps began to drift through the night. They were drawing near. Then, as the Oldsmobile topped a rise in the road, they spied the first glow of the work lights atop the derricks of the Haber River field. Another mile and they saw a row of coal oil lanterns stretched across the road; and behind the lanterns, a line of men holding lengths of iron pipe; and behind them, a row of horsemen. To one side of the road were a lighted tent and a motorcar with its lamps burning.

Ross stopped the Oldsmobile and turned to Owen. "How many men do you make it?"

Owen stared at the line. "Enough."

"Suppose we leave the road and outflank them?"

"They've thought of that. That's why the cavalry."

Ross clucked his tongue in thought, then said, "Then it's right through the middle. . . . Okay, boy, I'm dealing you out."

"Because you don't like the odds?"

"Because you were right. We got to think about Leah. And Tana."

Owen shook his head. "I'm staying."

While they were talking, the car which had been parked beside the tent coughed into life; it swung around the barrier of men and lanterns and advanced toward the Seadons. It came within the glow of the Oldsmobile's lamps, and Ross recognized the occupants. Billings, the secretary, at the wheel, and G. G. Haggerty beside him, holding a megaphone. Haggerty smiling, confident, as relaxed as if he were aboard his private railroad car.

"You're a man of your word, Mr. Seadon," he called. "But this is as far as you go."

Ross shouted back, "We'll see, Mr. Haggerty! We'll see!"

"That you will!" Haggerty laughed. He gestured to Billings, and the car swung around and headed back.

Ross left the Oldsmobile and walked back along the line of buggies and wagons. Even in the darkness he could make out some of the anxious faces looking down at him. It was not going to be a night of heroes. "All right, boys," he said, "pour your kerosene." He waited while they obeyed, then: "No matches until we hit the line. Nobody on foot; stay on wheels. Understand?" Heads bobbed silently. "Above all, don't crowd us. Keep back until it happens."

He returned to the Oldsmobile and put it in gear. The car moved slowly forward toward the line of Haggerty's men. At a hundred yards from the line it stopped and Ross nodded to Owen. "Not too far, not too close," he said. "One on each side of the road."

Owen produced two pieces of lead foil from his pocket and burrowed down into the pail between his legs and brought up the vial of fulminate of mercury. He measured the pellets into the foil, closed the foil into two tight balls, tied each with string, and added a lead sinker for extra weight. Then he stood up and threw.

Two mushrooms of orange fire leaped into the night; two ear-numbing roars merged into one; two blasts of heated air swept outward in a curtain of dust. Behind the explosions men were running, men were crawling, men were tumbling from their rearing horses.

The Oldsmobile plunged forward, followed by the buggies and buckboards and wagons. Haggerty bawled through his megaphone at his scattered ranks, and the nearest and bravest threw themselves at the column, only to retreat under the rain of flaming torches. Then a second wave. This time men were pulled from the wagons, a horse reared and a buggy spilled over and a buckboard collided with it. Now it was flailing pipes against torches. Hair and clothing flamed, bones broke, bodies fell under pounding hooves. Finally two of the wagons broke through the melee and raced into the oil field after the speeding Oldsmobile. The target had already been agreed upon. Led by Ross and Owen, the men circled the wooden derrick; torches arced through the night; the derrick flashed into flames.

Then, from somewhere behind, above the crackle of burning

timber, Haggerty's voice boomed through the megaphone. "All right, Mr. Seadon! Enough! Let's go sign some papers!"

The oilmen filed into Haggerty's tent one by one. Some with puffed eyes or broken noses or loosened teeth, but all grinning at the stack of legal papers spread out on the table before them. The contracts were clear and simple; Pacoil guaranteed, without condition, to buy all oil produced at a price of fifty cents per barrel for a period of two years.

When the last name had been signed, Haggerty beamed and held out his hand to the Seadons. "You boys didn't disappoint me. It was a thumping good fight, and I enjoyed every minute of it."

Ross was suspicious of such gallantry. "But you did expect to win?"

"I certainly did!"

"Then why did you have all these contracts ready and waiting?"

Haggerty chuckled. "I always carry an extra deck, just in case." He looked thoughtfully at the Seadons. "Now you tell me something. Would you honest to God have burned down every derrick?"

"If we had to," Ross said. "Of course, all Owen and I ever talked about was Seadon Number Five."

Haggerty's eyes glazed momentarily. "*Your* well?"

Owen grinned. "We were going to pull the derrick down anyway. It was a dry hole."

It was a victory with qualifications. Pacoil had gained control of four Weston producers; it could not be driven out, and it had put a ceiling on the selling price for crude oil for the next two years. But there are always two ends to every piece of string. The very next day Harry Buhlenbeck announced that the Bank of Weston would reopen its loan window; the market price for oil stocks leaped upward, doubling and tripling within a single day; the Pioneer Hotel was besieged with reservations from drummers for drilling supplies. And Weston had an authentic hero. The *Weston Weekly* devoted an entire page to Ross Seadon and his "fiery defeat of the forces of greed." The story was picked up by the metropolitan newspapers, and Liz Barnard mailed a clipping from the *Los Angeles Times* which paired the photographs of Ross and Haggerty and captioned them "Victor and Vanquished." Liz attached a note: "Congratulations, dear! Didn't I tell you?"

If only she had been there to share it, Ross thought. But at least she had sent her mailing address.

> Dear Liz—
> In spite of all the hurrahs, I guarantee we haven't heard the last of Mr. Haggerty. The wounded bear is always the most dangerous. Meanwhile, we're pumping oil again and drilling two new wells on your lease. You'll soon be getting some very fat royalty checks to squander.
>
> Love.
> Ross

"And how are my favorite arsonists?" Father Barrie greeted the Seadon brothers as they accompanied Leah from Mass the following Sunday. "I hear that one of you has kindled another flame outside my parish." He smiled slyly at the three puzzled faces, then narrowed his attention to Owen. "Nothing to confess, my son? Must I rely entirely upon Father Anselmo?"

Owen's face brightened cautiously. "I've heard that name . . . somewhere."

"Have you now?" He winked at Ross. "Father Anselmo has asked for my character reference, on behalf of certain parishioners who appear to hold tender sentiments—"

He got no further. Owen emitted a whoop. "The Delgados!" He seized Father Barrie's hand. "Father, everything depends on you! Please! Even if you have to stretch the truth . . ."

Father Barrie laughed. "Fine advice to give a man of the cloth! And a bit late. The deed is done and in the mail."

That evening the impetuous Owen left for Rancho El Encanto. Two days passed without word. Then a third. On the fourth day Ross received a telegram.

LOCATED TWO MORE LEASES SESPE AREA   STOP   I CAN DOUBLE
THEIR PRODUCTION   STOP   SELLERS WILL TAKE TEN THOU-
SAND CASH TWENTY THOUSAND STOCK SEADON OIL STOP
STRONGLY URGE WE DEAL   STOP   OWEN

"But what about Tana?" Leah asked when Ross showed her
the telegram. "He hasn't told us anything."

"I think he has. Why do you suppose he wants to take on
more leases over there? It gives him the perfect excuse to live
with the Delgados."

The day following Ross's authorization to buy the Sespe
leases, Owen wired again:

CONGRATULATE ME   STOP   AND PRAY FOR SHORT ENGAGE-
MENT.

Six months was the absolute minimum, he reported when he
returned to Weston. "Tana and I begged and argued until we
were blue, but her mother wouldn't budge. She wants the
whole damned rigamarole—parties and bridal showers and the
Seadons coming over to be houseguests and meeting sixteen
thousand relatives."

"Good! I'd love it," Leah said.

But Ross hedged. "Better count me out. There's too much
going on here. Tim Beakley thinks he's going to bring in a new
field west of the Springs. I want to pick up some leases, just
in case."

Beakley proved to be right, and his discovery triggered a
new inflow of money and men and drilling rigs. The stocks of
the oil companies, the old reliables and the new hopefuls, were
a daily wonder, defying belief and the law of gravity. There
seemed not a cloud on the horizon when Owen escorted Leah
to visit the Delgados; but when they returned to Weston, only
two weeks later, they found Ross with a long face.

"The railroad just doubled their freight rate for Weston oil.
It's kicked hell out of everything."

Owen understood immediately. "Christ, fifty-cent oil isn't

fifty cents when we got to pay double freight rates. And what if the rate goes up again?"

"It probably will," Ross said. "The word around town is that G. G. Haggerty is behind it. Maybe, but there's no way of really telling. Whatever, we can't take it lying down."

Owen made a sound of disgust. "Another torchlight parade and burn down the railroad?"

"Uh-uh. We make ourselves independent of the railroad. We build a pipeline."

Ross called a meeting of the drillers' association and outlined his plan. A fund should be set up to hire surveyors and engineers to examine the practicality of a pipeline westward to the shores of the Pacific. If it proved feasible, then the drillers should form a company and issue stock and bonds to finance the project. To Ross's surprise, there was little opposition.

"Ross knew how to handle G. G. Haggerty," Tim Beakley told the gathering, "and I say, let's follow him again. Sure, it'll cost millions, but we'll lose millions with those damned freight rates. This way, we'll own our own transportation. So let's go!"

The meeting broke up early, so that when Ross and Owen drove back to the house they were not surprised to see lights in all the downstairs rooms. The front door hung open. Why not? It was a hot night. Then, as they went up the front steps, they heard the high-pitched gabbling of the Chinese in the parlor. Below their excited treble there was another sound, a wordless moaning and sobbing.

It was Leah, huddled on the sofa, arms around her knees, stockinged feet splotched with blood. Ah Sing and Sammy Lee, ranged behind the sofa, were watching Hop Gee dab a wet cloth at Leah's bleeding shoulder.

Ross and Owen dropped onto their knees beside her and she clutched their hands. "I didn't know! . . . I never realized! . . ." she gurgled. *"How could he?"*

Ross looked up at Hop Gee, who nodded and led the servants from the room. At first it was impossible to get anything intelligible from Leah; the words came out in a jumble of hysteria.

"It was awful! Horrible! Oh, I'm so cold, cold!" Ross told Owen to telephone for Dr. Pixley, but Leah stopped him with a wild "*No!* Nobody must know!"

Ross shook her. "Nobody must know *what?*"

"Harley!"

"What about him?"

"He . . . he came by . . ."

Ross glared at Owen. "Sure! The bastard knew we were at the meeting."

Owen frowned. "What happened, Sis?" She looked wildly about the room, as if seeking an avenue of escape. "You've been seeing him behind our backs, haven't you?"

She swallowed guiltily. "I was just so bored. I thought it was harmless. . . . Tonight, I knew he'd been drinking . . . but I thought it would be all right to drive out to the Weir . . ."

"Go on," Ross commanded.

"That's . . . that's where Harley asked me to marry him. I said no, I wouldn't. Then he took out a bottle. Absinthe. He started drinking and talking crazy. Was there somebody else? And who was it? And he was going to kill him."

Owen looked at the torn dress. "Did he . . . you know . . . do something to you?"

She wagged her head. "I was afraid he would. I got out of the car and started walking. Then he came after me. He said he'd drive me home. But he didn't. He knew where to go . . . and what time it was. The road along the railroad tracks. I saw the light coming down the tracks, and Harley shouted that if he couldn't have me, nobody would. Then I jumped."

The brothers stared at each other. Then Ross asked, "So Harley's dead?"

"I don't know! I heard the train whistle . . . and the crash. I just ran and ran. All the way home. . . . Whenever I saw somebody, I hid in the bushes . . . so they wouldn't know."

Ross got to his feet and went to the telephone and asked for the county hospital. Yes, they had admitted a Mr. Harley Stewart. And his condition? Shock, cuts, bruises, a broken arm, an undetermined number of fractured ribs. Ross hung up without identifying himself.

Owen listened to Ross's report and shook his head. "You know what they're going to say when this gets around? A lovers' suicide pact."

Ross eyed him coldly. "Worried about the Delgados?" Owen's flush was answer enough. "All right. I'll see what I can do."

Wilmot Caruth opened the front door, blinked sleepily at Ross, then invited him in. Caruth was in his nightgown; but his wife, wandering in from the kitchen with a jelly glass of amber fluid in her hand, appeared dressed for a ball. As she swept unsteadily toward Ross, Caruth took her elbow and escorted her from the room.

When he returned he smiled awkwardly. "Prosperity can be hell on a woman when she has nothing to do. Especially in this town." He paused and frowned uncertainly. "But I doubt you came here to wish me pleasant dreams."

Ross described what had happened to Leah and the report from the hospital. "What I've told you," he concluded, "I expect you to forget."

"Naturally." Caruth nodded. "But *why* are you telling me?"

"I want a favor, Wil. I can't go to the hospital and talk to Harley Stewart. Somebody might connect it with Leah. But you could go see him—a lawyer looking for a suit against the railroad."

"What do you want me to tell him?"

"That I want him out of town as soon as he can walk. And if he ever mentions Leah's name, his next stop will be the cemetery."

Caruth pursed his lips. "I don't like threats, Ross."

"It's not a threat. It's my personal guarantee."

"But suppose the engineer of that locomotive saw Leah jump from Harley's car. He wouldn't know who she was, but he'll certainly put it in his report. He'll have to."

"Let him. But you get to Harley tonight. And tomorrow see that you accidentally bump into Sloppy Weather Smith. You ask him if he knows which girl at Madame Devereaux's was out with Harley."

Caruth's eyes squinted with amusement. "Uh-huh. That ought to give the tongues something to wag on." Then he laughed. "God almighty, you sure missed your calling, Ross. What a shyster you'd make!"

Ross waited until the next morning to talk to Leah. When he came into her room, she was still in bed, Hop Gee's breakfast tray on her lap. Her eyes were puffed from a sleepless night, one cheek was swollen and blue.

"I want the truth," Ross began. "You've told us everything about last night except *why* it happened. Did you lead Harley on?" Her eyes drifted to the window. "*Did* you?"

"Yes."

"Oh, Christ!"

"It was a game, don't you see? I never thought he'd take it like that. How could a man want to kill himself over me?" She shook her head and shivered. Shocked, awed, proud, and flattered, all in one. She who could sing Verdi, who knew the plots of all the melodramatic operas, could not believe that she had been the prime mover, the center, of her own tale of passion.

"But *why*, damn it! What ever put the idea in your head?"

She fidgeted with the breakfast tray; she picked up the coffee cup and set it down again. "I knew that Harley used to board with Liz Barnard . . ."

"Yes?"

"I knew he saw her sometimes."

"You also knew Liz was my girl."

"That was why. I knew that Harley was common. I thought common enough to talk . . . tell me things. That maybe sometime he and Liz had . . ." Her eyes went toward the window again. "I wanted to know what she was like. In bed."

He did not repeat the conversation to Owen. Yet he could not close his mind to the situation. Leah's motive in leading Harley Stewart on was unforgivable; but if she had followed up on her singing career, as she had wanted to at one time, perhaps she would not have taken out her frustrations in envying Liz Barnard. The basic problem, Ross decided finally, was Weston. A crime-ridden boom town. There was no outlet for a respectable young woman unless she escaped into marriage and filled her days with babies. Yes, it was Weston. Liz Barnard had fled it. Helen Caruth had in another way. The memory of Wil's alcoholic wife was a warning of what could happen to a desperate woman.

Later that day the brothers discussed the situation in their office. "In a way," Ross said, "we should be grateful for last night. Suppose Leah had told Harley she'd marry him. That's the kind of brother-in-law we don't need—a broken-down oil scout and crook to boot. He'd be telling us how to run the the Seadon Estate Company and how Leah should vote her stock."

"I thought about that," Owen conceded. "But God knows, she can't go on living an empty life. She needs a husband."

"That's what I've been chewing on all morning," Ross said. "We want her to have somebody we can respect, who will treat her right. Somebody with brains and money and position. Does that suggest anybody?"

Owen pulled on his earlobe and thought. "Not around Weston."

"What about San Francisco?"

"Dave Marcus!" Owen grinned at the idea. "Hell, yes! He's the best friend we have, and he's already got a case on Leah. . . . But how do we get them together?"

"That's no problem. Let's assume that this pipeline idea pans out. Then I'll be going to the city to talk to Dave and the Montgomery Street boys about a bond issue. That's the time for me to take Leah along. After Harley Stewart, Dave ought to look pretty damned good to her."

But the pipeline project dragged along from one month to another. The surveyors' reports and the engineers' recommendations were revised and revised again and argued over by the drillers' association and not finally agreed upon until the week of Owen's marriage to Tana.

The wedding Mass was celebrated in the Delgados' private chapel at Rancho El Encanto. Ross was best man and Leah the maid of honor. Doña Felipa, through her tears, insisted it was the most beautiful wedding of her most beautiful daughter. At the wedding dinner, Don Jaime toasted the newlyweds and announced his dowry for Tana. It was 2000 acres of Rancho El Encanto. There Owen and Tana would build their home, he predicted, and there they would rear their many children. The day following, after the honeymooners had left for Del Monte, Don Jaime and Ross cantered over the rolling hills and gentle glens that composed the dowry. It was parklike, with live oak and eucalyptus and sparkling springs. But nowhere did Ross see an oil seep.

They leaned on the deck railing, Ross and Leah, and watched the wake of the ferry foaming backward toward the Oakland mole and the great gray train shed where they had transferred from one form of transportation to another. The morning was cold and windy and they shivered in their lightweight clothing. Then presently they walked forward along the deck and gazed westward toward their destination. Past the brown hulk of Yerba Buena Island fingers of fog were withdrawing from the Embarcadero and sifting seaward through the Golden Gate. Above the fog the windows of the shanties on Telegraph Hill and of the great mansions on Nob Hill flashed yellow in the morning sun. Neither brother nor sister spoke their excitement; it was enough to look and to listen to the thrashing of the big sidewheel paddles, the cries of seagulls wheeling and soaring overhead, the distant moan of the foghorns and the clang of channel buoys. The last time Ross had heard those sounds he had been homeward bound from Stanford, education uncompleted, condemned, he believed, to a life of clerking in his father's hardware. He still remembered the pain, the rage he felt, that his moneyed classmates would finish college and go on to certain futures, while he— What was he? A cipher. And now another ferry ride, and the cipher was Ross Seadon the oilman, with a letter in his breast pocket from the president of the Bay Steel and Engine Company:

> I look forward to your visit with keenest pleasure, and with confidence that we shall be able to meet your requirements. Believe me, sir . . . Very truly yours, Arnold Schroder.

The clock tower of the Ferry Building loomed above the bow. Bells rang, the great sidewheels reversed direction, the pilings along the ferry slip groaned with the first impact, the landing ramp dropped into position, the passengers pressed forward. Ross, with Leah on his arm, moved through the gloomy interior of the Ferry Building and came out into the sunlight of Market Street, where representatives of the city's hotels solicited customers and helped them into their waiting hacks. Ross chose the Palace Hotel, rather than the new St. Francis, partly for sentimental reasons (Val and Cathlin had stayed there), but more importantly because the Palace was the unofficial headquarters of the Southern Pacific Railroad. It was there, in the Palace Bar, that its agents entertained the state's lawmakers and newspapermen and bought their drinks and votes and editorials. If all went well, Ross himself intended to have a story to hand out, in the very camp of the enemy.

He liked Arnold Schroder from the moment they shook hands. The president of the Bay Steel and Engine Company was, as his five hundred employees thought of him, "plain as an old shoe." "Plain" was also an apt description of his features. Serious gray eyes, sparse gray hair, a thin mouth from which jutted a seemingly endless chain of cigars. He worked in his shirt sleeves in an office that was no more than a partitioned space in the planning department, which was where Ross spent the afternoon going over with the company engineers the proposed pipeline route and specifications for pumping plants and power lines.

"I'd like a week to complete our bid on the project," Mr. Schroder said at the end of the meeting. "Would you be able to stay over until then?"

"I plan to," Ross said.

"Good! Then perhaps some evening you'd do Mrs. Schroder and me the pleasure of dining with us."

"Thank you." Ross glanced at a framed photograph of two women on the rolltop desk. The older woman, he decided, would be Mrs. Schroder. The younger, blond and pretty, must be the daughter.

Mr. Schroder saw Ross's glance and said, "And if by any chance Mrs. Seadon is with you . . ."

"I'm not married. But I'm sure my sister would be delighted."

"Then it's settled." Schroder's face brightened. "Come to think of it, Phyllis—Mrs. Schroder—is planning to have a few friends in this Sunday. Would that be convenient?" Ross assured him that it would be. Then Schroder had another thought. "Is there anyone else you'd like us to invite?"

Ross seized on it. "Do you know David Marcus?"

"I should hope so! His bank has financed quite a number of our customers."

"And Henri Laprebode? I understand that he's still . . ." Ross hesitated, not wishing to say "alive."

Schroder understood and laughed. "Yes. Very much so. Eighty is not old, you know, if you're Henri Laprebode. He's the city's leading institution." It was plain that Schroder was impressed by the two names; Ross Seadon was no country bumpkin.

That evening a written invitation from Mrs. Schroder was delivered to the Palace Hotel. The hour would be eight o'clock, the dress formal. A carriage would be sent.

Both brother and sister had suffered an attack of nerves at the sight of the butler opening the door of the mansion on Van

Ness Avenue. Then, in a moment, their confidence returned. David Marcus was crossing the marble foyer, kissing Leah's cheek, clasping hands with Ross, and escorting them arm-in-arm into the parlor.

Most of the other guests, Ross noted, were of Arnold Schroder's generation and clearly among the leaders of San Francisco business. Best of all, they were interested in Ross Seadon. Karl Neilson, head of the Neilson Shipping Line, indicated that his fleet included tankers which could transport oil to the various refineries once the pipeline had been completed to the coast. Holgar Thorsvan, the timber baron, foresaw the possibility of mammoth wooden trestles to bridge ravines and canyons along the pipeline route. Both men pressed Ross to accept their own private wrappings of Havana cigars and invited him to lunch at their clubs. Ross was buoyant at this immediate acceptance as an equal—and then irritated when someone tugged his elbow and said, "You gentlemen must excuse us. I need Mr. Seadon's opinion." It was Louise, the Schroders' daughter.

"I didn't need rescuing," Ross protested as she guided him across the room.

"Perhaps not," she said, "but *I* did—from their wives. Besides, I do want your opinion." They passed through an archway into a garden room green with ferns and palms and twittering with canaries. Louise tossed her head. "What do you think?"

Ross glanced about. What was he supposed to see? Then his gaze returned to Louise. The face he saw before him had none of the pastry prettiness which he associated with blondes; the high cheekbones were sharply modeled, the mouth firm and yet feminine, the eyes an unusual pale golden brown.

She tossed her head again, this time impatiently. "The windows! They're Tiffany. We just had them installed."

Ross scowled at the swirling multicolored glass. "I like them," he said, not meaning it.

"I doubt it." She smiled. "May I have a cigarette?" With

162

that request, Ross understood; the Tiffany windows were simply a ploy to get him alone. He opened his case; she selected a cigarette and bent toward his match. As she did so, he saw her eyes slide toward the parlor and focus on Leah, who was basking in the attention of David Marcus and a rather too elegant young man named Oliver Eakins.

"Your sister is quite the success," Louise observed with a tinge of coolness. "Very attractive." Then a frown. "Ollie obviously thinks so."

And obviously the wrong man for Leah, Ross reflected. "Tell me something about Eakins," he said.

"Oh, we've known each other for ages. Ollie invests. Utilities, railroads. *And* he really likes our Tiffany windows." Ross saw that she was examining him with a curious intensity. "You know, you're really not what I would expect."

"In what way?"

"Well, there's no six-shooter on your hip, and no high explosives in your pocket." She laughed. "At least, I hope not."

"So you've been talking to Dave Marcus."

"Purely feminine curiosity."

He wondered. It could be an indication of more than passing interest, which was both flattering and disturbing. *When* had she talked to Marcus? This evening, or sometime earlier? If earlier, it implied a closeness between them that could interfere with Ross's plans for Leah.

Then he was conscious again of Louise's scrutiny. "I've never met a man who wanted to blow up an oil field. Especially the great Mr. Haggerty's oil field."

"And now that you have, what do you think of him?"

Ross's directness startled her and she shifted her gaze to the top of his head. "I really can't say. I haven't made up my mind." She laughed lightly. "Besides, we're being much too personal, and there *is* a party going on."

As they returned to the parlor, Ross saw a short white-haired man, a new arrival, stare at him and then raise his cane and point. "There! That is the young man I met almost fifty years ago!" It was a declaration intended to startle the room, and did. Henri Laprebode limped forward and put his free arm on Ross's shoulder. "He is exactly the same! The hair, the eyes, the nose, the height, the strength. The one difference is that then I called him Val Seadon." Men and women smiled, as if relieved that Laprebode had not gone suddenly senile. He dropped his voice. "My boy, did you know that I brought your dear father and mother together?"

"I know. I'm honored to meet you, sir."

"You should be! I am responsible for you, and for your lovely sister." He looked toward Leah. "Yes, I see Cathlin in her, too." The old Frenchman's eyes misted behind his pince-nez; in another moment, Ross thought, he would break down. Then the emotional moment passed. Dinner was announced.

At the table Ross found himself seated directly opposite Louise. From time to time they bantered lightly; then, toward the end of the meal, Louise turned serious. "Tell us about the oil business, Mr. Seadon."

"It's like any other business."

"I should think not. Most wealth is a slow, patient accumulation. Like my father's. And the others'." She indicated the rest of the table. "No, I'm sure there's a difference. Old money is not dramatic. But you, you drill a hole in the ground, and there you are—a millionaire."

"I'm not, Not by a very long shot."

Her lips pursed. "But you intend to be?"

"As quickly as possible."

"And then?"

"Then a second million. And a third."

"Bravo!" Arnold Schroder called from the head of the table. "And when you are a millionaire, Mr. Seadon, will you go on living in Weston?"

"No. San Francisco." He glanced toward Leah, who was listening. "And my sister, too."

"I can hardly wait!" Leah beamed.

"I can imagine," Louise said dryly. Then she smiled at Ross. "Mr. Seadon, I've made up my mind."

"About what?"

"I think you know."

It was past midnight when the party broke up. As the carriage moved down Van Ness Avenue, Leah peered back through the window at the marble steps that they had ascended a few hours before.

"We're different people, aren't we?"

"So you felt it, too," Ross said.

"Oh yes!" She settled back in the seat and Ross adjusted the lap robe over their knees. "Glad to see Dave again?"

"Oh, always. But Ollie was more fun."

So it was "Ollie" already.

The carriage passed under a gas lamp at the street corner and Leah watched the light play on her brother's face. Before it retreated into the shadows again, there was a question she must ask.

"Do you think you might ever call on Louise?"

"Yes," he said. "Tomorrow afternoon."

Chapter 12

"'T H E C I T Y that never sleeps" was the proud boast of San Francisco, and one which Ross and Leah found to be no over-statement. Following his call on Louise (disappointing; both were tired from the night before), Ross and Leah were dinner guests with David Marcus and his family; the next night they sat with the Schroders in their private box at the Orpheum; another night there was a moonlight cruise on the bay in Karl Neilson's yacht, with Ross escorting Louise and Oliver Eakins with Leah. The daylight hours were equally crowded. Ross spent a week touring the bond houses along Montgomery Street to listen to their proposals for financing the pipeline. When he returned to the Palace Hotel at the end of the day, Leah would be bubbling with news of her own activities. "In just two blocks along Kearny Street, I saw John Drew and Maurice Barrymore and DeWolf Hopper. Ollie introduced all of them to me." Another day it was the literary life. She had seen Jack London and lunched with Oliver Eakins and his

North Beach bohemian friends and it was "terribly atmospheric." Ross scowled at that account.

"I'd say there's too much Ollie Eakins and not enough Dave Marcus."

To which Leah replied, "Ross, I wish you'd stop pushing Dave at me. I'm not a piece of acreage to be signed up. I want experience. Anything and everything. I want to *seethe* through life!"

And seethe she did, until finally the frenzy of activity and the overrich food brought Leah down with a hard cold and she agreed that it was wise to spend a day in bed. And so being on his own, Ross decided it was the ideal time to take up David Marcus on his promise to initiate him into that unique San Francisco experience known as the "Cocktail Route." It was a tradition which traced its beginnings back to the 1880s, and it had evolved through the years into an itinerary as rigid as a railroad time schedule. It began at the recognized hour, five o'clock, at the recognized first stop, the Reception Saloon on Sutter Street, near Kearny. There the merchants, bankers, attorneys, politicians, and newspaper editors gathered before the long mahogany bar and called for their personal bottles of liquor which stood in gleaming ranks on the shelves behind. David Marcus' bottle was bourbon. From it the bartender poured three fingers and repeated the measure for Ross.

The two friends raised their glasses to each other, then David asked, "How are you coming with Bay Steel?"

"Schroder wants a few extra days for his bid. I think he's nervous that his Los Angeles competitors might undercut him."

"I hope not. Bay Steel could use the business."

"They'll get it. Regardless of the figure, I want a San Francisco outfit."

"For personal reasons?"

Ross understood his meaning but evaded it. "San Francisco is headquarters for everything; that's why Seadon Oil is going to move here . . . and maybe the pipeline company, too. I want as many friends as I can make."

"Then you'll be selling your house in Weston?"

Ross shook his head. "Owen and I will take turns down there. He'll commute from Ventura, and I'll go down from here, and we'll need someplace to stay. Besides, the house is part of Ma and Dad. We grew up there, and Hop Gee and Sammy Lee and Ah Sing have grown old there. It's their home, too."

"Not good business, but damned fine sentiment." David smiled. "How about some free lunch?"

They drifted over to the adjacent counters where white-jacketed waiters were dispensing the specialties of the Reception Saloon—baked ham and terrapin in cream and sherry sauce. David introduced Ross to some of the men clustered around the food; then it was time for the next stop, the Occidental, at Sutter and Montgomery. Again, one bourbon and a sampling of oysters. Then Dunne Brothers, at Eddy and Market. Bourbon and crab legs. And the Baldwin, the Peerless, the Cardinal. Bourbon and bourbon and bourbon.

"Enough!" Ross groaned, leaning against the bar of the Cardinal. "I feel like I'm turning into a walking distillery."

"You'll get used to it," David assured him. "You have to, because this is how the real business of the city gets done." It was true. At each bar David had introduced Ross around and afterwards ticked off each man's role in the interplay between the city's business leaders and the social cliques. Few had to push; life was easy and secure, the men complacent. They would be no match for a Ross Seadon.

Finally they arrived at the last stopping place, splendid in mahogany and red African marble and bronze fixtures, and blue to its vaulted ceiling with cigar smoke. The bar of the Palace Hotel. David pointed out William Randolph Hearst, out from New York to visit his home town, who was trading jokes with Ambrose Bierce, his editor. Just beyond them, to one side, was someone more interesting from Ross's point of view. G. G. Haggerty. The man beside him, Billings the secretary, motioned toward Ross, and Haggerty raised his glass in salute. Then, deciding that was not enough, he pushed through the crowd and shook hands.

"I hear you've been a busy boy around town." He smiled affably. "How's the pipeline coming?"

So Haggerty had heard. San Francisco could not keep a secret. "Too soon to say," Ross said.

Haggerty's intense black eyes moved toward David Marcus, then back to Ross. "You know, you don't need bankers and bond houses. I can fix you up with all the financing you need."

"Uh-huh." Ross nodded. " 'Come into my house,' said the spider to the fly."

Haggerty laughed pleasantly. "It's a very nice house, friend. And for you, the latchkey is always on the outside." He clinked his glass against Ross's and strolled back to Billings.

Ross stared after him. "When Haggerty gets friendly, I get nervous. I'd rather he swung at me."

"He will at the right time," David replied. "He's a hater with patience."

A little later they encountered the president of Bay Steel. Arnold Schroder clapped Ross's shoulder. "Good Lord, I haven't seen you since when?"

"Ages, sir," Ross replied, playing the game. "Not since last night."

"That long? Well, well, don't be such a stranger." He winked and said he was on his way home and proved it by disappearing into the lobby.

Ross turned back to David. "I really like him. A fine man."

David squinted thoughtfully. "And maybe a fine father-in-law?"

Ross rolled the ice around in his glass and listened to the clink. "What do you think of her, Dave?"

"A nice girl."

"That all?"

David paused and considered Ross with a solemnity born of eight bourbons. "I just wonder, Ross, if you're not confusing things. You've had a pretty exciting time up here. Pretty rich fare. Naturally, you're all heated up."

"Some of the best things happen when you're heated up. The mistakes come out of boredom. Something like that almost happened with Leah." Ross purposely brought in a reminder of his sister; if they could talk about the possibility of Louise, why not Leah?

David followed his lead. "You think we could go upstairs and look in on her?"

Ross grimaced. "She's got a running nose and red eyes. I don't think she'd appreciate it."

"I guess not. You know, the last week, seeing Leah, seeing her outside that damned Weston of yours . . . seeing her bloom up here—her sheer joy of living . . . Well, I guess you know what I mean. How I feel about her. Maybe always have and didn't know it."

This was better, much better. "I kind of had a hunch."

"Oh, God damn it! You suppose she'd have me?"

"I sure hope so," Ross said quickly. "Put it up to her."

"That's the hell of it. I can't!" He slammed his glass down on the bar. "It's my family! Don't you understand?" He saw that Ross didn't. "I'm Jewish. My sisters married Jews, and I've got to. My parents insist on it. God, it's miserable!"

Swift and blunt, there it was. In all the years of their friendship, Ross had never considered the possibility of such an obstacle. "Well," he sighed. "I guess we're all in the same boat. Leah is Catholic and can't marry outside the Church. I always assumed that if she found a Protestant, or a Jew, that he would join the Church. That's what my father did."

"He wasn't a Marcus." David dismissed the subject with a moody smile. "Well, partner, you've seen the Cocktail Route. All except the grand finale. Which will it be? Love at a parlor house, or boil out at the Hamman Bath?"

Ross shrugged. "Why not both?"

"Henri Laprebode was certainly right. You are *l'oiseleur*," Louise declared with an emphatic bob of her head. It was a

170

beautiful afternoon, and Ross, at the wheel of her father's red 1905 Cadillac, had joined the parade of carriages and motorcars in the Sunday ritual of a drive through Golden Gate Park.

"Huh! And I thought the old man was my friend." Ross sniffed. "What's a . . . a whatever-you-call-it?"

"*Oiseleur*. A bird catcher. One who can charm the birds out of the trees."

It didn't follow, Ross thought. He had merely attempted to entertain her with humorous stories of Weston. "It doesn't follow," he repeated aloud. "Somebody who charms the birds out of the trees is a flatterer."

"And you are. You try to amuse me, and that flatters my sense of importance. It makes me feel good." A hint of a frown crossed Louise's face; she had not meant to go so far. She fell silent and Ross contented himself with watching the Sunday procession. Men in bowlers and straw hats in the carriages, men wearing driving caps in the motorcars, society women with cartwheel hats bedecked with flowers and bird plumage. But none was dressed as smartly as Louise—or so Ross thought —in her beige alpaca suit with black passementerie. More than once a carriage or a motorcar approached from the opposite direction and a man would tip his hat to Louise and stare hard at Ross. Louise would acknowledge with a nod and, in some cases, identify him for Ross's benefit. A member of the Blood Horse Association. A yachtsman. The master of the revels at this year's Bohemian Club High Jinks. All were, as Louise put it, "old money."

"Does it matter whether it's old money or new?" Ross challenged. "A dollar is always a dollar."

"Not quite. Old money means you know who you are, what you are, and what is expected of you." She paused as if analyzing the truth of her definition. "Most old money in San Francisco is only second generation. I never realized how really old 'old money' could be until I went East and saw all those great houses on Fifth Avenue and at Newport. . . . But someday *we* will be just like them."

It seemed to Ross that her stress on "we" included him; it

was personal, almost in a family sense of the word. Warm and comforting. Only lately had Ross realized his loneliness. The deaths of Val and Cathlin had left an aching void which he had tried to fill with Liz Barnard, only to have her leave him and build a life around Philip, that boy she had adopted. Owen had married, and it was only a question of the right man for Leah. Then what? The prospect of empty evenings was grim and frightening.

"There they are again!" Louise exclaimed, breaking in on his thoughts. She was pointing toward a carriage which had swung in from a side road. The occupants were Leah Seadon and Oliver Eakins. The four had lunched earlier at the Cliff House, then separated with a promise to meet again for dinner at The Poodle Dog.

The two women waved to each other, then Louise said, "There's something I've been curious about ever since we met. Why isn't Leah married?"

Ross smiled. "She asked me the same question about you."

"I almost was. I was engaged."

"You broke it off?"

"Death broke it off. Tom was mountain climbing in Yosemite, and fell."

"When was this?"

"Two years ago. . . . At first I thought I'd never get over it. But one does." She paused and looked sideways at Ross. "You will, too."

Was this a feminine wile to gain his confession? Ross wondered. There were times when Ross had felt the loss of Liz Barnard as a man might an amputated leg; the body still received messages from the phantom limb. But surely that was behind him now. The past was the past; the present was blond with pale brown eyes.

"You still haven't explained why Leah isn't married."

"She's choosy."

"Good heavens, what's the matter with Dave Marcus? That first night, at the party, I could see he was gone on her. Yet here she is, out with Ollie, who isn't interested in any woman and never will be. Does she know so little about men?"

Ross avoided the question. "Dave can't marry Leah. It's got to be a Jewish girl."

"Has he said so?"

"To me, yes. So . . . that's that."

"Hmmm. Well, I certainly know scads of men. Want me to blow the bugle?"

"Would you?"

"Of course. It would be fun to watch. And in return . . ." She fluttered her eyelids coquettishly.

"Yes?"

"Heavens! don't you have any imagination?" She pouted her lips playfully. "I thought you were the man who got his way, even if it meant burning down an oil field."

Ross grinned, and when the car came to the next side road he turned off and followed it to Stow Lake. He parked by the water's edge, and they watched a swan convoy its young across the rippling blue. Then, after a moment, Louise raised her parasol, and behind the lacy screen Ross bent toward her up-turned face.

The following day Arnold Schroder submitted the bid of Bay Steel for the pipeline, and Ross, leaving Leah at the Palace Hotel, returned to Weston to present the figures at a meeting of the drillers' association. In addition, he recommended that Braithwaite and Company, on Montgomery Street, should underwrite the bond issue in the amount of six million dollars. The meeting voted approval and appointed Wil Caruth, who was secretary and general counsel, to accompany Ross back to San Francisco to sign the contracts. Two evenings later Ross and Caruth stood drinks for the newspapermen in the Palace Bar and handed out the formal announcements. Whether by accident or design, neither G. G. Haggerty nor any official of Pacoil or of the Southern Pacific Railroad was present.

Later that same evening Ross went to the house on Van Ness

Avenue and talked to Arnold Schroder in the privacy of his library. Schroder stood with his back to the grate of coals and listened gravely. When Ross had finished, he took the cigar from his mouth and studied it with a frown.

"Let me ask one question, Ross. Would you be willing to come into Bay Steel as my assistant and someday, when I retire, take over?"

"I'm an oilman, sir. I know nothing about the steel business."

"I'll teach you."

"I understand. But I'm afraid not, sir."

Schroder twirled the cigar thoughtfully. "Bay Steel has been my whole life. It's been very good to me. If I had a son, he would carry on the business. But since I don't have, I've always hoped that Louise's husband would take my place."

Ross felt his body grow heavy with disappointment. "I would feel the same way if I were in your place. But I'm me, and I'm selfish."

"Aren't we all?" Schroder returned the cigar to his mouth and drew on it. "Of course, I've got quite a few good years ahead of me. At least I hope I have." He exhaled, and the corners of his eyes began to crinkle. "I suppose . . . I suppose I could hang on until my grandson is ready."

Ross gave a start. "You mean I have your permission?"

Without answering, Schroder strode to the library door and opened it. In the hallway beyond, Ross saw Louise twisting her hands. Schroder beckoned. "Come on in, hon. Ross has something to say to you."

"I'm going back to Weston," Leah decided when Ross told her of his engagement.

"Why, for God's sake?"

"I should think it would be obvious. You'll be spending all your time with Louise. I'd just be a fifth wheel."

"Oh, Christ, don't talk like an abandoned child. There'll be bridal showers and parties and dinners. They'll be going on for three months, and you're bound to meet somebody. Hell, you could be married before I am."

"And if I'm not?"

He sighed. "That's up to you. I can't live your life for you." It sounded brutal, and Ross felt brutal; but he refused to accept the guilt Leah seemed determined that he assume.

Then Leah's mood passed. She seemed to warm to Louise's gestures of friendship. Louise asked her to be bridesmaid of honor; she included Leah in every bridal shower, and at the luncheons and dinners she seated her next to the unmarried men. She consulted Leah about Ross's likes and dislikes and even asked her opinion on the redecoration of the Schroder house for the wedding reception. Best of all, Leah began going to dinner with Jerry Braithwaite, the junior partner in the bond firm which had underwritten the pipeline issue. Then, in the final week before the wedding, she began to complain of headaches and asked to be excused from parties. Ross would return to the Palace at the end of the evening to find Leah sitting in the bay window of her room staring down at the Market Street traffic or asleep in a chair with an empty brandy glass.

The wedding Mass was celebrated in the evening at St. Ignatius', on Van Ness Avenue. It was both the Schroder church and the pride of San Francisco's faithful; its vast interior glowed with paintings and frescoes and stained glass, its altarpieces glittered with gold and jewels. Owen Seadon was best man, and Tana joined Leah among the bridesmaids. Don Jaime and Doña Felipa made the journey from Rancho El Encanto, and there was a delegation from Weston. The Wil Caruths, the Ted Buhlenbecks, Sloppy Weather Smith, Tim Beakley, and—at the insistence of Ross—Hop Gee, Sammy Lee and Ah Sing. After the ceremony, as the bride and groom went gaily up the aisle, Ross caught sight of a young woman smiling at him, a young woman with paprika hair. For one startled instant Ross hesitated; then his grip on Louise's arm tightened and they swept by. Louise, he hoped, had not seen Liz Barnard's slow, sly wink.

The reception at the Schroder home was hailed by the

Chronicle and the *Examiner* as, along with the wedding, one of the social highlights of the season. An orchestra played; Dale Lantry, the society photographer, fired tray after tray of magnesium powder for group pictures; butlers poured jeroboams of champagne; the guests dined from a buffet which began with caviar, proceeded to roast pheasant, and ended with *croque-en-bouche*. Louise and Ross danced the first waltz together; then Louise with her father, and Ross with Leah. Shortly before ten o'clock Ross sought out Owen, who was telling a story to David Marcus.

"Well, it's time, boys. Louise and I are going out the back way. Keep the party going."

"Have a wonderful honeymoon," Owen said.

"And don't get seasick." David grinned. He was in on the know, that Mr. and Mrs. Ross Seadon would spend their wedding night on Karl Neilson's yacht, at anchor scarcely two miles away. The following day they would leave for Colorado Springs.

Ross whispered a final aside to Owen: "Keep an eye on Leah. She's hitting the champagne."

Leah looked over the shoulder of her dance partner at the dark-eyed laughing woman who was waltzing with Owen. Tana's waist was thick, very definitely thick, Leah thought. Probably five months along. How soon would Louise find herself in that condition? Just as rapidly as she could. Louise had that look about her, the brood mare. Leah frowned; what a morbid thought. She needed another drink. The dance ended and she drifted away from her partner. She saw David Marcus coming toward her and she shook her head. No more dancing. A servant passed with a tray of champagne glasses; she took one and wandered toward the garden room. Good, it was deserted. She felt like being alone.

Then she realized that she was not. Rising above the ferns, she saw a curl of cigarette smoke. Then a man's head appeared. It was Dale Lantry. He was interesting-looking, Leah decided.

He reminded her of a courtly Southern gentleman rather than a photographer. His sideburns were tinged with gray and he spoke with a softness that was surely Southern, which it was. As he smiled and came toward Leah, it occurred to her that he had included her in an unusual number of photographs. At least this time he was not lugging that cumbersome big black box.

"Catching your breath, Miss Seadon?"

"Like you. You've certainly been busy this evening."

"My job." He watched Leah finish her champagne. "Would you like some more?"

"Please." As he turned to go, she added, "Bring a trayful."

When he returned, Lantry carried a bottle and two glasses. Leah downed Lantry's first pour and held out her glass for a refill. "Somehow, I don't see you as a photographer. You look more like . . ." She groped fuzzily for the right words. "Like, you know . . . a painter. A court painter. For royalty."

"Odd you should say that. I began as a painter. But photography pays better."

"It always comes down to money, doesn't it?"

"Not always." Lantry smiled. "The camera can capture the instant better than any brush. I don't mean those miserable things where you look white-faced and staring. That's because of the magnesium. But if I use natural light, soft, filtering through tree leaves, or like here—" He touched the frond of a potted tree fern. "That's the way I would try to capture you. With mood and beauty."

" 'Capture.' I like that word," she said and held out her glass again. "It would be nice to have something like that. A real portrait."

Lantry responded eagerly. "I'd consider it an honor. If you really mean it."

Leah smiled vaguely. "A portrait I could keep and look at when I've gone to wrinkles and lumps and sags." Lantry started to protest the thought, and she cut him off with a laugh. "Woman's fate, Mr. Lantry. But a portrait doesn't change. If

I could look at it and say, That's the way I was on the deliriously happy night of my brother's wedding."

Lantry blinked. "Tonight?"

"Tonight."

"But I've used up all my plates." He paused helplessly. "Besides, it wouldn't be fair to try it at a party. Perhaps tomorrow, when we're both fresh, you could come to my studio . . ."

"Tonight," she repeated. "At your studio."

Leah saw his expression change; it was the look that she wanted. "I am going to pose for you, Mr. Lantry. In the nude."

She stood looking out the window of the one-room studio. Below, just beyond the foot of the hill, she could discern the moonlit yacht harbor and the black shapes riding at anchor. Which one was it? Perhaps that one. Or over there. Then, deciding it really didn't matter, she turned and went back to the bed and stretched out beside Dale Lantry. She let his mouth wander over her breasts for a while, and then she said, "Dale, will you marry me?"

She saw his head come up in surprise.

"Well?"

"You're joking, of course."

"Was I that bad?"

"Good God, no!"

"All right then. You said I was beautiful. And young. And you'd never forget this night. You even cried."

"But you could have your pick of men. Every unmarried man at that party—"

"Bores!" She sniffed. "You're different. You're gentle . . . sensitive . . . cultured." She meant manageable.

He shook his head. "Your brothers wouldn't allow it. They wouldn't accept me. Not the Seadons." He spoke the name with awe.

"They couldn't help themselves." Her hand went out to caress him. He sighed and glanced around the cramped room with its battered furniture and boxes filled with camera equipment. "I've got a little savings. Perhaps I could swing that two-room flat upstairs."

"The Palace Hotel. They have suites on the top floor."

"I see." For the first time he was decisive, emphatic. "No. I won't live off your brothers."

Leah laughed and drew his face down to hers. "You won't have to, darling. I will."

The wedding, a modest affair at St. Mary's, followed that of Ross and Louise by exactly one month to the day. "How the hell could Leah do this to us?" Ross muttered to Owen after the ceremony. "A half-baked photographer!"

"Who cares?" Owen answered. "As long as she loves him."

"Love, hell! It's just pity for a failure!"

Chapter 13

I T W A S Opera Week, the gayest week of the social season. Every newspaper covered the arrival from New York of the Metropolitan Opera Company in their special railroad cars; every new edition carried the latest raptures of the musical greats about the Queen City of the West; the leading restaurants vied with one another in confecting new dishes in honor of their famous visitors: Cherries Caruso, Salade Fremstad, Pommes à la Scotti. The opening performance at the Grand Opera House on Monday, April 16, was a dazzling production of the voluptuous *Queen of Sheba*. Ross and Louise Seadon and the Arnold Schroders shared a box with Dale Lantry, who had come stag because Leah was in the last month of her pregnancy and had chosen, sullenly and resentfully, to remain in the suite at the Palace Hotel. Very pregnant women, very proper women, in the year 1906 simply did not make a public display of their condition. For the same reason Leah declined to attend *Carmen* the following night, or the opera galas—not even the party given by the Schroders—and had to content herself with reading newspaper accounts of the great affairs to be. Women would wear their finest jewels and gowns specially created for the evening. And Leah's husband would see it all, hurrying from party to party as he photographed the famous of music and society. It was enough to embitter any woman on the subject of motherhood.

Ross and Louise knew that the affair at the Schroders' would be a late night (it did not end until after two in the morning) and had decided in advance to stay over in one of the guest rooms rather than to return to their own apartment. They slept poorly, pulses pounding from the conflicting effects of champagne and coffee. Ross remembered turning over in bed and hearing dogs barking and howling and the frightened whinny of a horse somewhere. He opened his eyes and saw that dawn was breaking. Then he heard another sound—a deep angry rumble. It semed to come from nowhere and everywhere. A moment later the bed jerked and heaved, french windows banged, a floor lamp toppled, pictures crashed.

"Earthquake!" Louise shrieked, clutching at Ross.

They leaped from bed and staggered across the bucking floor. They reached the hall door, but it had jammed shut. All they could do was to hold each other as the violence grew. The room, the whole house, was pitching and heaving like a ship in heavy seas. Timbers groaned, bricks ground against each other, plaster ripped and fell. Then, as suddenly as it had begun, it was over. There was silence. Silence broken only by the clang of church bells, still swinging in their belfries.

"Thank God! Oh, thank God!" Louise breathed. "I've never felt anything like—" She finished with a scream.

It was the second shock, even more severe. The chiffonier slid toward them, spilling out its drawers; the chandelier swung against the ceiling and showered down prisms. Outside there was a thunder of falling brick as the chimney collapsed. The hall door that had been jammed swung open, and Ross pulled Louise out into the hallway, where they staggered along like drunken people. The rolling and jolting intensified, and Ross felt his stomach rise and thought he would vomit. There was an explosion of glass. "My Tiffany windows!" Louise wailed. She sank to her knees and crossed herself. "Hail, Mary, full of grace..."

Then again silence. It was over, finally and truly over. Ross, Arnold Schroder, and Baldwin the butler—all in their night-shirts—inspected the damage. Every clock had been thrown down, its hands stopped at 5:13; mirrors and pictures and chandeliers had crashed; the grand piano had moved across the music room; the Tiffany windows, as Louise had guessed, were no more. The house itself seemed structurally intact. But the electricity had failed, the telephone was dead, the gas was off. The cook reported there was no water in the kitchen; she wondered if it was all right to light the coal stove for break-fast. "Who can eat?" Schroder grunted. "My stomach's moved up to my bald spot." It seemed marvelously witty, and every-body laughed with a kind of hysterical relief. "Everybody get dressed," he added, "and out into the street, in case there's another one."

The street was filled with their neighbors, some in night clothes, some half-naked, all babbling of their experiences. One gentleman had donned his opera attire of the night before, tails and boiled shirt, but had forgotten his trousers. Every chimney on both sides of Van Ness Avenue was down; here and there a porte-cochere had collapsed or a roof had sagged; but all in all, Van Ness Avenue had come through remarkably well.

Arnold Schroder cranked his Cadillac and called to Ross, "I've got to see what happened at the plant. Want to come along?"

"Yeah. You can drop me at the Palace." He was thinking of Leah and Dale Lantry. After that he would check on the offices of the Seadon Oil Company in the Call Building.

They went down Van Ness and passed St. Ignatius', where Ross and Louise had been married. The belltowers were gone, and the stained-glass windows. They turned eastward and stared dumbly at the growing signs of devastation. Streetcar tracks were scrambled like limp spaghetti; broken power lines writhed on the pavement and flashed blue fire; water geysered up from broken mains. Entire buildings had crumbled into rubble. They passed a milk wagon half buried under a slide of bricks, the horse on its side, kicking and screaming, the driver lying dead beside it. They saw policemen carrying a child out of another ruin, his stomach skewered through by a length of metal.

"My God!" Schroder groaned. "We've had quakes before, but nothing like this."

Ross's answer was a gasp as he pointed at the sky to the south and east. Pillars of black smoke were rising into the morning light—a dozen, a score, a half hundred. The earthquake had been but the preliminary; now fire, with all the city's water mains broken.

The drive from the Schroder home to the Palace, ordinarily a trip of ten minutes, consumed half an hour. Market Street was choked with debris, with people, with vehicles, with dashing ambulances and fire wagons and police motors, all with bells ringing or horns blowing. Then the Palace, miraculously whole. The thousand guests, in all stages of undress, milled in the street and called out the names of missing mates and children. A short rotund man, whom Ross recognized as Enrico Caruso, waved a framed photograph of Theodore Roosevelt and shouted in his famous tenor, "My voice! I've lost my voice!"

Ross leaped from the Cadillac, gestured good luck to Schroder, and pressed through the crowd. At the hotel entrance the police turned him away; only hotel personnel were permitted inside.

Then he saw one of the assistant managers pushing toward him. "Don't worry, Mr. Seadon! The Palace rode it out like the queen she is. No danger of fire, either. We have our own reservoir. Tonight everybody will be back in their rooms!"

Ross ignored the optimism. "Have you seen my sister? Mrs. Lantry?"

"She's with her husband."

"Where?"

He pointed toward a streetcar, derailed and abandoned. The hotelman was crazy, Ross thought; but he would look.

Leah was alone, huddled in a seat, a blanket about her shoulders. At the sight of Ross, she half rose and clutched his hands and kissed them. "Oh, Ross! I'm so frightened!"

"Everybody is. Where's Dale?"

"Gone for a doctor."

Then he saw that sweat was streaming from her face, her eyes bulged with pain. She was in labor.

He left the streetcar and returned to the crowd. Out of those hundreds of men, one must be a doctor. But none was. A policeman said every physician had gone to the Mechanics' Pavilion, which had been designated the main emergency receiving station. What to do? Wait for Arnold Schroder to return with the Cadillac? If he could. Then Ross saw a dray wagon nosing through the crowd; it was loaded with injured. Yes, the driver said, he was going to the Mechanics' Pavilion and he could take Leah and Ross. For fifty dollars.

The great vaulted hall of the pavilion echoed with the cries of the injured, many of whom had been brought from the demolished Central Emergency Hospital across the street. Some were insane and were roped together in screaming groups of three and fours. Doctors and nurses, many of them injured themselves, bent over the wounded and beckoned to a priest or minister when the case appeared hopeless. Finally one of the physicians came to Leah, asked the frequency of her pains, and told Ross she might be delivered in six hours. Certainly no sooner. "She'll be fine. I'll have a nurse keep an eye on her." He started to turn away, then looked at Ross. "Where's her husband?"

"Here, I think. I'll look for him."

But there was no sign of Lantry, and Ross decided he should

go to the offices of Seadon Oil in the Call Building. When he stepped outside the pavilion, he saw it was already too late. The separate columns of smoke had merged into a single black curtain stretching from south of Market to the Embarcadero and north to the financial district. The Call Building was eighteen stories of flame.

The loss of the Seadon Oil Company's headquarters barely registered with Ross. He was in shock without realizing it. He knew vaguely that he should get word to Owen in Ventura, but how? Telephone service was out, but perhaps the telegraph lines still functioned. If he could find an office or a hotel which could send the message . . .

While he was debating, he felt the earth move under his feet. Another quake, not heavy, perhaps a "settler," he told himself. Or the prelude to something worse. The telegram could wait. His place was with Louise. He turned and started to trudge up Van Ness, keeping to the center of the street, just in case. It was strange, he thought, how few people were about. Then he noticed a line of trucks and wagons approaching, each flying a red flag. Dynamite carriers. That explained the empty street. Several more blocks, and more trucks and wagons bearing soldiers from the Presidio.

An officer on horseback detached himself from the procession and rode toward Ross. "You! In the wagon!"

"What for?"

"Fire fighting!"

Ross laughed. "With what? Watering cans?"

The officer gestured to his men, and two of them leaped from a wagon and came toward Ross with rifles and fixed bayonets.

Ross was only one of hundreds of conscripts. He had only a hazy idea where they were; somewhere south of Market, near the waterfront, and dangerously close to the flames. At first he unloaded dynamite, which was passed from hand to hand until it reached the intended target. But the explosions which were intended to snuff out the fire just as often hurled firebrands to buildings still untouched. When the dynamite was exhausted, the fighters beat at the advancing flames with gunny sacks soaked in beer from abandoned saloons. Nothing helped; block by block the men were forced back. Blasts of superheated air scorched through the streets and alleys as if blown by a giant bellows. Ross's lungs ached from smoke; his feet felt blistered from the heat of the cobblestones. Once he was almost buried under the collapse of a warehouse. Another fighter was not so lucky. Ross heard his screams for help and clawed through the rubble until he found him pinned under a fallen girder. "Don't let me burn! Don't let me burn!" the man begged. Ross heaved against the great weight but could not budge it. It would take three men, he decided, and called to the nearest fire fighters. Then he heard gunshots behind him. He whirled and saw a soldier with his rifle still raised. "That's murder!" he cried.

The soldier glowered back. "General Funston's orders. Shoot looters on sight."

"But he was one of us!"

The rifle swung toward Ross. "You want to be a looter, too?"

First the quake, then fire, now blood lust.

It was dark by the time Ross managed to slip away. When he finally reached Van Ness Avenue, the street was jammed with refugees streaming north toward the safety of the beach. They went in buggies and on foot, in wheelchairs and on crutches, with pushcarts and baby carriages and wheelbarrows piled high with belongings. Two men pushed an upright piano; a woman clutched the family Bible and a vial of holy water. A child carried a birdcage with a dead canary.

But at least all was well at the Schroders'. While Louise clung to Ross and thanked God for his safe return, Arnold Schroder reported that the Bay Steel factory was reduced to a block-long heap of twisted girders.

"But you're insured?" Ross asked.

"For fire, not earthquake. And anyway, most of the insurance companies will probably go bankrupt. If they even exist." Schroder was referring to the rumors that the entire nation had been leveled; Los Angeles and Portland had been destroyed; New York and Chicago had been swept away by tidal waves.

After washing up, using water from a goldfish bowl, and eating a supper of sandwiches, Ross felt somewhat restored and his thoughts turned to Leah. He and Louise, he said, would take the Schroder carriage (the Cadillac had been commandeered by the military) and go to the Mechanics' Pavilion and wait for Leah's delivery; then they would bring her and the baby back to the house.

But long before they reached the pavilion, they could see orange flames leaping from the huge roof. "Everybody's evacuated!" a policeman shouted. "They're in Golden Gate Park!"

They found Leah stretched out on the grass, in one of the long rows of injured. Beside her, swaddled in a towel, was a baby girl.

"Where's Dale?" Leah whispered. "I can't leave without Dale."

A nurse gestured to Ross, and he followed her through the ranks of the injured. They came to a separate group, lying with arms and legs in stiffly contorted positions. The nurse pointed toward one of the bodies. "He was found under some bricks. Will you tell her?"

Leah read the truth on Ross's face. "I guess I knew all along," she wept. "He gave his life to save mine, to save his child." She dried her eyes and went on in a dreamy manner. "I've already decided what to name her. Dale. After her father. It's the least I can do to honor his memory."

Ross sensed the rebuke intended for him, the brother who had disdained Lantry for his lack of worldly success.

By midmorning the cruel wind which had blown all day intensified and fanned new waves of fire across the city. Black smoke towered two miles into the sky. Ashes carpeted Van Ness Avenue and sifted through the broken windows of the Schroder house. Outside, the endless column of refugees was showing the first signs of panic; people no longer clung to their possessions; they cast them to the ground and hurried on like a routed army fleeing the advancing enemy. It was clear by now that the entire city was threatened, and Mayor Eugene Schmitz called a meeting of the leading citizens at the Fairmont Hotel to consider how San Francisco was to be saved. Arnold Schroder and Ross attended. But the meeting solved nothing. General Frederick Funston, the Army commander, recommended wholesale dynamiting and shelling by his artillery; the business leaders raged back that the general would destroy the city more certainly than the fire.

Shortly before midnight the meeting broke up, and Ross and Schroder joined the throng on the crest of Nob Hill and watched the great crescent of flames below. Wherever they looked, south, east, north, a thousand fiery mouths were devouring everything in sight. The Palace Hotel, with its acres of marble, its bronze statutes and crystal chandeliers; the towering City Hall; the magnificent Church of St. Ignatius with its paintings and frescoes; the Emporium and Maison Française; the Grand Opera House; the theaters and music halls; the great banks; the proud hotels; the churches; the famous restaurants; the saloons of the Cocktail Route; the parlor houses; Barbary Coast; Chinatown. Serpents of fire writhed through the streets, fireballs rolled over rooftops, flaming shingles and timbers arched skyward. Every gust of wind brought the stench of burning flesh, human and animal. The noise was like nothing Ross had ever heard, a fiendish chattering, hissing, humming din of devastation. The dull crump of dynamite was matched by the sound of saloons exploding with their stores of alcohol.

The crowd watched in dazed silence. Here and there someone broke into hysterics. Finally Schroder turned to Ross and shook his head. "There won't be anything left except up here." He swept his arm to include the Fairmont Hotel and the great rococo mansions of the railroad barons and Comstock kings— Stanford, Hopkins, Huntington, Crocker, Flood.

But by dawn they, too, were gone. Only the Flood mansion remained, and the blackened shell of the Fairmont Hotel. Then the flames pushed on to the west.

The second day brought false hope. Dynamite had contained the fire some blocks to the east of Van Ness Avenue. People began to tell each other that the Western Addition would be saved, and certainly the Mission District. A trainload of doctors and nurses arrived from Los Angeles. The warships of the Pacific Fleet dropped anchor in the bay, and marines and sailors came ashore with food and medicines and joined in the fight against the flames. Surely, victory was in sight.

Then the winds rose again. With the intensity of a gale, they drove the flames like a giant blowtorch. Window glass melted into molten pools; lead plumbing liquefied and ran in streams of fire. The earth itself seemed ablaze. And a new horror was added—bubonic plague, spread by the hordes of rats fleeing the burning Embarcadero and Chinatown.

Ross went with Arnold Schroder to another conference of the civic leaders. It produced only fresh bickering and new casualty figures. A quarter of a million were homeless, over six hundred dead, nearly five thousand injured. David Marcus was at the meeting and, despite the loss of his family's home and bank, still clung to faith in the future. The United States Mint, he told Schroder, had miraculously come through the flames, and its officials had promised to lend gold to the bankers. "So when this is over, Arnold, come around and we'll help you rebuild Bay Steel."

"What a marvelous friend," Mrs. Schroder commented when Schroder repeated the conversation at home.

"He's that. But what will I use for collateral?"

Ross answered, "You must have some stocks and bonds."

"Sure. A trunkful. Of every company that got shook down or burnt out."

"Then we'll mortgage this house," his wife said. "As long as we've got a roof, we can begin again."

Neither Ross nor Schroder mentioned that they had seen field artillery moving into place at the foot of Van Ness Avenue.

Dawn of the third day was barely distinguishable from night. Ashes sifted down from a sky in which the sun hung like a dull red ball. Those who remained in the city (300,000 had fled to

Oakland and down the peninsula) went about in a stupor of fatigue, or broke into fits of trembling from delayed shock. The wind had diminished, but not the appetite of the flames. In the afternoon they swerved westward and for the first time dynamite and artillery were heard on Van Ness Avenue itself. House by house, the troops moved down the avenue, sometimes planting explosives, sometimes aiming field guns. Just before nightfall there was a knock on the Schroder front door and a captain of artillery saluted its owner. "Sir, you have two minutes."

That night they joined the thousands on the beach. Ross and Louise, Leah and her baby, the Schroders and their servants. Here and there along the sand there were bonfires with people crowded around; most simply hunched in blankets and watched the racing flames.

Sometime during the night Louise crawled into Ross's arms. "I'm sorry, darling," she whispered.

He did not reply. His eyes were fixed on the glow in the sky, on what had once been San Francisco, the city where his parents had met, the city which he had planned to conquer.

"I'm sorry, I'm sorry!"

Finally he looked at her. "About what?"

"You thought you had married an heiress. The only dowry I've brought you is ashes."

Ross smiled softly and smoothed the blond hair away from her eyes. He kissed her cheek and felt the wet of her tears. "The luck of the draw, honey." He kissed her again. "There's always another."

BOOK
THREE

Chapter 14

Throughout the spring and summer and fall of 1915 Ross and Louise Seadon looked down from their home on Pacific Heights at the assemblage of towers and domes and spires of the Panama-Pacific International Exposition. They could see the forty-four-storied Tower of Jewels, an astounding confection of bad taste festooned with plaster statues of eagles and gods and goddesses; they could see the Grand Concourse decked with the flags of twenty-five nations and the fountains that danced before the Chinese Pavilion and the Florentine Court. At night they could watch the circling lights of the giant Ferris wheel and the fireworks which punctuated the darkness with blossoms of red and green and blue and yellow.

The exposition's official purpose was to celebrate the opening of the Panama Canal, "the wedding of two oceans," which brought the Pacific Coast 15,000 sea miles nearer to the Eastern Seaboard. To the people of San Francisco, there was a deeper symbolism—the triumph of Life over Death. Nine short years after the worst disaster ever to befall an American city—"a modern Pompeii," newspapers of the nation had mourned at the time—here San Francisco stood again, gleaming on its seven hills. New homes, new office buildings, new factories, new theaters, new hotels. The gutted St. Francis and Fairmont hotels had been restored; the Palace Hotel had been rebuilt. As had the Bay Steel and Engine Company factory, thanks to a loan from the Marcus bank. Mr. and Mrs. Arnold Schroder entertained as lavishly as ever in their new house on Van Ness Avenue.

The city had never been more festive; visitors filled the hotels from every part of the state and nation. The Seadons entertained weekly, sometimes nightly; they took their guests to the exposition to hear Paderewski play and John McCormack sing, to gape at Charlie Chaplin and Theda Bara, up from Hollywood. By fall, the dinners and outings were beginning to pall even on the party-loving Louise.

"I'll be glad when the exposition's over," she said one evening to Ross as they were dressing for dinner at the new Poodle Dog. "I'm exhausted with entertaining people."

"Careful," Ross warned. "Owen and Tana are in the next room."

"That's different. They're family. We can relax with them." Louise held a choker up to her throat and examined the effect in the mirror. "Oh, pshaw! Didn't I wear these opals last night?"

"Sure. And they looked great."

"All right. Then if you'll fasten the clasp . . ."

Ross came up behind her and glanced into the mirror at their twin reflections. They were, he thought, still a handsome couple after their ten years together. Louise's face was without a hint of line, although her blond hair had darkened somewhat and was now almost the color of his own. Here and there in his sideburns he could see a vagrant gray hair; but, thank God, he was not thinning on top. And so far he had avoided a paunch, which was an accomplishment in a city that lived for its stomach.

He fastened the clasp. "No, don't," Louise said. "I'm going

to wear my pearls." He unfastened the clasp. "I'm so exhausted I can't make up my mind about anything. We both need a real long rest, away from everything. Business, the house, the children." She crossed to the vanity and opened her jewel case and took out her string of pearls. "You know, Europe is beautiful in the fall."

Ross watched her incredulously. "Lou, when you go to your father's office, what do you see on the wall behind his desk?"

"Why, a map of Europe."

"Uh-huh. And why does he keep moving those lines of red and blue pins around over Belgium and France?"

"Oh, really, that's just Father's way of keepng up with the war. It's a game with him."

"Some game. Ten thousand men die every time he moves a pin."

"We don't have to go to Europe proper," Louise pursued. "Ingrid and Holgar Thorsvan are going to England and Scandinavia."

"England's got zeppelin raids, and Scandinavia is short on food. Besides, the *Lusitania* is all booked up." Ross gave his wife a playful slap on the hip.

"Don't be grisly, dear."

"I thought I was being familiar."

Louise eyed him curiously. "You seem to be in a jolly mood tonight. Did you hire some ravishing new secretary?"

"Better than that. One of the belly dancers from the exposition." Then he turned serious. "England is out, Lou. Any passenger liner could be another *Lusitania*. We'll do our sailing on the ferry to Sausalito."

His declaration was lost on Louise; her attention was on the confusion of children's voices in the hallway. She went to the door and opened it; outside her son and daughter were playing tag with Tana's children.

"Maggie! What did I tell you?"

The nurse's voice floated back from a distance. "Yes, mum. They're on their way to bed now."

Ross looked at his watch. "Hell, let them stay up. They're not babies."

Louise shut the door. "They're overtired, overstimulated. They stayed much too long at Leah's. I couldn't drag them away earlier, because it *was* Tom's birthday party and Leah was sweet to give it for him. But if I had known what it was going to be like . . ." She paused for a rueful shake of the head. "I wasn't going to tell you about it until tomorrow, but Tana may bring it up herself. She was as shocked as I was, especially with her own children there."

Ross gazed absently out the window at the glowing lights of the exposition. *You're in a jolly mood tonight. Did you hire some ravishing new secretary?* But he was not in a jolly mood. He was out of sorts. No, more than that. Melancholy. He had lunched that noon with David Marcus, who had just brought his wife Ruth back from the Mayo Clinic. Her case was hopeless, David had told him, and then went on for two distressing hours to relive his years with Ruth, their happiness, their lack of children, their unspoken agreement to pretend there was a future to be shared.

Ross sighed at the memory and turned away from the bedroom window. Louise was slipping into her evening wrap. What was she saying?

". . . Oh, I should have suspected when Leah was using candles and lanterns. I thought they were just for atmosphere. Then I went into the bathroom and the lights wouldn't turn on. And right in the middle of things, when the children were eating the cake and opening their favors, there was this banging on the hall door and some man was yelling he wouldn't leave until Leah paid her grocery bill. The children didn't hear, they were laughing so much. Except poor Dale. What a way for a daughter to grow up! Anyway, Tana and I went through our purses, and then we sneaked out through the kitchen door and paid him off. What does Leah do with her money? She's got plenty for somebody like that thing we saw her tangoing with at the St. Francis. He with his diamond stickpin. I'll bet she bought it for him. From Shreve's, probably—if they haven't closed her account." Louise paused to examine herself in the mirror again. "You know, I think I'll wear the opals after all. What do you think?"

"Good," Ross said. "The pearls are fine."

The following afternoon Ross and Owen visited the exposition to hear a lecturer at the Electric Pavilion speak on hydroelectric power versus oil-generated energy. It proved a waste of time, and the two brothers left the pavilion in a mood of frustration. They wandered to the midway with its fortunetellers and freak shows and weight guessers. They bought hokey-pokey ice cream cones and tossed nickels to a monkey performing to the strains of a hurdy-gurdy. Finally they stopped at the counter of a shooting gallery where a boy with heavy horn-rimmed glasses was expertly knocking down a procession of metal ducks. Beside him, watching, was a woman wearing a stylish "hobble" skirt and a straw cloche over her red hair.

"*Liz!*" Arms flung about her waist, lips kissed her cheeks, hands grasped hers. "Why didn't you let us know you were in town?" Ross demanded.

"It's our first day. I was going to stop by your office later in the week."

They had not seen one another in three years. They smiled and laughed and assured one another that they had never looked better; nothing had changed.

Owen glanced at the boy gaping at them. "Lord, Philip's almost as tall as you, Liz."

She nodded proudly. "He's going to be a six-footer. How many do you have now, Owen?"

"Three."

"And you, Ross?"

"The same two. Tom's going on nine and Ginny's seven."

"Really? Somehow, I always thought you'd raise a baker's dozen." Liz spoke lightly, but her expression betrayed her surprise. It was unnecessary, Ross thought, to explain the obvious:

Louise could have no more children. A tubular pregnancy had settled that possibility.

Owen noted that Ross was still holding Liz's hand. He turned to the boy. "Say, Philip, have you been on the Ferris wheel yet?"

"No, sir."

"Then come on!" He grinned meaningfully at Ross and Liz. "Meet you in an hour. By the fountain at the Turkish Pavilion."

Liz hooked her arm through Ross's, and they began to walk toward the Avenue of Palms, away from the din of the midway. At first their conversation was awkward as they sought to bridge the gap of years. There would be a spasm of talk, then silence, then another attempt. Philip was in his first year of high school; his grades were excellent. Yes, it was a pity he had to wear glasses. No, she still had not told him he was adopted; she never would. He seldom asked questions about his father; he was simply a man who had died shortly after Philip was born.

"We stopped by Weston on our way up," Liz said. "I wanted Phil to see where my money comes from."

"Did you go out to the lease?"

"Yes. I had no idea you'd put down so many more wells. I should have guessed, from the size of my royalty checks. And the way Weston has changed! A new hotel, another bank, all those office buildings." She shook her head wonderingly. "I missed some of the old faces. They told me Wil Caruth is up here now."

"Yes. He's head of our legal department." Ross named others they had known who were now dead. Sloppy Weather Smith, Harry Buhlenbeck, Slim Perry. He realized sadly how many others were no more, friends unknown to Liz but cherished by him. Henri Laprebode, Don Jaime Delgado, David Marcus' father. Too many, far too many. Then he was conscious that Liz was watching him quizzically.

"Are you satisfied, Ross?"

"About what?"

"Your life."

"Why not? Seadon Oil is one of the five biggest independent

oil companies in the state. We just bought out Tim Beakley and merged his company with ours. We're pumping in four counties. We've got a refinery, a couple of tankers, and next year we'll have our own string of gas stations."

"That's not what I meant."

"Well, I've got a twelve-room house on Pacific Heights, a fine wife, and two good kids. I belong to the Bohemian Club, and Louise must be on every damned charity list in town. We've even got ourselves a chauffeur." He laughed. "Does that answer your question?"

Liz looked into the sky at a flight of pigeons circling through the mist of one of the fountains. "In a way."

"What about you?"

She crinkled her nose, and Ross was conscious of the freckles that he used to kiss during those love-filled afternoons of long ago. "I have Philip. And that little house in Hollywood."

"What about a husband?" Liz dismissed the question with a shrug. "You know, Philip is getting to the age when he ought to have a man to guide him."

"Perhaps. There *is* a man around . . . from time to time."

Ross frowned at the implication. It reminded him unpleasantly of Leah, the Merry Widow of Russian Hill. "You said you were going to stop by the office. Any special reason?"

"Yes. You remember Harley Stewart?"

"Vividly." Another unpleasant reminder.

"He came to Hollywood last week. He wants to buy my interest in the lease. Said he'd pay me fifty thousand dollars."

"It's worth more than that."

"Even so, I was surprised Harley had that sort of money."

"He doesn't. The last I heard, he was working for G. G. Haggerty." Ross had not thought of Haggerty in years; not since he had cut his association with Pacoil and gone East. Texas oil was Haggerty's play now. As for Harley Stewart, Ross had seen his name in the trade journals identifying him as land agent for Pantex Oil, Haggerty's company. But in Texas, not California. This was all very strange.

199

Liz broke into his thoughts. "If it's really Haggerty buying, how much would he pay?"

Ross sniffed. "Don't you ever think of anything but money?"

"Of course. Money lets me think of other things. How much?"

"Maybe eighty thousand. Maybe a hundred. But damn it, you're not selling—unless it's to the Seadons."

"A hundred thousand," she repeated softly. "That's a long, long way from the three dresses I sold you in the Pioneer Hotel."

The hour had fled, and Owen and Philip were waiting outside the mosquelike Turkish Pavilion. Just before they joined them, Liz smiled wistfully at Ross. "Whatever comes, we did have some good times together, didn't we? They were good days. They were fun."

"Yes," he said softly. "They were."

"You think Liz might sell to Haggerty?" Owen asked, lolling on the leather sofa in Ross's office.

"Oh, she's tempted by the idea of a big lump sum. But it's only a temptation. She won't turn her back on old friends."

"Harley Stewart may have been talking to Liz on his own account."

"As spite work, maybe. After that mess with Leah, and me running him out of town, he might want to even things. He could have put the idea in Haggerty's head." Ross tilted back in his swivel chair and gazed absently out at California Street and the cable car that, like a giant caterpillar, was creeping up the shoulder of Nob Hill. "What stumps me is why Haggerty wants a minority interest in one of our own leases. It's not his style. He's whole hog or nothing."

Owen yawned languidly. "That's why I think Harley was talking for himself. He didn't care whether Liz would sell or not. It was just an excuse to look her up." Owen saw his brother's face darken. "Why not? Didn't he use to board with her? And buzz her around in his car? Hell, Liz is still a damned fine-looking woman. Harley just might—"

"Oh, shut up!" Ross swung forward in his chair and drummed his fingers on the desk. "Give me a hundred dollars."

"For what?"

"To match the hundred I just mailed Leah."

"Oh, God! When is she ever going to change?"

"Never, I'm afraid."

The fall of 1915 passed into winter and winter into spring. Henry Ford had built his one millionth automobile. Industry across the nation boomed with orders from Britain and France for guns and oil and food. California fruits and vegetables—and beef from the Delgado rancho in Alto Valle—flowed eastward through the Panama Canal and on across the Atlantic. The wells of the Seadon Oil Company, and of every other company, were pushed to the limit to supply fuel for factories, railroads, and shipping lines.

"I'm sure we can afford a summer place down the peninsula," Louise decided.

"Sorry," Ross said. "Owen and I are cutting our salaries so the company will have more money for expansion."

In late April 1916 Wil Caruth stalked into Ross's office and laid a folder of contracts on the desk. "I've been going over these Salt Creek leases. Do we really intend to drill those properties?"

"Absolutely!"

"In the next four months?"

"No. That's why we want to renew the leases."

Caruth slumped down into a chair opposite the desk. "Tim Beakley just phoned from Weston. He says the landowners won't renew. They say as soon as the leases expire—and that's only four months away—they're going to sign with somebody who will actually drill."

"Hmm. Sounds like somebody's been talking to them." Ross thought a moment. "Call Tim back and ask if he's heard of anybody nosing around Salt Creek." Caruth rose to go and Ross added, "Tell Hattie to get me Owen in Ventura."

When his brother came on the line, Ross repeated the conversation with Caruth and ended with a question: "How many drilling crews have we got working?"

"Nine. I can't spare any of 'em, if that's what you're thinking."

"We could hire outside contractors."

"There ain't none. Everybody's working. Unless you want to pay panic prices, which we damned well can't afford."

"Call you back."

In late afternoon Caruth returned with a report from Tim Beakley. Several of the Salt Creek landowners admitted that they had been approached by a land agent named Harley Stewart, acting for Pantex Oil.

"So now we know." Ross sighed. "Haggerty's back in California. But why Salt Creek? Nobody's ever drilled the area. Owen is the only one who ever got excited about it. He practically clubbed me into taking those leases. What's Haggerty's game?" He ran a hand through his hair and frowned at Caruth. "Any ideas?"

"None. I guess we just kiss thirty-six hundred acres goodbye."

"Not yet. Let me sleep on it."

Several days later Ross learned the extent of G. G. Haggerty's fresh interest in California. It was spelled out in the boldface headlines of the *Oil Daily*.

G. G. HAGGERTY RETURNS TO GOLDEN STATE
PANTEX BUYS FIVE WESTON OIL OUTFITS
SUCCESSFUL BIDDER FOR LOS ANGELES COMPANY
VENTURA PRODUCERS APPROACHED

Ross's reaction to the news surprised himself. He was not dismayed; rather, he was stimulated. If Seadon Oil was to be challenged by new competition, let it be G. G. Haggerty. In the years since they had first clashed, Ross had seen other promoters just as calculating, just as ruthless, but without Haggerty's style and imagination. He was a man to be feared and yet respected. Oil, like gold and silver before it, attracted the spoilers and pirates who struck without bothering to run up the Jolly Roger. At least Haggerty always ran up his colors.

That was Ross's mood in the morning. In the afternoon he stopped in at Braithwaite and Company for his daily review of the ticker tape. Seadon Oil had dropped from 15 to 13½. The next day it closed at 12¼. Ross tore off a section of the tape and carried it into Jerry Braithwaite's office. Braithwaite was more than Ross's broker; he was a friend of years' standing. Blond, blue-eyed, he had a boyish expression that belied his role as one of Montgomery Street's most astute operators.

"What's going on, Jerry?" Ross began. "Who's selling Seadon Oil? And why?"

The broker scanned the ribbon of paper. "I've been wondering myself. Maybe that news about Haggerty and Pantex is scaring investors. People remember that feud you and he had going."

"Then they ought to remember something else. I won."

"I'm talking about the psychology of the market. For instance, you ought to do something about your board of directors. It's really just you and your brother. The rest of the board are all employees. If you put some old San Francisco names on the board, it would show strength, it would give the public confidence."

Ross considered. "Would you go on the board?"

"If you had some other good names." Braithwaite grinned at his own self-approval. "Say, like Oliver Eakins."

Ollie. Louise's friend, Ross thought sourly.

Braithwaite went on innocently. "Your father-in-law would be right, too. Schroder might bring in his crowd. Thorsvan and Neilson and—"

"No," Ross cut in. "This is a Seadon fight. I'm not asking anybody to hold my coat while I slug it with Haggerty."

Still, he could not ignore what was happening to the Seadon stock. If it continued to fall, it would affect the company's ability to raise cash, to expand, and even to meet Haggerty's challenge. The situation called for a dramatic gesture. It was then that Ross's thoughts went back to the Salt Creek leases. That night he telephoned Owen and persuaded him that it was worth the gamble. The following day he sent a telegram to G. G. Haggerty in Dallas:

IMPORTANT WE TALK EARLIEST CONVENIENCE   STOP   PLEASE ADVISE WHERE   STOP   ROSS SEADON.

When Haggerty arrived in San Francisco, Ross diplomatically suggested that they not meet at the Seadon offices; instead, they would lunch at the Bohemian Club. Both men were conscious of the change in their relationships. Ross, once nervous and defensive when he had met Haggerty aboard his private railroad car, was now assured and relaxed in the oak-paneled dining room of his club. The waiters and the wine steward respectfully murmured his name and sprang to light his cigarettes. Fellow members of the club, passing the table, nodded pleasantly. None of it was lost on Haggerty. Once so domineering, he was now open and friendly, equal meeting equal.

At the beginning of the meal they talked in generalities, of the rebirth of San Francisco, the end of the Southern Pacific's tyranny in the state, which had been brought about by Governor Hiram Johnson. And, inevitably, of the war in Europe.

"We're going to be in it, you know," Haggerty said. "The first excuse Germany gives us."

Ross disagreed. "The *Lusitania* was a pretty good excuse, but nothing happened. Wilson said we're too proud to fight."

"That was last May. But what did Wilson say this January? Let's have a bigger Army and a Navy second to none. 'Preparedness' he calls it. But preparedness for what?"

Ross laughed. "All right, we can't convince each other. Let's talk about something we know for sure." The moment had come; but he would ease into it gently. "I understand you tried to buy Liz Barnard's interest in our Mirage Springs lease."

"Last fall, yes."

"Why?"

Haggerty turned up his palms in an all-inclusive gesture. "So we could do this. Talk to each other. Maybe put an idea in your head."

"You could have picked up a phone or written a letter."

"People come to me. I don't go to them."

This was the old Haggerty. Ross felt a twinge of unease. He had a proposition to put to Haggerty; now, it appeared, Haggerty had something of his own. *Maybe put an idea in your head.* What idea? Behind those black eyes, those enameled eyes which betrayed nothing, the brain was devising something devious.

The important thing, Ross decided, was to keep the initiative. "In other words, you want to talk about those Salt Creek leases."

Haggerty opened his cigar case, selected a Corona Corona, snipped the tip with his cigar cutter, lighted it, inhaled, exhaled, and smiled through the bluish haze at Ross. "You know one of the greatest assets Seadon Oil has? Your brother. Owen's got just about the best nose for oil in the business. Every place he says there's oil, by God there *is* oil."

"At least that's one thing we can agree on."

"And yet he hasn't drilled Salt Creek. Why?"

"We still got four months to go."

"What about drilling crews? What about a million dollars for playing-around money?" Haggerty rolled the cigar around in his mouth and smiled again. "When I play poker, I always see that my opponent has got his back to a mirror. In other words, I know your whole situation."

The moment had come. "All right, I admit it," Ross said. "We don't have the crews or the money. But it looks like you do. So you can wait four months and pick up our leases, or you can save four months and come in with us right now—and have the benefit of Owen's nose for oil. We drill the leases jointly. Pantex pays half, drills half, and gets half the production."

Haggerty's eyes gleamed with amusement. "I imagine you'd

like that. So would the public. Haggerty and Seadon Oil are working together; they're the best of pals. The stock market would lap it up." Then his eyes hardened. "I don't give a tinker's dam about Salt Creek."

Ross caught his breath; it was almost as if he had received a kick in the solar plexus. If Haggerty did not want Salt Creek, why had he been wooing the landowners?

"Let's talk about the war some more," Haggerty went on smoothly. "You know what's going to win the war for the Allies? Oil. Oil for the navies and the supply ships, gasoline for airplanes and tanks. And where's it going to come from? You tell me."

"Well, Russia has the Baku Field," Ross supplied. "Holland has oil from Sumatra. Britain has Burma and Mexico. France is buying from Texas."

"Uh-huh. But oil from Sumatra and Burma has to go through the Suez Canal, which Turkey is trying to grab off for itself and the Germans. So the Allies got to protect themselves; they've got to build up other sources. One of them is California, the biggest oil-producing state in the Union." Haggerty paused to draw on his cigar and blow a smoke ring. "Now you know why I bought those Weston producers, and the stuff around Los Angeles and Ventura."

It was a moment before Ross could digest the implications. "Are you saying you've got marketing contracts with the British and French?"

"For everything I can deliver. And a bankroll running into the millions. British pounds, French francs." He smiled sweetly. "So I don't want to waste time wildcatting around Salt Creek. I want *proven* production. Right now. All I can get. And that includes the Seadon Oil Company."

Ross sat back in his chair and stared at the tablecloth. Now he understood. Haggerty's play for the Salt Creek leases was simply part of his war of nerves, to prove to the landowners the weakness of the Seadons. And the stock market was agreeing.

"Well, friend, how about it? Are you with me?"

Ross grimaced. "I seem to spend my life saying no to you, Haggerty. I told you years ago Seadon Oil is not for sale."

"I'm not talking sale. I'm talking merger. Seadon is as big in California as Pantex is in Texas. Between us, we'll be a power in the whole Southwest."

The prospect was dazzling. But Ross knew Haggerty. He would propose a marriage of equals; and once the vows were exchanged, Seadon Oil would be Bluebeard's Wife. All that would remain would be bones bleaching in the Texas sun.

"Sorry," Ross said, finally. "The answer is still no."

He waited for the counterargument, for fresh blandishment, for bluster. He remembered the first time he had refused Haggerty, the red flooding up into his cheeks, the venom in his eyes.

But now . . . nothing. Only the grinding out of the cigar in the ashtray, Haggerty rising from the table, brushing crumbs from his vest. He looked down at Ross with Olympian calm. "I'm going to be in Mexico the next three weeks. When I get back, we'll announce our merger."

Then he stalked out of the dining room.

Ross sighed and patted his shirtfront. He had heartburn.

Chapter 15

''Sure, Haggerty's after our scalps, and sure, he's still griped over that night we almost burned down his oil field. So what? He can't touch us.'' Owen's voice was thin and wavering over the long-distance line.

"He can't?" Ross echoed. "Take a look at the stock market. Beakley says there's a whispering campaign all over Weston: 'Sell Seadon and buy Pantex.' And people are doing it. But if we drill those Salt Creek leases and bring in a new field, that'll show everybody. We've got to fight Haggerty with headlines!"

Ross could hear his brother grunting an aside to someone in the Ventura office. Then he was back. "I think you *want* to tangle with Haggerty. If you're that bored, take a vacation. Take Louise and go somewhere."

"Listen, Owen—"

"I will *not* move my crews! I need every man and every dollar for proven production."

"All right, okay." Ross sighed. "But you will be here for the meeting?"

"Yes. I'll be there."

It was a special stockholders' meeting to elect new members to the board of directors of Seadon Oil Company. The threat of Haggerty had convinced Ross that Jerry Braithwaite's advice should be followed. San Francisco names must be added to the company. Oliver Eakins and Holgar Thorsvan, allied with the Schroder family, were balanced by Ross's own friends David Marcus and Jerry Braithwaite. The reaction of the stock market was immediate; Seadon oil stock rose five points, completely erasing its earlier loss. Then, with Owen safely back in Ventura, Ross made his next move.

It was not the best of seasons to see David Marcus. Ross had barely persuaded him to assume a directorship in Seadon Oil; the business world had palled on David since the discovery of his wife's cancer. Now he sat behind his desk, worn-eyed and remote, while Ross detailed the importance of Salt Creek. Finally he finished and David asked, "You have no absolute proof that there's oil at Salt Creek?"

"Not absolute. But Owen hasn't made a mistake yet."

"Still, it's a speculation. A million-dollar speculation. That's the only way I could present it to my loan committee." David cleared his throat in embarrassment; it was the first time he had not gladly come to the aid of the Seadons.

"Then what do you recommend?" Ross asked.

"As a banker or as a director of your company?"

"Both."

"Forget Salt Creek. Let Haggerty have it."

Ross started to rise, and David waved him back. "There's something else. I hate to bring it up, but it's serious." He hesitated unhappily. "Did you know your sister has a loan with us?"

"*Leah?*"

"It's almost a year overdue. We've granted her two extensions, but the loan committee won't approve another. Unless it's paid off, the bank will move against her collateral. I certainly don't want to see that any more than you do. Especially because of the nature of her collateral."

"My God, she *didn't!*" The only possible collateral Leah could furnish was her stock in the Seadon Estate Company. "How much did she borrow?"

"Twenty thousand. And there's delinquent interest."

"Good God, Dave, you should have come to me in the beginning. Leah has absolutely no sense about money."

"So it seems. But at the time, it appeared a sound commitment. Leah told us she expected Seadon Oil would be paying large dividends to the Estate Company, so we assumed there'd be no problem in liquidating the loan. Now it develops you've only been paying token dividends."

"Because we're plowing everything back into the business. Oh, that damned little fool!" Ross sighed heavily. "All right. I'll take care of it. But on one condition, Dave. That you never lend Leah another dollar."

"I'm sure we won't."

The music of a phonograph sifted through the apartment door. A waltz from *Swan Lake*. There was another sound which Ross could not identify, a dull thumping. Then it stopped and he heard footsteps running to the door in answer to his ring.

"Uncle Ross!" Dale Lantry threw her thin arms around his hips in a childish hug. The flush on her face, together with her white satin ballet slippers, explained the thumping sounds.

"How's my ballerina?" He grinned, tousling her dark hair.

She laughed for answer and drew him into the apartment. "I'm showing Mother what I learned today." With that she pirouetted across the parlor toward Leah, reclining on a wicker chaise longue. Leah was in her at-home costume, a wrapper. Her feet were bare and her hair, still chestnut brown, was caught back and fastened with a rubber band. She was, as usual, smoking a cigarette. Nothing had changed, Ross noted; the parlor was exactly as he had seen it on previous visits. Magazines strewn over the divan, sheet music scattered on the floor beneath the piano bench, a framed photograph of her latest male interest in the bookcase.

"Sherry?" Leah asked, indicating the decanter on the tabouret beside the chaise. Ross said no and turned, at Dale's pleading, to watch her attempt an entrechat. She was a graceful child, Ross thought, more so than his own Ginny. But at least Ginny was free of Dale's nervous intensity, that hallmark of an only child.

"That's enough, dear," Leah said. "It's time for your shower." Dale protested that she wanted to stay and talk to Uncle Ross; then seeing her mother's dark look, she mumbled defeat and obeyed. Leah waited until she heard the slam of a distant door, then said, "You didn't sound very happy on the phone. What's wrong?"

Ross produced a fold of paper from his breast pocket and dropped it onto her lap. She glanced down and recognized the stock certificate of the Seadon Estate Company.

"You knew I'd have to pay off your loan, didn't you?"

She flushed. "Dave had no business to tell you—"

"The hell he didn't! You knew I'd have to bail you out. And you didn't give a damn!"

"No! I thought . . . Oh, I don't know what." She broke off, feeling confusion, guilt, cornered. "Dave is our friend; I didn't think he'd do anything. I thought I could renew the loan year after year, as long as I paid the interest."

"You didn't even do that! Christ, twenty thousand dollars! What did you do with it?"

"Lived. Took care of Dale . . . and other things."

Ross sniffed resentfully at the implication of "other things." "I've talked it over with Owen. From now on you're going to live on an allowance. We're going to send you a check every month out of our own pockets. It'll be enough, but not for fancy men and big parties and buying sprees. Those days are over."

"Is that what you tell Louise?"

He scowled at the thrust. "I'm taking her in hand, too.

There's a difference, anyway. Louise has my salary from the oil company."

"Has she ever!" Leah swung herself up from the chaise and began pacing aimlessly, hands on her hips. "If you want to face facts—which you seldom do—the only trouble is that I'm a woman. If I were your brother instead of your sister, I'd be working in the company right along with you and Owen. I'd have a salary, too. But no, it's got to be an allowance, because I've committed the crime of being a woman. 'Behave, Leah, behave!' That's all I ever hear. You won't let me just *be!*"

Ross wandered to the bay window and stared out. The afternoon fog was groping its way through the Golden Gate; the black shape of an outbound freighter dissolved into the smothering whiteness. The bleakness of the scene sent his eyes back toward Leah. She was still pacing, as though she were restraining an inner panic, Ross thought. She was twenty no longer; she was past thirty. Her life was as meaningless as that of some moth caught between a kitten's paws.

"I know you're lonely, Sis," he said quietly. "It's hard to raise a child all by yourself. God knows, Owen and I want you to be happy. If you could just find yourself . . ."

"Or a husband. That's what you really mean." She smiled wearily. "I embarrass you, don't I? You and Louise. At least with Owen and Tana I'm out of sight. Perhaps I should be out of sight of everyone." She paused and nodded to herself, as if deciding. "Would you and Louise like to keep Dale for me?"

He eyed her sharply. "For how long?"

"Who knows? The Canadian Red Cross is taking American volunteers."

"Oh, don't be a damned fool!"

"It would be in keeping with everything I do, wouldn't it? Anyway, I've been thinking about it." She saw Ross's expression of alarm and laughed for the first time. "I frightened you, didn't I? I really did."

She had. He remembered the headlines that seemed to repeat themselves almost every week: GREAT BATTLE! HEAVY

LOSSES! Some were Canadian battles. Last year it was Yyres. This year it would be somewhere else.

Leah was beside him now, her arm around his waist, her head on his shoulder. "Don't be frightened. Promise me."

"You're not going anywhere," he said huskily. "You're staying here."

She went on tiptoe and kissed his cheek. "Oh, Ross, Ross, we could have had such good times together. If only . . ." She ended with a sigh.

When he reached the street, he heard Dale's voice calling down to him. He looked up. She was leaning from the bay window blowing kisses to him. In the background he could hear Leah's piano. He recognized the melody and remembered the lines that Leah had sung so often: "In the garden of tomorrow/Will the roses be more fair?"

He frowned uneasily. There were roses in Picardy.

"Ross, what's this new trouble we're supposed to be in?" Tim Beakley was calling from Weston.

"What are you hearing?"

"Nothing definite. But Harley Stewart is spreading it around that something's supposed to come out on us next week."

That, Ross reflected, would be when G. G. Haggerty returned from Mexico. Meanwhile the price of Seadon stock was to be driven down again. And it was working. The stock had risen after the election of the new San Francisco directors; now it was sagging once more.

Ross stared at the telephone speaker and pondered. Perhaps Haggerty had given him the idea he needed. "Tim?"

"Yeah?"

"Hang around the office. I may have something for you to do."

He put down the phone and summoned Hattie MacFarland to bring him the latest statement of his brokerage account with Braithwaite and Company. It showed he was "long" $190,000 in bonds of the United States Treasury. There was no debit balance. A handsome sum—all that he had accumulated in twelve years of labor—but still far from enough. How was it to be done? Ross left the office and walked around the block. Then around the block again. On the third circuit he began to chuckle, then to laugh, then to guffaw.

He returned to his office and telephoned Dallas. He must be completely certain of Haggerty's whereabouts. Anson Billings, the ever-faithful secretary, said yes, Mr. Haggerty was still in Tampico; he would be back next week. Was there a message? No, it would keep.

Ross called Tim Beakley back. "Here's what you do, Tim. You go out in the fields and hire three drilling contractors. I know it won't be easy, so look for guys who are finishing one job and haven't signed on for another yet. Tell them we'll sign a one-year contract and pay a bonus of twenty-five per cent."

He heard Beakley's whistle of amazement, then his awed question: "Christ, what's Owen found?"

"Nothing. But you and I will. We're drilling Salt Creek."

The following morning, at exactly nine forty-five—almost noon and lunchtime in Dallas—Ross Seadon rode the elevator down to the ground floor and strolled across the lobby to the board room of Braithwaite and Company. It was the usual midmorning calm. Clients and onlookers were lounging in the customers' chairs, idly gossiping about their stocks and the day's news. The marker boy, on the raised runway in front of the quote board, was dreamily erasing one set of figures and chalking up another. Jerry Braithwaite, in his glass-enclosed office, was leaning back, hands behind his head, joking with his secretary. The customers' men hunched over their desks, bored, waiting for telephones to ring. Several, seeing Ross, smiled and nodded as he sauntered toward the ticker telegraph. The tape was clicking out of its glass dome in a listless trickle.

Ross ran his fingers along the tape until he found the symbol for Pantex Oil. It was $19\frac{5}{8}$. He glanced around the room. There was only one important speculator in sight. Henryss Barstow. Yawning and scratching his chest. Ross looked at the clock above the quote board. Ten minutes to ten. Time. . . . In Braithwaite's office he saw the secretary answer the telephone, then speak to Braithwaite, who rose from his desk and peered out into the board room. He located Ross and gestured. Ross went toward the office, keeping his pace casual.

"It's your secretary," Braithwaite said, handing him the telephone.

"Here I am, Mr. Seadon," Hattie chirped. "You said to call at ten minutes to ten."

Ross's face went grim. "*What?*"

"I'm sorry. It's really nine minutes to—"

Ross flashed a look of alarm at Braithwaite. "Hattie! Don't say anything more. This is coming through the switchboard. I'll call you back."

He flung a "Thanks, Jerry" and hurried out into the board room toward the bank of pay telephones near the street entrance. He slipped a coin into the phone and glanced back at the office. Braithwaite was gesticulating to one of his brokers on the floor. The broker nodded and got up from his desk. Ross dialed. By the time Hattie's voice came on the line, the broker had sidled up to the neighboring telephone and was running his finger down a page of the directory.

"Are you absolutely *sure*, Hattie?" Ross's tone was hushed and intense. "My God, I can't believe it!" At the other end, Hattie's bewilderment reminded him of a chicken being pushed off the nest. "How'd you hear, Hattie? . . . I see. I see. . . . Do they know if it was an accident? . . . Uh-huh. Uh-huh."

His eyes turned toward the lobby entrance to the board room. Wil Caruth was coming through the door. Right on time. "Thank you, Hattie— No, wait! I'll want to send flowers. Can you take care of it? Good! And include my card."

He hung up and faced around to Wil Caruth, who greeted him with "What did you want to see me about?"

Ross scowled a warning. Caruth and his damned booming courtroom voice. "*Not a word!*" Ross muttered and caught Caruth's elbow and piloted him in the direction of Henryss

Barstow. As they neared Barstow, Ross shook his head sorrowfully. "You know, only two weeks ago G. G. Haggerty and I had lunch at the Bohemian Club. He was full of plans for Pantex. It was going to be one of the biggest. I never heard a man so confident."

Caruth opened his mouth and Ross gave him a savage dig in the ribs. Then they were past Barstow, and Ross whispered, "Get back upstairs, Wil. Don't see anyone, don't talk to anyone until I tell you."

"Ross, what in God's name—"

"*Go!*"

Ross watched Caruth disappear through the door, then he wheeled and hurried into Braithwaite's office.

"Jerry, I've got a hundred and ninety thousand dollars in U.S. bonds with you. How much margin can you give me for a stock at about twenty dollars? The absolute maximum?"

Braithwaite blinked and scratched some figures on a notepad. "I make it about forty thousand shares. That's a hell of a big buy."

"Not buy, Jerry. I want to sell *short*. I want to short forty thousand Pantex Oil."

The pencil slipped from Braithwaite's fingers. "Holy Christ! What's happened?"

"*Now*, Jerry! *Do* it!"

Ross waited to see Braithwaite scribble the order, then he strode quickly through the board room. Henryss Barstow was already huddled with the broker who had stood next to Ross at the public phone.

He stepped out into Montgomery Street and inhaled the crisp air. It was a beautiful morning for a stroll. He turned south toward Market Street, pausing to drop some coins into the cap of a blind pencil seller. At the corner of Post he turned west to Union Square. He stopped at Benny's flower cart and bought a carnation and fixed it in his lapel. "Nice day, ain't it, sir?" Benny said.

"Couldn't be better!" It was also a good day for a haircut at the St. Francis Hotel. Finally he sauntered back to Montgomery Street and stopped in at one of the brokerage houses where he was not known. The board room was jammed with excited traders, all staring at the quote board and the latest figure for Pantex Oil. It had dropped from 19⅝ to 16½. Ross wandered north again and looked in at another office. Pantex 15⅛. He decided it was time for a shoeshine. Then a third broker. Pantex 14 even. At ten minutes past noon he returned to Braithwaite and Company. He could barely push his way into the board room. Traders, brokers, onlookers all focused their eyes on the marker boy as he erased the price for Pantex and substituted another: 12⅝.

Jerry Braithwaite saw Ross coming and jumped up from his desk. "Jesus God, Ross! I thought you were my friend! Why didn't you tell me about Haggerty?"

"What about him?"

Braithwaite's jaw sagged. "Well, was it heart or an accident or suicide?"

"Business first, Jerry. I want you to buy in my short on Pantex."

"Very smart, I say." Braithwaite nodded. "Even if it goes lower tomorrow, you've made enough profit for one day."

"About three hundred thousand, I figure. Let's use that to buy twenty-three thousand Pantex."

Braithwaite's face paled, his eyes rolled. "*Buy?*"

"Buy. And use my bonds to pick up sixty thousand more. Make it eighty-three thousand all told."

Braithwaite slumped down into his chair and groped for an order pad. He paused, pencil poised, and stared up at Ross with a pitiful expression. "Ross, just one thing. You *did* say Haggerty was dead, didn't you?"

"Me? How the hell would I know?" Ross cocked his head to one side at Braithwaite. "You know, Jerry, you don't look well. Not well at all."

The following morning's *Chronicle* carried in the financial section a story datelined Tampico, Mexico. G. G. Haggerty, in the best of health and the worst of tempers, attributed the rumors of his death to spite work on the part of an envious competitor. Pantex responded with the leap of a startled deer and closed the trading day at 20⅛—at which price Ross sold his 83,000 shares. He had made a gross profit, before commissions and interest, of $880,000.

Of one thing he was confident. He would not see or hear from G. G. Haggerty for a long time. If ever.

He telephoned Louise to have the cook chill a bottle of champagne for the cocktail hour. Afterwards they would dine at Tait's and go dancing at the Rose Room of the St. Francis. Yes, there was something very special to celebrate; and no, he would not give her a hint. He wanted to see her face when he told her.

Louise was waiting for him in the library. With her, unexpectedly, was her father. This was even better, Ross declared; the Schroders must join them for the evening. In his elation and with the ceremonious opening of the champagne, Ross ignored the fact that Arnold Schroder did not accept the invitation.

"All right, congratulate me." Ross grinned, touching his glass to Louise's.

"I do!" She laughed, eyes dancing with anticipation. "But whatever for?"

"I just made eight hundred and eighty thousand dollars in the stock market. That's what for."

Her reaction was all that he could have wished. First stunned disbelief, then eyes widening with hope that it might be true, then acceptance of the marvel. Her arms went around his neck, her mouth pressed kisses, her words jumbled delight. "How incredible! How wonderful! How perfect! Now we can really buy a summer place down the peninsula!"

"Not yet," he warned. "I'm turning the money over to the company for our drilling program. When we bring in Salt Creek, you can buy the whole damned peninsula!" He winked at Schroder. "Ask me how I made eight hundred and eighty thousand dollars."

"That's why I'm here," Schroder said quietly. "Louise, my dear, if you will excuse us."

"I certainly will not! I won't miss a single word. Go on, darling!"

But Ross wavered. For the first time he was conscious that Arnold Schroder was not sharing in his triumph. "Looks like you've heard something, Arnold. I suppose Montgomery Street has got all sorts of stories—"

"No. Just one."

"What are they saying?"

"That you lied to Henryss Barstow. That you told him G. G. Haggerty had died suddenly."

"I most certainly did not!"

"Then what did happen?"

Ross sketched it quickly, beginning with Haggerty's whispering campaign against Seadon Oil and ending with "All I did was beat Haggerty at his own game. As for Henryss Barstow, he eavesdropped on what I was telling Will Caruth and jumped to conclusions—the conclusions I wanted."

Louise bobbed her head in agreement. "You see, Father? Ross didn't lie; he just . . . he just gave an *impression*. I think it was marvelous!"

It was a mistake. Schroder's face was stony now. "A lot of people lost money on that 'impression,' as you call it. Important people. Henryss Barstow and a good many more. Ross, in all the years we've known each other, I never suspected this side of you. What you did might go in Weston, a lawless frontier town. But in San Francisco we play by different rules. Civilized rules."

"I see." Ross bridled. "I'm some sort of a buccaneer, is that it?"

"If you want a name for it, yes."

Ross saw Louise's alarm, but he was past caring. Her father or no, he had been blooded and would draw blood in return. "So it was civilized rules when the Comstock kings put out newspaper stories that their mine was played out, when they shorted all the stocks and made fortunes, then bought the stocks back for almost nothing and ran more stories about great new ore finds and made still another killing. It was okay to publish outright lies that bankrupted hundreds and sent them to the madhouse. It's High Finance when Old Money does it. Tip your hats, folks, to their grandchildren! So refined, so moral, so respectable!"

By now they were squared off like two pugilists, with Louise a frightened referee shrinking in the corner. "Using the past is no defense for the present," Schroder said stiffly. "There are certain standards of behavior expected of gentlemen. In any case, I've found out what Eakins and Thorsvan wanted to know. You can expect their resignations from Seadon Oil."

"Good! Fine! Great! Tell them from me to go hang their harps from the weeping-willow tree!" Ross swung toward Louise. "Let's hear from you. It's different now, isn't it, Lou? Now that dear Ollie and Holgar are having moral gut aches!"

"Ross, I won't have any part of this."

"Oh, but you can't help yourself. Come on, tell me! Whose side are you on?"

Louise's face became a duplicate of her father's. "Well, I say it was stupid to risk all our savings, all those bonds, in a ridiculous fight with Haggerty. We could have lost everything."

"Really? The first time we met, you were pretty goddamned proud that I had licked Haggerty. Oh yes, I was the bullyboy. But that was when your Old Money friends didn't have to duck the shit."

"*Ross!*"

He wheeled and strode toward the doorway. Then he glared back. "In case you're wondering, dinner and the Rose Room are out."

In the entrance hall, as he slapped on his hat, he heard whisperings above him. Tom and Ginny, wide-eyed, were staring down through the balustrades. Then he heard another sound. The front doorbell. He flung open the door and saw a taxi pulling away from the curb—and before him, Dale Lantry, holding a suitcase.

"Uncle Ross! Uncle Ross!" she wept, thrusting a note into his hand.

Dear Ross and Louise:
Love Dale and keep her safe. Will write often. Always,
Leah.

Chapter 16

THE LIGHTS of Oakland slid past the dining-car window. Outside, at street crossings, Ross could see the headlights of cars waiting behind the crossing guard with his red flag and warning lantern. The Southern Pacific *Owl* was moving slowly; but once beyond the city, it would hurl itself with growing momentum into the eastern hills toward Tracy Junction, then swing south into the San Joaquin Valley. Only two weeks before, Ross thought, two short weeks, Leah had taken another train from that same Oakland depot. But she had gone north toward Carquinez Strait, then through Sacramento, past Dutch Flat, and on across the Sierras and the great plains to the East. Ross had received one postcard from her, mailed in Toronto. The Canadian Red Cross had accepted her, she wrote; she would be trained as a nurse's aide: "That's the bedpan brigade, but at least it will get me overseas. After that, we'll see."

It was hard to think of Leah and bedpans; it was still harder to think of her gone. Through the years, Ross had known comfortably that any time he wished to see her he could swing aboard the California Street cable car, drop off on Nob Hill, and walk north to Russian Hill. In a way, he believed, he missed his sister more than her own daughter did. Dale was wrapped up in the excitement of a new home, queening it over Tom and Ginny, who were awed by their cousin's worldliness. Living with a bohemian mother, she already had one foot into the adult world.

The past two weeks, Ross reflected, had been the most disillusioning period he had ever experienced. Oliver Eakins and Holgar Thorsvan had resigned as directors of Seadon Oil; and when their departure was noted in the press, the Seadon stock began to sink again. The word had gone out along Montgomery Street that Ross Seadon was too aggressive in business; he was dangerous. Jerry Braithwaite avoided him whenever he came in to look at the ticker tape; so did the members at the Bohemian Club.

Even David Marcus, who understood that Ross's fight with G. G. Haggerty was a matter of survival, was disappointed in him. "You remind me of what some French general said of the British charge at Balaclava. 'It is magnificent, but it is not war.' "

And Louise. Most of all Louise. "You see what you've done to us? Everybody else has got their invitations to the Candlelight Ball. I dread to think what sort of Christmas season we're going to have."

By the time Ross ordered dessert and coffee, the train had traversed the Livermore Valley. The man who had sat opposite him during the meal rose and left, and now Ross could see the diner at the next table. She was facing toward him, engrossed with the menu. She was young, perhaps twenty. Neither pretty nor unpretty, hair brown, nose upturned. It was her eyes that suggested to Ross that he had seen her before. The outer corners of the lids tilted upward, giving a slightly Oriental effect. Her dress was primly correct, a gray traveling suit with a lace dickey at the throat. Yes, he was certain he had seen her somewhere. At the moment when he decided that, she looked up from her menu and their eyes collided. She, too, had seen Ross before.

He paid his check and went back to the observation car and found a seat. He asked the steward for a bourbon and Shasta and began leafing absently through the magazines. At least the last two weeks had taught him something about himself, he mused. Something which Louise had summed up only the night before. "Every man in our circle plays billiards, but you play poker with Wil Caruth or some old crony from Weston. Other men go yachting or horseback riding on Sundays; you want to drive around and look at gasoline stations."

It went beyond that, Ross realized. He was not a joiner, a belonger; he was not truly a clubman. He was an oilman. A gambler. His club and his family were the people of Seadon Oil, from office boy to field roustabout. Eleven years in San Francisco, and only now did he see himself as he truly was. Owen had been smarter, more realistic. Thank God it wasn't too late. Tomorrow Ross would be back in Weston. Tim Beakley would be waiting with the drilling crews, and Owen was coming over from Ventura. "I need Salt Creek," he had told Owen. "I've got to prove myself. If I make mistakes, Tim will pull me out."

And Owen had understood. "You raised the money. It's yours to spend."

Ross heard the metallic clang of the vestibule door and saw her enter the observation car. The girl from the diner. There was only one vacant seat, between two flashily dressed men. Salesmen, undoubtedly. She hesitated, then went to the magazine rack, selected one, and sat down. Ross watched the salesmen appraise her, look at her left hand. There was no wedding ring. One of the men leaned toward her and started to talk. Apparently he was telling her a joke, which he laughed at and which she did not. Ross closed his magazine, signaled to the steward, and ordered a bourbon to be delivered to the girl. He watched the steward present the tray to her and nod in his direction. She looked surprised, then inclined her head in thanks.

The men beside her frowned. Why hadn't they thought of the gambit? Somewhere, Ross repeated to himself, he had seen that girl before. Possibly on this train. Yes, that was it. And he suspected why.

He rose and carried his bourbon out onto the observation platform. The wicker chairs were unoccupied, and Ross selected one in the corner nearest the green trailing light. He inhaled the warm air, thick with the sweet scent of clover fields, and judged that the train had entered the upper reaches of the San Joaquin Valley. A moment later the door opened behind him. He fought the impulse to look around.

She stood at the brass railing sipping her drink and watching the twin ribbons of steel spin out behind the platform. Ross waited a moment, then got up and moved to the railing beside her. "Ever see this country in daylight?" he half shouted over the clack of the wheels. She shook her head, without looking at him.

They were silent awhile. The acrid smoke from the locomotive streamed past overhead, reflecting green and red as it passed the trailing lights on either side of the platform. "Going all the way to Los Angeles?" Ross shouted. She nodded. "I've seen you on this train before." No response. "Or was it on the Coast Route? On the *Lark?*" She glanced at him quickly, understanding his questions. She knew that he knew. She lifted her glass, drained it, and threw it over the railing. Ross, at first startled by her gesture, arced his own glass into the night. "I'm tired of shouting," he said. "Let's go back to my room."

She followed him docilely through the observation car, past the stares of envious eyes. She waited for him to open the vestibule doors, then swayed behind him along the aisles of curtained berths until, in midtrain, they reached his stateroom at the end of the car. As they entered, they saw the porter had already made up the berth. The window was open, but the blind was pulled down and clattered in the wind. The girl surveyed the room, impressed by its size, the walnut paneling, the dressing mirror, the couchette, the private lavatory.

Almost immediately there was a knock on the door, as Ross had anticipated. He opened the door and saw the white jacket, the porter's black face smiling with elaborate innocence.

"You getting off at Weston, suh?" Eyes skirted Ross's shoulder to the girl seated on the edge of the berth.

Ross's wallet was already out. "Yes. Wake me in plenty of time."

"Sure will, boss. Sleep well, suh."

Ross locked the door, extracted several more bills from his wallet, and held them out to the girl. "Will this do?" She took the money, counted it, nodded, and stuffed it into her handbag.

"When you get to Los Angeles, what will you do?"

"Some shopping. See a picture show."

"And take the northbound train tomorrow night?"

"The *Owl* or the *Lark*."

"And in San Francisco?"

"Some shopping. See a picture show."

"What's your name?"

"June. And yours?"

"Benjamin Franklin."

She smiled for the first time. "I thought I'd seen you in some history book." Her eyes slid toward Ross's valise and suitcase with the gilt initials R. S.

"Tell me something," Ross resumed. "You're a good-looking girl. Why do you do this?"

"To make money. Why do you?"

"To forget money."

"Then you must have an awful lot."

"Never enough."

It had been a long time since a strange woman had undressed for Ross, and he watched with an anxious intensity. First the jacket, then the shirtwaist, then the camisole, then the petticoat, then the corset, then the shoes, then the stockings. It was a good body, a fine body, really a bargain.

He undressed and slid between the sheets beside her. He felt happy, happier, he thought, than in many a year. "So your name is June, like in the poem."

226

"What poem?"

It was a joke from his college days, which he had never found the right occasion to use. Until now.

"I don't remember it all. Just the lines that apply: 'And what is so rare as a night in June?/Then, if ever, come perfect lays.'"

She snickered. "You're funny, Mr. Franklin."

"What's with you and Louise?" Owen asked, that first morning in Weston.

"What's with me and San Francisco?" Ross replied, and explained with the minimum of detail. "But everything will work out," he concluded. "I just need a change of scene for a while."

That afternoon he and Owen and Tim Beakley drove the eighteen miles of dirt road and the four miles across open range to Salt Creek. In spite of its name, there was no water except during the winter rains; the balance of the year it was a dry gully wandering through flat scrubland where small herds of cattle disputed the forage with the native elk.

"I still say it's ridiculous to sink three wildcats at once," Owen said, surveying the arid landscape. "It just means three chances to bring in dusters."

"That's the oil game," Ross said. "The main thing is we'll hold on to the landowners. When they see our rigs working, they'll renew those leases."

Owen turned to Beakley. "Remember, it's going to be deep stuff, so don't spud in just anywhere; drill the sandblows first."

"Damn it, stop backseat driving," Ross snapped. "This is my baby."

It had been understood between them that Ross would spend some weeks, perhaps months, in Weston and would conduct company business from the local office. Knowing this, Owen had brought Hop Gee and Ah Sing from Alto Valle—where they had been part of Tana's staff for the past several years—to reopen the old house on Central Avenue. For Ross it was a return to the carefree days of his youth.

At the office the work went smoothly, and at Salt Creek it was as stimulating as the early days of the Haber River field.

All three wildcat wells were spudded in on the same day, and Ross saw to it that the landowners were on hand to witness it. After that it was simply a matter of fountain pens squiggling signatures to the new leases. Weston's faith in Seadon Oil mounted, and so did the buy orders for its stock. "They're onto something big, those Seadon boys" was the word in the oil offices and saloons along Central Avenue.

Perhaps it was no coincidence, Ross thought, that he began to get regular telephone calls from Louise. She missed him; the children were fine; there was a letter from Leah. Ross asked Louise to forward it to him. Accompanying the letter was a snapshot of Leah in a khaki Red Cross uniform, looking trim and purposeful. Her training was almost completed, she wrote; she would be sailing soon for England. She gave a post-box number in Canada where Ross and Owen could write to her.

Late one night, almost two in the morning, Ross was awakened by the telephone. It was Louise. She was at the Weston railroad depot with the children; could Ross pick them up? "I wanted it to be a surprise," she said on the drive to the house. "The children have been nagging me for weeks. 'When is Daddy coming home?' So with school vacation, I thought, Why not? Besides, it's time we got all this silliness behind us." She did not need to define the "silliness"; Ross understood and agreed. They distributed Tom and Ginny and Dale in the various bedrooms and then went to their own. Louise put on a new negligee, French and expensive, and a new perfume, French and expensive, and boldly led Ross to bed.

They were pleasant days. The old house once more echoed with children's voices; there was rummaging in the attic and trooping about in bits of Cathlin's finery and Val's old hats; Hop Gee carved cricket cages for the girls, and Ah Sing built a Chinese war kite for Tom. One day Ross rented a touring car and drove his family out to Salt Creek to see the new wells. The temperature was over one hundred, but Louise gallantly insisted she preferred it to the cold and dampness of San Francisco. The wells were "really very exciting"; Weston, which she had seen only once before, during her first year of marriage (and had disliked intensely), was a "lovely little town." She praised Ah Sing's cooking and ate pigs' knuckles without a wince.

Her appreciation of everything began to grate on Ross like the steady dripping of a faucet. "Don't lay it on so thick, Lou," he said one night at dinner. "I'd feel more comfortable if you'd hate something."

"But I don't. Really, I don't." She smiled around the table at the three children. "You know, this is what we should do back home. All eat dinner together. It makes us a closer family." There were cries of agreement and clapping, until Louise added, "The children are old enough. We don't need Maggie any more." Then there were groans.

On the final night in Weston, when they were in bed, Louise said, "Father wants you to know he's sorry for the things he said. If you'd like, he'll be glad to go on your board of directors."

Ross raised up on one elbow. "Did he volunteer this, or did you ask him to?"

"I asked him. I told him nobody can go through life without making mistakes. You made a bad one, and we did worse in not standing by you."

Ross bent down and kissed her. "Tell Arnold you're all the support I need."

He returned to San Francisco with his family. As they got off the *Owl* at the Oakland station and Louise and the children waited for him to point out their luggage to the redcap, a voice behind him sang out, "Well, *hello*, Mr. Franklin!" For an instant he did not connect the greeting with himself. When he did, June was already swinging jauntily down the platform. A close thing, Ross thought with relief. And then he saw Louise's face.

For a day or so he half expected her to bring up the subject of the girl; when she did not, and her attitude remained easy and serene, he convinced himself that his wife's glare at the girl had been no more than the reaction of a respectable woman at the sight of a prostitute. Besides, June had said "Mr. Franklin"; she might have been hailing some other man at the station. And so he dismissed the subject.

A subtle change had taken place in San Francisco during Ross's absence. For generations the city had been like a beautiful woman who spent her days admiring herself in the mirror; now it was beginning to look from its windows at the great world beyond the Sierras. There was a martial spirit, evidenced by American flags fluttering above doorways and on rooftops; newspaper editorials and cartoons denounced Germany for its submarine warfare and praised President Wilson for his protests against it. Yet, at the same time, there was a yearning for peace, again mirrored in the newspapers, which approved Wilson's campaign slogan for the coming Presidential election. "He kept us out of war" appealed to the voters with its implied promise of no involvement in Europe, and irritated those who had already committed themselves. In Leah's first letter from London she wrote, "We've got to get into this, Ross. Civilization is at stake. Only cowards will turn their backs on the greatest adventure in history." Ross suspected that the "adventure" had a personal meaning for Leah. She enclosed a snapshot of a gray-haired man in officer's uniform and scribbled on the back, "His name is Scott Marston. Captain, Medical Corps."

In another letter to Owen, she sent a photograph of Scott and herself standing on Waterloo Bridge. "We didn't meet over a bedpan," she wrote. "I've been transferred to Administration, which means filing things. I'm pestering Scott for one more transfer, the ambulance service."

"I know Owen said it would be deep stuff. But how deep is deep?" Tim Beakley brooded when Ross returned to Weston. "All three holes are down two thousand feet and *nothing*."

"And the deeper we go, the more it costs," Ross agreed. "Okay, let's cut our losses. Pull the rigs and try new locations."

This was Election Day, 1916. The following morning the *Weston Daily* (graduated from a weekly) ran banner headlines:

REPUBLICANS WIN
CHARLES EVANS HUGHES NEXT PRESIDENT
WILSON LOSES IN CLOSE CONTEST

But the following morning the newspaper reported that the vote tally of California was incomplete and the outcome in doubt. On the third day after the election the newspaper carried the official result:

CALIFORNIA ELECTS WILSON BY 3773 VOTES
PEACE PLATFORM WINS STATE

Somewhere in France
January 26, 1917

Dearest Ross:

Your letter just reached me. I'm saddened about Ruth Marcus and will write my sympathy to Dave. I know what he's been through, for I see it here every day.

Scott and I are assigned to the same Base Hospital. On our way here we got to see Paris together. Even with the war, the City is more beautiful than anything I had dreamed.

You asked me to tell you what my life is like. I can't. The Censor would be unhappy. But remember that morning when you found me in that streetcar on Market Street —and later in Golden Gate Park when Dale was born with all those people on the grass? But this time I'm not frightened. This time I can help those who are. Yes, your kid sister has finally found herself. To think of all those wasted years and all those futile men I turkey-trotted after!

Please, please, please, send me a snapshot of Dale, and tell her I love her. As I do you and Owen.

Leah.

P.S. How are things at Salt Creek?

They were dismal. By the time Ross read Leah's letter he had abandoned the second group of wells and grimly embarked on yet another three, like a gambler at the crap table determined to throw the dice again and again until he made his point.

In February Germany announced "unrestricted" submarine warfare, and President Wilson broke off diplomatic relations. In March the U-boats sank three American ships, and Wilson called a special session of Congress. "The world must be made safe for democracy," he said, and Congress agreed. On April 6 the United States entered the war.

The next week Owen arrived from Alto Valle. "I know we're both over military age," he said to Ross, "but we can still do our part. A barrel of oil is as necessary as an artillery shell. We've got to increase production."

Ross nodded agreement. "Then give me a hand out at Salt Creek."

"Not on your life. I want your crews over in Ventura. From now on we drill the sure stuff. No more farting around after maybes."

"Damn it, Owen, you're the one who was so hot on Salt Creek!"

"So I was wrong. I'm not the all-knowing God. I want those drilling crews."

"Okay. I'll give you one of them."

"All!"

In the end they compromised. Salt Creek would continue with a single crew overseen by Tim Beakley, and Ross would return to the San Francisco office; the old home in Weston would be closed again and Hop Gee and Ah Sing would go back to serve Tana and Owen at Rancho El Encanto. Secretly, Ross was glad; he could devote himself to the business he knew best. He was appointed to the government's War Industries Board and worked on the allocation of California's oil production. The war effort involved everyone he knew. Arnold Schroder's steel mill turned out shell casings and turbines for the Liberty freighters being built across the bay; Jerry Braithwaite and Dave Marcus led Liberty Loan drives; Louise and her friends rolled bandages and served coffee and doughnuts to the draftees boarding the troop trains decorated with banners and chalked bravado: ALL ABOARD FOR BERLIN! KAISER BILL HERE WE COME!

By the spring of 1918 the war had lost its glamour. Russia had surrendered to the Germans, the First British Army had been crushed, and Washington issued a second draft call. By summer the lights of Market Street were dimmed to save energy, and there were no motorcars on gasless Sundays. People were learning to pronounce Château-Thierry, and black wreaths were appearing on doors and in windows. Somewhere in France Leah wrote a note that touched Ross by its brevity.

> Dear Ross:
> Scott is dead. His ambulance was going up to the lines when a shell hit.
> I'm working in a forward unit now, wherever we can set up—a farmhouse, a church, a school. I miss you. Love.
> Leah
> P.S. We were to be married next month.

One day in the fall Ross finally faced the reality of Salt Creek. Tim Beakley had drilled five consecutive dry holes in addition to Ross's own nine. "There's no point going on," he told Wil Caruth. "All I've done is burn up a half million dollars and make a fool of myself in front of everybody. And to cap it all, I proved to G. G. Haggerty, without his spending a penny, that Salt Creek is worthless. God, how he must be laughing!"

"Then you want to quitclaim the leases back to the landowners?" Caruth asked.

"Today. Before I leave the office. After that I may go out and get drunk."

But he didn't. He went directly home, intending a quiet dinner with Louise. As he closed the front door, he heard a child's scream, then the slam of a door upstairs and footsteps running. He started up the staircase and met Maggie hurrying down.

"Don't, Mr. Seadon! Please don't!" Her words, her pale face, then a second scream sped him up the remaining stairs and along the hallway to Dale's room. He flung open the door. Dale was bent across Louise's lap, struggling and shrieking as a hairbrush came down on her bare buttocks.

"Louise! Stop it!"

She looked around, face flushed, eyes ugly. "She's going to the convent! I won't have a twelve-year-old whore in my house!"

The hairbrush raised again and Ross seized it. Dale flung herself from Louise's lap and threw her arms around Ross's hips, weeping and trembling.

"What in God's name do you think you're doing?" Ross shouted.

"Look at her!"

For the first time Ross saw that Dale was wearing a night-dress, and there were circles of rouge on her cheeks.

"Show him!" Louise hissed. "Show him what you did!"

"No! I was just pretending for Tom and Ginny!"

"All right, *I'll* show him. See this!" She pointed to a cube of incense smoking in a dish on the nightstand. "And this!" She held up a brandy glass, half filled. "And this!" She thrust a cigarette between her lips and flung herself onto the bed. "This is what our children saw!" Cigarette in mouth, brandy glass raised, Louise attempted the smoldering expression of a courtesan. The effect was less seductive than comical.

"For God's sake, Lou, have some sense of proportion. Dale was just playing grownup."

"Was she? And where did she get those ideas? Playing the harlot like her mother!" She saw the fire in Ross's eyes and cried, "Yes! I said harlot!"

Ross's hand swung and Louise's head snapped to one side. "That's right, defend her!" she shrieked. "The two of you are alike! Leah with her fancy men, and you with your little sluts on the train! And God knows where else!"

He seized her shoulders and shook her. Thank God Dale had

escaped from the room and was, he hoped, out of earshot. "Get hold of yourself. So there was a girl on the train. How can you be jealous of a woman who sells her body? How can you take it out on a child?"

"Because I can't stand any more! Oh, God! God! God! All the years Leah disgraced us before my friends, all the smirks I had to endure! And now you and your lechery! It's a wonder you haven't infected me with some disease. The Seadons are rotten, all of them! Rotten!"

An hour later Ross checked in at the St. Francis Hotel and ate dinner in his room. He could taste nothing; he could feel nothing. It had all happened with the speed of a tornado, coming out of nowhere, without warning, destroying everything.

In the evening he left the hotel and crossed Powell Street to Union Square. He wandered the gravel paths and shivered in the evening chill. He thought about telephoning Louise, then abandoned the idea. He could not think what to say to her, and he did not want to hear more of her fury. He left the square and walked up the east side of Powell Street. He passed a cable car rattling its way down the hill; he passed newsboys shouting the war news, a blind fiddler scraping his bow. He heard none of them. He had made a mistake, he told himself, in not taking Dale with him; he could not abandon the child in that house of hate. He must go back and bring Dale to the St. Francis. He glanced around, hoping to see a taxi. There was none. Then he remembered the taxi stand outside the St. Francis; he would cross to the opposite side of Powell and thence down to the hotel. As he stepped off the curb, he did not hear someone shout "*Runaway!*" He did not hear the woman scream. He did not see the automobile plunging downhill directly toward him.

Chapter 17

THE HOSPITAL waiting room and the corridors were quiet; the last visitors had left hours ago; now there was only the waiting. Arnold Schroder sat holding his daughter's hand and listened to her disjointed talk. The rain outside. How she had felt when the police had telephoned her. What she had told Owen when she telephoned him at Alto Valle. He thought there was time for him and Tana to catch the northbound *Lark* in Santa Barbara. On and on she talked. The years she and Ross had shared . . . her pride in the man who had seemed afraid of nothing . . . the outing they had planned for that weekend. Thank God her mother was staying with the children that night. Tom and Ginny really did not suspect what had happened, did they? Only Dale. In some way she seemed closer to Ross than his own children.

Louise would lapse into silence, then think of some incident that had happened years before: what Ross had said, what she had said. She mesmerized herself with trivia in order to blot out the memory of the quarrel of a few hours before. She wished that she could confess it to a priest. No, she must never tell anyone. Suppose Ross had been so upset over her outburst that he had walked blindly in front of that motorcar? Suppose he died? Or suppose he lived but his brain was permanently damaged? She shivered. How could she ever atone?

A surgeon came from one of the operating rooms, the one where they had taken the other pedestrian who had been hit by the motorcar. The surgeon shook his head. The man had died.

Shortly before midnight another surgeon appeared, the one who had been operating on Ross. It was over, he said; he had cut an opening into Ross's skull and had relieved the pressure on the brain. How long he would remain in a coma could not be estimated, nor could the final outcome be predicted.

Arnold Schroder took his daughter home, where she slept fitfully and had nightmares. By dawn she was up and dressed and telephoning the hospital. Ross's nurse said he was still in coma but "holding his own." She would not return to the hospital, Louise decided, until Owen and Tana had time to get from the depot. They were there in the waiting room when she arrived. Tana embraced her tearfully and said she had prayed all night for Ross. Louise stared guiltily at the tiny figure clutching her rosary; her anguish for Ross seemed more than her own.

Tana saw that Louise was dry-eyed. "My dear, you must cry. It is required."

"Why? Tears can't change things."

Tana looked surprised. "But they are necessary. Tears are the measure of our love."

She felt the reproach in Tana's words. It was easy for her to talk. She knew nothing of what had passed between Ross and herself. If she told Tana—which was unthinkable—she would not have believed her; it would be beyond her. Tana was too secure in her marriage, completed in her husband and her children.

By nightfall Louise reversed herself. She must talk, she must unburden to someone who would be on her side. Her parents. But when she relived for them her scene with Ross, Mrs. Schroder was puzzled. "You've never been given to hysteria, my dear. Ross is a man, with a man's weaknesses; but surely your marriage can't come apart over trifles."

Mr. Schroder was more pointed. "Everything you've told us, hon, is just trying to rationalize the irrational. You must have acted out of fear. But fear of what?"

She thought about it, and then suddenly the answer came to her. "I had one hold on him. Social position, our circle of friends. Those things mattered to Ross in the beginning. Until that fight with Haggerty. He threw over everything to win, and when he did, he was free of us. Then and there I lost him."

Her father snorted. "Nonsense! Bushwah! I never thought a daughter of mine would throw in the towel before the first bell. You can get him back, if you want to. The question is, Do you?"

"Yes," she said. "I do."

The next morning she returned to the hospital. Owen and Tana were in the waiting room again. One of the doctors, Owen said, reported that Ross had come out of coma. His mind was confused, but that was to be expected. Perhaps Louise could see him later that day, after the doctors had completed some tests.

While Owen was talking, a redhaired woman hurried into the waiting room. Owen saw her and went toward her. He put his arms around her and kissed her cheek. Something he said caused her to dab her eyes and exclaim, "Oh, thank God!"

"Who is that woman?" Louise murmured to Tana, who was watching intently.

"I have not met her," Tana whispered, "but she has red hair, so she must be the one Owen calls Liz Barnard. She used to live in Weston. An old friend."

Not old, Louise thought. Nor did she wear a wedding ring.

Louise remembered vaguely Ross mentioning her name. Some business connection. But business connections do not burst into tears and thank God.

Owen brought Liz over and introduced her. They shook hands and Liz said, "I just got off the *Owl*. I read about Ross in the papers."

Louise stiffened. There was no mention of Ross in the morning's papers; that had been the day before. "Where did you read it?"

"The *Los Angeles Times*." Liz flushed, realizing the implication. "I was coming to San Francisco anyway. On business. So I thought I would stop by."

It was a lame recovery which deceived no one. By that evening Louise had put flesh upon the skeleton of her suspicions. Ross's obsession with Salt Creek and his stays in Weston were an excuse to be with Liz Barnard. She was the woman he had loved before Louise, and now again. Owen knew. Tana knew. Everyone knew except Louise. In her fevered imagination she pictured her husband and his paramour writhing in sexual ecstasy, and found justification for everything that she had shrieked at Ross. It would be better if he had been killed and her humiliation ended. No, she dared not think such a thing. It was wicked; it was a sin, a matter for confession. But still . . .

The doctors permitted her to see Ross the following day. His head was heavily bandaged, his broken arm in a sling, his waist encased in a plaster cast. He was in a great deal of pain, and his mind was unclear; he would not understand what she intended to say. She put it off from day to day and spent her time at the hospital in polite conversation with Ross's visitors. David Marcus, Wil Caruth, Tim Beakley.

One day she saw Owen talking earnestly to Liz Barnard, who was still in town. Louise watched from a distance as Owen gestured and Liz listened intently. He scribbled notes on an envelope, which Liz tucked into her handbag. What was going on? Louise wondered, and then decided she did not care.

During the second week in the hospital, Ross himself brought up the subject of their marriage. He led into it so obliquely that Louise was caught unawares.

"Have you put Dale in the convent?"

"Not yet."

"You won't have to. I've talked to Owen. He and Tana will take her until Leah gets back."

"I wish them luck."

"At least it's a temporary solution. But for you and me, I'm afraid there is none. It's over, isn't it?"

She sat there looking at him, only inches away and yet uncounted miles. "Yes, it's over."

"It's hell being Catholic."

"Not for me," she said. "If you mean divorce, that's impossible of course."

"Then a legal separation?"

"No. I care about appearances, even if you don't. Eventually it will come out, but right now I'm not ready for it."

"What about the kids?"

"You can see them whenever you wish. If you can find the time."

"I'll make time. I want to see they get the proper education. Finishing school for Ginny, probably Eastern, then some good college. Prep school for Tom, then Stanford. After that he'll go into the oil business with me. Naturally I'll take care of all your living expenses—within reason. If you go in for something really extravagant, I'll expect you to look to your father."

She felt cheated. Ross had taken over, had planned everything, and the scene which she had detailed so carefully in her mind, the cutting remarks she had rehearsed, all were pointless now.

"Someday," he went on, "you'll meet another man. When you do, you may change your mind about divorce."

"I won't. Marriage is a holy sacrament, something which you seem to have overlooked with all your adulteries." There. At least she had scored that much. But he merely smiled quietly; nothing she could say would matter any more. She rose from her chair, went to the door, and looked back. "It's hard to believe all I've ever been in your life is an episode, something enclosed in parentheses."

"If so," he replied, "a damned fine-looking one."

In the hall outside, the tears came at last.

Ross was discharged from the hospital at the height of the great influenza epidemic. At first it had been greeted lightly and people laughed at the popular jingle "I had a little bird named Enza. I opened the window and in-flu-enza!"

But by October, when Owen came to San Francisco to accompany Ross to Alto Valle for his recuperation, the cautious were going to work with gauze masks over their mouths; theaters were closed and public gatherings shunned. Twenty-five million Americans were ill, one half million were to die. One of them was Ross's secretary, Hattie MacFarland.

For the first few days at Rancho El Encanto, Ross did little more than move from his bed to the sitting-room couch or out to the wide veranda for an hour of sunshine. He was an irritable invalid; he cursed the sling around his broken arm, the taping over his ribs, the dressing on the side of his skull which Tana changed daily. He fretted when Wil Caruth, temporarily in charge of San Francisco operations, failed to report on affairs, and resented it when he did. Then gradually he began to accept the idleness, to enjoy it, to savor the slow passage of the hours, free of problems and decisions.

He discovered it was pleasant to be surrounded by children, and he realized sadly how little time he had devoted to his own son and daughter. Owen's son Eugene was thirteen. He was quiet and thoughtful, with Owen's features. Carla, twelve, was blessed with her mother's eyes and oval face. Angela, ten and pudgy, was the family cut-up. Leah's daughter Dale was Ross's favorite and knew it; with her cousins she might sulk, but in his presence she was a shooting star of gaiety. Already she showed intimations of beauty, and more than intimations of possessiveness. "Tío Ross," she would say, borrowing her cousins'

Spanish, "tell us a story about Grandpa Val," and she would arrange the other children in a semicircle on the floor facing Ross.

Sometimes Tana would join the listeners and prompt Ross to retell the story of the San Francisco earthquake, which she called "the day the earth sighed." She was little changed from the girl Ross had met fifteen years before: still slim and smooth of face, her ability on a horse not lessened by the years. Yet there was a subtle difference. In her youth she had been a rebel against the Latin strictness of her parents; now as a mother herself, she was as firm as Doña Felipa. She reprimanded her children in Spanish and praised them sparingly in English.

By the second week in November it was clear that the war was almost over. Ross followed the reports in the *San Francisco Chronicle*, delivered by mail to Rancho El Encanto: the surrender of the Austro-Hungarian armies, the Kaiser's abdication, revolution in Berlin, the Allied armies advancing everywhere. At two o'clock in the morning of November 11 the telephone rang. Louise, in San Francisco, asked for Ross. "Germany has surrendered!" she cried. "Church bells are ringing and sirens blowing! There are bonfires on Twin Peaks and Telegraph Hill! I wish you could see it."

"So do I," Ross said. "How are you, Lou?"

"Fine. Just fine."

"And the kids?"

"Right now, screaming with excitement. And you?"

"Almost back to normal. . . . Well, thanks for calling, Lou."

The past did not die easily, he thought. For either of them.

Several days later Ross had his first serious business talk with Owen since he had arrived at El Encanto. Seadon Oil, he said, should move its headquarters from San Francisco to Los Angeles. Southern California was enjoying more than a war boom; its industry had grown to twice that of the northern part of the state. Los Angeles owned more motorcars than any other American city and consumed more gasoline. And there was the infant aircraft industry. Glenn Martin had pioneered it by building planes in an abandoned church in Santa Ana ,in 1909; now Ryan was turning them out in San Diego and the Lockheed brothers in Santa Barbara. "We've got to go where the market is," Ross concluded. "Who knows? Maybe we'll even do some wildcatting down there. So what do you say?"

"Consider it done." Owen grinned.

One day a telegram came from Toronto.

AM CIVILIAN AGAIN   STOP   PLAN WEEK IN SAN FRANCISCO
TO BUY WARDROBE   STOP   AM I WELCOME AT EL ENCANTO
LOVE   LEAH

Tana arranged a special dinner for her arrival, and that night the three Seadons sat at the same table for the first time in as many years. Everyone talked at once, the children babbling of the presents Leah had brought, their elders firing questions about London and Paris and carefully avoiding reference to Dr. Scott Marston or Leah's experiences behind the lines. They must have been shattering, Ross thought, noting the tremble in her fingers, the cigarettes she lighted one after another, and her frightened start when Ah Sing dropped a pot in the kitchen. Now and then during the conversation she would fall silent and lean over to kiss Dale beside her or to pat Hop Gee's hand when he served her.

Afterward, when the children were coaxed to the playroom, they gathered in the sitting room before the log fire. The talk drifted from Ross's accident and his separation from Louise (the cause not defined) to the fiasco of Salt Creek and plans for the Los Angeles headquarters. Leah listened absently, as if there was something on her mind. Then during a lull, it came out with a rush: "I think I should tell you, I've left the Church."

Ross was the first to react. "Why?"

"It happened to me in France. Every death was meaningless. Both sides prayed to the same God for victory, they called out to the same Our Father Who Art in Heaven . . ." She broke off with a shrug. "Pointless, all so pointless."

"I can understand your mood, Sis," Owen said. "But it will pass. You're just suffering from emotional shell shock."

"Whatever. I *have* left the Church."

Tana shook her head agitatedly. "No. You *think* you've left the Church, but the Holy Church will not leave you. Never! *No puede ser!*"

"We'll see. I wanted you to know how I feel, because I'm marrying outside the Church." There was a stir, and she added, "You'll say I'm living in sin; but don't forget Ma did, too, until Dad finally took instruction." She saw the frowns and turned defiantly to Tana. "Wouldn't you have married Owen without the Church's sacraments?"

"Not then. No." Tana looked shyly at her husband. "But now, if I thought there was no other way . . ."

"Oh, the hell with all this theory," Ross burst out impatiently. "We're yammering about everything except who's the man."

Leah relaxed with a smile. "Well, I didn't spend all my time in San Francisco buying dresses. I saw quite a bit of Dave Marcus."

Her brothers gave a simultaneous whoop, then they were hugging and kissing her and tumbling out their reactions. Dave Marcus, at last, after all these years. Both married to different mates, both bereaved, yet finally finding each other.

"What do you mean you don't believe in God?" Ross said. "You'll be marrying in front of a rabbi."

"No, I won't. Dave understands how I feel. His parents are dead and his sisters don't care, so it'll be before a judge."

Exactly as it had been with Cathlin and Val, Ross thought. The generations repeating themselves. "Anyway, it's absolutely great," he said aloud. "I was afraid maybe you'd never forget Scott."

"I never will. I love Dave because he's so much like Scott."

She shrugged defensively. "Maybe you think that's unhealthy. Then let it be. Time will tell."

Ross enjoyed working early at the office on Saturday mornings, before the usual start of business. At 7 o'clock there was little street traffic and he could drive in five minutes from his apartment near Westlake Park to downtown Los Angeles; and at that hour there were no secretaries, no telephone calls, to interrupt his thoughts. But on this particular early morning, there *was* a telephone call. At first Ross did not recognize Owen's voice, for he was speaking barely above a whisper.

"I'm at a garage on the West Side, Ross. It's a party line and I don't know who may be listening in, so don't ask questions. Just meet me at Salt Creek."

"*Salt Creek?*" The name caused a twinge in Ross's stomach. "What the hell for?"

"I said no questions. Just meet me as soon as possible."

It was an exhausting six-hour drive in the big open touring car. First through the San Fernando Valley, then the steep grades and hairpin turns of the Ridge Route over the Tehachapi Mountains, followed by the long boring straightaway to Weston and then the side road toward Salt Creek. How he hated that last stretch, Ross thought to himself, the reminder of all those futile trips he had made in years past. What was it for this time? Had some other oil company drilled and found oil? No, if it were that, Owen would not have been so guarded over the telephone. But then what?

He judged he was about fifteen minutes from Salt Creek when he saw a Model T Ford pulled to the side of the asphalt. A woman was standing beside the car and waving at him. Ross had braked to a stop before they recognized each other.

"*Liz!* For God's sake!"

"Ross! Oh, you're an angel of mercy!" She climbed in beside him and kissed his cheek. "I ran out of gas, and just about hope. I must look an awful mess."

She did. Face heat-flushed, red hair hanging in damp strings, perspiration trickling down her neck.

"What in God's name are you doing out in this hell's half-acre?" Ross demanded.

"Getting my brains fried, mostly. Your brother phoned me in Hollywood and told me to get up to Salt Creek."

"Huh! He told me the same thing. But what's Salt Creek mean to you?"

"An oil well, I hope." She paused to mop her brow with a handkerchief, then said, "Shall I tell it to you from the beginning?"

"No. I prefer mysteries," he said grumpily and put the car into gear.

"There's no mystery. Remember when you had your accident last year and I came to see you in the hospital?"

"Sure."

"Well, one of the times at the hospital I happened to tell Owen I was worried about money, because my old Mirage Springs lease was pumping out. I asked Owen if he had an idea where I could pick up another lease that might turn into something good. Owen told me about Salt Creek."

"Did he tell you I'd drilled fourteen dusters?"

"He did. Owen said he still had faith in it, but he couldn't justify spending any more money on land rentals or wildcats. He said if I was willing to gamble a little money—"

Ross interrupted with a snort. "A little! Salt Creek swallowed over a half million dollars!"

"It's only cost me thirty-eight hundred and forty."

"To do what?"

"To buy twelve hundred and eighty acres at three dollars an acre. Owen told me some of the landowners had mortgaged their land to the Bank of Weston, planning to pay off when you brought in your wells. And when you didn't, the bank foreclosed. Owen said maybe the bank would be glad to get the land off their hands. That's the way it worked out."

Ross glowered through the insect-spattered windshield. He could guess the rest. "So Owen's been drilling for you."

"In spare time. We worked out a deal. I was to give your

company a lease and he'd send over a crew from Weston whenever it was between jobs. That's the way it's been, three or four days' drilling every now and then for the last six months." She paused and looked anxiously at Ross. "He *has* found something, hasn't he?"

"Well, I don't think he asked us up here for the scenery. But damn him, why didn't he tell me from the start?"

Liz crinkled her eyes. "Haven't you heard of the Seadon pride? If he drilled a dry hole himself, you wouldn't ever hear about it."

"Well, at least *you* could have told me."

"And just how often have I seen you?"

"Not since the hospital," Ross reflected.

"Oh, I hope Owen's done it, really done it," Liz went on wistfully. "If I can just be sure of three hundred dollars a month, that's all I ask."

"You're that short?"

She nodded. "I've got a boy to raise, remember. Philip will be going to college in another couple of years. I wish I could have brought him along today, but he's off on a weekend camping trip with some of his high school class. Did I tell you he's an Eagle Scout?"

Ross shook his head vaguely, thinking of other things. Despite Liz Barnard's needs, he did not relish the thought that Owen might have succeeded where he himself had failed. If there was an oil strike, let it be small.

The touring car swung off the paved road and began to cut across the open range toward Salt Creek. Finally the wooden derrick came into sight, and Ross recognized it as the abandoned rig at the very last well he had drilled. All that had been done was to return the boiler and engine and water tanks and put a new tarpaper roof on the bunkhouse.

Ross stopped the car, and he and Liz trudged toward the drilling platform, where several tool pushers were fastening an extra length of drill stem into place. Owen, dressed in khaki trousers and shirt and laced boots, was seated cross-legged on the edge of the platform, playing a game of solitaire. He looked up and nodded casually toward Ross and Liz. "Did she tell you?"

"She did. It's nice to be let in on your little operation," Ross said coolly. He glanced around at the familiar scene; toolies lowering drill, the foreman grunting orders, the engineer smoking a corncob as he lounged against the bull wheel. He noted with satisfaction that a sump had not been dug for possible oil; there was no smell of crude, nothing to promise more than another duster. "What's so damned exciting?"

Owen flipped over a playing card and assigned it to its proper place. "I read over all your logs. The deepest hole you dug was this one, twenty-six hundred feet. Not much deeper than a farm outhouse."

Liz tittered nervously at the comparison and Ross scowled. "Where are you now?"

"Thirty-four hundred."

"And?"

"Take a look at the bailer." Owen nodded toward the metal pail alongside the walking beam.

Ross dug his fingers into the sand-filled bailer and brought up a handful; he squeezed it into a gray ball and sniffed it. Then he carried it back to Liz and she smelled it. "Thank God!" She laughed.

"Don't get your hopes up too much," Owen warned, but now there was a twinkle in his eyes. "So far we've only got a trace, but maybe when we get down a few feet more . . ." He looked toward the foreman. "You ready, Mike?"

"Ready!"

The foreman signaled to the engineer, the great bull wheel began to revolve, the walking beam rose and fell. . . . An hour passed. Then two. The sun was sinking toward the western hills. "I hope we find something before dark," Owen said.

"Just find it," Liz said.

"Hell, yes." Ross nodded. "For that we'll stay all night."

The drill stem began to vibrate. "Damn, we're back into

rock." The foreman glowered. The vibration increased and the drill stem recoiled from the barrier far below.

"Shit!" Owen muttered. "I thought from the bailer we were right over it. Must have been just a pocket."

Another hour. The sun was chinning itself against the distant hills. Owen frowned at the foreman. "Mike, do you smell something?"

Mike moved to the collar of the drill hole and put his head down. "Gas!"

"How much?"

"Plenty! Cut the smoking, boys!"

"I don't like it," Owen muttered to Ross. "We got to keep the boiler lighted to drill, but if we get too much gas up here..."

He stopped in midsentence. The drill stem was recoiling again. Each time before, the iron stem had moved upward only three or four inches, then settled back. Now it was mounting higher and higher, coming up with an ugly metallic hum. Owen, Ross, and the foreman gazed at it like men in a trance. The platform underfoot began to shudder, the timbers overhead strained and groaned. The drill stem was still rising, coming fast now, with a baleful screech. Then there was an ominous rumble below.

Owen flung up his arms and bawled, *"Let's go! Run for it!"*

It was needless advice. The drilling crew was already tumbling from the platform. The Seadons caught Liz, jumped, and raced across the work area to the open range. When they stopped to look back, the drill stem had shot to the top of the derrick, collided with the crown block, smashed it, and was rocketing upward into the sky. Then, with a deafening roar, all thirty-four hundred feet of drill iron began to follow.

"Down!" Ross yelled, recognizing the danger. They threw themselves flat on the earth and covered their heads with their hands. They could hear the drill stem exploding into the sky, cracking apart, and whistling downward in a deadly hail. After the drill came thirty-four hundred feet of iron casing—soaring, breaking like so many giant soda straws, then crashing downward on all sides with a terrifying bang and clang. For the first time in years Ross whispered a Hail Mary.

Then, finally, silence. The Seadons and Liz got cautiously to their knees and stared. It might have been a battlefield; lengths of pipe and drill stem, timbers from the derrick, chains, and belts were strewn for a quarter of a mile around. The derrick itself was gone. Owen's car and the bunkhouse were smashed heaps. "My God, I thought it was the end of the world," Liz breathed. "What's down there?"

As if in answer, the ground started to shake, and with a yawp like some prehistoric monster, mud, shale, sand, and rocks began to spew up from where the derrick had stood. Then a blast of black spray. It took on form and substance. At first a thin finger, wavering and beckoning, then growing thicker, enlarging itself into a glistening column of black that soared fifty feet, seventy-five, a hundred feet, until it could go no higher and broke and cascaded downward to spread across the earth in a black tide.

Ross, Owen, and Liz gazed at it in dumb awe. It wasn't possible, Ross thought. After all those years of heartbreak, of Nature's defiance and G. G. Haggerty's smug derision, Salt Creek had finally come in.

He heard a shriek. Liz Barnard was on her feet, arms outstretched, red hair flying, running toward the spreading oil. She reached it, bent down, cupped her hands in it, raised them high, and cried, "It's ours! It's ours! All ours!"

Ross and Owen and the drill crew joined her, whooping and laughing. They linked hands and kicked and capered through the flowing black. Liz slipped, fell, and pulled the Seadons down with her. They rolled and splashed and struggled to their knees, clothes drenched with oil, faces smeared with it, hair clogged with it. No one cared. They hugged each other, kissed each other, and shouted until they were hoarse.

Owen was the first to come to his senses. "God almighty! The boiler!" It was still in place, fire burning, under that rain of oil.

The Seadons sprinted to what remained of the toolshed, found buckets, filled them from the water tank, and raced to the boiler and kicked open the firebox. Another trip to the water tank, more buckets, and the flames were snuffed out.

They were barely in time. There was another explosion from the well, a second bombardment of rock. The gusher was tearing at its mouth, enlarging it, and vomiting up a still greater pillar of oil. Its diameter now was the thickness of a man's waist. "This isn't a gusher!" Ross yelled at Owen. "It's a hemorrhage!"

The foreman was alongside them now, shouting over the roar. "We're going to drown the whole county! Get me men to build a dam!"

That night every Seadon Company worker from Mirage Springs and Haber River was rushed to the scene. Volunteers came from farms twenty miles away, from Weston's railroad yards, and even rival oil companies, to fill sandbags, to man tractors and plows and throw up dirt embankments. At first they worked by the light of a quarter moon in which the great gusher appeared like a mammoth snake with an iridescent skin, hissing upward into the night. When the moon went down, they worked by the headlights of motor cars; but as fast as they built one catch basin, it filled and another had to be thrown up.

Sometime during the night Ross returned wearily to the touring car. Liz Barnard was sitting on the running board watching the workers and listening to the gusher's eerie splashing in the darkness. Ross seated himself beside her and put his arm around her waist. "Tired?" he asked.

"Exhausted."

"Still excited?"

"More than ever." She gazed upward to where the top of the gusher was lost in the night. "How long can this go on?"

"God knows. You've heard of Union Oil's Lake View gusher?"

"The world's greatest, wasn't it?"

"Even bigger than Spindletop. About forty miles north of

here. Lake View came in at a hundred and twenty-five thousand barrels a day. Before it finished, it blew nine million barrels into the sky. The odds must be a hundred thousand to one against another. But tonight I'd say the odds are one to one." He paused, hearing Liz's strangled sobbing. "Hey! What's wrong?"

"All I . . . all I wanted . . . was three hundred dollars a month!"

Three days later the great gusher still gave no sign of abating. The laborers and tractors were gone now, and in their places were the tents of hundreds of boomers who had come to traffic in leases and percentages. The more cautious went about in rain slickers and sou'wester hats to shield against the gray fog which misted down from the tireless geyser. No one dared smoke, and drivers of motorcars prudently turned off their engines half a mile away. There was a curious dreamlike quality to the scene, unlike the first frantic rush at the Haber River field and at Mirage Springs; even the boomers seemed awed by the gusher. The ultimate tribute came from Harley Stewart, who followed Ross around like a hungry courtier, compared him glowingly to Harry Sinclair and E. L. Doheny, and hinted that he was anxious to defect from Pantex and G. G. Haggerty.

It was on that same third day that Liz Barnard brought Philip up from Hollywood to view the spectacle that had transformed their lives. As they made their way through the crowd, Ross spied them and came over. He barely recognized Philip as the boy he had met at the Panama-Pacific Exposition in 1915. True, he still wore horn-rimmed glasses, but the owlish expression was gone. He was tall and muscular, his voice had deepened, and he shook Ross's hand with the grip of a grown man.

"A fine-looking kid," Ross commented after Philip had excused himself for a closer view of the gusher. "He's going to be a real heartbreaker."

Liz nodded uneasily. "I know. I'll be fighting off every fortune-hunting mother in the state."

Ross grinned. "How about yourself? How many proposals of marriage have you had the last couple of days?"

She gave him a quick look. "I've stopped counting."

They were still talking when they saw Philip returning through the crowd. He had removed his glasses and was wiping the oil mist from the lenses with his handkerchief. Ross frowned. He hadn't seen Philip without glasses since when? Childhood. He looked different; there was something about the face, the eyes, something familiar . . . something . . .

At that instant Liz's hand clamped his wrist, her fingernails dug into his flesh. "*Not a word!*" she whispered.

"But my God!"

Her fingernails dug deeper. "*Do you want me to hate you the rest of my life?*" She turned toward Philip and waved. "We'll be back in a moment, dear! Don't wander off!"

They made their way behind a tent and Ross burst out, "Did you think I'd be blind forever? Adopted, *hell!* Philip is *you*, he's *me!* God in heaven, he's my first-born!"

BOOK
FOUR

BOOK
FOUR

Chapter 18

DALE LANTRY liked Los Angeles. She liked the clear warm days; she liked the absence of fog, which had so often depressed her in San Francisco; she liked being able to go about the campus at USC in summery skirts and blouses; best of all, she liked the nearness of Hollywood and its movie stars. In short, as she summed it up to her sorority roommate, Los Angeles was the bees' knees. Dale's mother and stepfather had argued in favor of Mills College, across the bay, but she had held out for the Los Angeles university. "San Francisco thinks everything exciting stopped with The Fire; but this is 1924, and Los Angeles is absolutely the place to be."

In the end her mother had agreed with her. After all, Dale would not be entirely on her own; her cousin Eugene, Owen's son, was a sophomore at USC and could keep an eye on her, and off campus there would be Dale's Uncle Ross. "She's not interested in boys," Leah had decided, "so there's nothing to worry about." Worry, on any subject, no longer engaged Leah. With her discovery of New Thought, she had put aside her wartime cynicism and now denied the possibility of evil; she "knew the Truth" about every threatening problem, and so dispelled it.

This, Dale's first semester at USC, proved Leah's conviction that her daughter was male-proof—at least so far as those she had met on campus with their boring talk of Red Grange and other football heroes. Nor did Dale warm to her sorority sisters, who talked about the men who talked about Red Grange. The one treasured exception was her roommate, Audrey Sommers (called "Aud" by Dale and "Odd Aud" by everyone else, for no reason whatever). She was a pleasant-faced brunette who laughed easily and was a willing audience for Dale's enthusiasms for The Theater (meaning the gods and goddesses of nearby Hollywood), the poetry of Edna St. Vincent Millay, and the novels of Kathleen Norris and Michael Arlen about "girls who dared." Aud considered it a special distinction to room with the girl who was the cousin of Eugene Seadon. "My knees absolutely stammered," she confessed after her introduction to Owen's son. "Gene's so terribly Latin, like Valentino."

"Naturally," Dale agreed. "His mother is a Delgado. They were grandees who came over with the Viceroy from Spain."

And so with this community of interests, the two girls were inseparable. Many a Saturday afternoon they would take the bus to Pershing Square and transfer to the double-decker for Hollywood—and their Mecca, the Hollywood Hotel. Old, vaguely California Mission in architecture, it possessed a priceless feature for Dale and Aud: a wide veranda where the film stars lolled in wicker chairs between shootings. On various walk-pasts, the girls had identified Jack Holt, Harold Lloyd, Douglas Fairbanks, and Mary Pickford. A block to the east was their second shrine, Grauman's Egyptian Theater, where on one memorable afternoon they saw Cecil B. De Mille's *Ten Commandments*. Afterward, on that same afternoon, being full of purse and chocolate malts, they saw a second movie at the Hollywood Theater and, coming out, raised their eyes to the second floor of the building on the opposite side of the street, the Cafe Montmartre, where saxophones moaned and men in tuxedos and women in chiffon floated past the open windows. Somehow, some way, some night, Dale and Aud vowed to each other, they too would dance past those windows, and, God willing, they would be in the arms of movie stars.

There was one pleasure which Dale did not share with Aud— the Sunday afternoons when Uncle Ross, in his chauffeured Pierce Arrow, would call for his niece and nephew. There was no consistency to Ross's appearances; but whenever, they would include excursions to the new Seadon Oil drilling areas—Santa Fe Springs, Playa del Rey, Signal Hill. Sometimes, and more to Dale and Gene's liking, there were visits to the amusement piers at Long Beach and Venice. And always, without fail, an inspection of Ross's great house which was nearing completion on a mountaintop behind Beverly Hills. The day would end with an excellent dinner at a roadhouse or speakeasy—perhaps the Sunset Club in Santa Monica, or Marcel's in Altadena, where Volstead agents were not likely to intrude—and Ross would talk fondly of the old days in Weston and San Francisco. Both Dale and Gene understood their importance to their uncle; they were substitutes for his own absent Tom and Ginny.

"It's a shame they can't be with him," Dale remarked to Gene one evening after they had returned to campus. "You think Uncle Ross and Aunt Louise will ever get together again?"

"Nope," Gene said.

"And never get divorced?"

"Nope."

Shortly after this conversation Leah telephoned Dale from San Francisco; she and David Marcus were coming to Los Angeles for Ross's housewarming, she said, and Dale and Eugene were invited. No, they could not bring dates. "We want you and Gene to spend your time with the family, not lally-gagging around with people you can see every day."

As one approached the Beverly Hills Hotel from the east along Sunset Boulevard and looked to the northern hills, "Ridgemont's" slate roof and four stone chimneys could be seen rising above a screen of newly planted black pine. The house, like most of those in the Beverly Hills area, was something of an architectural absurdity—a Tudor mansion appropriate for the damp English countryside which found itself transplanted to a hilltop where yucca had once bloomed and coyotes barked and rattlesnakes defied all intruders. The exterior was red brick with oak trim, the windows mullioned, the glass leaded, the massive front door recessed under a stone archway. A flagstone terrace, with potted privets stationed along the balustrade, entirely circled the house. More flagstone, in descending levels in the rear, led to the swimming pool, the greenhouse, the aviary, and a five-car garage.

An east wind, strong, dry, and warm, was blowing when Dale and Gene arrived in Ross's limousine. Caterers in white jackets were arranging trestle tables on the terrace for the buffet to come; others were erecting a striped cabana in which the musicians would play, while still others were adjusting strings of multicolored Japanese lanterns which bobbed and curtsied with each gust.

Ross, still in gray flannels and shirt sleeves, greeted his arrivals on the terrace. "Damn, I hope this wind dies down. If it turns into a Santa Ana, we'll have to move everything indoors." He led the way into the great entry hall. "You kids are the first here, so I'd say that entitles you to the grand tour."

"Where are Mother and Dave?" Dale asked.

"Forgot them. Upstairs, taking a nap or something." Ross winked. "You never can tell about old folks. . . . Now this little hideaway the architect calls a living room. More like an aircraft hangar, I say."

Considering its scale, Ross was barely exaggerating, for the cathedral ceiling soared two and a half floors. The dining room, more intimate, was formal and crystal-chandeliered; the orchid conservatory was a tropical bower; the billiard room was paneled in rosewood. Ross saved to the last his favorite, the library. Its walls were scant on books but profuse with paintings and photographs. There were views of the Seadon Oil tankers, the refineries at Ventura and Wilmington, the ten-story Seadon Oil Company Building in downtown Los Angeles, and dominating the whole room, a painter's re-creation of the Salt Springs gusher that had propelled Seadon Oil into the front ranks of California oil companies—and had paid for Ridgemont.

"It's all kind of sad," Dale said when she joined Leah and her stepfather. "This great enormous house just for Uncle Ross to live in alone."

"He's likely to have company," Leah said. "At least Tom and Ginny. If anything can wean them away from their mother, Ridgemont will do it."

It was, in fact, the chief reason for Ridgemont. Louise, wealthy from Ross's separation agreement, had sought to bind their children to her by trips to Europe during school vacations, a roadster for Tom, endless parties and gifts for Ginny, and finally, a country estate at Woodside, near Palo Alto, convenient for Tom at Stanford and an easy commute after he graduated to her father's Bay Steel Company. It was a conspiracy, Ross declared, between Louise and Arnold Schroder to divert Tom from his rightful place in Seadon Oil. "But so help me God, they won't get away with it. I'll outbid them. Tom goes with me. And Ginny too. I'll marry her to the richest bachelor in the State of California!"

By dusk and the arrival of the first guests the east wind had increased to a full-fledged Santa Ana which whipped the Japanese lanterns, billowed women's skirts, and blew the musicians' sheet music from their stands. The party moved indoors; the buffet tables were set up in the dining room and bars in the library; the musicians crowded into the recess of a bay window in the great living room; the Oriental rugs were rolled up and the furniture pushed back for the first Charleston—"Yes, We Have No Bananas." There were over three hundred guests: relatives, friends, oil people, politicians, bankers, even several priests. There was Liz Barnard, who arrived in furs and emeralds, and chattered about her newest purchase of Wilshire

Boulevard real estate. There was G. G. Haggerty, materialized out of faraway Texas (and uninvited), who presented Ross with a solid silver punchbowl and introduced his third bride.

"How did you know about this shindig?" Ross asked.

Haggerty winked. "Was there ever a time I didn't know what you were up to?"

"Yes. When you went off to Mexico."

"Once! Just once, you son of a bitch!"

And, of course, there were Owen and Tana. "This isn't a home," he growled, "it's a damned monument."

"I know," Tana agreed. "Somehow, it doesn't seem like Ross. Unless he's changed."

"He *hasn't*. It isn't him at all. How can you square all this froufrou with the man who cried over Hop Gee?"

Owen's reference was to the death of the aged family retainer. First it had been Ah Sing, earlier in the year, then two months later Hop Gee had suffered a massive stroke. Owen had telephoned from Rancho El Encanto, and Ross had walked out of a business meeting and raced the hundred-odd miles to Hop Gee's bedside. The old man, barely conscious, had rallied for a few moments, long enough to know that Ross was there holding his hand, calling him for the last time "Lao-hu," Old Tiger.

The party was growing noisy. Groups linked arms and sang "Yes, sir, that's my baby; No, sir, I don't mean maybe," while others, dizzy with liquor, giggled and stumbled through the steps of the Charleston. Outside, the Santa Ana buffeted the windows and made animal sounds of rage. And outside, braving the wind, Liz Barnard and Ross talked confidentially on the flagged terrace.

"How often must we go over this, Ross? If Philip knew his father was alive, that I'd kept him from you, he would turn against me. I know he would"—Liz's voice broke with emotion—"and I'd lose all that matters in my life."

Ross sighed and stared out over the terrace to the lights

262

of Beverly Hills in the lower distance. It was almost word for word the argument they had had years before, that day at the gusher. "You're living in a dream world, Liz. One of these days Phil will look in the mirror and see me."

"Why should he? He's heard over and over that his father is dead. Why should he think you're any more than an old friend?" She slipped her hand into Ross's. "You can't know how many times I've called myself a selfish bitch. I wanted a child and I wanted my freedom. I got both and I've paid the price. You'll never know how lonely it's been. But what's done is done. I can't let Philip know I made him a bastard."

Ross held up their twined hands and looked at Liz's emerald ring. "I'm warning you, when Phil graduates from Harvard, I'm going to be there to see it. And if anything happens to you..."

"I'm prepared for that ," she nodded. "There's a letter in a safe deposit box. If Philip ever has to read it, I'll be past caring how he feels. Then you can have your son." She paused, considering her words, then gave a wry smile. "I guess I've just given you a motive for murder, haven't I?"

It was almost midnight. Dale Lantry drifted from room to room, feeling lost among these people flashing with jewels, powerful, mysterious, seeming to a college girl on a modest allowance even richer than they were in fact. She felt as dependent as the servants who filtered through the crowd with trays of canapes and drinks. It was silly, she told herself. She was a Seadon just as much as her self-assured cousins Gene and Carla and Angie and Tom and Ginny. The trouble was, they carried the Seadon name, whereas she was Dale Lantry.

Finally, in her boredom, she wandered into the billiard room, where Angie was watching her brother Gene practice pool shots. Dale yawned and glanced out the french window. There was Uncle Ross out on the terrace again; he was with a man she had not seen before. Ross, with his billfold in hand, was peeling off banknotes.

"Gene, what's Uncle Ross doing?"

Gene gazed over Dale's shoulder. "Paying off a bet, I guess." He looked more closely. "Nope, that's his bootlegger."

"You're kidding!"

"I saw him in the kitchen. He was lugging in cases of the stuff. Guess the party was running out of booze."

Dale examined the man with new interest. Although she could not see his face distinctly, he appeared young and slender. "He doesn't *look* like a bootlegger. He's wearing a tux like everybody else."

"What do you expect he'd wear? A sandwich board saying 'I am a bootlegger'?"

Dale continued to contemplate the subject of their discussion. "I wonder what he's really like," she murmured to Angie.

"Don't do it, Dale, " Angie whispered back.

"Is that a dare?"

"No. Because you'd take it."

Gene rapped his cue on the edge of the table. "How about some pool?"

"Oh, let's!" Angie agreed.

Gene selected two billiard cues from the rack, chalked the tips, handed one to Angie, and turned to give the other to Dale. "Hey! Where the heck did she go?" Then he saw the open french window.

Dale launched herself from the shadows of the big house in a series of graceful pirouettes in perfect time to the music indoors. "Picture you upon my knee. Just tea for two and two for tea." Hair swirling, skirt flaring, feet dancing over the flagstones, eyes carefully avoiding the man leaning against the balustrade. Then, as she drew near, discovery, elaborate confusion.

"*Oh!* I thought I was alone."

Only a sideways glance.

Yes, he was young, perhaps twenty-five. Black curly hair and olive skin. The glow of the Japanese lanterns overhead threw his eyes into shadow, but she could see his mouth; it was hard, possibly cruel.

"Waiting for somebody?"

A silent nod.

She scraped a pump on the flagstone uncertainly. Her study of Emily Post had not disclosed the etiquette of conversation with a bootlegger. It was all a stupid idea. The problem was how to get back indoors gracefully. With dignity. And hope that Gene and Angie hadn't witnessed her snub.

"Well . . . when you meet your somebody . . . maybe you'd like to come inside and join the party."

"I came from a party. I'm going back to it."

"What's wrong with this one?"

"It's dull."

How rude could he be? It was an insult to Uncle Ross. "What's so special about yours?"

"Mack Sennett, Constance Talmadge, Antonio Moreno, Lon Chaney."

"It's a *movie* party?"

"Sure."

"Well." She recovered. "Well, I suppose actors and actresses *can* be fun. But we are, too. . . . Why, I was dancing out here with a fellow and he told me to take off all my underthings so he could think of dancing with me naked."

"Huh! What kind of guys do they let into this party?"

"Bootleggers." She saw him flinch. "You brought the stuff into the kitchen, and my uncle came out here and paid you."

"Mr. Seadon is your uncle?" Uneasy, but impressed.

"He is." Dale stared at the nearest potted privet, then at the one beyond. "I've really forgotten which . . ."

"Forgot which what?"

"The bush where I hid my underthings."

His eyes appraised her doubtfully. "How old are you?"

"Enough. My name's Dale Lantry. What's yours?"

"Joe Carvalo."

The exchange of names seemed to relax him. Dale felt her victory and went on confidently. "While you're waiting for your friend, we could dance a little."

He hesitated, weighing the idea, then stepped toward her.

They had barely begun to foxtrot when Dale felt his hand explore her back and find her brassiere strap.

"So you hid your things in a bush? You lie about everything?"

She tossed her head defiantly, then said in a rush, "Joe, I'm sure my uncle wouldn't mind if you brought your friends to our party. He might even thank you."

"So that's what this is all about. No dice."

"All right, then we could go to your party. Not just me, but my cousins Tom and Gene and Carla and Angie. We'd follow you in our own car, with our own chauffeur. We wouldn't bother anybody for autographs; we wouldn't be any trouble at all."

He was wavering, Dale was sure of it. Then someone coughed and Joe looked around and saw a man standing under one of the Japanese lanterns. He nodded and Joe walked toward him and they began to talk. Who was that man? Dale wondered, and then remembered the white-haired judge who had been loudly telling jokes all evening. Now he was not joking but talking rapidly while Joe jotted notes on a pocket pad. Finally the judge finished, shook Joe's hand, and turned back toward the house. Joe stood a moment gazing back at Dale, then he came toward her and held out his notepad and pencil. "Give me your phone number."

"But the party?"

"Not tonight."

She scribbled her sorority's number and handed it to him. "You won't call," she said. "You're afraid of my uncle."

"Let's say I'm not stupid." He hesitated, then tilted her chin upward with his forefinger and studied her face. "On the other hand, I like girls with tall eyelashes."

At least he had noticed.

Chapter 19

DALE REGRETTED telling Aud about Joe. At first it had been thoroughly satisfying to dramatize for her roommate the scene on the terrace at Ridgemont; then as the days stretched into weeks without The Phone Call, Dale's disappointment went from humiliation to anger. "Stop asking about him, Aud!" she would snap. "I don't give a darn about him. Who cares about a bootlegger?" Then, almost three months from the date of the housewarming at Ridgemont one of the sorority sisters called Dale to the hall telephone.

It was Joe. "Want to see some movie stars?"

"Oh, I don't know. Perhaps." Cool and distant.

"Saturday afternoon?"

"Where?"

"It's something they call a tea dansant. The Cafe Montmartre."

The Montmartre!

It was exactly as she had fantasized; no, even better. The

headwaiter unfastening the red velvet rope and escorting them to their table; champagne in an ice bucket; gliding about the floor while the band played "The Sheik of Araby"; being introduced to Mabel Normand and Gloria Swanson and Milton Sills and Richard Dix. Dale noted that Joe did not mention her last name; she was simply "Dale." No one used Joe's last name either, except the headwaiter, who had addressed him as "Mr. Carvalo."

Joe gave no explanation for inviting her after all those months, nor did he tell her what he had been doing. "Out of town," he said to one of the actresses who had wondered where he had been; "Mexico," he said to another. In both cases Dale saw that special intensity in the exchange of looks, that glitter to the eyes, and recognized its meaning; she had seen it, as a child, pass between her mother and certain men. Dale was aware, too, that both actresses had examined her with undisguised feline jealousy.

"You see much of your uncle?" Joe asked abruptly as they returned from the dance floor.

"Uncle Ross? Oh, yes. I'm his favorite niece."

"You hope so."

"I know I am."

"Are you going to tell him about seeing me?"

"Do you want me to?"

"No."

"Then I won't."

It was the most extended dialogue they had had, and Joe followed it up with another question. "How long can you stay out?"

"Ten o'clock, that's our sorority curfew . . . unless we get special permission from the housemother and tell her where we'll be and who we're with."

"Okay, we got time," Joe said. "Let's go."

They drove out Wilshire Boulevard, past the Old Soldiers' Home, to Santa Monica, and ate dinner overlooking the beach at what Joe called a "speak." Afterward they strolled under the palm trees and cypress which lined Palisades Park. Joe had returned to his silent mood, which suggested to Dale that he was struggling with some great secret burden; perhaps he was another Mr. Rochester, she thought, having just read *Jane Eyre*.

Then without warning, he swung around and faced her. "I wasn't in Mexico. I was in a hospital."

"Oh, Joe!" A flood of sympathy. "Was it serious?"

"Three slugs in the gut serious."

Haltingly, he told her. He had driven to San Diego with his partner and waited in a cove of the beach to take delivery of a load of liquor coming ashore from a rumrunner up from Mexico. Somebody else knew; there had been shots in the night; his partner was killed and the liquor hijacked.

Dale was appalled. "How in the world did you get into such an awful business?"

"It's money."

"But suppose there's another shooting? . . . Joe, you can be more than a gangster."

He looked down at the waves cresting on the beach below. "I'm working on something." He turned back with a smile. "Then maybe you can mention me to your uncle. *Maybe*, I said."

Joe returned Dale to the campus shortly before ten. As she stepped out of the car, he said, "Next time I call you, do something about that curfew."

Slater Dougal lounged in the walnut-paneled board of directors' room of the Seadon Oil Company, chainsmoking cigarettes and waiting for the decision that was being made in the next room, the office of the president. Dougal was a lanky man in his mid-thirties, with eyes that shone with a boyish innocence which belied the fact that he was one of the Midwest's most successful independent oilmen, who had assembled a group of failing operations into the highly respected Tri-State Oil. Dougal had come out from Tulsa with the company's officers to inspect the Seadon Oil properties, of which his company would become a part owner if Tri-State agreed to a merger. Now it was dealing time, and the first move depended on the men in the next room. They were a savvy bunch, Dougal thought. The Seadon brothers had proved that when they came back to Tulsa and eyeballed Tri-State; and Wil Caruth was an attorney with no flies on him, either. Tim Beakley might be a bit behind the times, but he was a good old ham-fisted wild-catter who knew how to make hole. The only Seadon director Dougal was edgy about was David Marcus; the San Francisco banker had given him the fish-eye when they had been introduced that morning. Dougal recognized his voice on the other side of that door; the words were indistinct, but certainly emphatic.

"It's your oil company, boys," Marcus was saying, "but I am married to your sister and I owe it to Leah to protect her interest. I just don't like the deal." He gazed through the cigar smoke at Ross behind the desk and Owen hovering beside him. Wil Caruth and Tim Beakley, sprawled on the leather sofa, watched Marcus pace the room as he went on. "I'm not objecting to the price. Fifteen million is probably fair if Tri-State's properties are what you say they are. But Oklahoma, Kansas, and Wyoming are one of Pantex's major markets. You're thumbing your nose at G. G. Haggerty—"

Ross interrupted. "Sure, we are. And if it means another fight with old Pickles and Vinegar, let it happen. We don't give a damn."

"You better give a damn. You want to offer Tri-State fifteen million in Seadon Oil stock. Suppose the Tri-State shareholders take your stock and sell it on the open market and Haggerty buys it up?"

"Owen and I have gone into that. Haggerty won't spend fifteen million to be a minority shareholder. He knows the Seadon Estate Company owns the controlling interest in Seadon Oil; he'd just be the tail of the dog."

Marcus leaned his hands on Ross's desk and looked down at him. "Remember the night you were crossing Powell Street and

270

that runaway car got you? Suppose something like that happens again, and this time you aren't so lucky. Or suppose you and Owen are driving out to one of the fields in the same car, and you get hit by a truck. Both killed . . ."

Owen laughed uncomfortably. "God, you're a ray of sunshine."

"I'm being realistic. There would be nobody to run Seadon Oil. That's how a minority owner could wind up running the whole shooting match—and it could be G. G. Haggerty."

"All right," Ross decided. "We won't buy Tri-State for stock. We'll pay cash." He smiled up at Marcus. "You got fifteen million in your hip pocket?"

Marcus shrugged. "The bank can handle five million. Somebody else will have to pony up the rest."

"Okay. I'm going East next week. I'll talk to some of the New York shylocks." Ross rose from his desk and went to the door of the board room. "Come on in, Slater."

Slater Dougal listened to the proposition as Ross sketched it and smiled at the figure of fifteen million. It was, he said, three million higher than the figure Mr. G. G. Haggerty had offered. He was certain that he could persuade his stockholders.

"But there is one condition, boys. If I swing my people into line, I want to be elected vice president of Seadon Oil in charge of mid-continent operations. I know the Midwest, and you boys don't." He paused and watched the surprised faces. "And that condition includes a three-year contract, and an office right here on your tenth floor."

Ross grunted. "How the hell can you run the Midwest from Los Angeles?"

"The last I heard, the trains were still running both ways. I sort of cotton to the Coast; I want to move my family here. The staff we got in Tulsa can stay on and see to the day-to-day stuff." Dougal smiled silkily. "Remember, I've spent a week studying your operations, and I'd say you're running shorthanded on the top level. You need a good old chore boy."

There was a moment's silence; cigars were puffed, feet

shifted, then Owen spoke. "Slater, you mind stepping outside again?"

When the door closed behind Dougal, Owen shook his head. "He's too full of ideas for me. He talks like a lion tamer, but I got a hunch he wants to own the circus."

Ross grinned. "Don't we all? But we want Tri-State, so Slater Dougal is our new vice president."

So far as anyone knew, Ross had gone East for the sole purpose of arranging added financing for the takeover of Tri-State Oil. The second reason, although unspoken, was to attend Philip Barnard's graduation from Harvard. Ross sat beside Liz Barnard in the audience and watched the file of young men, capped and gowned, pass the rostrum to receive their diplomas; and when it was Philip's turn, he felt all the emotions natural to a father, compounded with the frustration of a father who could not declare himself. He was that ambiguous creature, a friend of the family.

Perhaps Liz had anticipated his feelings, for while they were waiting for Philip's turn, she had taken an envelope from her handbag and whispered to him, "Put this in your pocket. Don't look now." But he had. Inside were various snapshots of Philip —on his child's tricycle, in Boy Scout uniform, in high school track suit, then as a Harvard freshman, a sophomore boating on the Charles, a senior in the glee club. Ross squeezed Liz's hand in thanks. At last she was sharing their son. "I want a copy of Phil's graduation photo, too," he murmured, and she nodded.

It was curious, looking at the photos. In the earlier years there was the resemblance to Ross which he had recognized that day at the Salt Springs gusher; now it had faded until one could barely detect it. It was Liz who was dominant—the red hair, the blue eyes, the freckles across the bridge of the nose. And yet as Ross watched Philip during the milling congratulations at the end of the ceremony, there *was* a resemblance. Not physical, but in mannerism—the same enthusiastic laugh, the habit of tugging his earlobe in thought, the toss of the head when making a point in conversation. By whatever name, he was a Seadon.

Philip's graduation present from Liz was a trip to Europe in the company of several of his classmates. On the night that the *Leviathan* was to sail from New York, Ross invited Philip and his mother to a celebration dinner in the Oak Room of the Plaza Hotel. Again he was the outsider, the fifth wheel, while mother and son chattered about Europe, the sights in store, the people Philip must look up that Liz had met on her own trips abroad. Finally, toward the end of the meal Ross found his opening.

"What are your plans, Phil, when you get back?"

"Well, a couple of the guys are going into their dads' firms in Wall Street. They say there ought to be a place for me. I've got some names and addresses."

So it would not be back to the Coast. Yet why should he? New York was the loadstone of the new generation, drawing the brightest and strongest, and rewarding them as no other city could.

Ross passed off his disappointment with a smile. "If it doesn't work out the way you want, remember, there's always a place for you in Seadon Oil."

"Thank you, sir." Philip clasped his mother's hand. "We both want you to know how much we appreciate all you've done for us. And your brother, too. Without the Seadons, none of this would be happening." He hesitated shyly, "I hope I'll always be able to come to you for advice."

"You can count on it, son."

There was a bon voyage party aboard the *Leviathan* in the cabin which Philip was sharing with three classmates. Everyone was jammed shoulder to shoulder, laughing, jostling, spilling bootlegged champagne; mothers and sisters were misty-eyed, fathers and brothers shouting advice about Paris and its oooh-la-la girls. Then the ship's warning blast and stewards shouting, "All ashore!" The stay-behinds trooped down the gangplank, paper streamers arced from the ship's railing, the band on the promenade deck blared, hawsers were cast off, propellers churned.

Ross and Liz, arm in arm, stood at the end of the pier and watched the great ship swing wide in the Hudson River and glide down toward the bay.

"It's strange," Liz said, sniffing back her tears. "In all the years Phil was away at Harvard, I never felt separated from him. Tonight I do."

"Because from here on Phil is on his own. He's a man."

"I suppose." She looked down the waterway at the fading lights. "God, I feel so alone."

Ross cleared his throat to cover his own emotion. "I think we need a drink."

"Oh, I'm sick of speakeasies. Would you have a bottle?"

It was a sultry night. Heat lightning somewhere to the north flared into the dark bedroom which overlooked Central Park. Liz propped herself on one elbow and looked down into Ross's face. "If you're counting, don't tell me."

"Tell you what?"

"How many years it's been."

It was twenty-odd, Ross reflected. They had gone to bed less from desire than to console each other for times long gone. It had been good for them; their bodies, they discovered, were still youthful, still attractive, still responsive.

"You know," Liz said, "I think Phil suspects there's something between us. Not in the past, but going on right now."

"Hmm. I kind of got that idea myself, the way he looked at us at the dinner table. Would it upset him?"

"Probably. He's at that age when all mamas are supposed to be mothers superior. He knows I'm not, of course, but we both pretend." She glanced toward the window as the room flared into light again. "In your case, I think Phil would make an exception. He admires you tremendously."

"I hope so."

"Not that he understands you. He asked me once why you

don't get a divorce and remarry. I told him you and Louise are Catholics, but it didn't make sense to him."

"You should have given him the old saw: Why buy a cow when you live next door to the dairy?"

She laughed. "That's one of the nice things about being a millionaire, isn't it? There's always a free lunch." She gave him a playful peck on the nose. "Confession time. Why don't I ever hear about your affairs?"

"Because there aren't any."

"Oh? What's this, a class reunion?"

"It doesn't count. You said 'affairs.' I'm too busy for all that rigmarole. I'm not about to have someone asking 'Why didn't you ring me yesterday?' Or 'Where were you last night?'"

"I know. It can be a bore. But I'd hate to spend my life taking cold showers."

"I don't." Ross wished she would get off the subject, but if he had to spell it out for her . . . "When it reaches that point, I just pick up the phone and in a few minutes there's a package at the front door."

Liz shook her head. "It sounds awful. Don't you miss affection?"

"Sometimes." Ross sighed. "Sometimes very much."

A month passed before Joe Carvalo phoned Dale again and invited her to dinner. It was sunset when they drove across town to Hollywood Boulevard and then west through the residential area until the boulevard dead-ended at a crossroad which appeared to wind up into a canyon. He swung onto the canyon road and said, "Most people call this Laurel Canyon, but in the business we call it Rumrunners' Alley. When the cops are chasing you, all you do is duck up here and get lost on a side road."

In spite of herself, Dale glanced around; no one was chasing them. "Are we going to where you live?"

He nodded. "Some people are stopping by. You might like to meet them."

"Movie people?"

275

"What do you want, a guest list?" He looked at her somberly out of the corners of his eyes. "If you're scared, I'll take you back to school."

"School." That detestable word; she wasn't a child. And not scared, not really. Her mother had gone to strange places with strange men and nothing had happened. Something, but not terrible; just the things that Edna St. Vincent Millay approved of. That was how poetry got written, wasn't it?

The road twisted and rose rapidly, then Joe turned off onto a side road which climbed even more steeply. Dale caught glimpses of shingled cottages huddled among pine and eucalyptus. The homes of poor, she thought, or outlaws. Then onto a dirt road which ended at an iron gate. There was a chain-link fence and two German police dogs barking, first in challenge, then in greeting. Joe unlocked the gate and drove up through the eucalyptus until a house came into view, then around the house to the rear where a plumber's truck was parked. Joe used it, he said, for deliveries in "delicate situations." The house itself was indistinguishable from the others she had seen—small, shingled, with a half story to the rear which nestled into the slope of the hill. The interior was rustic—a sitting room paneled in redwood, a leather sofa, several easy chairs, a fireplace with the logs ready for lighting. At the far end of the room, stairs climbed upward toward what Dale assumed must be a bedroom. She could see the kitchen through an archway to the right, and a table where Joe probably ate.

"Don't you get lonely living by yourself?" Dale asked. If it was by himself.

"Not here long enough," he said, going into the kitchen. She followed him and watched him open the icebox and chip at a block of ice. He dropped the ice into two glasses and carried them to the counter and filled them from a bottle of gin. He handed one to Dale. "You take it straight, don't you?" he said, seeing her hesitation.

"Oh, sure." It was a new experience and she shivered as the alcohol scalded down her throat. "When will your friends be here?"

He held out a dish of salted nuts. "Pretty soon."

They went back into the sitting room. Joe lighted the logs and gestured her toward the sofa. "Now," he said, "let's talk about Dale Lantry."

Perhaps it was the relaxing effect of the gin, or Joe's reassuring interest in her; in any case, she found herself being quite witty about her college studies, about Aud, and, with a second glass of gin, about her childhood. Her birth during the San Francisco fire, her father's death in the quake, her mother's war service in France; they were not Dale's accomplishments, yet she dwelt on them with the pride of a miser exhibiting his gold.

The telephone in the kitchen rang and Joe went to answer. "The bathroom's upstairs," he called over his shoulder. A hint for privacy, and a welcome suggestion.

When she came out of the bathroom, she heard Joe's distant laugh. It was not the between-men sort of laugh, she thought; it was man to woman. Probably one of those actresses she had seen at the Cafe Montmartre. One who had come to this house with Joe. It didn't make sense; he had the pick of Hollywood, and yet tonight he was out with a college kid. Why? And why was she resigned to the outcome? No, not resigned to it—desiring it, to be initiated into the mystery, to know, to experience, to be the equal of those actresses.

"You okay?" Joe's voice echoed up the stairway. She hurried down. Did she know how to cook? he asked. A little, she said, following him into the kitchen. He handed her a can of beans and a can opener. She heated the beans in a pot while Joe fried two steaks in a skillet. That was their dinner, consumed while they sat cross-legged in front of the fire with a bottle of red wine. Everything was perfect, Dale thought: the blazing logs, releasing their eucalyptus scent, the cozy room, the pleasant fuzziness in her head, the man who had chosen her to be beside him. She wished she could put a giant bell glass over them and preserve this moment intact forever.

"You ashamed of being out with a bootlegger?" Joe asked suddenly.

It startled her; how could he break the mood? "Of course not. Besides, you said you're getting out of it."

He tossed his head, neither confirming nor denying. Then he saw her glance at her wristwatch and he smiled coolly. "They're not coming."

"Your friends?"

"Yes." The smile continued. "You knew that all along."

She turned her eyes to the fire. "I wasn't sure."

"You knew. And you didn't give a damn." The smile melted. "Go on, say it. 'I didn't give a damn. Not one holy damn.'"

She shook her head; no matter how curious she was to know what other women found in Joe, she would not humiliate herself.

He regarded her, tight-lipped, then got to his feet. "Let's go."

"What?"

"I'm taking you home."

It was unbelievable; he was putting on his coat. "Joe, what's wrong? If there's something I said . . ." She scrambled up and went toward him, eyes brimming. "Joe, not like this. Next week is the end of the semester. I'll be going back to San Francisco. I'll be gone all summer—"

"And you want something to remember, right?" He seized her and brought her mouth to his. It was a long kiss, hard and brutal. And a revelation. Then he released her. "That's want you want, isn't it? And a lot more. All right, little rich girl, beg for it!"

"Never!" Her Seadon pride was flaring now. "I won't sink to your level. I won't be one of your dirty little whores!" As she spat out the words, she had visions of being thrown out the door, having to elude the watchdogs, climbing the fence, tramping down strange roads in the dark, hitchhiking back to campus.

At least he spared her that. As he let her out of the car in front of the sorority, he gave her a knowing grin. "I can wait. Let's see if you can."

Dale fidgeted in the confessional booth, tugged at a lock of hair, and chewed on a thumbnail, as she recognized the cold disapproval in Father Morrison's words—he who had inveighed in the pulpit against Sigmund Freud, hip flasks, saxophones, and rumble seats. It was not enough that he had pronounced a penance of an unbelievable number of Hail Marys and Our Fathers and one whole day of fasting; in Dale's agitation, it seemed as if his voice brayed like a foghorn to advertise her transgression to the farthest corner of the church. Then, finally it was over as he dismissed her with "Go and sin no more!"

For a day or two Dale believed it might be possible, just as she had believed during her summer vacation in San Francisco that she could erase Joe from her memory. She had filled her days with tennis and swimming and horseback riding and her evenings with theater and lectures and parties, until both her mother and stepfather began to fret that she might wreck her health.

Then Dale had returned to USC for the new semester, and Joe telephoned again. She had accepted eagerly, and they had gone straight to the house in Laurel Canyon, and to bed. The experience had been vaguely disappointing, and the guilt sharp. Until Father Morrison had lessened it with his heavy penance. Then Joe called again, and Dale decided she would test herself; she would insist on an evening of friendly conversation and nothing more. But the conversation had soon palled and she found herself following Joe upstairs to the bedroom. This time there was no disappointment; she understood fully why those actresses had looked at Joe with glittery eyes. The fact that he was still a bootlegger no longer concerned her; it added spice; he was outside the law, a rebel.

Her affair settled into a routine; every weekend she spent with Joe, signing out at the sorority with an explanation to the housemother that she would be with her uncle Ross or visiting her cousins at Alto Valle. She no longer cared about the movies; Joe was her drama, her hero and villain. She felt deliciously wicked, superior to poor old Aud and all her other virginal classmates; while they drudged at their studies, Dale dreamed of the next weekend and fresh abandonment.

Late in the fall Dale received a telephone call from San Francisco. Leah and David Marcus were shocked by her grades. How could Dale have made the dean's list for two semesters and now have failing marks? It was the work load, Dale said. The sophomore year was harder than the freshman, and she had been plagued with one head cold after another; but there was nothing to worry about, she would make up her grades. Her mother seemed a bit dubious and asked, "Are you in love?" which Dale dismissed with a laugh.

The next day—was it a coincidence?—Ross invited her to a swimming party at Ridgemont and pointedly asked her to bring a date. She thought Uncle Ross looked surprised when she appeared with her cousin Gene; and why did he ask if she was still going to confession?

Then, the week following the swimming party, Dale's roommate announced that Gene Seadon had taken her out. Gene with humdrum old Aud, the girl he couldn't see for sour apples? It was very strange, even suspicious. "You didn't tell Gene anything about me and Joe, did you?" Dale asked. She saw Aud's eyes turn away. "*Aud!* What did you tell him?"

"Why, nothing, really."

"Oh, Aud! How *could* you?"

The two men sat on opposite sides of the big desk in the library at Ridgemont. Ross tense and angry, Joe Carvalo relaxed and amused as he scanned the private detective's report. Everything was detailed: Joe's links with other bootleggers; an arrest and a six-month jail sentence; two Hollywood divorce cases in which he was named; the hijacking at San Diego and hospitalization; the ongoing affair with the actress Juanita Torres; and the times and places of Joe's meetings with Dale during the two weeks that Ross had had him under surveillance.

Joe finished reading the detective's report and tossed it onto the desk. "I suppose you went to all this trouble to have something to show Dale."

"If I have to."

"Go ahead. I've told her everything."

"Including Juanita Torres?"

Joe's eyes flickered. He shook a cigarette out of its case and lighted it. "I thought I was here to talk about Dale."

"You are. And ten thousand dollars."

"She's worth more than that."

"But you aren't." Ross watched the sulky hesitation. "Fifteen thousand if you leave Los Angeles permanently, and by tomorrow."

"I'm afraid that doesn't fit in with my plans."

"All right. Then the family will ship Dale out of state. We'll find an Eastern college."

Joe blew a cloud of smoke toward the ceiling and watched it. "You miss the main point. Dale is in love with me, or thinks she is, which is just as good. Ship her out of state. In a week she'll be right back in my bed." He lowered his gaze to Ross. "Let's stop beating our chests and talk like businessmen. I'm tired of collecting bullets. I want out of the booze line. But it isn't easy with my background." He smiled with mock apology. "Unless, of course, you happen to have an opening in Seadon Oil. Not just any job, but something right for the future husband of your favorite niece."

Ross hunched forward in his chair, scowling. "If you marry Dale, we'll have it annulled."

"On what grounds? She's legal age. Besides, Dale wouldn't go along. So let's keep everything clean. Let's close the deal and make Dale a June bride."

"And if I say no?"

"Then I'll just have to bring Dale out in the open. After we've hit a few local hotels, your society friends will know she's a bootlegger's piece. Maybe a pregnant one, too."

Ross thought that if he were only fifteen years younger, he

would break every bone in Joe's body. Instead he had to say, "I'll talk it over with the family. I'll get back to you."

"I'm sure you will."

After Joe had gone, Ross sat and gazed about the library at the symbols of Seadon achievement—the painting of the Salt Springs gusher, the photos of tankers and refineries and ribbon-cutting ceremonies. Wealth was supposed to guarantee security; if not happiness, at least untouchability. The Seadons had warmed themselves at the fire of that illusion, while all about them, in the darkness of the jungle, beasts of prey marked their every move and waited to pounce.

Ross picked up the detective's report and read it through again. The man had been thorough, meticulous in detail; everyone was named, with date and hour and address. It ought to convince Dale—if it did not have the opposite effect and rush her to Joe's defense. She was a proud girl, in a dangerous emotional state.

Ross concentrated on the last page of the report, the most damning. Nowhere did it indicate who had prepared the report, nor for whom. Dale was mentioned by name only twice, and twice more referred to as "client's niece." Just four references. Easy to remove with the point of a penknife. Ross smiled to himself. He tore off the page, cut four neat rectangles, folded the page, and placed it in a plain envelope. Then he sealed it and addressed it to Juanita Torres.

Chapter 20

PEOPLE OUGHT to have more consideration, Dale told Joe, than to call up on a rainy Saturday night and want a case of liquor delivered within half an hour. Business was business, Joe replied. And loneliness was loneliness, she retorted. So, rather than stay behind, Dale accompanied Joe, seated alongside him in the plumber's truck which he used for squeamish customers. By the time they returned to Laurel Canyon, the rain was approaching a cloudburst. The windshield wiper was useless and Joe had to peer out the side window to guide the truck up the dirt road, which was now a churning channel of water and debris. Then at last the gate and the two German police dogs barking. "Crazy mutts!" Joe grunted. "Coming out in this rain, must be a coyote around." Joe set the parking brake and got out and splashed to the gate. Dale watched him unlock it and swing it open and gesture "down" to the dogs. Then, as he turned back toward the truck, there was a loud crack. For an instant Dale thought it was thunder, until she saw the shattered window glass in her lap. Then a second crack, and the windshield exploded. She shrieked and threw herself flat on the seat. She heard three more gunshots in rapid succession. Then only the rain drumming on the roof of the truck. She raised her head timidly and stared through the broken windshield. Joe was face down in the mud; one of the dogs was licking his outstretched hand.

She dropped to her knees and cradled his head in her arms. It was already over; blood from his lips mingled with the rain and washed into the mud. Somewhere in the darkness down the road a motor started up and faded away.

She stood up, drenched and shivering, numb to all thoughts except one. Not that Joe had been murdered, not that someone had waited in ambush, but that those first two bullets had been meant for her. Should she run to a neighbor for protection? No. The nearest house was at least five minutes on foot. And they would call the police; there would be a scandal. But she had to get away, and she must leave no clues. First her overnight case in the bedroom; after that she went rapidly through the sitting room and picked up her lipsticked cigarette butts and dumped them into her handbag. She scoured more lipstick off a drinking glass in the kitchen. At least, she thought, she had learned something from all those crime movies. What else now? The keys to Joe's roadster. It would never do to drive the plumbing truck; all that smashed glass would attract attention.

When she reached the main Laurel Canyon road, she followed it down to Sunset Boulevard and turned east until she found a dark side street. Before she abandoned the car, she wiped her handkerchief over the steering wheel and the door handle; all that remained now was to find a drugstore somewhere along Sunset. And a pay telephone.

Ross listened grimly to Dale's sobbing account as he drove her back to Ridgemont. It was, he thought, an eerie echo of that night of so many years before when her mother had wept out the details of Harley Stewart's attempt to kill her under the wheels of a Southern Pacific train. Everything was the same hysterical jumble—Dale's sorrow for Joe, terror at her own near death, comfort at the sight of her uncle, Joe alive, Joe in the mud. "He said he was getting out of bootlegging. But they wouldn't let him! They tried to get him in San Diego, then just waited for another chance. But why did they want to kill me too? Why me?"

Ross flinched inwardly. Juanita Torres must be mad. He had expected her to confront Joe, and probably Dale. He had counted on the knowledge that Joe was sleeping with another woman to bring Dale to her senses. But murder!

"The main thing," he said finally, "is to keep your name out of this mess. Did anyone see you at the house? A neighbor?"

"No. They're too far away."

"How about your sorority? Anybody know where you were?"

"I think Aud guessed. But I told the housemother I was spending the weekend with you."

"And you are. If anybody asks questions, I'll say you've been with me the whole time."

It was a sleepless night for niece and uncle; Dale in grief, Ross in worry. Where was Juanita Torres? At some police station blurting out a confession? Perhaps claiming temporary insanity and producing that page from the detective's report? Thank God, it couldn't be traced. Unless the detective came forward.

Sunday morning's radio news gave an answer of sorts. Joe Carvalo, a bootlegger and rumored friend of certain film actresses, had been killed in a gangland shooting. Police were questioning suspects.

So Dale had been right, after all. Or, Ross wondered uneasily, had the police accepted the obvious because it suited their convenience? In any case, Juanita Torres was not implicated and so, in effect, Ross was absolved. *Kyrie eleison.*

"Oh, my poor poor baby!" Leah wept when Ross delivered Dale in San Francisco and reported what he had dared not trust to the telephone. David Marcus was less sympathetic. "You've seen the last of USC, young lady. Your next school will be where they keep you under lock and key."

"Oh, no!" Dale wailed. "Not a convent!"

"It's that, or where my sisters went. Convent or finishing school in Switzerland. Take your choice."

It was Switzerland.

Dale's involvement with Joe Carvalo produced two side effects. The first was when Gene told his parents of the affair. "That settles it," Owen said. "We're not letting *our* kids off the leash. If Gene and the others want to go to college, they'll do so living under our roof. We're moving to Los Angeles."

The second effect was that Ross began to think of Europe. Everybody was going or had been. Leah and David were escorting Dale to a finishing school outside Lausanne; Tom and Ginny had toured Europe with Louise; Philip Barnard had gone with his classmates; his mother made it an annual habit. It was high time for Ross Seadon. "Why not?" Owen agreed. "Slater and I can run the store. And next year we'll trade off, and Tana and I will go."

Europe, Ross discovered, was giddy with prosperity, fueled in part by the flood of American tourist dollars. Ross reveled in the luxuries of the great hotels, the Excelsiors and Carltons and Grands and Ritzes, with their marble bathrooms and heated towel racks and clouds of servants. London fascinated him, for it was the nerve center of the great international oil companies: Shell Transport, Burmah Oil, Anglo Persian. The financial pages of the newspapers were like a roll call of the oil nobility: Sir Henri Deterding, Lord Cowdray, Sir Chester Beatty, "Mr. Five Per Cent" Gulbenkian. It was in London, as Ross crossed the lobby of the Savoy, that he encountered none other than G. G. Haggerty. "Well! What are you doing out of the playpen?" he greeted Ross.

"Same as you. Business," Ross lied.

Haggerty gave a lukewarm "Oh?" and added, "I'm just in from Venezuela. Got me a nice little concession there that the

Johnny Bulls want to bankroll." He smiled triumphantly. "Not here, boy. Throw up outside."

Ross intended to complete his European tour in Rome, but first there was Switzerland and Dale. Lausanne reminded him of San Francisco, if one omitted the French Alps in the background. Lake Geneva, with white sailboats skimming over its sapphire waters, needed only the Golden Gate; and the hills to which Lausanne clung required only cable cars to complete the similarity. Uncle and niece spent their first morning together tramping the up-and-down streets while Ross brought Dale abreast of family gossip—chiefly Owen and Tana's move to Los Angeles and Ginny's coming marriage to a relative of Ollie Eakins. What the young man did for a living was unclear, but Louise had said his family was in Montana copper and he was a star polo player. Ross had promised to be back from Europe in time to give Ginny away and to arrange for a generous dowry.

"Have I changed much, Uncle Ross?" Dale asked that afternoon as they were strolling the foredeck of the lake steamer they had boarded for Montreux.

"Quite a bit," Ross said. Gone were the nervous mannerisms, the fidgeting with hair, and chewing of fingernails. She wore no make-up (her school was strict on that point), and she had abandoned the slinky walk which she had borrowed from Hollywood films. "At least on the outside," Ross added. "Inside, I don't know."

"That's where it's happened." She smiled gravely. "I've had a lot of time to think about Joe. He was part of my growing up. Without him—or what happened to him—I wouldn't be here."

"But you like Lausanne?"

"Except when I get homesick. But then I think how lucky I am to be in the same city where Voltaire and Dickens lived, and where Gibbon wrote part of the *Decline and Fall of the Roman Empire*. It's a wonderful place for writers."

"Tell me more about school," he prompted.

"Well, you saw the girls. Most of them are English and French. We get along well enough; but all they talk about is going home and marrying and settling into society. They're finished, all right. But I want more. A real college education, so I can make my own living."

Ross leaned against the boat's railing and stared. "What kind of living?"

"I want to write. No, don't laugh. I may sound like Mother and her singing 'career,' and I know work sounds simple when you've never done it. But I want to try, anyway." She unfolded her plan. One of the professors at school had told Dale that he and his wife would be glad to have her live with them if she wanted to attend the University of Lausanne; they were childless and would welcome her as they had other students in the past. And when Dale returned to America she would have the cachet of a European education to impress book editors. She was full of novels, she thought; there ought to be a story in an American girl studying in Switzerland, and the love story of herself and Joe Carvalo was surely the equal of Kathleen Norris. She might even sell it to the movies. "You know," she concluded, "I've always had a wild imagination. Maybe I can turn it into dollars."

"You just might," Ross said. "Have you written home about this?"

"Not yet. I'm afraid they'll say no."

In capital letters, he thought. Yet damn it, the girl should be given a chance. She had a tensile strength no one suspected. She was a true Seadon.

He saw her eyes appealing to him. "Don't write," he said. "I'll work on them."

"Oh, would you?" She flung her arms around his neck. "I'm glad you're my uncle; it's even better than being my father. There's just enough distance between us to make us close." She kissed his cheek and then his mouth, and for that brief moment Ross envied Joe Carvalo.

The wedding of Ginny Seadon to Gurney Forbes, Jr., did more than unite two young persons; it bridged the ten-year rift between Ross and Louise. They might never again live together as man and wife, but their rivalry for the affections of their children was at an end. Louise, everyone agreed, had chosen the right course: separation rather than divorce. She was still Mrs. Ross Seadon, with her country estate at Woodside, her art collection, her Catholic good works, her place in fashionable circles in San Francisco and New York and London and Paris. She enjoyed that unassailable position in Catholic society—The Wife.

It was an afternoon wedding in the Woodside parish church. Ginny's brother Tom was the best man, and Gurney Forbes's sister the maid of honor. As Ross escorted his daughter down the aisle and waited to give her away, he thought that for the first time in her life Ginny was almost beautiful. Perhaps not a Dale Lantry, and certainly without her cousin's magnetism; but she had, at least for that afternoon, the same blond radiance that had attracted Ross to Louise on that evening when he had first entered the house on Van Ness Avenue.

How little time he had spent with his daughter—and with Tom, too. Brief visits when he was in San Francisco on business, Christmas and birthday checks, an occasional long-distance call. A father *in absentia*. Well, he would make up for it now. Ginny and Gurney would honeymoon on the *Franconia*, a round-the-world trip paid for by Ross; and when they returned to San Francisco, they would furnish their apartment at Sloane's and send him all the bills.

Ross and Louise were sitting together during the Mass when she whispered to him, "Tom wants to talk to you."

"What about?"

"He'll tell you. Just don't jump down his throat." Had he ever? Louise nodded, as if reading his thought. "Be patient. He's overawed with you; thinks he can't measure up."

It had never occurred to Ross; he was as blind as his own father, who had never realized his son's feeling of inadequacy.

The wedding reception was held on the oak-dotted lawn which fronted Louise's house. It was there, after the wedding party had posed for the photographer, that Tom finally approached Ross. "Sir, would it bother you if I didn't finish at Stanford?"

"It damn well would." Ross caught himself; there he was, jumping down the boy's throat. "Look, son, maybe you don't appreciate how important it is nowadays to have a diploma."

"I do. But I want it from the Colorado School of Mines."

Ross felt his heart bound. The Colorado School of Mines was famous for one category of graduates—geologists. "You're sure, son? The world is full of geologists. We can hire them by the gross."

"I don't care. I want to work with you. And Gene and Uncle Owen."

So it was not to be the Bay Steel Company; Louise and her father had lost. That explained the faint coolness which Ross had detected in talking with Arnold Schroder. The boy was sharper than he had given him credit for. Bay Steel would have been a comfortable berth, but it could never equal the opportunities of Seadon Oil. If it was a selfish decision, Ross cared not one whit; at last he had a son with whom he could be open—not like Philip, his true first-born, with whom he was forced to play the empty role of family friend. From this day forward it would be Tom and Ross, together, inseparable.

When he finally spoke, there was a huskiness to his voice. "All that matters right now, son, is that you've made your choice. But before you decide on petroleum geology, I think it's time you knew where Seadon Oil is going. Tomorrow I'm getting together with Owen and Dave Marcus and I'm going to spring something on them. I'd like you to be there. *If*, that is"—he put his hand on Tom's shoulder for emphasis—"if you give me your word that what you hear goes no further. Not a word to anyone. Okay?"

"Yes, sir. I understand, sir."

"And no more 'sir' stuff. It's 'Dad.' "

They met in David Marcus' office high above Montgomery Street. Ross had given no clue as to the purpose of the gathering nor why Tom Seadon was present, or Owen's son Gene, who had been invited by Ross as an afterthought to forestall any feeling of family favoritism.

Ross stood behind a club chair, resting his elbows on its back, and addressed himself to Gene. "Before we get started, I want you to give me the same promise I've got from Tom. You will not repeat anything said in this room. Not to your mother, to your sisters, not to anyone, any time, anywhere. If you can't make that promise, I'll have to ask you to leave."

Gene swallowed and glanced at his father, who gave a snort of impatience. "Of course he promises. Why the hell all this drama?"

"I'm coming to it." Ross smiled leisurely at the expectant faces. "You know, I learned a lot in Europe. It's a hell of a big world and a hell of a big market for oil. Stuck off here in California, we think Seadon Oil is the big cheese of independents— which it is, west of the Rockies. But that's just a beginning. We've got to become a major; we've got to go international." He paused to relish the effect. Tom and Gene, with the innocence of youth, were properly impressed; but for Owen and Marcus it was here-we-go-again time. Ross resumed. "I learned something else in London—why G. G. Haggerty didn't put up a fight when we moved into the Middle West with Tri-State. Haggerty's got bigger fish to fry; he's taking Pantex into Venezuela."

Owen kicked a shoe thoughtfully. "When's he going to learn? He got his fingers burnt in Mexico when they nationalized, and it'll happen all over again."

"Maybe. And maybe not. Standard and Royal Dutch are pouring tens of millions into Venezuela, which means they must feel pretty safe. Personally, I hope Haggerty hits it rich in Lake Maracaibo. I'd love to have him do our work for us, because . . . because Seadon Oil is taking over Pantex."

David Marcus leaned back in his desk chair and cleared his

throat; Owen scowled; Tom and Gene blinked. Ross laughed at their reactions. "No, I haven't been hitting the poppy pipe. You want to know how we do it?"

"If it's not too much trouble." Owen sniffed.

"All right. Remember when we took over Tri-State Oil and Slater Dougal told us Haggerty had made an offer for the company? Haggerty was going to buy Tri-State for Pantex stock, so he had to show Slater the books. What Slater saw was very interesting, although I didn't really think it through until I got to Europe. It seems Mr. G. G. Haggerty owns only three hundred thousand shares of Pantex."

"Out of how many?" Owen asked.

"One million. The company has ten million dollars in preferred stock, about half of it issued to Haggerty, and bonded indebtedness of thirty million. But all we care about is the common stock, because it has voting control. With one million common, all we have to do is buy five hundred and ten thousand shares and we got the company."

Marcus reached for a scratch pad and pencil. "What's the price of the stock?"

"Forty-seven dollars on yesterday's market."

Marcus scribbled the figures and multiplied. "God, that's twenty-four million dollars."

Owen snorted. "Just about twice the cash reserve of Seadon Oil. It's impossible."

"For Seadon Oil, yes." Ross nodded. "But you and I and Dave are buying it personally."

"Oh, Jesus, Mary, and Joseph!"

Marcus shook his head. "I don't know how many millions you boys got, but I'm just a poor banker."

"Could you raise one million?"

"If I bust a gut."

"Okay. And Owen can kick in two, and I'll go two. Five million is all we need on margin." Ross glanced at Owen. "You don't believe it?"

"Hell, no! For Christ's sake, Ross, if we tried to buy five hundred and ten thousand shares at forty-seven, the damned stock would jump to a hundred. It would be clear out of reach."

"I know that. So we take our time; we nibble at it. We buy every week, every month, maybe for a year, maybe for two years. Sure, we'll drive up the price after a while, and it'll get more expensive for us. But the stock we've already bought will be worth more, too; we'll have more borrowing power. And when the day comes that we've got our five hundred and ten thousand shares, we turn them over to Seadon Oil and the company pays us in stock equal to whatever Pantex is selling at—"

"Slow down a minute," Marcus broke in. "Before we turn over our Pantex stock, we'd have to pay off our margin to the brokers. Where do we find the money?"

"Hell, that's easy. Once it gets out that we've sewed up Pantex, every bank in the country will be glad to lend us the cash. That's the least of our worries."

Marcus gazed out the window at Telegraph Hill and hummed thoughtfully. "And all I'd have to put up is one million?"

"That's all. One million to make five million. Maybe even more. . . . And you and I, Owen, at least ten million."

Owen rubbed his chin. "There's just one worm in your apple. When we start buying up Pantex stock, our names are going to appear on the transfer books. When Haggerty sees what's happening, he'll go into the market and buy up the stock himself."

"He would if he knew, but he won't. We aren't transferring the stock into our names. Dave knows how it's done."

Marcus slapped his hand against the desk. "Street certificates!"

"Right! We let the stock stand in the names of the brokers. We have Dave place all the orders, so the Seadons are kept out of sight. Let's say Dave buys a block through Jerry Braithwaite. The only name that will show on the Pantex books is Braithwaite and Company. The same with brokers in Los Angeles, New York, Chicago, all over the country. Haggerty won't have an inkling." Ross grinned at Owen. "What do you say, boy?"

"Maybe. I don't know. I keep wondering, if Pantex is such easy pickings, why hasn't somebody else pulled it off?"

"Because nobody has had the guts. Or the imagination. . . . So how about it?"

Owen sighed. "Let's break for lunch."

They ate and returned to the office and reviewed the project step by step. Possible pitfalls were re-examined, rates of margin interest were computed and how much in Pantex dividends would be received during the buying campaign. By midafternoon even Owen was convinced. "I'd give anything"—he chuckled—"to see Haggerty's face the day we walk off with his candy bag!" All that remained was to sign a memorandum of partnership and an authority for David Marcus to act as agent for the Seadon brothers. The following morning he would telephone Jerry Braithwaite and place a buy order for five hundred shares of Pantex Oil.

Ross and Tom said goodbye to Owen and Gene outside the Marcus bank and then strolled down Montgomery Street. "You see now," Ross said, "why it's a waste of time to become an oil geologist. We don't need to find oil, just grab the companies that got it."

"Then you're saying that Uncle Owen is old-fashioned."

It was not the reaction Ross had expected. "In some ways, yes. But you notice he went along with me. Owen is smart enough to change with the times."

Tom understood the implication. "Okay. I'll stay on at Stanford."

"Good. And switch your major. Go for a law degree." Ross saw his son's look of consternation. "I know. It's late in the game; it may take an extra year of college, but I want an attorney in the family."

"Why? You can hire the best there is. I want to work with you, Dad."

"You will be. Right in Wil Caruth's department." He slipped his arm around Tom's waist. "And when the right time comes, I'll see that you're more important than your old man. Don't ask why or how; just trust me, son."

Chapter 21

Ross's trip to Europe had provided him with a larger vision for Seadon Oil; but meanwhile, until the shares of Pantex had been accumulated, what to do? The day-to-day routine was without challenge; and whenever a problem did arise, Slater Dougal was there to solve it. Dougal was more than the vice president in charge of Midwestern operations; he was a tireless worker in public relations. He attended Chamber of Commerce dinners (which bored both Ross and Owen) and delivered speeches on civic affairs which somehow managed to become panegyrics on Seadon Oil; he instigated the first annual picnic for the company's employees; he even found a town house just off Wilshire Boulevard, in Fremont Square, for Owen and Tana and their children. Slater Dougal was, in short, invaluable—and an irritation. "God, I wish Slater would relax," Ross grumbled one day to Owen. "Every time I go to the men's room, I expect to see him there with a towel and a whisk broom. Christ, if he'd just take up golf!"

Owen laughed. "Or a mistress!" A few months later Ross had cause to remember Owen's joke, for it was Ross himself who embarked on an affair.

Kay Vanleigh, according to Personnel's report, was thoroughly qualified to be Ross's new executive secretary. Her shorthand was excellent; her typing speed was seventy words per minute; she spoke French and German; she was twenty-three and unmarried; her personality was rated "pleasing." There was one negative comment: "May cause friction among staff." Translated, she was pretty. The eyes were dark and lustrous; the hair black and cut in bangs; the mouth smiling yet strong; the legs, highly visible in the new fashion of short skirts, beyond reproach.

It had come about by accident. First a shy kiss on Ross's birthday; then late work at the office and a nightcap at a speakeasy; then Kay's sprained ankle and a taxi to her apartment. But why this girl? Ross asked himself. He knew a dozen attractive women who were available, women with social background and financial independence, women who would not cause lifted eyebrows when they entered a restaurant on his arm. Perhaps that was it. Eyebrows did go up with Kay. Men looked at him with envy. He was not a burnt-out fifty; he could hold a girl young enough to be his daughter. She had given him back his own youth.

In the beginning he was puzzled by her own motivation. She was not a gold digger. She did not hint for jewelry; she was content with her tiny two rooms on Beaudry Avenue; she did not want a motorcar. "Kay, what *do* you want?" Ross finally demanded. "Don't you aspire to anything?"

"Yes," she replied. "To be secretary to the president of Seadon Oil. To be in the center of things." It was as simple as that; she was sexually drawn by his authority. Love did not enter the equation; it was power.

Above all, she was discreet. In the office there were no telltale glances, no terms of familiarity; it was always "Mr. Seadon" and "Miss Vanleigh." No one on the executive floor, Ross told himself, could possibly suspect. Kay was the model secretary who managed his appointments, took dictation, and wrote out checks for his signature. And who never questioned the purpose of the fifty thousand dollars paid each month to David Marcus.

One full year had passed since Marcus had made his first purchase of Pantex stock, and he and the Seadon brothers were scarcely a third of the way to their goal. Ross had not foreseen the great Coolidge bull market in which all stocks, good and bad, were soaring into the clouds. Pantex, which had traded at 47 a year before, now was 78, and each monthly payment to Marcus bought fewer and fewer shares. "Christ," Owen brooded to Ross, "we won't corner the market before the end of next year—and it'll take a hell of a lot more than five million. Every time Dave puts in another buy order, Pantex jumps five points."

"Let it," Ross said. "It makes the stock we already got just that much more valuable. Gives us more borrowing power. Next month instead of sending Dave fifty thousand apiece, we go to seventy-five."

But by the Christmas of 1927, Pantex was trading at 95; and on March 13, 1928—the day when Radio Corporation jumped 21 points—Pantex traded at 130. Then, on June 11, David Marcus telephoned Ross: "God Almighty, the stock market is coming apart at the seams. Pantex just dropped eighteen points."

"How's the rest of the market?"

"Worse. Especially the Giannini companies. Bank of Italy is down a hundred . . . Bank of America, a hundred and twenty."

"Holy Jesus! What's Jerry Braithwaite say?"

"He's shaking in his boots. But he thinks the worst is over."

"I agree. It's a buying opportunity. Tomorrow grab some more Pantex."

Ross's confidence proved correct; within a month the market reached new highs. Seadon Oil traded at an even 100, and Pantex at 155. The *Wall Street Journal* carried an interview with G. G. Haggerty in which he declared, "The investing public is buying Pantex for one reason—quality." Ross and Owen smiled. If he only knew. But when David Marcus came down from San Francisco for the annual meeting of Seadon Oil, he was disturbed. "Pantex is just too damned high. We ought to back away from it for a while, until the price comes down."

"I've been thinking the same thing," Ross said. "Meanwhile we can build up our war chest by trading some other stocks." He tossed a telegram across the desk to Owen. "I've subscribed to an advisory service in New York. This is what they're recommending."

Owen read the telegram aloud. "MILKING TIME FOR MOO STOP SPARKS ARE FLYING. What is this? Code?"

"Yep. Means sell National Dairy and buy Radio. Are you game?"

Owen rubbed his chin and looked at Marcus. "Are the dice hot or cold?"

"Hot. Let's roll 'em again."

Once more it was the right move. The price of Pantex sagged while the Seadon brothers and Marcus doubled their money in other stocks. Wall Street, it seemed clear, was another name for Easy Street; and after Herbert Hoover defeated Al Smith in the coming presidential election, then the sky would be the limit. After all, weren't the Republicans promising "a chicken in every pot, a car in every garage"? New brokerage houses opened on Spring Street and spread westward along Sixth and Seventh. One was a branch of Braithwaite and Company, on the ground floor of the Seadon Oil Company Building, with Jerry Braithwaite's son the office manager. Ross immediately opened an account. He had never felt more confident. Everything he did was right; nothing could stop him. Kay said so. And Owen and David Marcus. Even Arnold Schroder telephoned from San Francisco: "Ross, you have the Midas touch. What's good in the market?"

General Motors, Auburn Auto, General Electric, Radio Corporation. And Seadon Oil.

Everything seemed "good in the market." On all sides Ross heard stories of success. The elevator operators, the barber, the headwaiter at Goodfellows Grotto—everyone boasted he was on the road to Easy Street. All it took was a few hundred dollars on margin to control shares worth thousands. The servants at Ridgemont were infected. Brooks, the butler, and Mrs. Pryor, the housekeeper, came to Ross.

"Sir, Mrs. Pryor and I have got a bit put by, and we're wondering if it might not be wise to invest it in some good stocks. Perhaps you might have a suggestion."

Ross was fond of Brooks, who reminded him of a graying English rector. "Well, Brooks, if you go into the market on my recommendation, will you get out when I tell you to?"

"Of course, sir."

"Then Seadon Oil. You can't lose." It was a certainty; once Seadon Oil announced its takeover of Pantex, its shares would rocket.

In early December 1928 Owen and Tana proposed to Ross that instead of the annual Christmas party at Ridgemont they would reopen El Encanto and invite all the executives and family friends for an old-fashioned Spanish *Natividad*. When Ross agreed it was a spendid idea, Tana added, "And, of course, you will bring Kay."

"Miss Vanleigh?" Ross feigned surprise until he saw Tana's eyes dancing. "So you know?"

"Owen told me months ago, my dear. Everybody knows." She shook her head in reproof. "Sin is beautiful, is it not? But it is still sin, unless you marry."

"That's out of the question with Louise. Kay understands."

"But you love her?"

"What's love? She's . . . useful."

He was in a cynical mood these days; his daughter Ginny had divorced Gurney Forbes on the grounds that he cared more for his polo pony; now, one month after marrying a society bandleader, she was being named co-respondent by the wife of some stunt flyer.

If "everybody" knew about Kay, Ross decided, they might as well come out in the open; Kay would live at Ridgemont. She accepted the new arrangement with one proviso: that she remain Ross's executive secretary. She cared nothing about domesticity, she said; she would leave Ridgemont to the capable direction of Brooks and Mrs. Pryor. So every morning the chauffeur drove Kay and Ross to the office and picked them up every evening. Some nights they brought work home and Ross dictated in the library; other nights they entertained and Kay was the efficient hostess. "Well, aren't you the cradle snatcher," Liz Barnard commented to Ross when she met Kay for the first time. "What do your kids think of her?"

"Who knows?"

But he *did* know. Tom, now graduated and working in Wil Caruth's legal department, was polite but cool. Ginny, on a recent trip to Los Angeles with her newest lover, had taken one look and made an unpleasant noise with her tongue. On the other hand, Owen's son Gene, who came up frequently from the Wilmington refinery, treated Kay like a favorite sister.

And Dale Lantry, in her latest letter from Lausanne, wrote that she had the news from Leah. "Good for you! It's about time!" It was the same letter in which Dale reported she had sold a short story to *The New Yorker* about American expatriates in Europe, and on the strength of that she was going to remain abroad after graduation and become "a real foreign correspondent."

"I like Kay," Liz went on to Ross. "She's stylish. But you ought to get her some jewels."

"She doesn't care for them."

"That's odd." Liz examined the emeralds glowing on her own wrist. "That's very, very odd."

On March 26, 1929, the interest rate for "call money" rose from 9 per cent to 20 per cent, and the stock market fell sharply. Pantex Oil sank from 268 to 241. For the first time Ross began to feel queasy. Only last November, Radio, in which he was heavily committed, had traded at 400; but on December 7 it had lost 72 points in one single trading session. It was time to take a good hard look, and so Ross and Owen returned to San Francisco and ate lunch at the States Restaurant with David Marcus.

"All we need is another thirty-five thousand shares of Pantex," Marcus reported, "but even on margin, we'd have to put in another million, six hundred thousand."

"You think maybe if we wait, it'll drop some more?" Owen asked.

"It's got to. The whole market will. Business isn't that all-fired great. Schroder says orders are down at Bay Steel, and the same with a lot of other companies. God knows, the farmers are hurting. They bought too much land during the war, planted too many acres, and now they're suffering for their greed."

"So what do we do?" Ross said.

"Let's stick with our General Motors, Westinghouse, and Radio. There's bound to be a summer rally; then we unload and buy our thiry-five thousand Pantex." The banker waved at a man approaching the booth. "Speaking of the devil . . ."

Ross had not seen Arnold Schroder since Ginny's wedding and was disturbed at his appearance. His face seemed gray and caved in, and his shoulders hunched forward as if breathing were difficult.

He seated himself across from Marcus and, after a few halting pleasantries, said, "Dave, this new rate for call money—I hear some companies are turning over their excess cash to you bankers."

"They are."

"Would you be interested in Bay Steel?"

"Hell, yes. We'll take all the idle cash you got."

"Six million?"

"Sure. We're charging the brokers twenty per cent. I'll pay you half. Ten per cent."

"Secured?"

"By the brokers' best collateral. Nothing but blue chips."

Schroder extended his hand across the table. "I'll see you tomorrow."

After he had left the table, Marcus smiled at the Seadons. "I know what you're thinking. Six million would cinch Pantex. If it was anybody but Arnold . . . But you know how he is."

Ross nodded. Arnold Schroder frightened easily; at the first hint of trouble he might call the loan. "We can wait, Dave. This summer will do it."

But in July Pantex had climbed to 300. On the other hand, Radio, in which the Seadons and Marcus had invested over two million, was still slipping. Ross grew restive again; and when Liz Barnard attended the next party at Ridgemont, he took her aside.

"What does Phil think about the market?"

"He's nervous. He wrote me last week that his company is telling their people to take profits. He says Bernie Baruch is selling and going into gold and bonds. Phil thinks I should, too."

"Have you?"

"Yes. I just put a million into government bonds. I hope you're not in deep."

"Up to my ears."

It was the same evening that Liz gave Ross another snapshot of Philip. Boating on Long Island Sound, with his arm around the daughter of the president of his firm. "Anything serious?" Ross asked and Liz smiled. "Perhaps." Later, when the party was over and Kay had gone to bed, Ross added the photo to his special album and returned it to the top shelf in the library.

Ross repeated to Owen Philip Barnard's advice to his mother. "I think Phil's right," Owen said. "Let's cash in our chips and buy that last hunk of Pantex."

"But damn it, Pantex is three hundred and thirty. I'd like to squeeze a little more profit out of Motors and Westinghouse. Let's wait but keep our noses to the wind."

The wind appeared to blow fair. Wherever Ross looked, he saw optimism. Outside Grauman's Chinese and Egyptian theaters there were lines of people waiting to pay premium prices to see the new talkies; at the subdivision where Liz Barnard had invested heavily, bright-eyed salesmen were signing buyers for lots at $10,000 and up. In August the stock market soared still higher. In September *Ladies' Home Journal* published an interview with John J. Raskob, vice president of General Motors, under the title "Everybody Ought to Be Rich." The secret? Buy shares. The stock market took off again.

On a warm Sunday afternoon in October, Ross was lazing beside the swimming pool and watching Kay in the water. When Brooks brought a tray of highballs he said, "Begging your pardon, sir, but Mrs. Pryor and I have been wondering about the market."

"Yes?"

"Well, we've doubled our money in Seadon Oil, thanks to you, sir, and we thought perhaps we should buy more."

"For cash or margin?"

"Margin, sir. Our broker says we've built up a good bit of credit."

"Then go ahead. Seadon Oil is just about ready for a big jump." The Pantex takeover, of course.

Kay, listening at the edge of the pool, called to Ross, "Is there something you haven't told me about?" She saw his grin. "How many shares should I buy?"

"All you can."

It was Thursday, October 24. As Ross and Kay stepped from their limousine outside the Seadon Oil Building, they saw an elderly couple standing in the entrance of the branch office of Braithwaite and Company. The woman was crying and the man, probably her husband, was shouting at passersby, "Thieves! They're all thieves!"

Ross frowned to Kay. "Maybe I ought to have a look. Meet you upstairs."

At first he could not believe the figures being posted by the marker boys. General Motors down 8; Auburn Auto down 13; Seadon Oil down 11; Pantex down 16. And the morning was young.

Ross hurried to the office of young Braithwaite. "Dick, what's happening?"

"God knows. All I can tell you is I got a blizzard of sell orders."

He went upstairs to the executive floor, and Owen met him in the reception room. "Dave Marcus is on the phone. He says he can get us our thirty-five thousand Pantex at three hundred and ten."

"*Three hundred and ten?* I just saw it at three twenty-eight!" Then he remembered the late tape.

"Shall I tell Dave to buy?"

"Yes. . . . No! . . . We got to get out of our other stuff first. Let's wait for the turnaround."

By noon the ticker had fallen 104 minutes behind trading. Pantex was down 39 points, Seadon Oil 28. David Marcus telephoned again. "Ross, I got a margin call from Jerry Braithwaite. He wants seven hundred thousand."

"How much?" Surely there must be a mistake.

"Seven hundred thousand. We got to come up with it by tomorrow's opening."

For a moment all Ross could think of was the pulsing in his eardrums. "Dave . . . look . . . tell Jerry I'll have his office here sell some of our General Motors and Auburn. . . . What about the brokers in New York and Chicago?"

"I'll probably have wires from them any time. Ross, I think you and Owen should get up here tomorrow."

"Right. We'll take the *Lark* tonight."

"And bring your checkbooks."

The next morning the Seadon brothers left the Third and Townsend Depot and went directly to Montgomery Street and the offices of Braithwaite and Company. Customers stood five deep around the ticker telegraph, groaning as each new price came out of the machine. General Motors was down 9, Auburn Auto 17, Pantex 22, Seadon Oil 18.

They crossed Montgomery to David Marcus' office. The banker, haggard-faced and grim, showed them the telegrams from the brokers in New York and Chicago. They wanted $1,200,000 extra margin. "I couldn't get them the money by this morning's opening," Marcus said. "I figure they sold us out forty thousand shares of Pantex."

"Jesus Chirst!" Owen moaned and sank down into a chair.

Marcus went on. "I got that seven hundred thousand to Jerry. Cleaned out my bank account and all my government bonds."

Ross grimaced. "We'll give you checks for our share."

Marcus nodded and reached for the ringing telephone. He listened for a moment, then put his hand over the phone. "Jerry needs another eight hundred thousand."

The Seadons stared at each other; their bank accounts would be drained. Ross took the phone from Marcus.

"Jerry? Ross Seadon. That Pantex stock you've been buying for Dave. Owen and I are in on it, too." He paused while Braithwaite stuttered his surprise, then: "Look, we're loaded with blue chips in our accounts with your Los Angeles office. But I'll be damned if we throw everything away in a panic market. Suppose Owen and I give you our personal notes?"

Braithwaite hemmed. "Well, I'm sure you guys are good for it. But I'll have to discount the notes at some bank."

"Okay, do it."

Ross hung up. "The next thing is to keep New York and Chicago from selling any more Pantex. Dave, can your bank telegraph say half a million in bankers' credit?"

"If you boys back it up, sure."

Owen made a strangling noise. "*How?* Ross, we're out of cash!"

"I know that. We'll have the Seadon Estate Company declare a special dividend. Leah can turn her share over to Dave."

Marcus frowned uneasily. "In other words, you'll give me your checks, and by the time they clear you hope you'll have the money?"

Ross smiled winningly. "Don't talk like a banker, Dave. Be Leah's husband, and my oldest and best friend. Okay?"

At noon, which was three P.M. in New York and closing time, the ticker was clattering four hours and eight minutes behind the final trade. When at last the machine went silent, Jerry Braithwaite tore off the tape and handed it to Ross. Pantex was down 55; Seadon Oil 41.

Ross sucked on his lower lip. "Where's this going to stop, Jerry? Is everybody crazy?"

"Completely. They've been nuts for years. Bellhops, scrubwomen, waiters, all playing on margin. Now they're called and it's you big boys who are suffering. The lambs are devouring the lions."

"And who's responsible?" Owen demanded. "You brokers chasing after commissions, the bankers greedy for twenty per cent interest."

Braithwaite gave a tired shrug; he had heard it all day. "Just tell me one thing: Do you still want to hold on to your Pantex?"

"Good God, yes!"

"Then I'll need more margin. A million six hundred thousand."

Owen blanched and Ross recoiled as if he had been struck. There was only one solution—liquidation. "Okay, Jerry," Ross said. "Phone your son in Los Angeles and tell him to sell the rest of my General Motors and my Radio. . . . Owen?"

"Yes. Mine, too."

On Saturday the market improved slightly. "Maybe we're out of the woods," Jerry Braithwaite said, and added, "I hope."

The Seadons decided to stay on in San Francisco to be with David Marcus for Monday's market. On Sunday morning Ross went to Woodside to visit Louise. Almost her first words were "Ross, I've lost a quarter of a million dollars."

"That all? You're lucky," he said. "How about Arnold?"

"Oh, he got out last week. But Bay Steel has six million on loan to Dave's bank. He's calling the loan tomorrow."

"Oh, Jesus God! He *can't!* He'll wreck the brokers!"

She fluttered her hands helplessly. "Father's still recovering from a stroke, Ross. He's got to have peace of mind."

The Seadon brothers ate Sunday dinner with their sister and David Marcus in the town house on Pacific Heights. The men silent and preoccupied, Leah talkative and confident. "There's nothing at all to worry about, my darlings," she said. "I've talked to my practitioner, and he's knowing the truth for us."

Owen sniffed. "We've got a bellyful of the truth."

"No. You're mesmerized by animal magnetism. Divine Love is our Abundance, full and overflowing."

When the Seadons returned to the Fairmont Hotel that night, they found a telegram.

PHILIP EXPECTS BAD MONDAY STOP DO YOU NEED HELP
STOP LOVE LIZ

Ross wrote the reply:

OVERWHELMED BY YOUR GENEROSITY STOP THANKS BUT
NO STOP LOVE ROSS AND OWEN

On Monday morning, October 28, the Seadons met in Marcus' office to plan their strategy before the market opened. The prime objective, they agreed, was to hold their position in Pantex. If necessary to maintain their margin, the three would liquidate all their remaining holdings—their General Electric, U.S. Steel, and Westinghouse. And if the market rallied, they might clear enough to buy back the lost shares of Pantex and even more. Today, they told themselves, they might claim the reward for three years of work—control of Pantex.

But the first figures on the tape confirmed Philip Barnard's fears. There were "gap openings" on the downside. Hour by hour prices crumbled. U.S. Steel, off $17\frac{1}{2}$; Westinghouse, off $34\frac{1}{2}$; General Electric, off $47\frac{1}{2}$; Pantex, off $62\frac{1}{4}$.

At midnight lights still burned in the offices along Montgomery Street as weary brokers and clerks struggled to catch up on their paperwork and to telegraph fresh margin calls. In David Marcus' office the Seadons watched the banker complete his computations.

Finally he threw down his pencil. "We're not only sold out in New York and Chicago, we owe the brokers over three and a quarter million."

Owen sucked in his breath and stared at Ross. "Should we call Liz?"

"And pull her down with us?" He pondered a moment. "Dave, any chance the bank can help us out?"

"None. We're stuck like everybody else. Schroder called his loan and I had to squeeze the brokers. All I got back was forty cents on the dollar."

Ross was not concerned with other people's troubles. "Then we ride it out alone. We still got a hundred and five thousand Pantex."

Marcus nodded. "Until Braithwaite calls for more margin. Only a rally can save us."

Ross stood at the hotel window and looked down at the lights at the foot of Nob Hill. It was two in the morning, and Montgomery Street was still working. He thought of another night, twenty-three years before, when he had watched from almost the same location, outside the Fairmont Hotel, as the financial district had gone up in flames. Then there had been the crackle of combustion; tonight there was silence. The cables had stopped in the slots down California Street; the ferries and freighters slept in their berths; the only sound was the fretful hoot of a switch engine as it tugged freight cars along the Embarcadero.

Suddenly Ross slammed a fist into his palm. "God damn that son of a bitch Haggerty!"

Owen poured another glass of bourbon and came to the window. "So it's his fault, is it?"

"No, but it doesn't stop me from hating that bastard's guts." He glowered defiantly. "Okay, spew it all out. I've been waiting for it."

Owen obliged. "You hate Haggerty because you can't bring him down. Because he's still got Pantex. You hate him because you've ruined Dave Marcus, ruined your sister, ruined me and Tana, the whole Seadon family—just so you could strut around the Big World Oil Man!" Owen's voice broke. "And I hate myself for letting you get away with it."

"Anything else?" Ross sneered. "Maybe tears? Prayers and Hail Marys?"

They were close to blows; then, as suddenly as it had flared, their anger faded. Ross reached for Owen's bourbon and tossed it down in one swallow. "We still got a fighting chance," he said. "Hell, we've been through rough patches before. Remember the night we loaded up that fulminate of mercury and took on Haggerty's armed guards? That all-out gamble at Salt Creek? We came through then; we'll come through now. There's *got* to be a rally."

Owen sighed. "Well, we'll know in just about five hours."

In five hours the dam broke. On previous mornings in the Braithwaite board room the crowd had reacted to the prices on the ticker with groans and curses; but on Tuesday, October 29, there was a stillness except for the clatter of the ticker and a clerk calling out the prices for the marker boys. Stocks were dropping five dollars between trades. Within minutes the tape was already running late; it would be, everybody saw, the heaviest volume in the history of the stock exchange. On the bulletin board a secretary chalked up flashes coming over the Dow Jones wire. The London and Paris exchanges had crashed. Commodity markets were in chaos. The Board of Governors of the New York Stock Exchange were in emergency meeting. The exchange would close for the next two days. But that would not save today. Jerry Braithwaite stood in his office doorway holding a telephone that connected directly to the trading floor in New York. The prices which he relayed to the white-faced listeners were five, ten, even fifteen dollars below those coming across the tape. A woman customer fainted; a man lunged at his broker with a cane. Ross and Owen chainsmoked and watched with churning stomachs for each new trade of Pantex. At eight A.M. it was down to 100. At nine A.M. Braithwaite asked for more margin and the Seadons shook their heads. Braithwaite sold 20,000 Pantex at 88. At ten A.M. he sold 30,000 at 72. At eleven A.M. he sold 30,000 at 61. By noon the Seadons and David Marcus had lost every single share of Pantex. Seadon Oil had dropped 58 dollars.

Owen turned to Ross. "I'm going home. I want to be with Tana tonight."

"How? Unless you fly."

"There's a first time for everything, isn't there?"

The brothers sat across the aisle from each other in the

309

cramped cabin of the Ford trimotor. Conversation was impossible over the roar of the engines, so they stared down at the vast open ranges of the San Joaquin Valley, at the dots which were automobiles crawling along Highway 99, at the rooftops of Weston, where they had started so many years before. As the plane climbed over the Tehachapis, Owen scribbled a note and passed it to Ross. "We're not just busted. We owe sixteen million."

Ross scratched his reply: "Wrong. Seventeen million."

The sun was setting as the limousine ground up the steep approach to Ridgemont. Through the screen of pines, Ross could see the majestic Tudor structure with its bay windows and soaring chimneys and stone ramparts. No one could take it away from him; he would hold on to it, no matter how. There had to be a way.

The limousine reached the crest and glided toward the house. It was then that Ross saw the people standing in a ring around the swimming pool. Kay and the servants. He told the chauffeur to stop and he got out. As he neared the pool, he saw Mrs. Pryor weeping; two men in uniform were tugging on a rope which descended into the water. Then a body broke to the surface. It was Brooks.

That night as Kay was undressing for bed, she called to Ross in the bathroom. "I saw a beautiful diamond bracelet at Brock's today. It's only nine thousand dollars." She waited. "Ross! What do you think?"

He was not thinking; he was vomiting.

BOOK
FIVE

Chapter 22

PRESIDENT HOOVER assured the nation that business was "fundamentally sound," and the soothsayers of Wall Street agreed. What if the October losses in the stock market were twice the nation's public debt and equal to the total cost of America's war against Imperial Germany? It was positive proof, according to the perverse logic of the day, that the United States was the richest nation in the world. As for those who had lost their life savings and those who had committed suicide—they must be regarded as by-products of Prosperity. Not everybody won at the race track or at cards; let the losers accept their misfortune. A new decade was at hand, and the 1930s would surpass all that had gone before.

The Seadon brothers took little comfort in such reasoning. Every passing day meant more interest to pay on their multi-million-dollar debts. Their first move was for Seadon Oil to declare a year-end cash dividend of what, to the stockholders, seemed staggering generosity. Seventy per cent of the dividend went to the Seadon Estate Company, which passed it on to the Seadon family. Ross and Owen received over four million dollars each, and Leah a similar amount, which she gave as an outright gift to David Marcus. The Eastern stockbrokers and the referee in bankruptcy for Braithwaite and Company were appeased, temporarily; but the drain of cash from Seadon Oil meant a halt to Ross's plans for expansion and Owen's for new exploration. The disappointment, coupled with their personal losses, brought a coolness between the brothers, which sometimes erupted into shouting matches. Everyone on the executive floor heard Owen's voice, audible in spite of the closed door, as he shouted at Ross, "You and your goddamned Pantex!"

In the spring of 1930 the stock market staggered upward again, and the optimists began talking about the new "baby bull market." It was a selling opportunity, the Seadons agreed, and the Estate Company sold off a large block of Seadon Oil stock and transferred the proceeds to the family members. "Another two million for each of us, and we'll be in the clear," Ross wrote to Leah, and added, "if the market holds." But it did not. By June, when the Seadons decided to sell another block, it was already too late; the market had begun the long sickening slide which was to make the lowest lows of 1929 seem, by comparison, dizzy pinnacles of optimism.

How to pay off the remaining debts? Ross's Ridgemont could not be sold for more than its mortgage, which would leave Ross with no equity; but there were the Oriental rugs and the paintings—a Renoir, a Degas, a Whistler—which the auction catalogue described as "from the estate of an owner of prominence." The five cars in the garage were reduced to one Packard coupe. The chauffeur was the first to be let go, then one by one the household staff, until finally there were only Mrs. Pryor and the cook. A single gardener battled the weeds and overgrown shrubbery; the exotic plants in the greenhouse shriveled to sticks; leaves matted the floor of the empty swimming pool. The gala parties were no more; entertainment was impossible when three-quarters of Ross's salary was assigned to his creditors.

The younger generation of Seadons watched with dazed disbelief as their world crumbled about them. Carla and Angela wept when Owen and Tana announced that the town house in Fremont Square would be sold, regardless of price, and the family would return to the economy of El Encanto. The girls did not want to leave Los Angeles and the friends they had made at college, so they chose the one remedy open to them— marriage. Carla, the eldest, eloped with Don Wharton, a pharmacy graduate; Angela took her vows with Ronald Buck, who had hoped to be a teacher.

"You'd think they'd at least marry boys who have jobs," Owen sighed to Tana.

"They will in time," she answered. "They're both bright, which is better than marrying stupidity with a paycheck."

In the end Owen decided that he could find a place for his sons-in-law in the company; Buck would work in statistics, and Wharton in marketing. That left only Gene to return with his parents to El Encanto, from which he commuted to the Ventura refinery while Owen divided his time between the various oil fields and an occasional check-in at Los Angeles headquarters.

The effect on Ross's children fitted their temperaments and circumstances. Ginny, living now in Honolulu as the wife of a pineapple grower, was mainly puzzled. "How could Daddy be such a failure?" she wrote to Tom. "Everybody said he was so smart. Or was he just lucky for a while?"

Tom wrote back, "Are you just finding out? Everything in life is luck—and mine is lousy. I got competition now not only from Gene but Carla and Angie's husbands. All three are waiting for the day when they can sit in the president's chair."

It was a fear which Tom voiced to his mother on one of his vacation trips to San Francisco. "Buck and Wharton are a couple of bootlicking schemers. They didn't marry those idiot girls just for love."

315

"That's no way to talk about your cousins," Louise replied. "They're very fine girls, and I'm sure they wouldn't encourage their husbands to try to displace you and Gene. When your father and Owen retire, you boys will step into their shoes."

Louise was gray-haired now, and with her pale amber eyes she looked at her son with the detachment of a woman disappointed by life. Her father was dead, the beautiful estate at Woodside was gone, and her art collection; now it was an apartment on Russian Hill which she shared with her widowed mother. The crash of 1929 and the aftershock of June 1930 had wiped out Louise's wealth; but at least there were still the dividends from Arnold Schroder's shares in Bay Steel Company, which allowed mother and daughter to live in modest comfort.

"Tell me about your father," Louise prompted. "Is he still happy with Kay?"

"I suppose. I don't go by Ridgemont any more than I have to. Dad's always got his nose in his account books, and Kay's glued to the radio. Christ, I got better things to do than listen to Amos 'n' Andy and Rudy Vallee."

Louise smiled. "Girls, I suppose. . . . When are you going to make me a grandmother, Tom?"

"There's plenty of time."

"No. There never is."

On these visits to San Francisco, Tom would look in on his Aunt Leah and David Marcus. Leah would show him a British or French magazine in which there was a new short story by Dale Lantry. And always there were snapshots. Dale and her French journalist lover on their bicycles in the Bois de Boulogne, mugging at the piano in their Paris walk-up, at the seashore at Deauville.

Invariably Leah would ask Tom the same question: "Everything's much better with Ross now, isn't it?"

"Not really, Aunt Leah."

"Of course it is. You mustn't believe the testimony of the senses, my dear. Divine Mind is your father's Supply. And ours too. All we must do is *believe*. St. Paul said, 'Faith is the substance of things hoped for, the evidence of things not seen.'"

After such affirmations, Leah would smile at her husband for agreement, and David would twist his mouth and stare out the window. Faith was difficult when 522 banks across the nation had failed in the single month of October 1931. Even the Marcus bank was affected by the growing unease; every day brought more and more customers to the cashiers' windows to withdraw their deposits. Overseas the situation was grimmer still. The great Kreditanstalt bank in Vienna had collapsed; Britain had gone off the gold standard and devalued the pound by 40 per cent. Faith—how did one spell it?

Matters were equally grim for the Seadon Oil Company. People no longer took the family flivver out for Sunday drives, and they rode streetcars or walked to work—if they had jobs to go to. Factories cut back production and used less fuel oil. As gasoline and oil sales fell away, price wars raged until gasoline was selling for less than it cost to produce. Seadon Oil cut back refinery runs, idled its tankers, and closed service stations. Ross dreaded to go to work in the morning and see the anxious eyes in the elevator. Who was to be let go today? Then in the spring of 1932 the unthinkable happened. Seadon Oil passed its dividend.

The following morning, after the board of directors had made its decision, Kay told Ross that she did not feel well; she would not drive to the office with him. When Ross returned to Ridgemont that evening he found her note on the vanity table.

> Dear Ross—
>   Please consider this my resignation and goodbye. I'm sorry you disappointed me.
>
>   Kay

"If Kay's that shallow, she's good riddance," Liz Barnard said when she arrived at Ridgemont in answer to Ross's phone call.

"The odd thing," Ross said, "is she didn't seem to mind my auctioning off the paintings and Oriental rugs and letting the servants go. I guess because outsiders didn't know what was going on. But when the company passed its dividend, she took it as a public disgrace. . . . How about a drink?"

Liz nodded. They went into the bar, Ross poured double bourbons, and they carried them into the library, which was Ross's refuge now that the living room was stripped of carpets and paintings.

Liz paused at Ross's desk and picked up a photograph he had cut from the *Los Angeles Times*. It pictured a blond young woman in a swimsuit waving from the deck of a yacht. Liz read the caption aloud: " 'The former Mrs. G. G. Haggerty aboard her yacht in Monte Carlo harbor.' "

Ross smiled fleetingly. "I'm keeping it to show Owen. She helped ruin us."

"How?"

"Well, we didn't know it at the time, but during the Crash a lot of that Pantex stock was being dumped by Mrs. Haggerty. She got it in a divorce settlement from old G. G. She cleaned him—and us indirectly—and now she's the queen of the Riviera."

Liz watched Ross down the rest of his bourbon and then eye the glass which she had barely touched. She offered it to him with a frown. "There's something more than Kay on your mind. Why did you want to see me?"

"To ask you for the name of a good real estate broker. I can't afford to keep Ridgemont."

She grimaced. "You couldn't sell it for more than the mortgage. You'd walk away without a dollar."

"No matter. Just give me a name."

Si Benjamin was a good man, Liz told him. He had handled her subdivision when people still had money to buy lots. But now he couldn't move even her business properties on Wilshire Boulevard. "Are you sure," she added, "that you aren't taking out your guilt feelings on Ridgemont?"

"What guilt?"

"For what you think you've done to your family. For being what you think is a failure."

Ross laughed for the first time. "Jesus, you sound like one of those what-do-you-call-them—psychiatrists."

"Perhaps. I've been to three. London, New York, and here."

"Why, for God's sake?"

"To cure me of headaches and sleepless nights." Liz looked steadily at Ross. "To help me with my guilt for what I did to you and to Phil in my cursed selfishness."

Ross put his arm around Liz's waist and kissed her cheek. "Did it work?"

"Yes. I learned that we can't get through life without making mistakes. I'm not God, and you aren't either. Forgive yourself." She returned Ross's kiss. "And *don't* sell Ridgemont. If nothing else, it's proof of what Ross Seadon did once—and can do again."

Philip Barnard was no longer thought of as a "comer." In the beginning it had been easy for a young man with a pleasing personality and a Harvard cum laude to rise rapidly in his Wall Street investment firm. Nor had it been a handicap to have a wealthy mother in California who channeled her stock purchases through her son. He had been the favorite escort of half a dozen girls from the "best" families; he had played tennis with them on weekends in the Hamptons and crewed aboard their fathers' racing sloops on the sound. Then came the Crash. Six months later Philip's firm failed, and he had been forced to take a position with another company. In 1931 it, too, collapsed. Month after month he made the rounds of other offices and heard the same story: "Sorry, we don't have any vacancies." . . . "Sorry, the position has just been filled." Several times the position had been taken by one of his former classmates. The Establishment was caring for its own. There were fewer and fewer tennis matches in the Hamptons and no more cruises on the sound. The girl he had hoped to propose to, when he found another job, married a man whose father was senior partner in one of the leading Manhattan law firms. Worst of all, Philip Barnard's savings were gone.

Liz glowed at the sight of her son stepping off the train in Pasadena. On the drive to her home she listened to his description of the situation in New York.

"There just *aren't* any jobs. My God, men and women are eating out of trash cans and sleeping in doorways and on the steps going down into the subways. And those who *are* working have their pay cut to where they can barely feed themselves. I was walking in Washington Square one night and a girl came up to me and said I could have her for a dime. A single dime! She was a good kid, too; she said she was working in a garment factory for a dollar twenty a week. I thought *that* was horrible, until I got on the train and saw how it was across the country. Every freight train was crawling with people. Not hobos, but decent-looking people. Men, women, kids. When the freights pulled into a station, the railroad detectives ran along clubbing heads and kicking crotches like they were so many mongrel dogs." He concluded with a sigh. "God! What's happened to America?"

Liz nodded understanding. "It's as unbelievable as American troops using tear gas and bayonets on our own war veterans." She was referring to the Bonus Army which General Douglas MacArthur had driven from Washington, D.C., only the week before. "I don't know. I'm almost ashamed to have a nice home and security."

It was more than a "nice" home; it was quietly luxurious, nestled at the foot of the Hollywood Hills on Franklin Avenue. Although Liz had lost over six hundred thousand dollars in the failure of a Hollywood building and loan association, and income from her Wilshire Boulevard properties barely covered the property taxes, the interest from her government bonds allowed her to live comfortably with a cook and maid.

Mother and son talked away the hours that first evening. Philip, Liz said, must live with her, at least until he married— to which he agreed; and he must manage her properties and direct her future investments—to which he said no.

"I'm not ready for charity, Mother. I won't be like all those gutless guys back East living off their families. I want to make it on my own, from scratch. Can't you understand?"

"I can. You're just as independent as I am. And as pigheaded. But do you have anything in mind?"

"Well, you remember that night I sailed on the *Leviathan* and Ross Seadon said I could always have a job with his company? I know those were different times, but the worst that can happen is that he says no."

"I doubt he will."

"Then I'll work my butt off for him. Sure, it means I'd be getting a job because he's a friend of yours, but I'll bet he'd fire me just like *that* if I didn't pull my weight. Nobody could ever say I got there through family pull."

Liz stifled a smile. "Absolutely nobody."

He would not sell Ridgemont after all, Ross decided. Phil Barnard, he told himself, was an omen of better things to come. All the frustrations of recent years melted away; everything seemed possible again. Even the healing of the breach between himself and Owen. Ross would have to make the first move, of course; and the news of Phil joining the company would have to be handled with tact. He could not be brought in on an equal footing with Owen's son Gene, nor even with his sons-in-law Buck and Wharton. Nor must Ross ruffle Tom's feathers. What was needed was a dramatic gesture.

Several days after Ross had hired Phil, Owen came down from El Encanto. When he entered the office, he saw a huge cake on his desk. Rising from the center of the cake was a miniature oil derrick of spun sugar, with a plume of brown spouting from the top of the derrick. Owen looked up from the confection as Ross strolled into the office. "What the hell is this?"

"An anniversary cake."

"What anniversary?"

"Anything you want to make it. Dad's discovery well, Mirage Springs, the Salt Creek gusher. Or maybe just in celebration of things to come."

Owen squinted at the cake as if he expected to hear ticking sounds. "What things to come?"

"Being ourselves again! Damn it to hell, Owen, we've been so busy trying to pay off debts, trying to hold the company together, we've forgotten what we are. We're oilmen! We didn't give a hoot about money in the old days, so long as we could make hole and find the stuff."

By now Ross was warming to his subject with the fervor of a revivalist at a prayer meeting. "Sure! I know I sound like an old geezer who's living back in boom times. I know every company in the business is fighting to keep from going under. We got price wars, we're giving away dishes with every tankful, we got millions of flivvers in garages instead of on the road; but it's going to change. The Democrats are singing 'Happy Days Are Here Again,' and I'm ready to believe them. Once we kick Hoover out of office and get on with Roosevelt's New Deal, you'll see a whole new mood in the country. People will be jumping in Old Lizzie and yelling, 'Fill 'er up!' And when they do, we got to be ready. We'll need every barrel of crude we can produce. So hang the money, let's start building up our reserves right now!"

"You mean, go wildcatting again?"

"I mean! Owen, you know you're the best there is. You could find oil in an old maid's glass eye!"

His brother poker-faced at the compliment. "Well . . . as long as we're talking, there's something I've been meaning to tell you for some time."

"Yes?"

Owen swallowed awkwardly. "The last couple of years I've seen the country's mighty brains, from the President on down, act like a pack of idiots. And the big boys of Wall Street turn out to be thieves milking the public. . . . What I'm saying is, I don't hold that Pantex deal against you any more. You couldn't help what happened. Compared to everybody else, you look pretty damned all right." He broke off and cleared his throat. "What in thunder brought this on, anyway?"

"I was coming to that. Who was our rabbit's foot all through the early days?"

"Rabbit's foot?"

"Our four leaf clover, our lucky horseshoe? Who brought us the Mirage Springs field? Who got us the Salt Springs gusher?"

"Why . . . I guess Liz Barnard."

"And suppose there's a second edition?"

"Huh?" Owen watched in puzzlement as Ross stalked to the closed door which separated their offices, opened it, and gestured to someone. Then Owen whooped. "Well, I'll be damned! I'll be doubled damned!"

The Seadon brothers were as one again. While Owen could scarcely credit Phil Barnard as a rabbit's foot, no matter; somehow the redhaired young man with the bright blue eyes and freckles had worked a magical change in Ross. He fairly tingled with energy and optimism. He would take Phil under his wing and see that he "got crude on his britches." Before assigning him to any particular department, the two would tour the refineries, the pipelines, the service stations, the tankers and loading operations, and then decide where Phil was best suited.

Ross saved Weston until the last. Only Liz could have appreciated the emotions Ross felt when he showed Phil the discovery well "my father" (*not* "your grandfather") had drilled on the banks of the Haber River. It was the sole remaining derrick, forlorn behind a fence, with a bronze marker describing its history. Only Liz could have understood why Ross opened the old house on Central Avenue and showed Phil through the rooms, still furnished, with sheets draped over the sofas and chairs. "You know what?" Ross said. "I'll bet we could stay here overnight. There must be sheets and blankets in the closets. Pretty musty probably, but what the hell, for one night . . ." For one night, then two, then three.

In the intervening days they toured the Mirage Springs field, still feebly pumping; then far to the west, Salt Springs, where the teen-aged Phil had seen his mother's gusher; then north a hundred miles to Coalinga and Kettleman Hills. It was hot and dusty and tiring, yet the hours sped by for Phil as Ross unfolded the lore of the business and spun story after story of the pioneer days of Seadon Oil.

On the last night, as the two men sat smoking on the front porch, Ross said, "Now that you got an idea of this cockeyed game, where do you think you'd like to try your hand?"

"I've been wondering myself. Someplace where I won't get in the way of your family. Tom, and Owen's sons-in-law."

"Hmm! What made you think of that?"

"Wall Street. I learned the hard way that blood is thicker than water—and a lot more poisonous."

It proved to be a self-fulfilling prophecy. Ross had barely returned to Ridgemont and unpacked his bags, when Tom Seadon arrived and faced his father. "Slater Dougal tells me Phil Barnard's being made assistant treasurer. Is it true?"

"It is. Phil's background is all in finance. Someday when things get better we may need his New York contacts." Ross watched his son's sullen expression. "He doesn't outrank you, Tom. Assistant manager of marketing is just as important."

"Maybe. But while you were gone, Uncle Owen promoted Gene from the refinery to exploration manager, Central Division. They're going wildcatting together. Christ, the next thing Gene'll be on the board of directors, and then Buck and Wharton."

Ross was tired from the trip and not in the mood for serious discussion. But it could not be put off; now was the time. He gestured Tom to a seat. "Tom, what do you want most out of life?"

"To be president of Seadon Oil . . . when you retire."

"Nothing more?"

"There isn't anything more."

"I wish I could say that. Businessmen used to be the gods of this country until they damned near ruined it. Look at the papers. Who are the new heroes? Who are the men who are going to pull this country together and go down in the history books? The men in Washington. That's why I wanted you to get that law degree. It's a leg-up in politics."

Tom's eyes widened. "You want me to be a . . . *politician?*"

"A statesman, by the time you're done. Governor of California, maybe senator, maybe even higher. I think you've got the stuff; so does your mother. We've talked about it every time we've seen each other. I haven't mentioned it to you before, because you weren't old enough to run for office. But now you're twenty-six, and you could go right into the House of Representatives." He searched Tom's face for a clue to his reaction; there was none. "Oh, I know it's too late for you to file for this fall's election, but for the next two years you can get your name in front of the public. You can speak at the Chamber of Commerce, get into charity drives, do volunteer work for this year's candidates. Just be sure they're Democrats, because they're going to be the winners."

Tom came out of his shock. "You really don't know anything about me, do you? It all sounds so easy. Speak at the Chamber of Commerce. But have you ever once heard me speak? No! Because I can't! You have the gift of gab, and so automatically I must have it, too. But I don't! I will not make a fool out of myself!"

"Who says you will? Look, Son, don't start off making three tracks in the mud, one of them your tail. Act like a winner. Why, Lord, the whole Seadon family will be behind you. We'll build our own political machine to support you. We'll give you the election on a platter."

Tom sprang to his feet, eyes flashing. "I see. It's a cooked-up job between you and Uncle Owen. Get Tom out of the company. Let Gene be president!"

"Oh, for Christ's sake—"

"Sure, it would be flattering to you to say, 'My son the governor . . . my son the senator.' Why should I believe your daydreams? I saw what happened with your grand plan for Pantex. The wizard who sits here in Ridgemont with walls and floors stripped bare and still two million in debt. No, thank you. I'll settle for what I know I can get. And damn anybody who tries to take it from me!"

Ross stood on the terrace and watched Tom's headlights disappear down the winding road. His shoulders sagged from weariness; he felt old, burned out, alone. Why such bitterness? Perhaps it was the stored-up resentment of a child of a broken marriage. Of a boy lacking security in the formative years. Or was it simply the disappointment of a son who had seen his father stumble and who could not forgive failure? Fathers and sons, sons and fathers. Natural enemies. . . . No. Not always. There was still Phil.

Chapter 23

LEAH MARCUS had known fear in the war zone in France. In the field hospitals she had trembled at the sounds of artillery barrages and bombing raids; but then at least she had understood what frightened her; she could see it, hear it, even smell it. What was happening now was invisible, except in its effect on her husband. Every evening when David came back to the apartment, he seemed more worn, more anxious, more withdrawn. At first—when was it? yes, mid-February—he had mentioned something about a "run" on the Detroit banks, which, he said, had been hard hit by the sagging auto industry. Then it had been Baltimore, then Chicago and New York. And now San Francisco.

"Nobody believes in the banks any more," David said. "I hear it everywhere—get your cash out. Buy gold. But damn it all, the gold's leaving the country, too. Europe thinks America is going down the drain, and they're calling home all their bullion."

Then, on March first, David had come home more despairing than ever. Pantex Oil had withdrawn all their payroll accounts from the San Joaquin Valley branches of the Marcus bank. "I don't know whether Pantex is scared, like everybody else, or if that bastard Haggerty is picking this moment to ruin me because I've been the main lender to Seadon Oil."

"Then it's up to Seadon Oil to help you," Leah replied. "Phone Ross and ask him to deposit every penny the company can spare."

"And have Ross lose it? Hell, I've even told my sisters to get their money out. And Louise Seadon, too. I can't drag them down with me."

The thought sent a chill through Leah. David had never talked like that even during the '29 Crash. It couldn't be; it just couldn't. She went to her practitioner and asked him to "work for Supply." Several days later the "demonstration" was made, she thought. But in a most unusual manner. On March 4, Franklin Delano Roosevelt announced in his inaugural address that "the money changers have fled from their high seats in the temple of our civilization," and on the day following he proclaimed a national bank holiday. Every bank would be shuttered until Monday, March 13.

Marcus brightened at the news. "That gives us a breather. If people can't get at their money, they'll come to their senses." And so it seemed. People regained their sense of humor; those with cash and those without were all in the same boat. Leah listened to the radio accounts of people buying groceries with IOU's and movie tickets with post-dated checks. Really, it was almost fun. Then, on Saturday, the federal examiners visited the Marcus bank and went over the books. That evening Marcus came home exhausted and white-faced. "They say we got too many delinquent loans. They won't let me reopen."

All day Sunday he brooded in the apartment. He sat at the dinner table and stared at the food he could not eat. "My father's bank, *my* bank," he repeated over and over. "We went through the Fire, the Panic of 1907, the Crash. And now, just

because we've got too many delinquent loans on the books . . ."
He broke off with a sigh.

Leah saw him grasp his left arm. "Dear, did you wrench your
shoulder?"

"Must have. The whole arm aches." He was cold, he said,
and put on his dressing robe. Leah drew the draperies to muffle
the moaning of the foghorns. She turned up the steam heat, but
still David shivered. She made him a pot of hot chocolate; at
least he could drink that. She turned on the radio, but it seemed
to make him nervous. Finally she went to the piano and began to
play "Just A-wearying for You." But it brought tears to David's
eyes; it was too sad, so she tried a ragtime. "Oh, the baboon
kissed the monkey's sister,/Kissed so hard he raised a blister."

David began to cough, and Leah made him put out his cigar.
But the coughing continued, and the pain in his arm. "It's hard
to breathe," he said. "I must be coming down with the flu."
That had to be it—all the strain of the past week, the worry, the
fear. The body was a mirror of the mind. Leah phoned her
practitioner; work for peace and joy. She helped David undress
and put on his pajamas and then got into bed beside him. If he
couldn't sleep, she told him, they could talk. About the good
times, those in the past and those that would come again.

"I'm glad we have no children," he said. "For the first time,
I'm really glad."

"But we have, darling. Dale is your daughter just as much as
if she had your blood. She loves you dearly." How often had
she repeated that to herself, to battle her guilt feelings for not
having given him a child. She had never been able to convince
herself that it was her husband's fault; it was hers, all those men,
all those too many men.

The coughing returned, hard, racking, and he had to sit up to
get his breath. Leah's concern grew. Although she no longer
believed in medicine, she said she would phone Dr. Rothman.
No, David would not allow it; the poor man needed his rest. It
was just the flu. The coughing passed, and he lay down again.
The grandfather clock in the hallway chimed midnight. The

coughing grew worse again. Leah did not care whether David liked it or not, she would call Dr. Rothman. She listened to the buzz repeat itself over and over again. Why didn't he answer? Was he attending some other patient? At a party? Out of town? Perhaps she should call a hospital. No, that was being panicky. "The only thing we have to fear is fear itself"—that's what President Roosevelt had just told the nation. Besides, David said it was just the flu, and he surely ought to know. She dialed her practitioner again; work against fear.

One o'clock. The coughing had lessened, but he was breathing in ragged gasps. She stroked his forehead and soothed him with words. "Remember the day we first saw each other? . . . I was coming down the stairs and there was that handsome boy in the entry. In Army uniform. Oh, you were such a man of the world with all your stories of the Philippines." She smiled to herself and clasped his hand; it was cold, so cold. "And then when we met again at the Schroders', I didn't pay much attention to you, because I just wasn't ready yet. But you knew it would happen eventually. . . .You *did* know, didn't you, Dave?" Silence. "Of course you did. We both had to marry someone else to find each other again. The main thing is that we did." She squeezed his hand for emphasis. There was no response. "Dave? . . . Are you asleep? . . . Dave?" She felt his wrist. Then his chest.

She closed her eyes, and her lips moved silently. Hail Mary, full of grace . . .

She drew the blankets tightly about them and buried her head against his shoulder. Time enough to call someone in the morning. This would be their last night together.

After the funeral service at Temple Emmanuel, after the rabbi had said the *Kaddish* at the graveside, after Louise and David's sisters and their husbands had said their goodbyes, Leah was finally alone with her family. Ross and Owen and Tana. They sat in the living room of the apartment on Russian Hill and talked of trivialities, avoiding the subject which had brought them together, as if by dwelling on the importance of the un-important they were affirming their own survival. From time to time Ross's voice thickened with a sense of unbearable loss; and whenever there was a lag in the conversation, Tana would reach hastily for a handkerchief. Leah herself neither spoke nor wept —until the telephone rang and she heard the voice of the over-seas operator. Ross listened intently to the one-sided conversa-tion. It was so thoughtful for Dale to call. . . . The flowers were lovely. . . . No, Dale must not come home. . . . Yes, perhaps she could visit her in Paris someday. . . . Yes, and Dave loved her, too. . . .

When Leah hung up, Ross's arm went around her. "I know this isn't the time to talk about it, but it will never be easy. . . . Dave told me he had a large insurance policy."

She nodded. "Enough to pay some of his debts, that's what the lawyer says."

Owen came forward. "Not all of them?"

"No."

Ross frowned at the floor. Another penalty for that damned Pantex deal. "Don't worry, Sis," he said. "You still got your Estate Company stock. We'll see that you get some dividends." His arm tightened about her waist. "And you're moving to Los Angeles. You're going to live at Ridgemont."

"And you're always welcome at El Encanto," Owen added.

"She certainly is," Tana said. "Come soon, my dear, and stay long."

Leah looked out the window with an unfocused gaze. "I wonder where he is."

Four months later Leah joined her daughter in Paris, and Dale wrote a chatty report to Ross:

It's perfect having Mother with me, although it means I had to rent a bigger apartment so she could have her own bedroom at a discreet distance from ours. (His name is André. He's a political journalist.) If you don't hear from me for a while, it'll be because I'm terribly busy with Mother and my first full-length novel. Sorry, not a hint what it's about.

P.S. Mother has taken up Spiritualism. Wouldn't you know!

In the two years that had passed since Phil Barnard had joined Seadon Oil, his relations with Tom and with Buck and Wharton, the husbands of Angela and Carla, had proved to be exactly as he had anticipated—strained. Yet, to Phil's surprise, this was not the case with Gene Seadon. Although they saw each other infrequently because of the distance separating Ventura and Los Angeles, they thoroughly enjoyed the times when business did bring them together. Perhaps it was the attraction of opposites, both physically and temperamentally. Gene dark and handsome in a masculine version of Tana; Phil redhaired and fair of skin like Liz. Gene with Owen's sense of the practical; Phil with a mixture of idealism and adventurousness that was a blend of Liz and Ross. Despite the differences, both friends shared a common enthusiasm, the outdoors.

It was natural, then, that they should decide to spend part of their vacations on a fishing and hunting trip into the Sierras. They met in Weston and loaded their camping equipment into the old open touring car which Gene had borrowed from El Encanto; then, turning off Highway 99, they drove northeast and followed the Haber River up into the rocky gorge where no trees grew, and higher into the cool upper meadowlands, and higher still into the tall pines, until finally they reached their goal—Lake Haber, blue and deep and cold. There for three days they let their faces go happily to stubble while they swam and fished and shot ducks.

It was on the drive back to Weston that the trouble began. They had turned off the Haber River road onto Highway 99 when they spied the dilapidated Ford with the Oklahoma license plates. It was pulled off the road and a young woman in a faded house dress stood beside it. A man's legs protruded from under the running board. Gene braked to a stop and Phil called, "Need help?"

The answer came from beneath the car. "If you got an extra transmission." The legs elongated into a torso, then the owner scrambled to his feet. "Guess it was too much of a load to pull." He gestured toward the interior of the Ford, where three Mexicans were crowded into the back seat. A man, woman, and a small boy. "How far to a garage?"

"Weston. About five miles," Gene said. "We'll give you a tow."

They attached the tow rope between the two vehicles; then, to ease the load, the three Mexicans squeezed into the back of the touring car along with the camping equipment. Mrs. Gordon, as she introduced herself, sat in front with Gene and Phil, leaving her husband to steer the Ford.

It was the all too familiar story that she told. The Gordons, like thousands of others before them, were foreclosed farmers who had left the Dust Bowl to find work in that land of second starts, California. Crossing the Tehachapis, they had seen the Mexican family thumbing for a ride. Where they were bound the Gordons had no idea, for they spoke no English. Gene's questions in Spanish provided the answer; the father had been a roustabout in the Los Angeles railroad yards until he had been laid off. They had relatives in the Salinas Valley, where they hoped to find field work.

The outskirts of East Weston were already in sight when the sheriff's car pulled abreast and signaled Gene to pull over. The two deputies who circled the cars, staring at the Oklahoma plates, at the three nervous Mexicans, at Gene and Phil with their three-day stubble, were cast to type. Big, beefy, hats tilted forward over suspicious eyes.

"Where you headed?"

"Weston," Gene said.

"No, you ain't. Weston ain't feeding no more vagrants."

Phil bridled. "What the hell makes us vagrants?"

The senior deputy planted his foot on the running board and

333

eyed Mrs. Gordon and the Mexicans. "Okies and greasers, that's what. So just keep heading north and do your starving in the next county."

Phil saw the expression on Gene's face at the word "greaser" and hurried to head off the explosion. "Look, officer, we both work for Seadon Oil Company. This is Gene Seadon and I'm Phil Barnard, assistant treasurer—"

"Sure you are! And this is your limousine"—slapping the hood of the old touring car—"and these ain't Okies and greasers, they're your secretaries and office boys."

Gene let go. "Damn it to hell, stop calling them greasers! They civilized California a hundred years before your people stopped eating out of a trough!" By now Phil was tugging at Gene's elbow, but in vain. "We can identify ourselves, and *you* damned well better, too. I want your names and badge numbers."

The deputies exchanged glances, and the senior said, "Looks like we got ourselves some real red agitators." Then back to Gene. "Okay, I guess you're going to Weston after all. Yessiree!"

It was past midnight when Wil Caruth, in answer to Phil's phone call, arrived from Los Angeles, shaking his white mane and roaring around the sheriff's office like King Lear with a toothache. "Mud-brained bastards! I practiced law fifteen years in this town and never heard of such an outrage!" After he had posted bail for Gene and Phil—and, at their insistence, for the Gordons and the three Mexicans—he warned, "Now not a word about this to anyone. Especially reporters." Futile words. Phil was already striding toward an eager-eyed youth with a notepad and pencil.

The following edition of the *Weston Daily* carried Phil's opinion that the Haber County sheriff's department was manned by bullyboys who belonged in Hitler's Brown Shirts. Further, according to Gene, the "Okies" were every bit as good as the down-and-outers who had settled Weston sixty years before;

and as for the Mexicans, he was proud that his mother was of the same blood.

"It's not exactly the kind of publicity I like," Ross said when Gene and Phil reported to his office in Los Angeles. "But I don't blame you, either. It's just what your grandfather Val would have done." He was speaking to Gene but mentally including Phil.

"Do you think he would have done more?" Gene asked.

"In what way?"

Gene turned to Phil. "It's your idea. Go ahead."

"Well, we did some thinking while we were in that jail cell. The Gordons are only one family out of thousands piling into the state. Farmers without farms, teachers without jobs, shopkeepers, bank tellers, bookkeepers, white people, black people from the South, our own Mexicans. Most of them with no place to sleep, some of them hungry and even close to starvation. We all know about it; we've seen it in the papers. But suppose they could get a roof over their heads; suppose they could plant vegetable gardens and maybe even raise chickens . . ."

Ross interrupted. "I thought you were talking about people who are flat broke."

"I am. Only the desperate cases. That's where Seadon Oil would come in. We could lend them the use of company lands that are pumped dry and just going to weeds."

Ross's eyebrows went up. "Hmmm! The old Haber River field . . . even parts of Mirage Springs. As I remember, there are still some of the old bunkhouses, and a couple of water wells. . . . But God, we couldn't handle everybody."

"We could set an example," Phil said. "Then the other oil companies might come in on it. Our only cost would be seed money and a few crates of baby chicks. And next spring they could plant cash crops, cotton and potatoes, and get a new start. Hell, it wouldn't cost half of what we spend on one radio commercial. We'd get it back ten times in good will."

Ross scratched his chin, and pondered. "It might be good business, at that. Let me think about it. I'll talk to Owen and

Slater. And I'll see what Wil Caruth says about squatters' rights."

Two days later Seadon Oil placed an announcement of the new project in the *Weston Daily*, the company service stations along Highway 99 passed out handbills, and Gene and Phil, using the last days of their vacations, set up a roadside stand to interview applicants. By the following week the old bunkhouses at Haber River and Mirage Springs had been filled; and over a hundred men, women, and children were hoeing the earth. By the second week, Seadon Oil set up fifty Army surplus tents to accommodate still more. Then the third week—and a band of nightriders.

Masked and armed with torches, they leaped out of trucks and fired the bunkhouses and tents and beat unconscious the few who tried to resist them. In Weston, in the front yard of the old Seadon house, there was a fiery cross and a placard on the front door: KATHOLICS KOONS AND KIKES—GET OUT!

Ross heard of it first, when the *Weston Daily* telephoned him. By midmorning Gene and Phil were in his office, irate and vowing to run down the guilty. "I don't think the Ku Klux Klan had anything to do with it," Gene fumed. "I think it was some of those damned bigoted farmers who think we're giving them unfair competition."

"No, it's the Klan all right," Ross said. "The West Side is an adder's nest of them. A lot of them are oil-field toolies that we had to lay off. This is their way of getting back at us. They know we're a Catholic family, and you say there were some Negroes and Jews in your encampments. In hard times, hate comes easy."

"Then we'll show them." Phil glowered. "We'll rebuild and bring in our own field security men."

Ross shook his head. "That would just guarantee bloodshed. No, this ends it. It was a great idea, boys, but in the wrong place and the wrong time."

It was and it was not. Newspapers throughout the state carried the story; editorials lamented what had happened in Haber

County and praised Seadon Oil and its two young officers for their humanitarian effort. Tana telephoned Ross and read him the editorials that appeared in the Ventura and Santa Barbara papers, which reminded their readers that Eugene Seadon was a neighbor and the grandson of the much admired Don Jaime Delgado. In Los Angeles both the *Times* and the *Examiner* interviewed Phil and quoted his view that there was one law for the rich, another for the poor. If it was not possible to build a new encampment for the so-called vagrants, Phil added, he proposed a fund-raising campaign to provide free clinics at the various San Joaquin hospitals to treat those migrants who were suffering from malnutrition and its side effects.

Ross read the newspaper interviews and called Phil into his office. "Are you serious about these clinics?"

"Completely."

"You're willing to devote your spare time to it?"

"With your permission, yes."

"Then count on a contribution from Seadon Oil. Put us down for five thousand. Okay?"

"*Okay!*" Phil lingered thoughtfully. "Then would you mind if at the next Chamber of Commerce dinner I went in place of Slater Dougal? I'd like to ask for their help."

"Fine! Fine!"

A very interesting development, Ross thought to himself. And more interesting, where it might lead.

In August 1935 Ross received a letter from Dale which bubbled about the acceptance of her novel by a Paris publisher. The letter closed with a less happy report on Leah:

> Frankly, I'm a little worried. Every few weeks she goes to London and comes back full of stories about David. She says she's "in contact" with him through a "marvelous psychic." I'm sure the man is a fraud and is just after Mother's money. I keep hinting to her that maybe she's been in Europe too long and ought to go back to California and visit you and Uncle Owen and Aunt Tana—

just to break this man's hold over her. If she did, of course, I'd miss her terribly, for she's been such good company, and she's so generous with André and me. (Last night dinner at the Ritz, to celebrate my novel.) Am I worrying too much, Uncle Ross? Write me what you think.

But Ross did not know what to write. He did not like the mention of the London psychic. He might be harmless, perhaps a man who had taken pity on Leah and told her what she wanted so desperately to hear; on the other hand, he could be Leah's Rasputin. There was really nothing to go on. Dale's idea of "generosity" might be magnified by her own lack of money —she barely supported herself by her writing—and so a dinner at the Ritz could seem a breathtaking extravagance. Besides, Ross reasoned, Leah's dividends from the Seadon Estate Company would go a very long way in Europe. In any case, Ross would discuss it with Owen; it might be prudent not to declare that extra dividend if Leah's share would find its way into unscrupulous hands.

It was still something of a novelty to the Seadon brothers to be solvent once more. Only three short years before, the family had been mired in debt and Seadon Oil limping from one financial crisis to the next. Now the nightmare was over. True, the Depression lingered on. There were still far too many millions out of work, companies were still failing; but, regardless, there was a new spirit in the land. Even those who damned Franklin Roosevelt as "that man in the White House" and "a traitor to his class" could not complain about the action of the stock market.

The shares of Seadon Oil reflected the new confidence; from the dark days of 1932, they had doubled in price by the summer of 1933. The Estate Company had sold sufficient shares to settle the brothers' debts and to free their salaries from assignment to creditors. In 1934 the stock of Seadon Oil had doubled again, and again in 1935, as investors watched the company's recovery. There was the new field in Alto Valle, another in Oklahoma; a fuel contract with the U.S. Navy, another with a railroad, another with an airline. More than all else, Seadon Oil, like its competitors, was benefiting from the rising tensions in Europe.

Germany's rearming and Italy's conquest of Ethiopia had inspired countermeasures by Britain and France. Clouds of new warplanes were taking to the skies, new warships were sliding down the ways, fleets were maneuvering in war games—all increasing the world demand for oil. The surplus of gasoline and crude had disappeared; now every company rushed to find fresh sources and to take over its competitors. J. Paul Getty was locked in battle with Standard Oil of New Jersey for control of Tide Water Associated Oil; H. L. Hunt was putting together an empire in the South; G. G. Haggerty had merged Pantex with a Louisiana rival and had leased a second concession in Venezuela. Haggerty's move in South America had rekindled Ross's sense of competition; and he and Owen, with Gene acting as Spanish interpreter, had journeyed to Caracas and contracted for their own concession on Lake Maracaibo. So in the summer of 1935 Ross's dream was finally accomplished; Seadon Oil was an international company.

Ridgemont shared in the new prosperity. Once more there was a full staff of servants; two new Cadillacs replaced the old Packard in the garage; there were Oriental carpets again on the floor of the great living room, and on the walls the beginning of a collection of French Impressionists.

"The leopard can't change his spots" was Liz Barnard's comment to Ross on his renewed prodigality.

"Look who's talking," he rejoined. "I spend on Ridgemont, and you've got the real estate bug again."

She had indeed. Her government bonds had been replaced by scores of rural acres in the San Fernando Valley; and when Seadon Oil discovered a new deeper pool on her Salt Creek land, she had used the royalties to buy controlling interest in a building and loan association which was heavily invested in new subdivisions.

"A leave of absence?" Ross stared at Phil Barnard, who stood on the opposite side of his desk wearing an expression that was a mixture of apology and excitement. "What for?"

"Well, I don't want to embarrass the company. It might be considered a conflict of interest."

"What would? Come out with it!"

Phil did, with a rush of words. "The Democrats have asked me to run for Congress this fall. The House of Representatives. And I've said yes."

It was no surprise, really, to Ross. He had watched Phil's outside activities snowball during the past year. First the fund raising for the medical clinics, then the local Democrats had invited him to repeat his success for their party. What an irony, Ross thought. The very career that Tom had rejected was now Phil's for the taking. If only he bore the name *Seadon* . . .

Ross rose from his desk and extended his hand. "All the luck in the world, boy. You'll be a shoo-in."

"I hope so. I'd like to do some good for the country, but I've got a selfish reason, too. I'd like to show my old Wall Street gang they guessed wrong about Phil Barnard."

"And maybe a certain girl?"

Phil laughed. "Especially her." Then he sobered. "The only bad thing about winning is what I'll lose here. I'll miss Seadon Oil."

Ross's throat tightened at the thought. "Everything has its price. . . . By God, this calls for a party! It'll be Ridgemont's best!"

And it was, eclipsing even the housewarming of twelve years before. Every important Democratic name in the city was on hand, as well as every Seadon except for the expatriates Leah and Dale. Liz Barnard was the typical mother of the candidate, alternating between laughter and tears. No one was more enthusiastic than Tom Seadon. "Phil can count on me," he vowed. "I'll work my tail off for him!"

To which Gene commented in an aside to Phil, "You're damned right he will. He'd even stuff ballot boxes to get you to Washington and out of Seadon Oil."

It was past two in the morning when the last straggler had left and Owen and Tana and Gene had retired to the guest rooms. Ross fell into bed without setting the alarm; tomorrow he would sleep late. As he reached to turn off the light on the nightstand, the telephone rang.

It was Liz. "Ross, I know you were probably asleep—I know I was—but I just got a phone call from your sister—"

"Leah? At this hour?"

"Well, it's morning in Paris. She sounded hysterical. Everything was all mixed up. She said she'd just got back from India, seeing some kind of a holy man there, and she found a notice in the mail from a bank in San Francisco—"

"Oh, God almighty!" Ross knew what was coming.

"She said she owes the bank two hundred thousand, and she wanted to borrow it from me. I said I'd be glad to let her have it, but—"

"No, Liz! *No!* I'll take care of it. But why the hell should she go to you?"

"Because she said she was afraid to tell you. She made me promise that I wouldn't, but I just said that to get the facts. It seems she's pledged her stock in the Seadon Estate Company. You know what that means."

Only too well. It was the old, old story. "Liz, did she give you the name of the bank?"

"The First Security."

"And the deadline for payment?"

"That's the worst of it, Ross. It's three weeks ago."

The First Security Bank of San Francisco occupied the offices on Montgomery Street that had formerly been the headquarters of the Marcus Savings and Trust. Abner Fogelson, the president, sat behind David's desk and watched the Seadon brothers leaf through the bank's correspondence with their sister in Paris.

"As you can see, gentlemen, we gave Mrs. Marcus every opportunity. I think we were most patient."

So it seemed. There was Leah's original loan application, made in June 1933, shortly before she had left for Paris. There was the note, due two years later. There was Leah's letter asking for an extension of time, then another, and another, and the last: "My financial adviser tells me I can expect a very large profit from an investment within the next two weeks which will more than take care of your loan."

What "financial adviser"? The London psychic? The ghost of David Marcus?

Ross looked up from the file. "We've been through this before, Mr. Fogelson. Our sister simply can't handle money matters."

"Are you alleging that she is incompetent?"

"She is," Owen said. "But not legally. In any case, you should have come directly to us."

Fogelson smiled bleakly. "If Mrs. Marcus had given us General Electric shares as security, I'm sure we would not have tried to collect the debt from General Electric. The matter was between her and the bank."

"All right," Ross said. "How much do we owe you, both principal and interest?"

"Why, nothing. We have disposed of the security."

The Seadons stiffened; then Ross leaned over the desk. "You sold stock worth millions for a two-hundred-thousand-dollar debt?"

"Well, naturally, we realized more than the face of the loan."

"I'll bet!" Owen sneered. "How much more?"

"That is a confidential matter."

"All right, then at least tell us where you sold it."

"That, too, is confidential. The buyer happens to be a very good customer of the bank. I'm sure the gentleman will make himself known to you."

"Gentleman?" Ross echoed. "Not a company? An individual?"

"Yes. As I say, he will make himself known when he asks the Seadon Estate Company to transfer the shares on its books. Then, if you desire, you could make him an offer for repurchase."

Ross felt ill; his stomach churned as a name raced through his brain. "Just tell us one thing, Fogelson. This very good customer of the bank—is it G. G. Haggerty?"

Fogelson's eyes flickered. It was answer enough.

Chapter 24

If it was Haggerty, and the Seadons were convinced of it, it was urgent that they buy back the Seadon Estate Company shares before he transferred them to Pantex Oil. Ross telephoned Houston, and Haggerty's secretary said he was in Chicago at the Stevens Hotel. Another phone call. The Stevens reported that he had checked out. No, no forwarding address. But when the Seadons returned dejectedly to Los Angeles, they found a telephone message waiting. Haggerty had called; he was at the Ambassador.

They found him on the hotel putting green. It had been ten years since Ross had seen Haggerty, and he was startled by the change in the man. His white hair had thinned to a wispy horseshoe connecting the ears; he had lost weight; the jowls of another day hung in wrinkles; and there were bags beneath the black marble eyes.

"Sure," he said affably, leaning on his putting iron. "I got the stock in the hotel safe. I could have mailed it to you boys for transfer, but I sort of looked forward to doing it in person. More satisfaction, you might say."

"How did you find out about the loan?" Owen asked.

"Oh, don't blame Fogelson. It was one of the bank's attorneys. An old-timer. He remembered the days when we were shivving each other in the headlines. So when your sister's loan came up for action, he got in touch with me. He knew I'd pay the highest price."

"Obviously a man of compassion and high ethics." Ross simmered.

Haggerty squinted at the afternoon sun. "I grew up reading old Ben Franklin. A wise old bastard. Gave me my first tip on lawyers. 'God works wonders now and then; Behold! a lawyer, an honest man.' . . . The Frisco gent wasn't one." His gaze dropped to the Seadons and he held out his putting iron. "Would you boys like to try a few balls?" He waited, then shrugged.

God, how he's enjoying himself, Ross thought. No need for the old bluster, no need for threats or cajoling; just quiet enjoyment of his triumph.

Owen lost his patience. "Look, that stock is the only thing our sister owns in this world. We want it back."

"Yes, I guess you do. The Estate Company controls Seadon Oil, and her stock is one third of that control." He smiled thoughtfully at Ross. "You were going to say?"

"We want it back. What's your price?"

Haggerty made a practice swing of the iron. "You know what I'd do if I were you boys? It isn't right for your sister to be out in the cold. I'd take some of your Estate stock and set it up in a trust fund where she couldn't touch it but would have the income. Just the dividends, which should be very handsome. In fact, as your new stockholder, I'll insist that they are." He watched Ross's scowl and shook his head with a kind of rueful sadness. "Remember when we first met . . . in my railroad car? If you'd gone in with me then, this wouldn't be happening today. I never forget a man who says no to me."

"And you never forgive a man who says *yes*."

"Hmmm! A point." Haggerty's air of sadness seemed to grow, as if the elation he believed he should feel had somehow eluded him. "You know, I don't have any family. Brothers and sisters all dead, wives gone, no children. Just a couple of cousins. When I was younger, I didn't give a damn. But now I do. So, in a way, I'm grateful the way things have turned out. I've bought me a family. The Seadons. . . ."

He was still elaborating on the notion as Ross and Owen walked away.

It was incredible to the brothers that their sister had opened the gates to their archenemy. Unknowingly, perhaps, but that was no comfort. Their main concern now was Haggerty's next move. His goal, it was clear, was an eventual takeover of Seadon Oil. But so long as the Estate Company did not dissolve and distribute its assets, there was no way for Haggerty to gain the underlying shares. He had, as he put it, bought his way into the family; but the Seadon brothers still controlled the Estate Company and could outvote him on every proposal. He was locked in. The day would come, the brothers reasoned, when Haggerty would tire of the situation and they could buy him out. Time was the game.

There was, of course, the problem of Leah. She had lost her birthright; she had no income, and Dale no prospect of inheritance. So it was that the brothers turned to the solution that Haggerty himself had suggested. Ross and Owen would each contribute 10 per cent of his shares in the Seadon Estate Company to an irrevocable trust which would be administered by a Los Angeles bank. Leah would be unable to touch the corpus of the trust but would receive the income for life; and after her death it would go to Dale and her own issue, if any.

"It's foolproof," Wil Caruth declared when he read over the articles of trust. "Of course, you boys realize that the trustees will have to pay out all the dividends they get from the Seadon Estate Company. That means Leah will still have an awful lot of money to toss around."

Ross grinned smugly. "Maybe ten or fifteen thousand a year,

that's all. The Estate Company is going to be damned niggardly with its dividends."

"You think Haggerty will sit still for that?"

"He can't help himself. That's the beauty of it. Old G. G. must have a small fortune locked up in his stock, and it won't earn him peanuts."

Caruth ran his fingers through his white locks. "Seems to me it's a two-edged sword. Haggerty misses out on big dividends, but so do you and Owen. What are you going to live on?"

"Our salaries. Owen and I just raised our pay to a quarter of a million dollars a year."

"I can hear the stockholders screaming already."

"We'll handle them. By the time they scream, Haggerty will be yelling even louder. He'll be begging us to buy him out. If it doesn't happen within twelve months, Wil, I'll buy you a haircut."

Tom Seadon had welcomed his mother's suggestion that he take her for a drive to Lincoln Park. It would allow him to state his case without interruption by phone calls or Grandmother Schroder with her endless memories of San Francisco "before the Fire." It was a fog-free afternoon, and they could catch glimpses through the park's green-black cypress and pines of the sailboats making white punctuation marks on the waters of the bay. Passing among them, like a swan towering above its cygnets, the twin-funneled liner *Chichibu Maru*, Yokohama-bound, glided toward the great span of the Golden Gate Bridge, now nearing completion. "Let's park for a moment," Louise said, indicating her favorite spot, which commanded an unobstructed view of the twin bridge towers which every San Franciscan proudly told visitors were the tallest in the world.

Louise removed her eyeglasses, wiped them with her handkerchief, and replaced them to gaze at the mighty structure. "Your Grandfather Schroder never lived to see it, but from the time I was a girl he used to tell me about the bridges we'd have someday. He used to draw me diagrams of how it would be done. The coffer dams, the caissons, the pylons, the cable-spinning machinery. He knew every detail." She smiled to herself. "Every day I look out the apartment window and watch the work and think, Wouldn't Father be pleased to know that his steel is in those bridges? Not all his, but enough . . . enough to keep Mother and me from want."

Tom twisted his fingers on the steering wheel, impatient with the diversion from his own problem. "Really, Mother, you sound like Little Orphan Annie. You could sell your Bay Steel stock for what? A million and a half?"

"I see you don't read the financial pages. Nine hundred and thirty thousand dollars. Even so, that's ten times more than in 1932, when I wanted to sell and Ollie Eakins talked me out of it. Thank God, I had enough sense to listen to him." She glanced sideways at her son. "So when you ask me for three hundred thousand dollars, that's almost half of your inheritance."

"But wouldn't you rather see me have it now when I need it the most?"

"I'm afraid you haven't convinced me."

What did it take? Tom wondered. Every day his position in Seadon Oil was growing less secure. Uncle Owen had promoted Gene to assistant vice president for production, Angela and Carla's husbands were rising in the company, and now Slater Dougal's son was on the payroll, too. Moreover, if Phil Barnard did not win a seat in Congress, then he would certainly return to Seadon Oil. Tom was being crowded. And now, most alarming of all, Ross had reduced his own stake in the Seadon Estate Company by transferring those shares to Leah's trust fund. Shares which ought to be part of Tom and Ginny's inheritance.

When he repeated that last point to his mother, Louise shook her head. "Owen's given up some of his stock too, but is Gene complaining?"

"That's because he never thinks ahead. But I can see what's coming. G. G. Haggerty weaseled his way into the Estate Company for one reason—it's a steppingstone to taking over Seadon Oil. At first Dad and Uncle Owen will be too strong for him, but Haggerty will want to make a gesture, so he'll hit those who can't fight back. Buck and Wharton will go, and probably Gene. And me for sure, because I'm the son of the president. Haggerty will show who's the real boss—unless I can buy enough company stock so he'll have to respect me."

"Tom, you've got a case of the bugaboos. And even if all this happened, three hundred thousand wouldn't impress a man like Haggerty."

"I know that, but it's a beginning. If I own a block of stock, I can borrow on it and buy more. Maybe even get a loan from Ginny. She's fat on her alimony, and I'd pay her interest and even a bonus if necessary."

Louise frowned. "If you're going to run to women to help you, why not go all the way? Marry Slater Dougal's girl and let her protect you."

Tom had considered it. And then thought of the wedding night and all the nights that would follow. *"What's the matter, honey? Is it me? Or can't you ever do it?"*

Louise broke in on his thoughts. "You've got to stop seeing things under the bed, Tom. I know Mr. Haggerty's reputation, but I know your father, too. Ross can handle him."

"Can he? Christ, I remember what happened with his glorious Pantex deal. Dad almost wrecked the family, and next time we might not be so lucky."

Louise's voice rose with irritation. "Tom, if I give you what you want, I'll never see you again." She waved away his protest. "Oh, yes. I know you better than you think. Your grandfather and I gave you your chance to go into Bay Steel. You would have been the big frog in a little pond, with nobody to threaten you. But you chose Seadon Oil because you wanted a bigger plum. Well, you've got it. And the headaches that go with it."

"All right, then just two hundred thousand."

Louise made a helpless shrug. "Don't you realize I'd have to give the same amount to your sister? I have to be fair with Ginny, too, and her children. Even though she doesn't deserve it."

"For God's sake, Mother, Ginny's fixed for life. All that

alimony and child support, and probably another husband around the corner."

"I know, I know. Three divorces and she still calls herself Catholic. When I was a girl," Louise continued, "dear old Henri Laprebode used to say, 'Whom the gods would destroy, they first make rich.' I didn't believe it then; wealth seemed so right, so uplifting to the spirit. But now that I've seen enough of the world . . ."

"Mother . . ."

"Yes?"

"You won't help me at all?"

She sighed. "You *are* my son. I'll give you what I can afford. One hundred thousand. And the same to Ginny. If she wishes to lend it to you, that's her affair."

The two women sat opposite each other in the drawing room of the *Super Chief* and watched the outskirts of the city glide past the window. It was Pasadena, where the travelwise would detrain rather than continue on through the boring railroad yards to the Los Angeles terminal. Dale opened her lizard handbag and took out her gold cigarette case. There was just time for one more smoke before they arrived. God knew, her nerves needed it. She lighted up and looked across at Leah. "Aren't you at all excited?" Her mother pondered a moment, then inclined her head slightly. It had been that way all the way over. A bundle of silence on the *Queen Mary*, on the *Twentieth Century Limited*, and now on the *Super Chief*. "Then for pity's sake, show it! Smile! We don't want Uncle Ross to think we're a couple of deportees."

More pondering. "Don't go to the hotel, Dale. Stay with us."

"Later. But not now." How often did she have to tell her? Leah belonged at Ridgemont and Dale where the studio had booked her, the Garden of Allah. It was Hollywood ritual, and she intended to enjoy it to the full. She had explained it all to Uncle Ross, over the phone in New York, and he had understood. But Mother, she acted as if she were being abandoned.

"Pasadena! Two minutes!" the porter bawled down the corridor. Dale rose and checked her lipstick in the mirror. Lord, she looked pale. Excitement was supposed to bring a blush to the cheeks, not a ghostly white. She fluffed the curls around her ears and wondered how Uncle Ross would like the change of eleven years. My God, really eleven? Yes, not since Lausanne. She knew he was gray-haired now; he had sent a snapshot. But still handsome and lean and erect. But what about her? She adjusted her sea-green Chanel jacket and appraised her face. Not too different, really. More mature, of course. No, "worldly," that was a better word. She had André to thank for that, and the others before and after. Especially after. After the stillbirth of her baby; after the despair, the guilt, the quarrels; after André's newspaper had sent him to cover the civil war in Spain. *C'est la vie, c'est la guerre.*

There were people passing along the train corridor now. Several glanced into the drawing room and smiled goodbye. Blond Constance Bennett, returning to her studio; then a darkly handsome young man who winked at Dale. Cary Grant, also studio-bound. It was still hard to believe that she had actually had drinks with the two stars last night in the bar car. Reading a copy of weekly *Variety* had been a good ploy, and then when the conductor had called her Miss Lantry, Cary had come over to her. Was she *the* Dale Lantry, authoress of *Unholy Triangle?*

The train shuddered, brakes squealed, the porter called, "Pasadena!" Dale and Leah followed the clot of passengers down the vestibule steps. As the porter handed Dale down, he shouted, "Miss Lantry's driver!" and a man in uniform stepped forward and tipped his hat. While Dale pointed out her luggage to the driver, Leah looked around anxiously. "Where's Ross? Where *is* he?"

Then a shout. *"Leah! Dale!"* He had been waiting at the wrong Pullman. A moment later they were in his arms, hugging, kissing, laughing. "Ross! Oh, Ross! Ross! Ross!" Leah wept. Thank God, some emotion at last.

Dale followed her mother and Ross to his Cadillac, where they babbled at each other until they had exhausted themselves. Finally Leah settled herself in the rear seat and Ross gave Dale a last hug and murmured in her ear, "Sure it's not your imagination?"

"I wish it were. Call me at the hotel."

"In an hour."

The studio car purred over the Colorado Street Bridge, south through Eagle Rock, west along Los Feliz. Past juice stands shaped like giant oranges, bakeries that were Dutch windmills, billboards promising thrills at Gay's Lion Farm, painless dentistry at Dr. Parker's, eternal rest at Forest Lawn. Then, finally, Sunset Boulevard and the Garden of Allah. The hotel did not live up to its romantic name, Dale thought. It was simply a collection of one- and two-story structures, with tile roofs and stucco walls, set among tall sentinel palms and shaggy cypress. There was the obligatory swimming pool, around which guests sunned and drank and spoke with hard New York accents about their radio "packages" and movie deals. But at least there were flowers in her room—red roses from Solly Braunstein, her producer. The card read, "Love and kisses, baby! My office tomorrow. Ten sharp." And there was champagne in an ice bucket and another card: "Love and kisses, baby! Write us a beauty!" This from Nat Fox, her agent.

The telephone rang. It was Uncle Ross. "She seems fine to me, Dale. Just sort of quiet. I don't think she needs a nurse."

"But what happens when she's alone and you're at the office?"

"She *won't* be alone. I've got a houseful of servants. I think she just needs to be taken out of herself. I told her Ridgemont's her home. She can redecorate, give parties, do any damn thing she wants. And when you get around to moving in with us, she'll really take hold."

"I'm not moving in, Uncle Ross."

"But . . ."

"I'm sorry. I just won't."

With her first week's salary, three thousand dollars, Dale bought herself a LaSalle convertible. After the second week, and another three thousand dollars, she rented a house on the

351

beach at Malibu and enlivened it with a Great Dane and a parrot that was obscene in four languages. During her third week the studio mail boy delivered a note from her old roommate at USC, Audrey Sommers, now Mrs. Edgar Tillson. Would it be possible to have lunch sometime? Knowing that it would please Old Aud, Dale chose the Brown Derby on Vine Street. The great barnlike room was filled to capacity—movie stars, radio stars, writers, producers, directors, orchestra leaders, all raucous with success and alcohol.

The two friends fell immediately into their old roles, the woman of the world and her dazzled retainer. How was that handsome cousin of Dale's? Gene? Oh, married. Yes, really, to a girl from one of the old Alto Valle families. . . . And all those years in Europe? Romantic, exciting, marvelous.

Then at last Audrey got up courage. "I've read your book."

"How did you like it?"

"Well-l . . ."

"You didn't."

"Oh, I did. I did. But it must have shocked your family spitless."

"They haven't read it. Families never do."

"I don't see how they dare make a movie out of it."

"They aren't. I'm rewriting a script somebody else gave up on. The studio wants something they call 'decadence with class.' Like Somerset Maugham, only different. Like Anita Loos, only different. Like Clare Boothe, only different. But enough of that. Tell me about your husband."

Audrey opened her purse and produced a snapshot which included their two children. Her husband owned a Nash automobile distributorship and they were divinely happy, which pleased Dale and yet depressed her. Then Audrey asked the inevitable: Was there a man in Dale's life, someone she might marry?

"Not yet. Nobody really interests me."

"Maybe you're still in love with Joe Carvalo. I got that from your book."

"Then you got it wrong. I still love my *times* with Joe. There's a difference."

It was, Dale thought, as if they were talking to each other across the centuries. When they parted, they promised to keep in touch with each other and knew that they would not.

She headed the LaSalle out Hollywood Boulevard and, in her mood of *triste*, she turned up Laurel Canyon and then onto the mountain road that led to the old house at the end of the road. Part of the chimney had tumbled down, the shingles were buckling, and there was a rag stuffed in a broken window. A small boy and a goat meditated on the porch steps.

Ross was convinced that Dale was mistaken about her mother. Leah might be an idiot about money matters, and gullible about spiritualism, but she was not mentally ill. She did not require a nurse. That was unthinkable for a Seadon. She was happy at Ridgemont; she got along well with Mrs. Pryor and the servants; she enjoyed rearranging the furniture and puttering in the gardens. When Owen was in town, he would join them for dinner, and it almost seemed like the old days back in Weston. True, Leah said very little, and when she was asked a question the answer was frequently a blank look. When an art dealer brought a new painting to Ridgemont, perhaps a Degas or Renoir, Ross would ask her opinion and she would stare at the work and struggle for words and finally throw up her hands. "Good God," Ross sputtered once, "just tell me if you like it or if you don't. Does it look like fifty thousand dollars?" The answer was tears.

Ross's increased spending on fine art was due to the new federal law which was aimed at breaking up family holding companies. Unless such companies paid out to their stockholders their entire net income, the Collector of Internal Revenue stood ready to tax it away. So it was that the Seadons' plan to prevent G. G. Haggerty from sharing in the wealth of the Estate Company had come to naught. The income had to be distributed—over a million dollars a year to Haggerty and almost as much to Ross and Owen, with the remainder going into Leah's trust fund, from which it was disbursed to her in twelve equal installments. It was the payments to Leah that first seriously aroused Ross's concern. Mrs. Pryor reported finding a ten-thousand-dollar check stuffed between the folds of a bath towel; another time it tumbled out of the bedroom chandelier; the next, it was a greasy wad in a jar of cold cream. Then, at breakfast or dinner, Leah began to ask Ross why he was so against her singing career. And why must he marry Louise? The past and the present grew more and more confused and distorted. Dave Marcus was still alive, Dale was still a child. Then one evening, arriving back at Ridgemont, Ross found Leah standing outside the grilled gate. She was clanging a handbell and holding a tin cup and wearing dark glasses; suspended from her neck was a placard on which she had scrawled, MY BROTHERS HAVE ROBBED ME BLIND.

"I told you she needed a nurse," Dale said when she arrived in answer to Ross's call. "She was the same in Paris. She'd go for months perfectly all right, and then suddenly she wasn't. I never wrote you about it, because I was there to watch her. One time I was just on the point of taking her to a Swiss sanitarium, and then, just like throwing a light switch, she came out of it. She was her old loving self, giving André and me presents, cooking our meals, and planning picnics."

"I talked this over with Owen," Ross said. "He thinks maybe, in some wild way, she's trying to get attention."

"No, it goes deeper. I can see that you haven't read my novel yet."

Ross looked embarrassed. "Your Aunt Tana said she started the book, then threw it away. I gathered you'd written something off-color, maybe trying to outdo the French, and I didn't want to know about it."

She smiled. "It's off-color because life is off-color. It's about me and Joe Carvalo, about the girl who inherited her mother's weakness for men and nearly wrecked her life."

"Oh, good God, girl!"

"Uncle Ross, you're blushing!" She laughed. "Why? Good Lord, the name Seadon has always been a six-letter synonym for sex." She saw Ross's jaw set with insult. "Seriously, I think that's the answer for Mother—a man. When I was little, she always had one around, sometimes two or three. Oh, I'm not talking an affair or marriage. Just somebody to fill the empty hours. Somebody she could look forward to seeing and doing things with."

"It's grasping at straws."

"I know. Maybe it won't work, but what's our alternative? A psychiatrist badgering the poor woman? Pills and hypodermic needles? Locked away in a sanitarium? She deserves our love, not punishment."

Ross mulled over the idea for several days. It would take a very special man. Kind, patient, understanding, and with his own need for companionship. Perhaps a widower. Several names came to mind, and when Ross telephoned Liz Barnard, she suggested several more of her own acquaintance. But how to introduce them to Leah? It would have to be handled with delicacy; it must seem to come about by chance. A party, that was the answer.

The guest list was carefully camouflaged by including all the officers of Seadon Oil and their wives. The Seadon family itself came en masse—even Ginny, who happened to be visiting friends in Palm Springs. For Dale it stirred memories of that first party at Ridgemont. Lanterns glowed on the flagstone terrace, a band played for the dancers in the great living room, champagne corks popped, and—thank you, dear Lord—Mother was smiling and laughing with one man after another.

Midway through the evening Dale found her cousin Gene in the music room talking to a circle of guests. No, not talking, almost addressing them. What was he saying? Dale sidled alongside, unnoticed. Of course, the civil war in Spain, Gene's enduring anguish. Dale noted that he seemed to be directing his words to a tall man with red hair. "For all any of us know," Gene declared, "some relative of mine, some Delgado, is being killed at this very moment. And for what? It's obscene, it's a return to barbarism!"

"And a rehearsal for the next world war," Dale spoke up.

"Nonsense! Never!" someone challenged, and then everyone was talking at once, and the man with the red hair was tugging at Gene's elbow and nodding toward Dale. Gene's introduction was blurred by the surrounding babble. Phil Barnard . . . best friend . . . junior congressman . . . home on vacation. Cousin Dale . . . from Paris . . . novelist . . . writer of movie scenarios. Why was the man staring so? And what intense blue eyes. Penetrating. Appraising. Admiring. Dale felt a strange sensation in the region of her stomach and she seemed to have trouble breathing. What was he saying? Something patronizing about the movie business. The old clichés. She heard herself reply with an acid bite. What was wrong with peddling daydreams? People couldn't spend every waking moment picking their sores. And wasn't peddling daydreams what politicians did best?

He threw up his arms in mock surrender. "*Kamerad!* Armistice!" Then Gene was linking arms with them and guiding them toward the nearest bar for more champagne.

"*Dale!*" It was Uncle Ross, gesturing to her. She excused herself. "It's working! By God, it's working!" He grinned and motioned her to follow. They reached the living room. "That's funny. Just a minute ago your mother was dancing with one of Liz's friends." Then they saw her, off in a corner, dabbing a handkerchief at her eyes. Ross sighed. "I guess it was too good to last. Sorry, Dale, go on back to the boys."

But they had wandered off somewhere. Dale felt a surge of relief. A chance to get hold of herself, that was what she needed. To stop acting like a swooning teen-ager. The man was probably married. No, that was right, Gene had made a point of it—elected without the usual wife and kids. Okay, what did it matter? What she really wanted was a breath of fresh air.

The terrace was deserted. In the nearby hills a coyote raised its voice in a wild yapping song. To the east, searchlights crisscrossed the sky; some Hollywood premiere or a drugstore opening. She drifted along the balustrade and gazed out over the lights of Beverly Hills. There were so many more now than on that first night, when she had met Joe Carvalo on this same terrace. She glanced at the potted privets; they had tripled in size. She smiled to herself, remembering how she had pirouetted across the flagstone, pretending that she did not see Joe. The band had played a fox trot, "Tea for Two." Tonight it was the new beat, a rhumba. "El Manicero—The Peanut Vendor." She began to sway to the rhythm. It was fast, too fast; she would dance in half-time. A forward break, a side break, a spin—

She stopped. There was the fiery dot of a cigarette in the shadows. Then the cigarette fell and was crushed under a heel. Phil came toward her, holding out his arms.

Chapter 25

LOUISE WAS dead.

It had been sudden. She had gone into the hospital for treatment of what was considered a mild case of pneumonia. It was nothing alarming; she would be discharged by the weekend. Then, two nights later, her mother telephoned Ross that Louise was failing rapidly. By the time Ross and Tom had landed at the San Francisco airport, and long before Ginny had flown in from Chicago, she was gone. The Requiem Mass was said at Old St. Mary's, the red brick church just below the Fairmont Hotel on the edge of Chinatown, where Ross and Louise had frequently worshiped after the earthquake and fire had destroyed their own St. Ignatius'. The depth of Ross's grief surprised his children, for they had perceived their parents in attitudes long abandoned. No longer husband and wife in the true sense, still they were friends. No matter their past differences, Ross's respect for Louise had never wavered; she had been a woman of high standards, an unswervable Catholic, an authentic lady. A rarity in any age.

One by one the old familiar faces were deserting him. And Ross was past sixty. His doctor said he had the body of a man of fifty, the mind of forty, and, jokingly, the appetites of thirty. If so, where was his old optimism? The times seemed out of joint, the world without logic. A passing mood, he told himself, that went with mourning. No, Owen felt the same way; Tana, too. All three agreed that reading the newspapers or listening to the radio news was more depressing than diverting. In October the stock market had crashed again; through the winter and into the spring of 1938 more millions of workers were being laid off and people were muttering about a return to the dark days of 1932. The reports from Europe were equally discouraging. The Nazis hounded German Jews and muttered threats against Czechoslovakia; Spain, with its civil war, seemed bent on national suicide.

On a smaller scale, on the personal level, Ross had more cause for dejection. Leah gyrated between manic happiness and despair. One week she and her "companion" would go on long drives to Palm Springs, Santa Barbara, Laguna; the next week she would lock herself in her room and refuse to see anyone. Tom Seadon was contradictory in another way. He had become engaged to a socially prominent girl in Bel Air, and Ross, highly pleased, had arranged Tom's promotion to vice president for marketing. The following month the engagement was broken off without explanation. Would Tom ever marry? Would he ever give Ross grandchildren? At least Ginny had done that—Kevin and Andrew. But what sad young boys, parked in a Catholic parochial school in San Jose while Ginny flitted from Newport to Palm Beach to Havana and God knew where.

In the past whenever Ross had felt dejected about Tom and Ginny, he had been able to console himself with the thought of Phil Barnard. Now even he threatened disappointment. Phil had stopped by Ross's office and announced his intention to switch political parties and run for re-election as a Republican congressman.

"Why, for God's sake?" Ross demanded.

"A lot of reasons. The Democrats are too damned anxious to spend money. There are too many pinkos and too many sucking after the votes of labor and the unemployed. Hell, Ross, you know it's true."

"It is. I'm sick of the idea that if a man is rich he's guilty of some sort of a crime. But all the same, I wonder what happened to the young fellow who wanted to set up farms for the Okies around Weston."

"I'm not ashamed of it. It should have been done. But *then* is not *now*. The mood of the country has changed. Roosevelt's no longer the miracle worker. His NRA failed, his Brain Trust is a brain bust, he's packed the Supreme Court, and he's letting business go downhill. You know something, when Roosevelt appears in the newsreels, the audience hardly claps; in fact, I've heard boos and hisses. That sort of feeling sure can't help a Democrat up for re-election.

"Granted all that," Ross said, "if you switch to the Republicans, they won't trust you. And the Democrats will despise you. In politics, party loyalty comes before convictions."

"All right. Then I'll run as an independent."

Ross threw up his hands. "That will really finish you. I say stay with the Democrats and work for changes inside the party."

But it was clear to Ross that Phil was not convinced. He was enamored with the name "independent," the idea of freedom from ties. Just as Ross had been at the same age; just as his mother had been as a boardinghouse keeper in Weston. And his grandfather Val. It was in his genes.

It seemed impossible to cram one more body into Dale's Malibu house. Those guests who could not find standing or sitting room on the ground floor squatted on the stairs going up to the bedrooms, where still others hunched on the beds, or were chest to chest in the bathrooms and elbow to elbow on the balcony overlooking the moonlit beach. Everyone Dale knew, or

360

wanted to know, was at the party. Her producer, her agent, Elissa Landi, Peter Lorre, Mary Astor, Vivian Thorpe, Clifford Odets. Rudolf Friml, at the piano, tinkled through his score from *The Firefly*, barely audible against the tumult of talk.

"Tricky? He could get a sandwich off a chicken without breaking the skin." . . . "The United States just doesn't give a damn. Hitler marched into the Rhineland, took Austria, and what did Americans do? They sang 'Flat Foot Floogie with a Floy Floy'!" . . . "I'll tell you how dumb she is. She went into a bookstore and asked for that novel by the great Russian writer Mr. Tall Story. She called it *Worn Piece* and thought is was about a hooker." . . . "It's bluff. Hitler doesn't dare touch the Czechs, because France is their ally. That means England, too." . . . "Baby, he tells every girl he loves her. Anything with a hole. The romance of his life was a knotty pine fence!"

Phil Barnard felt he was odd man out. Who were Noël and Gertie and Talloo and Cole? He could not understand German, which seemed to be the second language of the evening. It was a by-product of Hitler, of course, whose rantings against German intellectuals and "decadent" artists had driven them to seek safety and work six thousand miles away in the motion picture studios, and so had resulted in a cultural explosion for Southern California that rivaled those in the artistic centers of New York and London.

Phil watched Dale circulate among her guests: a word here, a laugh there, and occasionally—not often enough—her eyes seeking him out from across the room. She was especially lovely tonight, he thought: the cream-colored Lucien Lelong gown, the chestnut hair in defiance of current styles, long and gathered in a swirl at the nape of the neck. But did she really enjoy all these shallow egotists—not the Europeans, but the New Yorkers and locals? Or was it just good business? Dale insisted that they amused her, gave her story material, and this had been the flashpoint of all their quarrels. They had even broken off seeing each other last year when Phil was about to return to Congress; now that he was back to campaign for re-election, they had been drawn together again. A case of go away nearer. Still, it was a scratchy relationship. If she weren't so damned independent, he thought. But then he was, too.

Ross was flanked on one of the sofas by the dark beauty of Mary Astor and the contrasting blond of Vivian Thorpe. He was grateful to be invited; it was pleasant to forget business and the problem of Leah and listen to the two actresses report their visits to San Simeon, where they had been guests of William Randolph Hearst. He was a dear old thing, the actresses thought, but how could he stand living in that enormous castle with all those moth-eaten tapestries and gloomy old masters?

"Does he have any Impressionists?" Ross directed the question to Vivian Thorpe.

"Impressionists? You mean, doing imitations?"

Mary Astor laughed. "Viv's pulling your leg, Mr. Seadon. Renoir, Degas, Monet, Manet, she knows them all."

Vivian nodded. "But I don't remember any at San Simeon, unless I missed them."

"I've got seventeen," Ross said, the old competitive spirit rising again.

"Really?" Vivian examined him as if he had announced he had seventeen toes. "Oh, I forgot. You're Dale's uncle with all the paintings. Her favorite uncle."

"Did she tell you that?"

She smiled curiously. "In a way."

They were interrupted by shouts of glee. Artie Belmer was taking off his clothes. Mary Astor leaned toward Ross and whispered that the actor had formerly been an artist's model; this was his standard party act for the benefit of certain of the male guests. It did not amuse Ross; he rose and excused himself from the two actresses and edged his way toward the door that opened onto the beach balcony. He lit a cigarette and went down the wooden steps onto the sand. As he strolled, he could smell the heavy musk of the kelp beds offshore. Now and then a seagull, sleeping on the sand, withdrew its head from its wing and watched his passage. Just how serious, Ross mused, was Phil about Dale? Or Dale about him? If they knew that they were first cousins . . . No, probably just a flirtation, a game to play.

He heard the crunch of sand behind him. He turned and recognized the blond hair of Vivian Thorpe. "I've had enough, too," she said, overtaking him. "When you get to be my age . . ." She let it trail off. Her age? Certainly not more than forty, Ross thought; not old at all. He had been conscious back at the party of her youthful figure. Her beauty, he had decided, was somewhat flawed: the nose a bit too prominent, the cheeks a bit too full, and gray eyes that should have been blue or brown. But that was quibbling. Why had she followed him onto the beach?

She supplied the answer. "That's my house over there. You feel like a tall Scotch and soda?"

"Sounds fine."

He followed her up the wooden steps to the porch, then into her kitchen. She opened the refrigerator and took out ice and found a siphon of soda. They carried their glasses into the sitting room, which might have been a duplicate of Dale's except for the theatrical posters on the walls, all of which featured the name VIVIAN THORPE.

"I was a London music hall girl," she said, noticing his interest. "Before that, plain Millie Huckaby from Sussex." She gestured him to a flowered chintz sofa, sat down beside him, removed her sandals, and shook the sand into an ashtray on the coffee table. "And you?"

"I thought Dale told you. A businessman. A widower." Ross frowned at a copy of *Unholy Triangle* on the table. "I hope you aren't going to read that."

"Just finished it. Borrowed it from Dale. I like to know something about my neighbors."

"Please don't hold it against her."

"Why should I? I wasn't shocked, if that's what you mean. I liked the heroine. I got the impression she was Dale herself."

"Oh, no. It's all fiction. Just trashy fiction."

"Then you wouldn't be the uncle in the story?"

"Good God, no!"

363

She nodded knowingly. "It was two other chaps, Your Honor." She studied him with amusement. "Too bad."

"Why?"

"Females are always interested in a man with a bad reputation. Gives a dog a good name."

Ross felt awkward; he wished that he had read Dale's novel and knew how she had described the uncle. And he was embarrassed because Vivian was being so personal, almost as if she were implying— Well, how else could he interpret it? Vivian Thorpe must be twenty years his junior; he ought to be grateful that she would say such things to a man of his age. He had been used to women throwing themselves at him; every wealthy man had that. But it had been a long time since. Certainly Vivian Thorpe did not need a wealthy protector, or whatever the term might be. Ross was aware of her jewels, the expensive beach house, her position in the film industry. Dale had mentioned something about an Oscar as best supporting actress. She could have her pick. No, simply chalk it up to her being an actress who enjoyed making startling remarks for their effect.

She laid her cheek against the top of the sofa and pouted at him. "Oh, stop looking so austere. You're not C. Aubrey Smith."

When he kissed her, her mouth replied with lazy pleasure, unhurried, savoring, approving. Then she pulled back. "Time to go."

"You want me to?"

"Yes. Hedda's at the party, remember. She'll be counting heads."

"Making a bed check?"

"To be blunt."

"Let her."

"Sorry. Neither of us needs that kind of publicity. Or my studio."

He rose reluctantly and went to the door opening onto the porch and looked back at her. She was watching him with a brooding expression.

"What's the matter?"

"I never met a man who owns seventeen Impressionists. What ever do they mean to you?"

"I'll explain sometime." He added, grinning, "If you promise you won't call me uncle."

Los Angeles baked in one of the hottest late Septembers in memory. Even the nights were hot, and people slept on their porches or in their yards or fled to the comparative cool of the beaches. But whether at home or office or seashore, every radio was tuned to the news broadcasts. Hitler had given the dreaded ultimatum. Unless Czechoslovakia surrendered the Sudetenland by October 1, the German armies would take it by force. All Europe braced for what seemed inevitable. French troops were pouring into the Maginot Line, the British fleet had put to sea, there were air raid drills in London, and bomb shelters were being dug in the Paris parks. The Pope had appealed for reason; President Roosevelt had sent messages to London, Paris, Berlin, and Prague to urge the cause of peace. The next forty-eight hours would decide.

At Ridgemont on the evening of September 28 Ross sipped his after-dinner drink beside the swimming pool and waited for Edward R. Murrow to begin his nightly broadcast with the familiar words "This is London. . . ." Ross felt lonely without Vivian beside him. Even Leah and her nurse would be welcome; but this was not one of his sister's "good" days, and she had already retired to her quarters and the release of sleeping pills. Ross's eyes fixed on the telephone at the foot of his pool chair. When would Vivian call? She had promised to shoo her two sons out of the beach house, where they had taken refuge from the heat of Pasadena and their dormitory at Cal Tech. But suppose they decided to spend the night? Hell, let them. Vivian certainly could invent an excuse to steal away for a few hours.

Dale was aware of their affair, which was inevitable when Ross's car could be seen parked just three houses to the east of her own. She was not only aware but enthusiastic for Ross's sake. So far it was a lighthearted arrangement. Vivian amused

Ross with her stories of the movie folk, and Ross's tales of the boom days in Weston bettered anything Vivian had seen on the screen. She had quickly dismissed the difference in their ages. "Darling, I've always liked older men. Why, at fourteen I wanted to seduce the Archbishop of Canterbury."

Ross had laughed. "You're a gallant liar."

"No. Just depraved."

Whatever, he knew that power was an aphrodisiac. Vivian was impressed when she saw the photographs in the library of the tankers *Val Seadon* and *Cathlin Seadon* and the map on the wall with red pins indicating the oil fields and refineries of Seadon Oil which stretched from California to Oklahoma and south to Venezuela. Still, he had the best of the bargain, a vibrant woman to take to dinner (always in an out-of-the-way place where they would not encounter movie friends), a woman who sincerely laughed at his jokes and told him she felt guilty to so enjoy herself when her countrymen were beset by the danger of war. . . . But why didn't she telephone?

Ross saw headlights swing up the driveway, and then Dale's LaSalle came into view. He turned off the radio and started toward the car. She was not alone; some man was getting out of the car with her. Phil.

Dale waved and called, "Isn't it wonderful?"

"What is?"

"Didn't you hear? It's on the radio right now! Hitler has invited Chamberlain and Daladier to meet him and Mussolini. Tomorrow, at Munich!"

Phil added, "Hitler's postponed mobilization. There'll be peace."

"Thank God! That calls for a drink."

Dale waved the idea aside. "We want to see Mother."

"I'm afraid she's already asleep."

"Then we'll wake her!" Dale paused. "Or is she . . . ?"

"Yes." He looked carefully at the young people. They were excited about something besides the news from Europe.

Dale threw her arms around him. "We're going to be married!"

366

Phil laughed at Ross's expression. "I told you he'd be bowled over!"

"Completely."

Dale bubbled on. "Remember now, it's a secret until after Phil's re-elected. I don't want him to lose the vote because he married a Hollywood writer."

"And what happens to the Hollywood writer?"

Phil grinned triumphantly. "I've convinced her there's just as much story material in Washington. She can write another novel, or maybe a play. All she has to do is finish out her contract with the studio, and by December she'll be free . . . and Mrs. Philip Barnard."

Ross smiled skeptically. Was it possible, his headstrong niece? On the surface, the battle of wills seemed over; she was radiant in surrender, a willing prisoner—on the surface. He kissed her and promised that he would give Leah the news in the morning. Then, shaking Phil's hand: "Have you told Liz?"

"No. We're on our way there now."

He was watching the LaSalle turn and head down the hill when the telephone rang. It was Vivian; her sons had left, finally, thank God. Hurry down. He couldn't, Ross said; something serious had come up, a business matter. Oh, bother! Then tomorrow night? Yes, without fail.

He wanted to telephone Liz immediately, but it would be wrong. She should hear from the kids firsthand. Afterwards she would surely call him; then they could decide. . . .

When Liz did telephone, her voice was thick with emotion. "It's perfect, Ross, absolutely perfect!"

"I hope so, but I've got my doubts."

"Why?"

"Dale, for one thing. Understand, I care more for her than my own Ginny, but she's been on her own too many years. She's willful; she won't keep her mouth shut; she's poles apart from Phil on politics; she'll be meddling in Phil's career."

Liz was silent a moment. "I thought you were going to object because they're cousins."

"I was coming to that. Heredity is nothing to fool with. Suppose Leah's trouble passes down to Dale later on, or to their kids."

"Suppose! Suppose the sky falls down. No, Dale brought that up herself. From what she's told me about her father, I'm sure his strength will cancel out any weakness from Leah."

Possibly so, Ross reflected. The Seadon brothers had never correctly appreciated Dale's father; they had considered him a financial failure and had underestimated his solid qualities, the same qualities which he had bequeathed to his daughter.

He heard Liz going on. "We aren't going to step between two wonderful people. Let's be proud and happy that our son chose a girl like Dale. My God, I can hardly wait to be a grandmother! . . . Now, how about coming over and spilling some champagne with me?"

"Another time, Liz. I'm ready for bed." . . . At Malibu, after all.

Prime Minister Chamberlain returned from Munich with the promise of "peace in our time," and the world sighed with relief. Czechoslovakia had surrendered the Sudetenland to Germany in exchange for Britain and France's guarantees of her new borders. Yet within the following ten days most of Czechoslovakia's industry was in Nazi hands, and by March 15, 1939, Hitler slept in Prague's Hradčany Castle. The governments of Britain and France, defaulting their guarantees, shrugged and looked the other way. But not so the common man. Dale Barnard, writing to Ross about her new life in Washington, D.C., quoted a furious letter she had received from the journalist with whom she had shared her Paris days. Chamberlain was "a lying dastard," according to André; Daladier "a disgrace to France." They were Hitler's most valuable agents; they had made him a hero to the German nation and had destroyed his political opposition, which had been far stronger than outsiders realized. "It is inevitable now," André had concluded. "There will be war before the autumn leaves fall. The excuse will be Danzig, but the cause will be Munich."

Ross wondered if Dale had shown André's letter to her husband, or had revealed their past relationship. But he did not doubt the prediction of war. "Let's hope it's not before September," Vivian Thorpe said to Ross one evening when they were discussing the possibility.

"Why September?"

"Because I've signed to do a film in England this summer."

"No, damn it, *no!*"

"Darling, I have to go where the work is. Besides, it's only for four months."

Ross groaned at the thought. "All right, I'll just have to find some business excuse to come over. When you're not shooting, you can show me the English countryside."

She shook her head. "We'd be recognized, and then the studio would have kittens."

They had been over the same ground almost from the start. Shortly before the release of each of her films, the publicity department would inspire rumors in the press of Vivian Thorpe's new romance with the male star. It was good box office; it sold tickets. But if her name were coupled with Ross's, the public's titillation would end.

Ross tried another tack. "If you stay in England till a war breaks out, maybe you couldn't get out."

"I will. If I have to swim." She kissed his nose. "They say absence makes the heart grow fonder. Think what it would be if I stayed away a whole year."

Then it would be over, Ross thought. Or they would be married.

Chapter 26

IN LATE August the Seadon brothers and Tana visited San Francisco to see the Golden Gate International Exposition. Compared with the city's great celebration in 1915, the new fair seemed small potatoes to the Seadons. There was, however, a macabre parallel. The exposition of twenty-four years earlier had been dampened by the war in Europe; now the certainty of another conflict overshadowed the exposition of 1939. And it was a certainty. Newspapers carried headlines of Hitler's threats against Poland; editorials worried about Germany's surprise nonagression treaty with Russia; letters to the editor expressed naïve shock at the pact between two supposed enemies, forgetting that it was Soviet Russia that had taught Hitler the value of concentration camps and the pleasures of Jewish persecution.

On September 1, the day the Seadons returned to Los Angeles, the Wehrmacht swept across the Polish border, and Britain and France declared war on Germany. But it was too late for Poland. On September 17, reeling from the combined German blitzkrieg and Stalin's attack from the east, Warsaw fell.

And Vivian Thorpe was still in England. Ross sent cable after cable urging her return to California and each answer read, "Soon." In October she signed to do a second film. "Home by February," she cabled. At least, Ross told himself, the Atlantic liners were still sailing; there was no bombing of London and Paris; the French Army sat in the bunkers of the Maginot Line braced for an attack which did not come. It was a "phony war," the newspapers decided, and so it appeared to be when Vivian finally returned. Ross made the mistake of meeting her at the Pasadena depot, and a curious reporter trailed Ross's limousine to Malibu. The following day there was a smirking paragraph in the movie section of the *Los Angeles News*. Vivian called Ross immediately. "Don't talk to any reporters," she said. "The studio is in an absolute froth, but I told them I would handle it."

She did in the next day's edition. "Mr. Seadon and I are just good friends. In my heart of hearts I have only one love, my work." It galled Ross to be dismissed so casually and with such a worn cliché, but that was show business. He wondered, too, who would be the first among the Seadons or his friends to come to him.

It was Tom, with his sister Ginny in tow. They were barely inside the door at Ridgemont when Tom demanded, "How long has this thing been going on?"

"Something over a year, if it's any of your business."

Ginny considered it was. "Do you know she's twice divorced?"

"Yes. With your own record, my dear, I'd say that's the pot calling the kettle black."

"Do you know about her two grown sons that she keeps out of sight?"

"I do. They're students at Cal Tech." Ross smiled grimly at his daughter. "Sounds like you've hired a detective."

Tom answered. "We didn't have to. I know a man with the

371

Merchants Credit Bureau. It's all on file, including that she's behind in her charge accounts. Dad, can't you see she's after your money? My God, she's twenty-two years younger!"

Ross fought to hold in his temper. "I suppose I should expect that from you, Tom. But I thought Ginny would have more grace. Viv doesn't give a damn about my age, so I'll thank you two to let me live my own life."

Tom's face hardened. "Then you're going to marry her."

"You'll be the first to know."

"Sure! That's beautiful! Then you'll adopt her brats and you'll bring them into Seadon Oil. Christ, she's young enough to even spawn some more. We'll have half-brothers and half-sisters all over the place!"

"I see. You're sweating your inheritance."

"Why shouldn't we?" Ginny shrilled. "Why should we be pushed aside for some scheming movie tart?" She saw that she had gone too far and retreated quickly. "Daddy, we're thinking of you. We don't want everyone saying there's no fool like an old fool. You're too fine for that. You deserve respect."

"Thank you for remembering that," Ross said dryly.

Owen's response to the subject of Vivian Thorpe was cautiously favorable. He and Tana would be pleased with any woman who made Ross happy. Had he proposed? No, not yet. He wanted to be completely sure of himself as well as of Vivian. He remembered all too well his confidence in marrying Louise and the pain of their separation. Further, Ross had to admit to himself, there was a certain justice in Tom and Ginny's position. At age sixty-four, he should put his house in order.

Wil Caruth listened carefully to Ross's solution. "Well, that certainly ought to shut up your kids," he agreed. "But are you sure you want to give up that big a slice of your Estate Company stock? You've already put ten per cent in trust for Leah; forty per cent of the remainder will cut your holdings almost in half."

"It's worth it for peace in the family. Hell, even with only half my stock, I can't possibly spend the income. Besides, if Tom and Ginny each get twenty per cent put into a trust, they can't fritter it away; it'll be there for Ginny's boys and for Tom's kids, if he ever has any."

Caruth puffed his cheeks in thought. "There's one angle I should point out to you. I helped your father put together the Estate Company, and I remember how strong Val was about keeping the family's assets within the family. If you and Miss Thorpe should marry, I'm not positive you could will her the rest of your Estate stock. She would be entitled to the widow's statutory share; but I think Tom and Ginny could sue for the balance. I'd sure hate to see a messy fight in court, dragging out all the dirty linen, maybe a charge of undue influence by an artful and designing woman." Caruth saw Ross about to protest. "Believe me, it could happen. When millions are at stake, people fight dirty. Filial love and respect go in the ashcan."

Ross laughed uneasily. "That's where this conversation belongs, in the ashcan. Tom and Ginny may have their faults, but they're still good kids. And Vivian is *not* a designing woman."

"Fine! Then my recommendation is this: Set up the two trust funds for your children, and go one step further. A premarital agreement."

"For Vivian?"

"For her, for you, for the good of everybody. Miss Thorpe would waive her claims to your estate and be satisfied with a nominal cash settlement and the position and privileges which she would enjoy as Mrs. Ross Seadon, which are certainly considerable. . . . Suppose I draw up a rough draft of the agreement and you can go over it with her."

Ross pulled his ear and thought. "No. It would be an insult."

"Maybe. But she's a woman of experience in the world; she might surprise you. And it would certainly prove to you, and to everybody, that the lady loves you for yourself and not your money. . . . If you really want to know."

Ross avoided Caruth's eyes. "Draw up the trust documents, Wil. Just the trust."

For many years the annual meeting of the stockholders and directors of the Seadon Estate Company had been an informal affair. Sometime in April, Ross and Owen and Wil Caruth, acting as secretary, would gather to look over the books and calculate the amount of dividends which the company would receive from Seadon Oil Company (whose own annual meeting was late in May); they would declare the Estate dividend, make an entry in the minute book, and adjourn *sine die*. But since G. G. Haggerty had become a shareholder, and with the establishment of Leah's trust fund, and now Tom and Ginny's, the Seadon brothers were forced to observe the niceties of corporate procedure. Notices of the annual meeting were mailed to Haggerty and to the bank that administered the three trust funds; the bank, in turn, issued its proxies to be voted at the meeting—one proxy to Ross to represent Leah's interest, another to Tom and a third to Ginny.

As he had hoped, Ross's gifts to his children had melted their antagonism; now there was a feeling of family unity and warmth. At the Estate Company meeting, held in the board room of Seadon Oil, Tom and Ginny were proud to share in the decision-making, and they voted their proxies with obvious satisfaction.

Haggerty, on the other hand, was taken aback by the addition of new Seadon faces; then, learning that they were there as representatives of their trusts, he recovered. "I wish I had children of my own," he remarked, "so I could do the same thing. It's damned lonely playing king of the mountain without kith or kin." He was particularly genial toward Tom. "Someday, young fellow, you're going to make a fine president for Seadon Oil." And gallantly to Ginny: "Wouldn't mind seeing a woman on the board of directors, either. Got a good head on your shoulders, young lady."

After the meeting Ginny remarked to Ross, "Mr. Haggerty isn't anything like I thought. He's nice. Don't you think so, Tom?"

"Yes. I'm surprised."

"Don't be." Ross sniffed. "We just voted a dividend that puts two million dollars in his pocket. Haggerty's niceness carries a hefty price tag."

The improved relations with his children encouraged Ross that the time was ripe to introduce them to Vivian Thorpe. They would meet at a small dinner party at Ridgemont, with Owen and Tana and, depending on her condition, Leah. No sooner had Ross telephoned the invitations than Liz Barnard called. Dale and Phil had arrived from Washington. When could they all get together? At the dinner, of course. Now the evening was an assured success. Dale was Vivian's friend; she would be well championed.

It was a success with qualifications. Although Vivian's stories of her London music hall days brought smiles to the table, Ross sensed the guarded reactions of Tom and Ginny. And afterwards, on the way to the living room for demitasse and brandy, Liz made an aside to Ross. "I wish she'd stop acting like she's running for public office."

"She's an actress," Ross replied.

"So was I. But I don't remember taking curtain calls every time someone cleared his throat."

There were compensations. Leah was enjoying another good spell; she sat beside Dale and held her hand and asked intelligent questions about life in Washington. It was fascinating, Dale said; the scramble for power was as frantic as anything in Hollywood, and she had already started a novel about it. Of course she would publish under a pen name to spare Phil any repercussions.

Her words were the cue for Phil. "I'd like to make two announcements," he said to the gathering. "First, I came back to Los Angeles for something besides a little vacation from Congress. I've been sounding out the local boys, and they've given me the green light. This fall I'm running for the U.S. Senate." He raised his hand to quiet the handclapping and looked at Ross. "I'm sorry I can't take your advice. I don't want any party ties. I'm running as an independent."

Ross looked thoughtful. "Well, I wish you luck."

"It'll take more than that, but I think I can swing it if I pick up the votes of some of the unhappy Democrats and Republicans. And especially if I can get the backing of the California oil industry. They ought to remember I was one of them a while back, and I'll stand up for their rights." He winked at Ross. "Would you pass that word in the right quarters?"

Ross bobbed his head and grinned. "Up and down the state. You can count on it." Then he remembered. "You said you had two announcements. What's the other?"

"That's the important one. Dale is expecting."

On May 10, 1940, Germany hurled its full might against Belgium and France; the "phony war" was over. On that same day, by a morbid coincidence, the stock transfer department of Seadon Oil reported that it had transferred 50,000 shares of company stock into the name of G. G. Haggerty. The next day the department received from banks in Chicago and New York an additional 171,000 shares which had been held as "street" certificates. These, too, were to be transferred into the name of Haggerty. Ross and Owen examined the certificates and noted their issuance dates; in each case they had been issued shortly after one of the annual meetings of the Estate Company. "So that's what the bastard was doing the last four years." Ross sighed. "Used our own dividends to buy Seadon Oil. Kept it all in dummy names, just like we did with his damned Pantex."

"But why does he pick now to come out in the open?" Owen wondered. Then he answered his own question. "Christ, the annual meeting!"

The officers and directors sat in a line on the stage behind the speaker's table. Ross, Owen, and Tom, seated in the center, gazed out at the audience and sensed a different mood than at previous annual meetings. In the past there had been a light-hearted expectancy of higher earnings and larger dividends. This morning there was a somber quiet; many of the stock-holders had brought the latest editions of the newspapers to the meeting and were comparing headlines. ANGLO FRENCH DISASTER! NAZI DRIVE TO THE SEA! One of the stockholders, also with a newspaper, was G. G. Haggerty.

376

The meeting opened with the address of the president and chairman of the board. Ross reviewed the past year's progress and gave his expectations for the coming year. Owen, as executive vice president, followed; and he reported field production and refinery runs and the experiments with artificial rubber made from crude. Then came the question period, and the Seadons fixed their eyes on Haggerty; this would be his chance to speak. But no; he sat quietly listening to the queries of stockholders and the answers from the stage. Finally Wil Caruth moved for the election of the board of directors.

"Mr. Chairman!" a voice boomed. It was Haggerty, on his feet. "May I have permission to address the meeting?"

"Certainly, Mr. Haggerty."

He made his way up onto the stage, carrying his newspaper under his arm. Ross adjusted the microphone and introduced the distinguished president of Pantex Oil Corporation. There was a buzz of surprise from the audience, then applause as Haggerty announced that because of his faith in Seadon Oil he had recently acquired 221,000 shares. "With such a holding," he said, "you might expect I am here to ask representation on your board of directors. But that is not my purpose. I wish, rather, to speak on a matter which I believe is on the minds of a lot of stockholders." He paused to open the newspaper which he had placed on the speaker's table, then he resumed. "Ladies and gentlemen, I speak to you as a man of somewhat advanced years. I am sixty-nine. I know the problems of age. I have been running the operations of my own company most of my adult life; but the time is coming when I shall have to turn over the reins to a younger man. Why? you ask. Because after sixty a man tends to make mistakes. Yes, I admit it. I've made my share." The Seadons lifted their eyebrows at each other; this was out of character. "In the case of Seadon Oil, we have a president and chairman of the board who is also getting along. Mr. Ross Seadon is sixty-four."

The audience stirred, sat forward, exchanged glances. "So what?" a man called from the rear of the room.

Haggerty picked it up. "So what? Just this. A man in his sixties sometimes tires of the daily pressure of business. He may seek outside interests which affect his performance as an executive. An outside interest that reduces his value to the company he is supposed to serve. Perhaps an outside interest, a diversion, that will remind him of his youth. His mind wanders from corporate affairs to personal affairs. Or to put it in the singular— *an affair*."

There were gasps of shock. "Shame! Shame!" someone called. Others hissed and booed.

Haggerty picked up the newspaper. "No, I'm not going to read you good people the war news. This paper was printed back in February. Like a lot of you folks, I don't confine my reading to the financial pages. I enjoy the movie section, too."

By now both Ross and Owen were on their feet and striding to the speaker's table. Ross snatched the newspaper from Haggerty and Owen shouted into the microphone, "Mr. Haggerty is out of order!"

Even without the microphone, and over the tumult in the audience, Haggerty's voice could still be heard. "All right! I see everybody knows what I was going to read. I say it's time for a new president. I propose a name you all know, a young man who has earned his spurs in this company, and who, I am confident, will not allow his private life to distract him from the business of this great company, a man who has been groomed for the office: Mr. Tom Seadon!"

First there was silence, then a confused babble. Wil Caruth seized the microphone. "Mr. Haggerty knows the bylaws of this company. The names of officers and directors who stand for election must be placed before the shareholders at least sixty days before the annual meeting!"

Haggerty shouted back, "We can have a write-in candidate! I'm voting my 221,000 shares for Tom Seadon!"

Ross bent over Tom, seated behind the speaker's table. "Did Haggerty put this up to you?"

"Of course not, Dad. He's out of his mind."

"Then tell them!"

Tom stepped to the microphone and disavowed his candidacy. There was a wave of applause. Owen turned to Ross: Did he want to answer Haggerty on his innuendo about Vivian Thorpe? No, he did not. Get on with the voting.

The company secretary tallied the vote. Out of ten million shares, slightly more than nine million were cast for the present management; 627,000 voted for Tom Seadon; the balance abstained.

"How crummy can a man get?" Owen muttered to Ross as they walked along the corridor of the executive floor. "Haggerty threw mud in your face and wound up fouling himself. He got absolutely nowhere."

"No," Ross said. "He got what he wanted. He planted an idea."

An hour later he called Wil Caruth into his office. "Wil, the time has come for me to pull Haggerty's fangs."

"Fine. How?"

"You remember explaining to me about a premarital agreement. I want you to draw it up. Today."

That evening Ross drove down to Malibu. Vivian welcomed him with a kiss and a dab at her eyes. "I'm glad you came. I need you to cheer me up."

"What's wrong?"

She gestured toward the radio in the corner of the sitting room. An English voice, worn and hoarse, was reporting from London the evacuation of the British and French forces from the beaches at Dunkirk. Vivian turned off the radio. "Belgium's lost, Holland's gone, France will be next, and then there will only be England. All alone."

Ross frowned; he could hardly have chosen a less opportune moment. But he would not put it off.

Vivian poured two straight Scotches and brought them to Ross, standing at the beach window. They clinked glasses and Vivian said, with an attempt at lightness, "Darling, you look like you're straight from the battlefield yourself."

"A good way of putting it." He took her glass and his own and set them on the coffee table and turned back to her. "Viv, the time has come to talk about us. I'm tired of this nonsense of us not being together all the time. I don't care about your damned studio and all those fake romances they dream up for you. You've got a real one, and I want us to live it. Let's get married."

She had not expected it, not then. For a moment she seemed frozen with surprise, then she was in his arms, laughing and trying to decide whether to call Hedda first or Louella. And wait till she told the studio to stuff it.

Ross dreaded to break the mood, but in fairness he could not turn back. He took her arms from around his neck and led her over to the sofa. He had rehearsed what he had to say, and he covered it quickly. Wil Caruth's advice, Val's desire that the family assets stay with those of Seadon blood, the avoidance of court battles. Great wealth entailed special responsibilities, which even two people in love must recognize. He took the premarital agreement from his breast pocket. When she had read it through, he said, "Naturally, I want you to show it to your attorney."

"Yes." She gave a tired smile and patted his arm. "It's been an emotional evening. I'm afraid I have a migraine. Would you mind terribly?"

He did; it was not the way a couple should celebrate their engagement. "I'll call you in the morning," he said.

"Do."

But it was Vivian who called Ross. Not in the morning, but that same night, shortly after he reached Ridgemont. "I've decided," she said. "I'd really prefer a younger man."

He told no one except Wil Caruth, who was entitled to know. But with the passing weeks, Owen divined that the romance had withered, and then Tom. How else to interpret Ross's sour disposition, his working late at the office, his sudden obsession with workouts at the Athletic Club gym? At the same time there was a parallel change in Tom. He grew more confident; he made small jokes in executive meetings; he was less prickly toward his cousin Gene; he began to put forth ideas on company policy and defended them with assurance. "Looks like Tom's finally found himself," Owen remarked one day. "I wonder what turned the trick."

Ross replied, "Maybe those six hundred and twenty-seven thousand votes at the annual meeting."

Others on the executive floor recognized the change and responded to it. Slater Dougal began to invite Tom to lunch and proposed that he speak at the next Chamber of Commerce dinner, he who had blanched at the thought of public speaking. "Damned good talk," Dougal reported back to Ross. "He did a neat job of tying in the oil business with national defense."

Defense was on everyone's mind. Paris had fallen and the Battle of Britain had begun. The Luftwaffe was ravaging London; rockets and bombs fell on the Houses of Parliament and Buckingham Palace. America looked on with growing anxiety. Colonel Lindbergh warned America First rallies that the nation must not embroil itself in Europe's quarrels, and he was echoed by Henry Ford and Ambassador Joseph Kennedy. But Franklin Roosevelt gave Navy destroyers to Britain, and Congress passed legislation for the first peacetime draft. The nation's jitters were not helped by Roosevelt's determination to break with historical precedent and run for a third term in the White House. Wendell Willkie, the Republican candidate, countered that Roosevelt was attempting to destroy democracy and would set up his own Royal Family. Once re-elected, others hinted, Roosevelt would imitate the last Democratic President and lead the country into war.

"Thank God I cut loose from the Democrats and went independent," Phil Barnard said one night to Ross toward the end of his contest for the Senate. Liz had invited Ross to dinner with Phil and Dale, both of whom were staying with her until the election.

"How do you feel the campaign is going?" Ross asked.

Phil made a face. "It's a crap game. A three-way fight. I may just splinter up the vote and come in trailing."

"You mustn't lose your nerve in the home stretch," Ross counseled. "It may be a close thing, but you've got the right people behind you, and the right money."

"Have I?" Phil jabbed a finger toward Ross. "What about Tom? You know he hasn't contributed a cent for my campaign? I asked him for five thousand dollars and he sneered at me! 'I'll give five thousand all right—but to defeat you.' That's what the S.O.B. said! I tell you, Ross, if he had been anybody but your son, I'd have flattened him."

Dale patted his arm. "He's just jealous, darling. You've always made Tom feel second-rate, which is exactly what he is."

That was true, as far as it went, Ross thought. But there was more. It was another example of Tom's new independence. He no longer feared the possible return of Phil to Seadon Oil; he had G. G. Haggerty on his side. It was disturbing; it was ominous.

Later that same evening Dale managed a private moment with Ross and asked him why he had not brought Vivian Thorpe. When he told her, sparing none of the painful details, Dale was downcast. "I wouldn't have thought it of her. All that fake sincerity, the scheming bitch!"

"I asked for it," Ross replied. "I wanted to believe so badly that I sold myself a gold brick." Then he changed the subject. "At least one of our romances has turned out right. You've never looked happier."

"I couldn't be! Phil is my safe harbor after a long and stormy voyage."

"And you get along with Liz?"

"Better than I ever dreamed possible. Before I married Phil I was petrified of her. All those tales Mother used to tell me when I was little were just a garble of jealousy." She paused and smiled thoughtfully at Ross. "Now that I know the truth, I can't understand how you let that lovely lady walk out of your life."

"It's a long story."
"Which you'll never tell?"
"Never."

Houston, Texas
Sept. 28, 1940

To the Officers and Directors
of the Seadon Estate Company:
    The undersigned owner of one third of the shares in the
above company requests a special meeting of the stockholders to consider a matter of great importance to all
concerned. It is suggested that the proposed meeting be
held in the second week of October, 1940, in an appropriate conference room of the Los Angeles Biltmore Hotel.

G. G. Haggerty

The Seadon brothers, both puzzled and curious, set the date
for the meeting on October 10 and mailed out the required
notices to the bank holding the three trust accounts. In due
course the bank mailed its proxies to Tom and Ginny, but there
was an unaccountable delay in furnishing Ross with its proxy
to vote Leah's interest. Finally, two days before the scheduled
meeting, Ross stopped by the bank to see its senior trust officer,
one T. Jeremiah Hazeltine.

"Perhaps I should have phoned you, Mr. Seadon. I shall attend
the meeting myself to represent your sister's trust."

Ross regarded the bleak eyes and the thin bookkeeperish
mouth with a feeling of disquiet. "Why this change of procedure?"

"The bank feels that it should retain its freedom of action
until we determine the majority view."

"On what?"

"Why, on the liquidation of the Seadon Estate Company."

Ross's jaw sagged. "Where the hell did you get that idea?"

"From Mr. Haggerty. He dropped by a week or so ago and
explained . . ." Hazeltine stopped and looked perplexed. "I as-

sumed you knew. I've already had conferences with your son and daughter."

"Get back to Haggerty. What did he tell you?"

"He believes the Estate Company has outlived its usefulness. He prefers to convert his holding directly into shares of Seadon Oil Company, because they are traded daily on the stock exchanges and have a known market value. I might add that the bank is inclined to agree with his position; and if your son and daughter go along with it, then we shall, too."

Ross's fist came down on the desk with a crash. "God damn it, man! Don't you see what Haggerty is after? Liquidate the Estate and he gets one million, seven hundred thousand shares of Seadon Oil!"

Hazeltine shifted uncomfortably in his chair; people simply did not raise their voices in the marble halls of finance, and particularly not in the hushed recesses of the trust department. "May I point out, sir," he murmured soothingly, "that the bank's duty is to administer its trust accounts in the best interests of the beneficiaries. In our opinion, Mr. Haggerty's proposal is sound, and I have recommended it to your son and daughter."

"They'll vote as Owen and I tell them to!"

"In that case, I see no cause for anxiety. However your children vote, the bank will follow suit with your sister's trust."

At least that was encouraging; Hazeltine could be swung in either direction. When Ross left the bank, he went directly to Tom's office and repeated his conversation with the trust officer. Why, he demanded, hadn't Tom discussed the matter with him? If he knew Haggerty was proposing the dissolution of the Estate Company, he should have reported it to Ross and Owen.

"I wanted to think it out for myself," Tom said. "I didn't want you and Uncle Owen pressuring me. That's what I told Hazeltine."

Ross felt as though ice were forming in his veins. "God almighty, Tom, the Estate Company is *us!* the Seadons! How could you even *think* of playing into Haggerty's hands?"

Tom gazed calmly at his father. "Because for once he's right.

Nobody knows the market value of the Estate stock, but Seadon Oil, yes. I want to know every single day how much my trust is worth."

"Bunk! That's no reason at all." Ross saw his son's look of defiance, the same defiance he had shown when he had learned of Vivian Thorpe. "Then you've decided?"

"Yes. I'm voting my proxy for liquidation."

"And Ginny?"

"Whichever way I go."

Minutes later Ross and Owen closeted themselves with Wil Caruth and computed the voting strength for the coming meeting. Out of the one thousand shares of Estate Company stock, Haggerty controlled 333⅓ shares; the trusts for Leah and Tom and Ginny totaled 186 and a fraction; the Seadon brothers, 480 and a fraction.

Caruth, who had been adding the figures, threw down his pencil with a grimace. "Yep, they outvote you by twenty shares. Not much, but it's a majority."

"Then we got to fight dirty." Owen glowered. "Let's file suit and break those trusts."

"They're irrevocable," Caruth reminded. "The only ground would be fraud, and there is none. You boys set them up and you're stuck with them." He shook his head ruefully. "Shakespeare called it. How sharper than a serpent's tooth it is to have a thankless child."

"Not thankless—greedy," Ross corrected. "But look, Wil, maybe Leah's trust could be different from Tom and Ginny's. Leah may not be quite right in the head, but if Owen and I went to her and explained our fix, I'm sure she'd go in with us and petition the court to dissolve her trust. And Dale would, too. Wouldn't that swing it?"

"Except for one catch. Contingent remaindermen."

"Who?"

"Legal double-talk for children yet unborn. The articles of trust specify that the corpus goes from Leah to Dale and then to Dale's issue. Right now Dale's pregnant, but her child can't appear before the court and express its wishes. Or any other kids she might have. You'd have to wait until Dale is past the childbearing age and her kids are all legal adults. By that time I think we'll all be more concerned about our seating arrangements among the heavenly host."

Suddenly Owen burst out. "What the hell's the matter with us? Ginny's our answer! If we can pull her away from Tom, we'll have our majority. Ross, talk to her!"

"She won't listen. I'm her father and therefore a cranky old fool."

"Then *I'll* talk to her."

"And be another old fool. Don't you understand? We're the wrong generation." Ross pondered what he had said. "Maybe Ginny *might* come around if it was somebody younger. Somebody she respects."

"Gene!"

"No. Too much rivalry with Tom. She'd discount anything he said. The same goes for Carla and Angie."

That left Dale Barnard. She was not only a beneficiary under Leah's trust, she was held in awe by Ginny and Tom—the maverick cousin who had carved out a career for herself without family help and who, the voters willing, would soon be the wife of a United States Senator.

Dale tried gallantly, although she could scarcely conceal her disdain for the pudgy blonde whose life was defined by her golf handicap, her bridge scores, and her affairs with other women's husbands. "I really don't care," Ginny told her with a shrug. "It's whatever Tom decides. Go talk to him."

And so she did. She dressed in her most flattering maternity outfit, had her hair and nails freshly done, and swept through the reception room on the executive floor to the admiring looks of businessmen waiting for their appointments. She accepted the chair that Tom pulled out for her and favored him with her most winning smile. She regretted, she said, that she had seen so little of Tom through the years, and told him how fondly she remembered the time when she had lived with her cousins in San Francisco while her mother was overseas with the Canadian Red Cross.

Tom listened politely to her preliminaries, but at the first mention of the Estate Company he cut her short. "You're wasting your time, Dale. Tomorrow I'm voting for liquidation."

"Oh, Tom, Tom"—she wagged her head—"don't you have any sense of family? If we go our separate ways, we dissolve into nothing. Family is everything; it's what holds society together. Otherwise we're no more than animals roaming our own little piece of the jungle." She saw his mouth tighten, his fingers twiddle impatiently with a pencil. "Tom, I'm not talking as Dale Barnard or Dale Lantry; I'm talking as Dale the daughter of Leah Seadon. I'm every bit as much a Seadon as you are, and perhaps value it more because of this." She patted the fullness below her jacket. "I'm not just another woman carrying another child; I'm carrying part of Grandfather Val's future. Without him, without his sons, you wouldn't be sitting here in this office. You owe everything you are to him, and to his sons, and you *can't* let Haggerty divide us." She stopped, winded and tense with emotion.

For a moment she thought her argument had carried the day; then she saw Tom's face harden. "Sentiment is one thing, Dale, but it's not reality. Not for me. Every share of Seadon Estate Company stock is fifty-one hundred shares of Seadon Oil. That's the reality."

"Figures! What do they matter?"

"Plenty. When the Estate dissolves, I'll have three hundred and six thousand shares of Seadon Oil in my trust. And Ginny will have another three hundred and six thousand. At the next annual meeting I'm standing for president, and we'll vote proxies for six hundred and twelve thousand shares. And Haggerty will back me with almost two million more."

"You believe that?" Dale cried. "He's just trying to drive a wedge between you and your father!"

"I'll gamble on it. Haggerty's old, he's already said he's getting ready to retire. Just as Dad and Uncle Owen will be doing.

That leaves just me and Gene in the running, and Haggerty's already come out for me."

Dale leaped to her feet, her voice rose to a shriek. "You'd turn your own father out of his company?"

"No. No, I wouldn't. Haggerty will do it. And when he does, I intend to be on the winning side."

"You despicable whelp!" Her hand stung Tom's cheek. "You unspeakable bastard!" She would have struck again but for the sharp kick and twist in her womb.

"Let's fire him! Boot him out of the company!" was Owen's explosive reaction after Dale had reported her scene with Tom. But Ross could not bring himself to sever the link with his son. "Boot him out, and we'll never get him back. He'll be Haggerty's man for sure. And more dangerous outside the company than in it."

In any event, the Estate Company was lost. When the Seadon brothers called the special meeting together in the conference room of the Biltmore Hotel, it seemed less a corporate proceeding than a memorial service. Neither Ross nor Owen spoke to Tom or Ginny, and they merely nodded to Jeremiah Hazeltine. G. G. Haggerty sat alone on the opposite side of the table, puffed on a cigar, and contemplated the brothers with amused satisfaction. Owen glared across at him with frustration and hatred. "You know," he said, "if I had my life to live over, Haggerty, there's only one thing I would have done differently."

"What's that?"

"The night Ross and I charged into your oil field, I should have shoved that fulminate of mercury up your ass."

Haggerty grinned contentedly and flicked his cigar ashes onto the tabletop. "I couldn't ask for a higher compliment." Then he turned to Ross. "And if *you* had your life to live over, you wouldn't have been so damned puking pure that night in the railroad car. That's what started us down this long, long trail." He nodded to Wil Caruth. "Mr. Secretary, I call for the vote."

Caruth polled the stockholders one by one, noted down the figures, and announced the result: the Seadon Estate Company would be liquidated.

Ross rose from the table and looked at Tom and Ginny with bitter eyes. "Well, you've done it, you two. You've destroyed your grandfather's company, you've destroyed my feelings for you, and you've handed Haggerty a million seven hundred thousand shares of Seadon Oil. Thank God, your mother never lived to see this day."

Haggerty had won the battle, but the Seadon brothers were determined to win the war. They would, they decided, drag their feet on the winding up of the Estate Company's affairs. It would not be difficult. Public advertising would be required for creditors (although there were none); final tax returns would have to be filed with the state and federal authorities; the corporate charter would have to be surrendered to the California Secretary of State. No matter how much Haggerty might fume, they would delay issuance of his shares in Seadon Oil until after the annual meeting in May 1941. This would buy them another year before the inevitable showdown, a year in which to plan their defense—and, God willing, to enjoy life.

It was an attitude common to most Americans of the day. More and more the prospect was accepted that somehow the nation would become involved in the war in Europe. Every passing month saw Britain's position grow more perilous. London was reeling under nightly fire-bombing; U-boats were sinking ever greater numbers of the ships transporting food and munitions from the United States—this in spite of the U.S. Navy, which was now openly convoying the supply ships. And there was growing tension in the Pacific. Japan lusted for the French holdings in Indo-China and the Dutch possessions in the East Indies. The United States, hoping to thwart such ambitions, declared an embargo against the export of scrap iron and steel to Japan, to which Japan retaliated by signing the Tripartite Pact, a military alliance with Germany and Italy. If the United States declared war on either European ally, then Japan would fight in the Pacific. So it was that Americans held precious every passing day of peace; the young men of military age jitterbugged and sang "Roll Out the Barrel" while they waited for their numbers to come up in the draft. Their elders hoarded sugar and bought new cars against the time when Detroit might convert its assembly lines to the production of tanks.

But all was not war and rumors of war. Phil Barnard was now the freshman senator from California (elected by a very narrow margin), and Dale had presented him with a daughter. When Phil phoned the news from Washington, Leah talked joyously of going East to see her granddaughter, which Ross opposed until he learned that Liz Barnard was going and could keep a watchful eye on his sister. But after several days Leah lapsed back into apathy—the trip was "too much trouble"—and Liz went on by herself. "Leslie is simply exquisite," she telephoned Ross from her hotel. "She's got red-gold hair and blue eyes and the slyest smile I ever saw! Guess who she looks like." Phil, Ross surmised. "Yes, and Dale, too. But that smile of hers is pure Ross Seadon!"

Rain in the month of May is a rarity in Los Angeles, yet rain it did on the morning of the annual meeting of Seadon Oil. It did little to encourage the spirits of the Seadon brothers. Nor did the sight of G. G. Haggerty seated in the front row of the gathering of stockholders. Once again during the question period Haggerty asked permission to speak, and Ross and Owen braced themselves for the worst. And once again Haggerty confounded them. He spoke glowingly of the future of Seadon Oil, of the part it must play in national defense, and of his growing investment in the company. He reminded the audience that at the last meeting he had owned 221,000 shares; shortly, he said, this holding would be increased by an additional 1,700,000, giving him a total stake of 19 per cent. There were murmurs of surprise, followed by applause. Haggerty bowed and started to walk away from the microphone. Ross and Owen stared at each other; was that all? No. Haggerty turned back to the microphone. "And next year, ladies and gentlemen, I'm casting my vote for Mr. Tom Seadon as your new president!"

"In a pig's eye!" Owen snorted after the meeting had adjourned. "Sure as God made green apples, he doesn't want Tom elected, so why does he keep dinging at it?"

"To divide and rule," Ross said.

"Then I say fire Tom. Today!"

"Sure! Just what Haggerty wants. Concrete proof to everybody that the Seadon family is in civil war. No, we just sit tight and sweat it out until Haggerty drops the other shoe."

It was a short wait. Exactly two days after Seadon Oil had issued its shares into the name of G. G. Haggerty. Ross and Leah were at breakfast at Ridgemont, she recounting in endless detail a dream of the night before, he grunting responses while he leafed through the morning paper to learn yesterday's closing price for Seadon Oil. It was 32¼. He turned to the next page and his eyes lighted on an announcement which was headed in capital letters: TO THE SHAREHOLDERS OF SEADON OIL COMPANY.

"*Jesus, Mary and Joseph!*"

Leah blinked across at him. "It was only a dream, dear—" He was already out of his chair and sprinting for the telephone in the entry hall. Before he reached it, it rang.

"Ross, have you—" Wil Caruth began.

"Just now. Three and a half million shares at forty dollars! Christ almighty, that's . . . that's a hundred and forty million!"

"I'm afraid it's our Armageddon," Caruth said theatrically. "What'll we do?"

"I don't know. Just round up everybody. I want them in my office in an hour."

Ross saw the crowd of newspapermen waiting in the reception room and avoided them by detouring through a series of connecting offices. When he reached his own, he found Owen, Wil Caruth, Tim Beakley, and Slater Dougal. The air was already thick with cigarette smoke as dense as the gloom on the four faces which turned toward him. "Well, boys," he greeted them, "now we know why Haggerty has been marking time. Pantex had to raise a hundred and forty million from the banks."

Slater Dougal scowled agreement. "And the banks aren't laying out that kind of dough unless they figure Pantex is going to win."

"They figure, sure. But it wouldn't be the first time bankers have guessed wrong." Ross glanced at the others. "Anybody add up how we stand?"

Owen held up a sheet of paper and read off the figures. Haggerty was already the dominant owner of Seadon Oil shares, followed by Owen, then the three trust funds for Leah and Tommy and Ginny, then by Ross himself. "As of today," Owen concluded, "Pantex can figure it's got nineteen per cent ownership, because Pantex is just another name for Haggerty. If it can corral three and a half million shares more, it'll own control."

Ross nodded absently. "Well, we knew this day had to come. The first thing we do is to hit the newspapers with an answer to Pantex. We tell the stockholders their shares are worth a hell of a lot more than forty dollars. We remind them that the Seadons built this company from scratch and they owe it to us to stand by the ship."

Slater Dougal sighed. "How many companies have made that appeal, and still gone down the drain?"

Owen countered. "At least it's better than just sitting here on our butts."

"Hold on," Wil Caruth said. "Maybe a little more butt time is just what we need. We're forgetting those trust funds for Ross's kids and his sister. They represent how many shares?"

"Nine hundred and forty-eight thousand," Ross said.

"Okay. If we can line them up on our side, we may be home free."

So they were back to that. Distasteful as it was, Ross paid another visit to the bank and T. Jeremiah Hazeltine. It was an unhappy meeting; Hazeltine was torn between sympathy for the Seadons and fear of commitment. The trust department, he said, must be guided by the "prudent man rule," yet he would not define which course would be "prudent." In the end the result was as before; the bank would be guided by the desires of Tom and Ginny, and their decision would determine the position of Leah's trust. It was clear, Ross saw, that Hazeltine and his advisers were intimidated by G. G. Haggerty and the powerful Eastern banks. Why risk the wrath of potential winners?

He returned to his office and consulted again with Owen and Wil Caruth. Ross would not, he said, go to his children and beg for their support; they had already proved their disloyalty in the liquidation of the Estate Company. "The only way we're going to win them over," he concluded, "is to prove to them we've got more muscle than Haggerty."

"Brave words, Ross"—Caruth smiled bleakly—"but *how?*"

"I don't know yet. Let's call an emergency meeting of the full board of directors—make it three days from now—and meanwhile Owen and I will do some skull work."

The following morning every major Pacific Coast newspaper carried Seadon Oil's appeal to its stockholders. Financial writers headlined their reactions. SEADON OIL COUNTERATTACKS . . . BATTLE OF OIL TITANS . . . CALIFORNIA VERSUS TEXAS. One of those who read the press coverage was Liz Barnard, who telephoned Ross and said, "I've got a block of ten thousand Seadon Oil, Ross. Count on them."

"Thank you, Liz. I was just going to call you anyway. I was wondering if you could get Phil to do me a favor."

"Name it."

"Well, do you think Phil has kept up any of his Wall Street contacts, the crowd he used to know when he was working in the Street?"

She laughed. "They're practically hanging around his neck. That's one of the advantages of being a senator."

"All right. Ask Phil if he can find out the terms of a bank loan made to Pantex Oil or G. G. Haggerty. Especially I want to know the date for repayment."

But information was no substitute for action. Before the directors' meeting, Ross and Owen personally called on the owners of the largest blocks of Seadon Oil stock—insurance companies, banks, pension funds—and argued their case for rejecting the Pantex offer. The responses were not encouraging; too many of the major stockholders confessed they had already accepted. "Our only hope is the little man," Ross concluded, and then belched. "Christ, this mess is giving me chronic indigestion."

Owen replied, "I'll trade you that for the trots."

On the morning of the directors' meeting, the *Wall Street Journal* carried an announcement by Pantex that it had already acquired over one million shares of Seadon Oil. The news was reflected in the faces gathered around the long walnut table in the board room.

Ross stood at the head of the table and began on what he hoped was a positive note. "Gentlemen, I see our situation as a magnificent opportunity. We're not here to plan a defense against G. G. Haggerty and his puppet Pantex Oil. We're going beyond that; we're going to destroy Haggerty for all time to come."

The listeners stirred uneasily, and Oliver Eakins, frail and trembling with palsy, interrupted querulously. "Ross, from the first day I met you, all I've ever heard was about you licking Haggerty. My God, almost forty years! Why don't you just quit? Let Haggerty have the damned company! You and Owen will still come out with more money than everybody in this room combined!"

"That's not the point," Owen rejoined. "We started this company; it's been our life; we're not going to throw it to the jackals."

Eakins threw up his hands in despair. "Who can fight a hundred and forty million dollars?"

"We can, Ollie," Ross answered. "It's borrowed money. It's

got to be repaid. I have word from a confidential source that Pantex has borrowed a hundred million from a group of New York and Texas banks, and G. G. Haggerty went in hock for another forty million. Both notes are payable in sixty days. So this is our strategy. We make an offer ourselves to our stockholders. We announce we'll buy a half million shares at five dollars above the Pantex price. That will force Haggerty to raise his own offer, and he'll have to go back to his bankers for another loan, which they won't like one bit."

Slater Dougal wagged his head. "I don't like it myself. We'll be imitating Haggerty, borrowing from the banks and then sweating out repayment."

"No banks," Owen answered. "We've already sounded them out and got the stall. So we use our own money. Twenty-two and a half million."

"But God almighty, that will drain away almost all our operating cash!"

Ross conceded it. "Survival doesn't come cheap, Slater. We pay a price, but we take a half million shares away from Haggerty."

When the proposal was put to a vote, and carried, only Slater Dougal and Oliver Eakins dissented. The final business of the day was a resolution submitted by Owen which would authorize the executive committee to take "any and all actions deemed necessary to protect the independence of Seadon Oil." This time the only no vote was from Oliver Eakins.

SEADON BIDS UP FOR STOCK was the next morning's financial headline. But from Pantex there was silence. And again the following day. "Just as I said"—Ross grinned—"Haggerty's having trouble with his bankers." But on the third morning Pantex increased its offer from forty to forty-eight dollars per share. That same morning Slater Dougal laid a sheet of paper on Ross's desk. It was Dougal's resignation.

Ross stared at it, stunned. "Slater, you *can't!* Not when we need you the most!"

"Sorry. I've been offered a better position."

"Who by?"

"Pantex. Plus a very special price for my ninety thousand shares of Seadon Oil."

"What?" Ross bounded out of his chair. "You son of a bitch! You lousy traitor!" His hands closed around Dougal's throat and thrashed him from side to side. Then Owen and a secretary rushed into the room and it was over.

The next morning's newspapers carried the story of Dougal's defection to Pantex, and quoted G. G. Haggerty to the effect that this was proof that Seadon Oil was a sinking ship. "We can't afford any more turncoats," Ross told Wil Caruth. "The next one Haggerty will go for is Tom."

"Has Tom said anything?"

"Hell, we barely speak. But he isn't going to swing those trust funds to Pantex unless we're sure losers. Here's what I've done so far. I've had Personnel put a new secretary in Tom's office; she's to listen to every phone call and report any conversation between Tom and Haggerty or Tom and the bank. Also any letters. Now what I want from you is a detective agency. I want Tom's phone tapped in his apartment, and Ginny's, too."

Caruth pursed his lips. "It's illegal, you know. As an attorney, I can't—"

"All right, all right! Just get me the detectives. You can tell yourself I want to find out when it's going to snow in Tahiti."

By the end of the following business week Pantex announced that it had bought two million shares of Seadon Oil, which, combined with the personal holdings of G. G. Haggerty, gave it 39 per cent of the company's shares. "There's only one out for us," Ross decided. "We've got to make a higher offer than Pantex. We've got to go for another half million shares."

"And the money for it?" Owen reminded. "Every banker is out to lunch when it comes to Seadon Oil."

Ross abandoned the idea and rubbed his forehead. "God, I don't know how much more of this I can take. I can't sleep, and when I do, it's nightmares. And on top of everything there's

Leah yammering at me about singing at the White House, or God wanting her to talk to Hitler."

"What you need is some normal home life," Owen diagnosed. "How about me bringing Tana down from El Encanto? We could put up here for the duration."

"It's a deal! Do it!"

Several nights later, in the small hours of the morning, Owen padded into Ross's bedroom and shook him awake. "By God, I've figured it out!" he crowed. "We can raise cash on the best asset we got—oil in the ground!"

Ross blinked. "You mean a production loan?"

"Right! We go to our biggest customers—the power companies, railroads, ship lines—and we borrow against future pumping. We pay it off with oil and we guarantee to deliver every barrel at today's prices over, say, the next three years."

Ross considered it with mounting excitement. "Lord, I can't see anybody turning us down, because if we get into the war, oil prices will shoot to the sky." Then he added a new idea. "Our tankers! We could sell them for cash, and then lease them back. We'd be millions ahead!"

They outlined the plan to Wil Caruth. "Sure, it's legal," he said. "The board of directors gave you power to take any and all measures. But don't forget, you're mortgaging the future."

"Or buying a future," Ross corrected.

By the following weekend the Seadons, after flying to San Francisco, Portland, and Seattle, had signed loan agreements with power, shipping, and railroad companies for forty million dollars and had sold the company's tanker fleet for an additional eighteen million. SEADONS UP ANTE FOR MORE STOCK was the headline in the *Wall Street Journal*, which also carried an interview with Ross explaining the source of the company's funds.

G. G. Haggerty's reaction was immediate and by telephone to Ross. "You stinking bastards! I'm onto your game! You're borrowing yourselves straight into bankruptcy!"

"How did you ever guess?" Ross chuckled. "If you ever do get Seadon Oil, all you'll find is scorched earth."

He had cause to regret that taunt, for the next day Pantex Oil ran a full-page denunciation of Ross, quoted his strategy of the "scorched earth," and appealed to the stockholders to sell to Pantex while there were still assets to sell. The sharpest reaction to "scorched earth" was from Oliver Eakins, who wrote a furious letter to Ross and resigned from the board of directors. A second director, George Bellhurst, declared the Seadons "crazed with blood lust" and called for their immediate removal from office. It was welcome copy for the financial editors. One considered the Seadons "brilliant generals of desperate ingenuity"; another suggested they were "committing corporate hara-kiri"; and still another asked, "Is Pantex buying a dead horse?"

It was that question which impelled Tom Seadon to one of his rare talks with his father. "Great God," he began, "the way you and Owen are running Seadon Oil into the ground, nobody will want it. The company will have to use all its earnings just to pay off those loans!"

"What's happened to your arithmetic?" Ross countered. "We only borrowed forty million. That's less than a quarter of our annual production."

"But it's the difference," Tom persisted, "between earning profits and just breaking even. What will the stockholders do for dividends? Christ, there won't be a penny coming into my trust fund, or Ginny's, or Aunt Leah's."

"So you'll all just have to live off your savings."

"But the other stockholders—"

"There won't be any others. By the time we're through buying out the public, there'll just be Pantex and us—and G. G. Haggerty kicking himself all the way to the poorhouse."

Part of Ross's prediction proved true. Seadon stockholders, frightened by the battle's intensity, gladly accepted the new higher price offered by the Seadons, and the still higher counter bid by Pantex. Every day counted now; every share was precious. Up and down the Pacific Coast, from San Diego to Seattle, and east to Denver and Tulsa, Seadon Oil branch managers and junior officers rang doorbells and wrote checks—and sometimes clashed with rival Pantex agents. At the home office

398

in Los Angeles, secretaries manned telephones to plead with stockholders. After business hours Ridgemont served as a command post, where Ross and Owen chalked up on a blackboard the results of the day's work, and where around the dinner table the family gathered, and Tana, like a tiny silver-haired matriarch, acted as hostess, said the grace, and thanked her favorite saints for the successes achieved and those still to come.

Then, one night in mid-July, Liz Barnard received a puzzling telephone call from Tana at Ridgemont. "It is time for old friends," she said. "Come. They need you."

Tana, red-eyed, met Liz at the front door.

"What's happened, Tana?"

"They will tell you."

She led Liz into the library, where Ross and Owen were slumped in club chairs. Both brothers were holding glasses of bourbon and staring moodily at the blackboard on an easel.

"Well, you two are a cheery sight," she began lightly. "What are you celebrating?"

Ross nodded toward the blackboard and a series of chalked figures. "There's the way we stand as of today."

Liz studied the tally. Pantex 44 per cent; Seadon Oil, 43 per cent; stock still in public hands 3.5 per cent. She glanced back at the brothers. "What's all the gloom about? Even if Haggerty got every single share of the public's stock, he'd still fall short."

Ross pulled himself up from his chair, went to the blackboard, chalked a line under the figures and added them. The total came to 90.5 per cent; not 100.

"Oh, God, I forgot." Liz sighed. "The bank. Those trusts." She crossed to the bottle of bourbon, poured a glass for herself, and took a swallow. "Ross, you've got to go to Tom and Ginny. Crawl, if necessary."

Owen gestured to several sheets of typescript on the table. "That came an hour ago."

"What is it?"

"Read it."

She saw that it was a detective's report, the transcript of a telephone conversation between G. G. Haggerty in Houston and Tom at his apartment.

MR. HAGGERTY: Tom, you still want to be president of Seadon Oil when I take over?

MR. SEADON: I'm counting on it.

MR. HAGGERTY: Then deliver me those trusts for you and your sister. Tell the bank to sell those Seadon shares to Pantex.

MR. SEADON: At what price?

MR. HAGGERTY: Sixty dollars a share.

MR. SEADON: I want seventy-five. And a contract of employment.

MR. HAGGERTY: Sixty dollars and no contract.

MR. SEADON: Look, you could appoint me president for a month, then fire me. I want five years guaranteed.

MR. HAGGERTY: I'll think about it. I'll be in Los Angeles next Friday. Meet me at the Biltmore Hotel.

MR. SEADON: Will do.

Liz frowned at the sheets in her hand. "Then it's over, isn't it? Unless you're willing to top Haggerty."

"Ross tried!" Tana sobbed. "Just now!"

He nodded confirmation. "I phoned Tom. I said I'd resign in his favor."

"Well?"

"He hung up on me." Ross folded his hands and stared at them bitterly. "I've always known Tom was ungrateful, but I didn't think he hated me. In a way it's my fault, I suppose. And Louise's, too. She wanted him to take over her father's steel company; I wanted him with me; I tried to push him into politics and run his life. We pulled and hauled at him . . . and now, at last, is the day of reckoning. Tom can show the world he isn't a monkey on a string."

"But that doesn't explain Ginny," Owen objected.

"Why not? She didn't have much of a father, either. She and Tom were always close, had to be, when they were kids, and it's never changed. . . . And so, here we are."

Liz gazed at the two brothers, stricken, defeated, their eyes wandering sadly over the photographs and paintings on the library walls. Seadon oil wells, Seadon pipelines, Seadon refineries, Seadon service stations—everything that was slipping from their grasp. Liz felt her eyes begin to fill, and she went up to Ross and took his hand. "Let's take a drive," she said.

The radio news predicted afternoon thunder showers, but no break in the heat which had oppressed Washington for the past week. President Roosevelt would host a party for members of the Senate Finance Committee and their wives that evening aboard the yacht *Potomac.* "Tell me something I don't know," Phil Barnard muttered, for he and Dale were to be among the guests. He flicked off the radio and checked through his briefcase to be sure it held the notes for the speech he would make that morning in the Senate. The telephone rang and he heard Dale say hello on the extension phone in the bedroom. He slipped on his seersucker jacket and went toward the nursery to kiss his daughter goodbye. As he passed the bedroom door, he saw Dale hold up the telephone and gesture to him.

"It's Liz. She wants to talk to you."

He stared at his wristwatch. Nine-twenty. And six-twenty in Los Angeles. Dale put her hand over the phone. "She sounds strange. I think she's been crying." She handed him the phone; he sat on the edge of the bed.

"Mother, what's wrong?"

"Everything. Can you fly to Los Angeles?"

"Why? What's happened?"

"Can you? Today?"

"Well, I suppose. If it's absolutely urgent . . ."

"It is. I want you to listen carefully, Phil. Don't interrupt me, just listen. And please, please try not to hate me. . . ."

They came together in the great living room at Ridgemont. Phil and Ross standing face to face, Dale to one side chain-smoking, Liz biting her lips as she watched the two men.

"But why, Ross? *Why?*" Phil's eyes were dark with reproach.

"Why all those years without a father? All those wasted years!" He raised a hand. "Oh, I know. Mother's explained over and over again. How she was afraid of marriage, afraid of the Seadons, afraid you might take me from her. But it still doesn't explain you. Didn't you give a damn about your son?"

Liz stepped between them. "Darling, *don't!*"

"But I've got to know!"

"Come," Ross said, taking his elbow and gesturing to Liz and Dale to follow. They went into the library and watched Ross climb onto a chair and reach to the top row of bookshelves. He extracted a heavy morocco-bound album, stepped down, and carried it to the center table. He motioned to Phil. "Here's your answer."

Phil turned the pages slowly and examined the snapshots of himself. In the crib. On a tricycle. In Boy Scout uniform. In a Harvard rowing scull. At commencement. He lingered over the graduation photo, then finally he looked up at Ross and said in a strangled voice, "I remember that day . . . the way you watched me . . . how sad you looked . . . I wondered why." He closed the album with a sigh. "It makes less sense than ever."

Dale reached across the table for his hand. "Maybe not to you or to me. But we can't possibly put ourselves in your father and mother's place. We can't judge the past by the now. If they made a mistake, what a price they've paid! My God, Liz's loneliness! And your father's! How he must have loved Liz to cheat himself of his place with you! And how she must love Ross to tell you after all these years, to accuse herself for his sake!" She rose and put her arms around Ross and Liz. "It was love, and it *is* love—and they deserve your honor and mine."

Phil took a breath. "All right. I'll do it."

"You understand what it means," Ross said. "Scandal. Ugly headlines."

Phil nodded. "If Mother can take it, so can I." He gave a hard laugh. "It's worth it just to screw that son of a bitch Tom. After all his conniving, God, it'll be beautiful!" He paused and gazed thoughtfully at the others. "No. That's not the real reason, not

402

the main one. When I was a kid, Mother avoided talking about the man I thought was my father, and I decided she was ashamed of him, that he was a failure, or maybe something worse. That was a lot harder to take than to know I was illegitimate. What's a marriage certificate mean, anyway? A piece of paper. It's blood that counts. To know that I'm a Seadon. And for the world to know it!"

Ross felt his throat tighten; he looked at Liz, who was dabbing at her eyes. "Well!" he began unsteadily. "Well, I think this is a night for celebration. Anyone want to go break out the champagne?"

Phil took the cue and steered Dale toward the hall doorway. When they were gone, Ross took Liz's hands in his. "I know what this must have cost you. But now, no more lies, no more excuses. We're free."

She looked at him shyly. "It's like starting all over again, isn't it?"

"We are. Does it frighten you?"

She laughed shakily. "No. I've learned my lesson, through loneliness and gray hairs."

He examined her with surprise. Gray? All through the years he had seen her in his mind as the fiery-haired girl with drifts of freckles across her cheeks. He raised his hand and traced his fingers through her curls. "Never mind, I like them," he said. "The rice won't even show."

In the two days before the arrival of Haggerty in Los Angeles, the Seadon brothers rode an emotional roller coaster. They would succeed; they would fail; there would be an unexpected delay; there would be an unforeseen speed-up of the end. Ross developed migraine; Owen could scarcely eat. They abandoned all pretense of normal business routine and waited from phone call to phone call from Ross's detectives, who were maintaining a twenty-four-hour surveillance of Tom and Ginny. They read the transcripts of every monitored conversation. There were three of importance: first Haggerty's call from

Houston to tell Tom that he had reserved the auditorium of the Biltmore Hotel for three o'clock on Friday and wished Tom and Ginny to be there fifteen minutes beforehand. Then Tom's call to Ginny repeating Haggerty's request, and their elated discussion of what it portended. And finally Tom's call to T. Jeremiah Hazeltine at the bank instructing him to join them at the auditorium.

"I don't like this auditorium business," Owen brooded. "Sounds like Haggerty is going to call a press conference."

Ross agreed. "Sure, to announce Pantex the winner. Haggerty loves dramatics, but also it's pressure on Tom and Ginny. He's hinting that he can pull it off without them. Both sides will bluff it out right down to the wire. And that's where we'll meet them."

"God"—Owen sighed—"I wish there were some other way."

"Don't we all?"

The brothers arrived at the auditorium thirty minutes before the hour and found it empty. They chose seats in the third row and waited. A hotel employee crossed the stage to the speaker's lectern and tested the microphone. A second man set up two flag standards behind the lectern and attached the state flags of Texas and California. Liz Barnard, Dale, and Tana came down the aisle and sat behind the brothers. A minute later Phil dropped into a seat beside Ross and propped a briefcase on his lap. "It's a press conference all right," he whispered. "I recognized some of the reporters and photographers out in the corridor."

It was that, and more. Men and women of middle age and beyond began taking seats. "Must be Pantex stockholders," Owen muttered.

"Yep"—Ross nodded—"here to watch their hero strut his stuff." Then Phil nudged him. Tom and Ginny were seating themselves in the front row. They stared at the Seadon brothers and put their heads together. Jeremiah Hazeltine arrived next, sat beside Tom, listened to his whisper, looked at Ross, and nodded politely.

Finally, by twos and threes, the newspapermen filed in, recognized Senator Barnard and the Seadon brothers, and began excited speculations. At exactly fifteen minutes before three a side door on stage opened and G. G. Haggerty appeared, bald head shining under the lights, a red carnation in his lapel. There was scattered applause, which he acknowledged with a bow. He searched the audience, saw the Seadons, frowned, then located Tom and Ginny and gestured to them. They rose, beckoned to Hazeltine, and all three mounted the steps onto the stage and followed Haggerty through the side door. At that same moment Ross signaled to Owen and Phil, and they, too, rose, strode down the aisle, and mounted the stage steps. Then it happened. Ross missed his footing and plunged forward onto his knees. He heard gasps from the audience, a scattering of titters, then Owen was helping him up. "Are you all right?"

"Good enough. Let's go!"

They went through the stage door, expecting to find an anteroom; instead it was a long corridor lined with more doors, all closed. Phil raced ahead, flung open a door, peered inside, then on to the next, and the next. Finally, at the last door, at the far end of the corridor, he waved to the Seadons.

They found themselves in what appeared to be a rehearsal hall. Tom and Ginny were seated at a long trestle table, reading a document. Haggerty, who was talking with Hazeltine, broke off and glowered at the intruders.

"Sorry, boys. If you think you can barge in here and put pressure on these kids, forget it!"

Tom scowled at Phil. "What the hell are *you* doing here?" Ginny, seeing her father, flushed and quavered, "Can't we go someplace else?"

"Why bother?" Ross demanded. "We know what's coming."

"Really?" Haggerty smiled. "Then you guys must like to suffer." He turned back to Tom. "The contract okay?"

Tom nodded and withdrew an envelope from his breast pocket and handed it to Hazeltine. Ross had thought that he was prepared for the scene, but at the actuality of it his chest tightened, his throat went dry. These were no longer his children; they might be strangers. He glanced at Owen, who was stony-faced; at Phil, who was opening his briefcase.

Hazeltine studied the letter, then looked at Haggerty. "I presume you are acting for Pantex Oil in the purchase of the trustee's shares?"

"I am. I have the company's certified check for the full amount."

"Then perhaps we should go back to the bank and we'll draw up . . ." Hazeltine stopped in mid-sentence as Phil thrust a document into his hand. "What's this?"

"A restraining order issued by the Superior Court." Phil handed him a second document, running to a dozen pages. "And this goes with it." Then he turned to Tom and Ginny and Ross and distributed copies. "You are all now officially served," he said.

Haggerty glowered uncertainly. "What the hell is going on here?"

Ross smiled and offered his copy. "Read it. It's fascinating."

Haggerty, Tom, Ginny, and Hazeltine frowned at the document captioned "Philip Barnard, Plaintiff. Petition of Natural Son to Share in Father's Estate." Pages rustled, eyes raced from paragraph to paragraph detailing the circumstances of the petitioner's birth, concealment by the mother of the father's identity, the plea to be recognized as son and heir and to share equally with his half-brother and half-sister.

Finally, Tom threw the complaint onto the table and sneered at Phil. "I always *knew* you were a bastard!"

Phil rejoined, "Even bastards have rights."

Ginny shrilled, "But not to one third of our trusts!"

Tom whirled on Ross. "For once I'm glad you made me study law. This garbage"—he pointed at the complaint—"is outlawed by the statute of limitations. It's outlawed by the passage of time."

Ross shook his head. "You didn't read Liz Barnard's supporting affidavit. Phil couldn't bring suit any sooner because he didn't know I was his father until three days ago. That's what I'll swear to before judge and jury."

"Hold on here," Haggerty cut in. "I don't give a damn about all this Seadon dirty linen. Senator Barnard can't touch those trusts. He's got to get his inheritance from his father. Ross is the one to shell out."

"Yes! That's right!" Tom cried, relieved.

Ross grinned. "*If* I had anything to shell out. Tell them, Owen."

"Ross has no assets. Yesterday I bought his entire holding in Seadon Oil. I bought Ridgemont and his art collection."

Haggerty's face went pale; his eyelids began to twitch. Then he asked Ross a question whose answer he already suspected: "What have you done with the cash?"

"It could be anywhere," Ross purred. "Maybe buried in the ground, maybe on its way overseas."

"It's a conspiracy!" Tom shouted. "We'll prove it in court!"

Haggerty seized his arm, then Ginny's. "Give Barnard his share, get rid of him! I'll make it up to you. You'd still have enough stock to swing our deal."

Hazeltine interrupted. "You're forgetting the restraining order. It forbids the trustee to dispose of any assets until there's a court hearing."

"*Until!*" Haggerty underlined. "We'll get the judge to cancel it; then Tom and Ginny can pay off Barnard."

Ross tensed; this was the one possibility he feared. Then Tom dispelled it. "I wouldn't give that skunk the paring of a fingernail! We'll fight him clear to the Supreme Court!"

Ross seized on it. "And that means two, three, maybe four years. Where will you be by then, Haggerty? Retired from Pantex? Bankrupt? Dead?"

For a moment it appeared Haggerty had stopped breathing, then he pointed at Hazeltine. "I don't need these kids. Just sell me those shares in Leah's trust."

Hazeltine looked dank. "After all this? If you'll excuse me, I have another appointment."

407

Haggerty slumped down onto one of the chairs. Tom and Ginny exchanged defeated looks and started to follow Hazeltine. "Tom!" Ross called. "When you get back to the office, clean out your desk."

"Gladly! I can get another job anywhere. But *you*"—he gestured at Phil—"you're finished! Nobody will vote for a bastard!"

"Won't they?" Phil retorted. "It's worth a million extra votes. The Senator who risked his career to save his father. The love child, the first-born!" He emphasized the words "first-born," and Tom wilted. It was the *coup de grâce*.

It was nearly over. Phil returned to the auditorium and the Seadons were alone with Haggerty. Ross almost felt compassion. In a matter of minutes the grand plan of years had collapsed, and with it, Haggerty. He had shriveled into an old man, the life gone from his black eyes, the authority from his voice.

"Ross"—he sighed—"you've pulled a lot of aces from your sleeve over the years, but Christ, an illegitimate son!"

"My one true son. And I have you to thank for it. Which I do, sincerely."

Haggerty sniffed at the sentiment. "It smells. It stinks. This whole thing." He eyed Owen suspiciously. "What did you pay for all of Ross's stock—one dollar? And another dollar for Ridgemont, and a dollar for his art collection?"

Owen suppressed a smile. "You said it, I didn't."

"Uh-huh. And when this mess with his kids is settled, you'll hand everything back to Ross. It's plain fraud. It won't stand up in court."

"Can you afford to wait that long?" Ross asked. "Can you hold off your bankers?"

"No. They want their money now."

"So how do you pay them? If you dump almost five million shares of Seadon Oil on the market, you'd drive the price into the ground. Your only out is to sell back to us."

Haggerty snorted. "What would you use for money? Cereal coupons?"

"Cash," Owen said.

"Talk! Bilge!"

"All it takes is a word from you," Ross pursued. "Just announce that you're selling back to Seadon Oil, and the cloud will be lifted off us; we'll be a good credit risk again. We can get bank loans or float a preferred stock issue that will pay you off."

Haggerty considered, then threw up his hands. "I wish to God I'd never heard the name Seadon! I curse the day we met!"

Ross smiled. "You want to step out onto the stage and tell that to the reporters?"

He did not move; it was past doing. When Ross and Owen left the anteroom, Haggerty was staring into space.

They walked to the speaker's lectern and surveyed the audience. There was a buzz of surprise, reporters readied their notepads, photographers raised their cameras. Ross grinned down at Liz, at Phil, at Dale and Tana, and winked. Then he bent toward the microphone. "Ladies and gentlemen, on behalf of Seadon Oil Company, my brother and I wish to make an announcement. . . ."

The day was clear and crisp; a strong westerly breeze sowed whitecaps across San Francisco Bay and caused the great Boeing flying boat to sway at its loading ramp. Ross and Liz were the last to board the Pan American Airways *Clipper* for the sixteen-hour flight to Honolulu. "Alone at last!" Liz sighed, sinking down into her seat in their compartment.

"At last!" Ross echoed. There had never been such a week of activity, he thought. First the negotiations for the return to Seadon Oil of its stock held by Pantex, then the all-night party in celebration, followed by the gathering of hundreds of guests for the wedding ceremony at Ridgemont. Yes, alone at last, as a honeymoon should be.

The four great engines coughed into life, one after another, the three-bladed propellers bit into the air, and the flying boat moved slowly away from its dock and swung to face into the west wind. The engines raised their voices from a low mumble to an angry bellow, the craft moved forward, rocking and plunging through the whitecaps. It gathered speed and sent up great spumes of spray as it rose higher and higher in the water. Then, with a mighty effort, it shrugged free and was airborne.

Ross pressed his face to the cabin window and gazed down at the city which so often had been a backdrop for the lives of the Seadons. The Embarcadero, where Cathlin had first stepped ashore, so poor and yet so rich in courage. Kearny Street, where she and Val ate chestnuts on a foggy night, and now lost to view in a thicket of office buildings. Nob Hill, where Ross had watched the city burn. North Beach, where he and Louise spent that homeless night on the sand. Pacific Heights, where they started life anew and Tom and Ginny had been born. The green of Golden Gate Park, where Leah had given birth to Dale. How many dramas the Seadons had played out upon that stage below.

Ross felt Liz's hand on his knee. "Darling, you're missing it!" He looked at her uncomprehendingly. "Right under us! The Golden Gate Bridge!"

"Sorry. I was thinking."

"Yes?"

"Oh . . . of times past and faces gone."

He turned to the window again and watched the silhouette of the city as it dwindled into the distance. No, he thought, times past and faces gone were never lost entirely. So long as one breathed, they continued on; and when mortality claimed one, still something of value remained in the consciousness of the generations that would follow. The past lived on, for the past was the memory of the future.

ACKNOWLEDGMENTS

The AUTHOR expresses his gratitude to Michael Korda, editor in chief of Simon and Schuster, for the three years in which he gave so generously of his encouragement and guidance toward the completion of this work. Appreciation is due also to Joan Sanger, senior editor, for her valuable contributions of balance and perspective in the final manuscript.